PRAISE FOR

A Bridge Across the Ocean

"I was utterly spellbound, beguiled, swept up in this ghostly mystery about the secrets kept during a time of war. I couldn't put it down."

—Jamie Ford, *New York Times* bestselling author of *Hotel on the Corner of Bitter and Sweet*

"Meissner illustrates the endless link between the past and present, the known and unknown, the flesh and the spirit, and all the mysteries therein. *A Bridge Across the Ocean* is a beguiling tapestry of storytelling and a unique look at one of history's most enigmatic ships, the *Queen Mary*."

—Sarah McCoy, *New York Times* bestselling author of *The Mapmaker's Children*

Stars Over Sunset Boulevard

"Susan Meissner deftly casts a fascinating friendship between two complex women against a glittering 1930s Hollywood backdrop. You will love this book for its very human characters and for its inside look at one of the greatest movies ever made."

—Marisa de los Santos, *New York Times* bestselling author

Secrets of a Charmed Life

"Rich with vividly drawn characters, places, and events . . . its themes of reinvention and redemption will strike a chord with readers."

—*Booklist*

continued . . .

A Fall of Marigolds

"A transportive, heartwarming, and fascinating novel that will resonate with readers in search of emotionally satisfying stories connecting past and present, and demonstrating the healing power of love."
—Erika Robuck, bestselling author of *The House of Hawthorne*

The Girl in the Glass

"A delightful tale that will take readers into the heart of Florence, Italy . . . Meissner blends Nora's, Sofia's, and Meg's stories with a deft hand, creating a layered work of art sure to enchant readers."
—*Publishers Weekly*

A Sound Among the Trees

"Meissner transports readers to another time and place to weave her lyrical tale of love, loss, forgiveness, and letting go."
—Karen White, *New York Times* bestselling author of *A Long Time Gone*

Lady in Waiting

"Both the history and the modern tale are enticing, with Meissner doing a masterful job blending the two."
—*Publishers Weekly*

The Shape of Mercy

"Potentially life-changing, the kind of inspirational fiction that prompts readers to call up old friends, lost loves, or fallen-away family members."
—*Publishers Weekly* (starred review)

A Bridge Across the Ocean

Susan Meissner

BERKLEY
NEW YORK

BERKLEY
An imprint of Penguin Random House LLC
375 Hudson Street, New York, New York 10014

Library of Congress Cataloging-in-Publication Data

Names: Meissner, Susan, 1961– author.
Title: A bridge across the ocean / Susan Meissner.
Description: First Edition. | New York : Berkley, 2017.
Identifiers: LCCN 2016037710 (print) | LCCN 2016043092 (ebook) |
ISBN 9780451476005 (paperback) | ISBN 9780698197862 (ebook)
Subjects: | BISAC: FICTION / Historical. |
FICTION / Contemporary Women. | FICTION / Literary.
Classification: LCC PS3613.E435 B75 2017 (print) |
LCC PS3613.E435 (ebook) | DDC 813/.6—dc23
LC record available at https://lccn.loc.gov/2016037710

First Edition: March 2017

Printed in the United States of America
1 3 5 7 9 10 8 6 4 2

Cover photograph by Richard Rutledge / Getty Images
Cover design by Colleen Reinhart
Book design by Kristin del Rosario

For June Boots Allen,
with love & gratitude

For the soul awakes, a trembling stranger,

between two dim eternities,

—the eternal past, the eternal future.

The light shines only on a small space around her;

therefore, she needs must yearn towards

the unknown . . .

HARRIET BEECHER STOWE, *UNCLE TOM'S CABIN*

Death is an impossible ending

It releases all the emotions of life

To roam the uninhibited skies forever!

And to endure all the spirits

Of other lifetimes

DENNIS A. BOOTS, 1948–1969

A BRIDGE ACROSS THE OCEAN

RMS *QUEEN MARY*

SOUTHAMPTON, ENGLAND

MAY 1936

The afternoon sun lies low and sweet among the clouds that hug the harbor, bathing the promenade deck in shimmering half-light. On the pier a brass band plays a happy tune as good-byes are said at the far end of the gangway. Men with cameras are jockeying for position to catch the best view of us pulling away from the dock.

Today is different than all the other days. I feel the change all around me. Something new is about to happen.

I study each person as they step aboard, but no one pays me any mind. They don't know I am here, so they do not stiffen at my touch or reach for me or gape wide-eyed in surprise or alarm. They alight on the decks, cheerful and carefree, joyfully reaching for glasses of champagne offered by white-coated stewards.

I drift among them all, unseen, unnoticed.

But then a woman with peacock feathers in her hat breathes in deep when I swirl about her, as though she has caught my scent and is mesmerized by it. Intrigued, I linger. Her eyes widen in surprise as she stands there at a portside railing.

"Where are you?" the woman murmurs, so soft it is almost like a whispered prayer.

She is speaking to me. She senses my presence. This woman is the first. I did not know this was possible.

"Don't be afraid," she says. "Where are you?"

I fold in closer to her. "Here," is what I want to say.

"Do you want to tell me your name?" she asks kindly.

And oh yes, how I want to. But I cannot.

"Have you been here awhile?" she asks.

I don't know the answer to this question. And that troubles me.

"It's all right. You can trust me," she says soothingly.

I want to trust her but I hesitate. Her questions fill me with unease. Another woman, this one red-haired and wearing a tweed coat, approaches. A wave of concern washes over her as she looks at the woman in the peacock-feather hat.

"Who in the world are you talking to?" says this new woman.

The woman who knows I am here startles. Her gaze darts about, as though she thinks I might scamper away at this intrusion. Instead, I move closer to her. The silken strands of the feathers on her hat ripple like sea grass under water as I draw near. She opens her mouth in awe and falters a bit.

"Are you all right?" the redhead says, as she grabs her arm.

"I am all right." The woman steadies herself.

"For the love of God, don't tell me there's a ghost here!" The redhead speaks as if her jaw is wired shut and she must spit the words out through her teeth. "This ship is new!"

"Not really. It took years to build, you know."

The redhead is angry. "And here I thought you'd be safe from all that on this ship," she grumbles.

"But I am safe. This one intends no harm."

"And how do you know that?!" the redhead snaps.

"I just do. She is young, this one. She doesn't know how she got here. I think she might be alone, poor thing."

I lift away at once to ponder these words. How is it that this woman *can know so much? I am surprised. Perplexed. Torn between wanting to know everything and know nothing. She senses my gentle departure.*

"She is leaving us," she says to the redhead as she looks beyond the place where they are standing.

"Fine with me." The redhead leads the woman toward a steward bearing champagne flutes on a silver tray.

But she looks for me as she sips, and the mooring lines are dropped, and the tugboats begin to pull us away from the dock.

I want to be near this woman, for she has spoken to my soul. And yet I feel as though the answers to the questions she has posed will be found in only one place: beyond the noise of the bands and the cheering crowds and the whirring planes overhead.

I ease up and away to where the bow points to the sapphire horizon. The sea stretches before me like a shimmering bridge, welcoming me across, inviting me to embrace all that I do not yet know.

One

SAN DIEGO, CALIFORNIA

PRESENT DAY

A friend's baby shower was the last place Brette Caslake expected to encounter a ghost.

The gauzy apparition wafted into the stylish living room, as if blown in on a breeze, the moment the pregnant guest of honor began to open her presents. Or perhaps the ghost had been loitering there by the mahogany bookcase long before the attendees started arriving, and it was just the gentle gust from the open window that had stirred the form, giving its edges depth and shape.

The moment Brette saw the ghost, she knew she'd stupidly let her guard down. She'd neglected to prepare herself to enter a structure she hadn't been inside before, and it was a mistake she hadn't made in a while. The high-rise apartment was a brand-new building, and that fact had lulled her into dismissing the hairs that had prickled on the back of her neck when she'd stepped inside—she'd remembered too late that a building didn't have to be memory-laden for a ghost to take up residence; it just had to be located at a place where the unseen membrane between this world and the next was delicate. As Brette silently berated herself for such a lapse of judgment, she made a second, far worse gaffe. She made eye contact.

When their pupils met, the ghost—an adult female in a plum-colored dress of a vintage Brette couldn't readily identify—opened its mouth in surprised alarm. Brette half-expected it to shriek from across the room. Ghosts, at least the ones Brette had come across, reacted to someone like her the same way people tended to react to them—with alarm. A yelp or two was customary, or a fearful shudder, or a perplexed stare of disbelief. Ghosts were unaccustomed to being visible when they didn't want to be seen, and they didn't always like being found out. For Brette, the feeling was mutual. Ever since a disastrous episode in college, she'd endeavored to ignore anyone she encountered who wasn't mortal. And avoiding eye contact was the first and best way of doing that.

Stupid, stupid, stupid.

She looked away and focused her attention on Lindsey, who was opening a gift from Brette's mother, Nadine, who sat a few chairs away. Nadine and Lindsey's mother had been best friends for years. A chorus of monosyllabic expressions of delight erupted from the other women in the room as Lindsey held up a trio of tiny smocked dresses; white, yellow, and pink.

"Oh, Nadine!" Lindsey gushed. "I love them. They are adorable!"

The ethereal image in the corner vanished, but only for a moment. Less than a second later it materialized in front of Brette, practically atop the gift pile on the coffee table. If it had had form and weight, it would have scattered the presents at everyone's feet. Brette had felt its energy as it made its move, and as she quickly cast her gaze to her feet, she emitted an involuntary gasp.

Not here! Not now! Brette inwardly demanded, but she only wished for a mere snatch of a second that the ghost would hear her silent appeal. Having them inside her head would be a nightmare. They always wanted something. Always. And half the time they didn't even know what it was.

"You are so very welcome," Brette heard her mother say, but she could tell that Nadine was looking at her, not at Lindsey. Her mother had heard her gasp. Everyone probably had.

At that very moment, the ghost lifted a pale hand toward Brette. The apparition's fingers were visible at the edge of Brette's limited field of vision as she stared at her shoes. She sucked in her breath even though she knew it would not touch her. She would be as flimsy to the ghost as its form was to her.

There was an odd pause as the attention in the room swung in Brette's direction. If she raised her head, she and the ghost would be at eye level, and there would be no way to pretend there was nothing there. At least there was no animosity emanating from the vaporous presence in front of her, thank God, and no evil intent. The apparition was not something dark and malevolent. It was merely an uneasy earthbound soul, stuck in a dimension it should have left long ago. Harmless.

"You all right, Brette?" her mother asked.

Brette turned her head toward her mother, keeping her gaze as low as she could. She put a hand to her brow. "Just a bit of a headache. Don't mind me."

The ghost leaned in, more curious now than startled, and Brette felt the skin on her arms and legs grow warm, as though electricity were passing through her limbs. She closed her eyes.

"You want an Advil?" said Lindsey's best friend, Allison, who was hosting the shower. "I have some in the kitchen."

Brette nodded, her eyes still closed. "That would be great."

She heard Allison rise from her chair and start to cross the travertine tile toward the kitchen. Brette longed to tell Lindsey to please, please continue opening her gifts. The sooner she wasn't the center of attention, the better. She opened her eyes carefully. The ghost was at her side, staring at her profile, perhaps trying to figure out what she was made of.

"Please don't let me spoil anything," Brette said to Lindsey as she rose from the couch to follow Allison. "I'll be fine. Really."

"Is she still getting those awful headaches she had in college?" Lindsey's mother asked Nadine in a low tone.

"Not so much anymore," Nadine said, but doubt cloaked her words.

Brette joined Allison in the kitchen but kept her gaze low and fixed. The ghost had swept into the room with them, but she didn't scan the corners to see where it had drifted. No doubt it was lingering at the far end of the granite-topped island, if the electrical charge emanating from that direction meant anything. Allison was at the refrigerator filling a glass with water. She turned and handed Brette the tumbler.

"Here you go."

From a cupboard above a tiered display of pastel macarons, Allison took out a bottle of Advil. "Two enough?" she asked, as she shook out the gelcaps and offered them to Brette.

"Sure. Thank you."

As she tossed the pills into her mouth, Brette sensed movement on her left. The hairs on her arm rose to attention. Her hand trembled slightly as she brought the glass to her lips.

"You sure you're okay?" Allison said, her head cocked to one side. "You can lie down on my bed if you want."

As Brette set the glass down on the counter, the ghost swirled into view. She knew what she needed to do.

"I'll be fine as soon as these kick in," she said. "But thanks. Is there a bathroom I could use?"

"Just down the hall and the first door on your left."

Brette smiled her thanks and headed out of the kitchen. She knew she would be followed. Inside the bathroom she closed the door, stood at the sink with her head down, and waited. A moment later she was no longer alone.

Slowly she raised her head to look at the ghost's reflection in the mirror above her head. It hovered behind her and to one side, by a sunlit window that sprinkled it with a muted, glitterlike shimmer. Brette saw for the first time that the ghost carried something in one of its hands: a baby doll with a cloth torso, hard plastic limbs. From the 1950s, she guessed.

"Where's Bess?" The ghost's mouth and lips barely moved, but its words were distinct in Brette's ears, and their airy tone was almost childlike. Pleading. Brette had encountered enough earthbound souls in her thirty-four years to know they were impossible to reason with. Logic meant nothing to souls stuck in the in-between realm, which was why she'd long since decided not to acknowledge their existence.

She was going to have to engage with this one, though, if she was going to get through the rest of the baby shower.

She lowered her gaze to the apparition's reflected midriff. She needed a second before looking into those questioning eyes.

"I don't know where Bess is," Brette murmured, quietly enough that no one in the living room could hear her. "Nobody here does. You must leave."

The ghost waited only a moment before repeating its question. "Where's Bess?" This time the tone was more fretful. Insistent.

Brette placed her hands on the marble countertop, willing its cold steadfastness to strengthen her. She tipped her head upward and looked into the ghost's face in the mirror. Its gaze was fixed directly on her own, eyes wide with expectation.

"I can't help you," Brette said quietly but firmly. "No one here can help you. You need to leave."

Then, without waiting for a response, she turned and charged through the diaphanous form, dispelling the vision as she opened the door.

Brette returned to the living room full of happy women, paper

hydrangeas, and plates of herbed hummus and pita chips. She ma-
neuvered her way back to the couch without so much as a backward
glance. If she could continue to ignore the ghost, it would physically
tire and leave. She pasted a smile on her face as she retook her seat,
nodding toward her mother to reassure her she was fine. Nadine
smiled back, but her eyes were full of questions.

Brette knew the little reprieve she'd been able to orchestrate for
her parents had most likely just ended. She'd enjoyed a long stretch
without them being overtly aware that she still saw and heard what
few others could, and almost as many years without an incident
of direct contact. She'd only just met Keith the last time a ghost
had spoken to her. They had been at a restaurant on their first real
date after meeting at a party. It had taken Herculean effort to ignore
the apparition that had somehow picked up on her ability and then
bobbed above their table to repeatedly ask her what day it was.
Brette liked Keith Caslake and had known she would eventually
have to tell him about her ability if things got serious, but it would
not be on that first date. Never on a first date.

"Is it happening again, Brette?" Nadine asked quietly an hour
later, when the shower was over and as they waited for the elevator
that would take them to the parking garage. Nadine's words were
robed with a mother's keen weave of sympathy and protectiveness,
as though she already knew the answer.

Brette wanted to assure her mother that it had been merely a
headache and nothing more. But she hated pretending to the people she loved most that she was just like everyone else.

"It never really stopped," she said.

Two

✳

Nadine waited until the elevator doors closed before asking Brette if the apartment building was haunted.

"No," Brette said. "It isn't."

"But you saw one at the shower, didn't you?" Nadine's gaze was on the digital screen in the elevator. She watched numbly as it clicked off the numbered floors. "A ghost."

Brette hadn't manifested her gifting in front of her parents in more than five years. Only Keith knew that from time to time she still saw them: on sidewalks, in buildings, in parks, on the beach, even inside churches. "Yes," she said.

"Is it . . . is it here with us? In the elevator?"

"No."

The elevator came to a gentle stop and the doors opened. Brette stepped out into the warm parking garage.

Nadine followed. "I honestly thought maybe you had found a way to make them go away. I was hoping you had."

Brette offered a wan smile. "I wanted you and Dad to think that. I've gotten pretty good at pretending I can't see them, but I was careless today."

Their shoes tapped an echoing staccato beat as they walked together across the concrete floor.

"What did it want?" Nadine said a second later.

"It doesn't matter."

They neared her mother's car, and Nadine's hand trembled as she pressed her remote to unlock it.

"Mom. You don't have to be afraid," Brette said. "I'm not. They don't scare me."

Nadine looked down at her feet before turning to face her daughter. "I know you're not afraid." But her expression was concerned.

"Then what?"

Nadine shrugged, and even in the shadowed confines of the parking garage, Brette could see her eyes were rimmed with tears. "It's been so long since . . . since I've seen you that way."

"You don't need to worry about me. Honestly. I can handle it." Brette crossed over to the passenger side and got into the car, closing her door with a resounding *thrump.*

Nadine opened the driver's-side door and lowered herself onto her seat. She said nothing as she closed her door and slid the key into the ignition.

The sound of the car's engine echoed around the low-ceilinged garage. A few moments later they emerged onto a sun-drenched street in San Diego's Little Italy.

"Does Keith know you still see them?" her mother asked as she turned onto Cedar Avenue.

"He doesn't ask much about it, and I really don't want him to. I just made a careless mistake this afternoon. Don't let it ruin your day, Mom. I'm not letting it ruin mine."

Nadine smiled weakly. She pressed a button on her steering wheel to activate a playlist, and Debussy filled the car.

The conversation shifted and the heaviness in the car seemed to lift. Her mother had never been one to discuss the Sight for longer than a few minutes, and that fact suited Brette far more now than it had when she was young. The Sight was a gifting Nadine had passed on to Brette, but she didn't possess the ability herself. It showed up only in female members of the family and hopscotched across generations with apparent randomness. Nadine's mother also had it, and so did an aunt, and there'd been a few distant second cousins, whom Brette had never met, with the Sight. As far as Brette knew, she was the last person in the immediate family who could see earthbound souls. Drifters, Aunt Ellen had called them.

Nadine had married Brette's father, Cliff, in her late twenties, and together they'd moved to San Diego from Minneapolis to take jobs in retail—she in human resources and he in sales—that paid well. They had been in no rush to become parents, so the story went, and waited for five years before casting off all forms of birth control. Brette had been born on Nadine's thirty-fourth birthday.

When she was a toddler, her parents began to tire of the relentless pace of the workplace. Cliff had no free time to play his guitar or write music or jam with his friends. Nadine wanted more time to experiment in the kitchen, grow an herb garden, and take interior decorating classes.

A couple of years later, Cliff inherited a substantial sum of money from his maternal grandfather's estate. He and Nadine quit their corporate jobs, bought a near-to-crumbling Victorian mansion in the charming coastal suburb of Solana Beach, restored the house, and opened a bed-and-breakfast. Nadine was finally able to indulge in culinary pursuits and decorating instead of personnel matters, and Cliff could at last spend the hours he wasn't tending to the inside sales job penning music that he sold for good money to recording artists who didn't write their own tunes.

Brette's bedroom off the kitchen had once been the maid's quarters. Her parents slept in what had been the original owner's private library. When they wanted a little privacy, a back porch off the kitchen—with ocean views—gave them a quiet place to relax. Mimosas and omelets were served to guests in the formal dining room, and the expansive living room was a common area for anyone who happened to be in the house in the evening to enjoy a drink and conversation before heading out to dinner. Cliff, a self-proclaimed wine connoisseur, liked to wow his visitors with robust Zinfandels and Cabernets crafted from old vines up the coast in Paso Robles. Cliff had given Nadine the naming rights to the B and B, and she settled on Willow House, an homage to the aging arroyo willow that stood squarely on the tiny front lawn.

The old house creaked and groaned with the changing seasons, and its walls were infused with the memories of forty thousand days. But Brette didn't see her first ghost in Willow House until she was six.

Her mother's aunt Ellen, a silver-haired spinster who smelled of cloves and Camay soap, had come for a visit after selling her Midwest home and before taking up residence in a stylish retirement village in Phoenix. She'd brought with her four trunks containing photo albums, picture frames, dishes, and stacks of lace and linens that had been her grandmother's and that Nadine had claimed for Willow House when Ellen called to announce they'd be sold at an estate auction if no one else in the family wanted them.

Brette had never met Aunt Ellen, as most of the extended family lived east of the Mississippi and were infrequent travelers to the West Coast. But she was curious about her after hearing snippets of a hushed conversation in the car between her parents a couple days prior to Aunt Ellen's arrival. It had been late in the evening, and the three of them were returning to Solana Beach following a wedding in Los Angeles. Brette had been faking sleep as they neared their exit off Interstate 5. If she was asleep when they got to Willow House, her father would carry her in—and she liked being carried in.

Brette hadn't been paying much attention to her parents' conversation until her name popped up in it.

"Do you think I need to tell Aunt Ellen to be mindful of what she says around Brette?" her mother had said. Brette cracked open one eye as she lay curled up in the dark on the backseat.

"Do you really think she'll say anything?" had been her father's quiet reply.

"No, not intentionally," Nadine answered. "But you know how it can be with older people who don't spend much time around kids. They say things too loudly and they don't stop to think who might be listening."

"But do you honestly think the topic will come up? I mean, if you don't ask Ellen for an update, then how likely is it she will even say anything about it?"

"Yes, but do we really want to take that chance? What if I ask her what she's been up to lately and she tells me—in front of Brette—that she's, you know, still conversing with the deceased?"

At six, the word *deceased* meant nothing to Brette. She'd continued to listen.

"Then don't ask her what she's been up to," her father had answered, almost playfully.

"Cliff, I'm serious!"

"So am I. Don't ask her. Don't ask her what she's been doing since the last time you saw her. Assume she's been watching *Jeopardy* and playing bunco and getting her hair done. Keep it about the right here and the right now. Take her to the zoo. Take her to Balboa Park. Take her to Coronado. Keep her busy with happy activities that have nothing to do with any of that other stuff. You bring it up and then it's up."

The conversation never went any further. But Brette's interest in her great-aunt had been piqued.

Two days later mysterious Aunt Ellen arrived. But six-year-old Brette saw nothing remarkable about her, though she followed her everywhere. Aunt Ellen was just a warm-hearted old lady who wore rosy-pink eyeglasses that dangled on a chain around her neck and who liked tea, not coffee. She didn't seem to converse with the deceased, whoever or whatever the deceased were.

One morning during the visit, Brette trudged up the attic's folding stairs behind Aunt Ellen, who'd insisted to Nadine that the box of old photo frames and empty albums wasn't too heavy for her to carry. She was leaving the next day and wanted to store the box for her niece where it wouldn't be in the way. There was a single window in the attic at Willow House, all the way at the back, and it let in the only natural light in the small A-framed room. When Brette entered the dim-lit space, just behind Aunt Ellen, she saw a boy crouched on the windowsill. His hair was tousled, his clothes were rumpled, and he wore no shoes. Sunlight dappled him, making him seem like nearly a shadow.

Brette's reaction was a mix of curiosity and surprise.

"Hey!" she'd said to the boy. "How'd you get in here?"

He cocked his head, seemingly both pleased and surprised by her question.

Ellen turned around, to peer first at Brette and then at the window. She looked surprised, too. But more alarmed than pleased.

"Who are you talking to?" Ellen said.

Brette pointed toward the window. "Him."

Ellen glanced toward the window again and then back to Brette. "Him?"

"That boy."

Ellen tipped her head in wonderment or concern or maybe both. "Can you see a little boy sitting on the windowsill?" She'd smiled in a strange way.

Even at six Brette could tell the smile was fake. Aunt Ellen was not happy with her. She didn't answer.

"No one is angry with you, sweetheart." Ellen knelt down and put her arms gently on Brette's shoulders. "Look at me, dear. Only at me. Did you see a boy on the windowsill?"

As Brette nodded, she caught movement out of the corner of her eye. The boy was coming toward them. But his feet were making no sound.

"Look only at me," Ellen said, and her smile was genuine now but her tone was firm. "Only at me. We're finished here and we're going to go downstairs. Let's play a little game, all right? You close your eyes and hold my hand and then tell me when you think we have reached the ladder."

But Brette hadn't wanted to leave the attic or play the game. She wanted to know how that boy had gotten inside their house.

"Why is he here?" she asked.

Ellen had tucked in her lip for a second. "He's just got the wrong house, Brette. That's all. I am sure he'll figure that out soon enough."

The wrong house, Brette wondered, and then she'd felt fear. She didn't know the word *intruder* but she'd felt its meaning within her. "Is he a bad boy?"

Ellen leaned in closer and locked her gaze with Brette's. "No, he's not a bad boy. That's not what he is. You don't need to be afraid of him. Do you understand? He doesn't want to hurt anyone."

The boy was suddenly right beside them and Brette couldn't *not* look at him. He looked as if he were standing in a tiny burst of mist, the kind that gathered over the ocean every morning. If she were to reach out and touch him, she thought, her hand would come away wet and he would not be there.

And then he suddenly wasn't there. He wasn't there at all.

Brette whipped her head around the room. Ellen's strong arms were still on her shoulders.

"Where did he go?" she exclaimed.

Ellen stood up straight and let out a long breath. "We need to go to find your mommy and daddy, Brette."

"Where is he?"

"Come along."

"Are you going to tell them about the boy?" Brette asked, still gazing about the little room, looking for the child made of mist.

Ellen took her hand to lead her back to the stairs.

"Yes," she said. "Yes, I am."

And her voice had sounded sad.

Three

Simone Devereux woke to the sounds of scuffling feet, voices shrouded in hoarse whispers, and the slamming of the wine cellar trapdoor. A sallow glow from a flashlight bounced off the wall opposite a staircase mostly hidden from her view by stacked wine barrels. She sat up on her makeshift bed as heavy boots clunked down the stairs. She expected to hear next the guttural shouts of the Gestapo ordering her in halting French to put her hands above her head or they'd shoot, and she felt strangely detached from the moment. Simone had imagined this day when the SS would find her. Her mind had played it out for her in different ways: Getting inside her empty barrel but forgetting the blanket. Getting inside her barrel with the blanket but leaving a bit of her clothing peeking out from the lid. Getting inside the barrel but having one German reach down to the pile of straw that was larger than the others and feeling the warmth left behind by her body. Or not getting inside the barrel at all and feeling the piercing bullets at her back as she tried to climb in. And the worst of all scenarios—the one her mind cruelly revisited over and over—safely inside the barrel with the blanket, the straw strewn about, but the Germans firing into all the barrels anyway, her blood mixing with the red wine as it spilled onto the dirt floor.

But the voices of the men descending into the cellar in the agitated manner she'd imagined a thousand times were strangely hushed, and it was this anomaly that kept Simone frozen on the straw and not dashing for cover in those seconds before whoever was coming down the stairs rounded the corner and saw her.

"Simone! We need your bed." Henri spoke her name in a tone that was both urgent and restrained from just beyond the wall of barrels.

She scrambled off the straw at the same moment that he rounded the corner, accompanied by two men she did not know. The winemaker shone the flashlight in Simone's direction, blinding her, but not before she saw that the strangers with him were carrying a fourth man covered in blood.

"Put him there!" Henri commanded, pointing to the mound of straw and the tousled blanket where Simone had been lying.

Simone watched in stunned silence as the injured man, wearing a uniform she did not recognize, was laid out on the cellar floor. He groaned and pawed awkwardly at his belt, reaching, it seemed, for something strapped to his pant leg.

"Take the gun," one of the men said to Henri. The winemaker removed the black pistol the man had been reaching for and tossed it to the straw.

Simone's blood ran cold in her veins. "Is he German?" she whispered.

But Henri seemed not to have heard her. He and the other men were tearing at the wounded man's clothes to expose his bloody torso. Simone saw dog tags attached to a chain around his neck and nestled in the hollow below his Adam's apple. They, too, shone with blood.

"I see it!" one of the strangers said. "He was shot here. Take off your shirt, Henri."

Henri began to unbutton his shirt with shaking hands. "Is the bullet still inside him, Sébastien? There is no doctor here we can trust."

The man named Sébastien turned the wounded soldier over, revealing his back and a hole, crimson and shiny. "The bullet exited here. That is good." Sébastien looked up at Henri. "Press the fabric here. I will see if Marie will come dress the wound. François, go find this soldier's parachute and get rid of it. Bury it if you must. See if he dropped anything else besides the camera. Take someone with you."

The man named François nodded and sprinted away as Henri knelt by the bleeding man and pressed his shirt to the man's side.

"Is your wife at home, Henri?" Sébastien grabbed the gun on the straw.

"Yes."

"We will need hot water and bandages. Maybe her sewing box. I don't know what Marie will want."

Henri glanced up at Simone. "Come hold this in place while I go fetch Collette."

The wounded man moaned. "Can I just go get Collette instead?" she asked.

"That is impossible and you know it. Come hold the shirt."

Simone got to her knees beside Henri. His hands were splotched with blood and she felt her gorge tumble inside her.

"Press here." Henri took her hand and placed it over the blood-ied shirt. Her hand was instantly sticky. Henri rose to his feet.

"You have anything stronger than wine?" Sébastien tucked the confiscated gun into his belt.

Henri shrugged. "We've some Armagnac. Not a lot. But some."

The man nodded toward the figure on the straw. "He's going to need it."

As Henri spun away to run up the stairs, Sébastien turned to-ward Simone.

"So you are the daughter of Thierry Devereux?"

Simone looked up from her grim task. The man speaking to her seemed like every other Résistance member she had known in her life, aside from Papa and Étienne: angry, driven, and fiercely in love with France. She said nothing. Papa had never mentioned a man named Sébastien before.

"Your father was a true patriot," Sébastien continued. "We have heard what he did. He was a very brave man."

His words were clearly spoken in admiration of her father, but coming from a stranger they made Simone bristle with a terrible sadness. This man didn't know her father. And he didn't know her. "I know what he was," she muttered.

The man took hold of his cap, removed it, and bowed slightly. "Sébastien Maillard. People around know me as the mechanic who can fix anything."

Could she trust him? Henri did. But Henri never talked about knowing her father. Henri never talked at all about the reason she was hiding in his wine cellar.

"You're not going to tell me your name?" He laughed lightly.

Simone hesitated for a moment. "You already heard my name. Henri said it."

Sébastien's smile diminished, but only somewhat. "Look, I don't care why you had to get out of Paris. But you need to know that if the Germans find this man here, they will likely kill Henri and Collette, and you, too. You need to understand that. They will kill you if they find you here with him."

Simone returned her gaze to the injured man. Despite the cuts and bruises on his forehead and cheek and the grim set of his mouth, he had a nice face. Handsome, even.

"He is not German?" she said.

"He's American. The Germans shot down his plane, and sooner

or later they are going to figure out that he survived. They will be looking for him. If you want to leave, now is the time."

Simone allowed a slight smile to frame her lips. "If I want to leave," she echoed.

"You think I am joking? You think you are safe here?"

"No one is safe anywhere. And the Germans already want me dead."

Sébastien cocked his head and an unmistakable look of approval mixed with equal parts doubt fell across his face. "Is that so? Why do they want you dead? Were you passing secrets for your father before he died?"

In her mind's eye Simone saw her father and brother jerking to the ground in front of the shoe-repair shop, their bodies riddled with Gestapo bullets. "You mean before they killed him? And my brother?"

The look of doubt on Sébastien's face slid away and his gaze intensified. "Are you Résistance, too, *chérie*?"

Simone didn't know what she was. She didn't answer him.

"How old are you?"

"I'll be eighteen on my next birthday."

Sébastien knelt down to meet her at eye level. That close, and with the weak light emanating from the flashlight, Simone could see that he was younger than Henri, older than her brother, Étienne, had been. Twenty-five, maybe. It was hard to tell. The occupation of France had aged everyone in different ways.

"What did you do?" Sébastien asked, his tone almost tender. "Why do the Germans want you dead?"

Simone looked down at her hands stained red.

"I killed one of them."

Four

✳

Papa taught her how to fire the gun.

A few months after the German armies marched into Paris, Simone's father had taken her into the shoe-repair shop's back room and shown her where he'd hidden a pistol inside a box of old polishing cloths.

"I do not know what the future holds for us, Simone," he said. "There may come a day when you will need to know where this gun is and how to use it."

She had just turned fourteen. She hadn't known that her father even owned a gun.

Her mother, Cécile, had been dead for five years, and while Simone missed Maman acutely, her father had carved a happy life for her and her older brother, Étienne. They lived above the shoe-repair shop in the seventh arrondissement on Rue de Cler. She had a number of close school friends living nearby. She enjoyed art class, and learning English, and the wonderment of imagining her first kiss with Bertrand Ardouin, a fellow fourteen-year-old who hadn't yet caught on that she liked him. She made the meals for her father and brother, mended their clothes, and decorated the flat at the holidays. In the evenings, the three of them listened to the wireless or played cards or read. Her life had seemed sweetly simple until the Germans came, and the radio was the first thing to go.

Papa repaired shoes. He was not a man who needed a gun.

When he lifted the pistol from the tangle of cloths, Simone could not help thinking how sinister it looked, with its shiny, beetle-black paint and trigger like a little devil's horn.

"I wish I had shown you how to use it when I showed Étienne," her father had said, shaking his head. "But I promised your mother I'd make sure to remember you were a girl becoming a lady. I knew she wouldn't have wanted you to go shooting with us that day."

He laughed, but it was a sad laugh, as though the memory of that pledge was both sweet and wrenching. He opened the chamber of the gun and shook the bullets into his palm.

"I keep it loaded, Simone, so you must be very careful to remember that this gun is always ready to shoot. But right now you can practice with it unloaded. I will put the bullets back in when we're done."

Papa held the gun toward her, but Simone did not stretch out her hand.

"I need you to take it, Simone."

"I'm afraid, Papa."

His eyes shimmered with tears. "So am I. I am so very afraid. That is why you must take it. You must learn what to do if you ever need to use it."

"Why would I need to use it?"

"Paris is not the city it once was. Things are different now. There might come a time when you must protect yourself from . . . from bad people who would try to harm you. You are a beautiful young girl, *ma chérie*, and the world is no longer a safe place for beautiful young girls."

He had not said the word *rape* out loud but she read his meaning. The streets were increasingly full of German soldiers and Gestapo officers—men in power, far from home and fueled by their victory over a defeated Paris.

She held out her hand and he placed the gun in it. The metal was surprisingly warm.

"There are only two things you need to remember," Papa said. "To keep your arm steady and your eyes open."

She nodded. The pistol lay in her open hand.

"Now hold the gun the way you've seen it done at the cinema, Simone. You can do this."

She righted the pistol so that its barrel faced outward and looped her fingers around the trigger.

Papa positioned himself so that he was standing just behind her. "Point the gun at the water heater. Use your other hand to help you control it."

Simone obeyed. The gun trembled in her hand.

Papa drew his arms around her. "Aim for the triangle-shaped smudge there, cock back the lever, and pull the trigger."

Simone leveled the gun's barrel toward the spot on the water heater. She pulled back the lever and then stopped. "I can't."

"Yes, you can. You must."

Simone closed her eyes. She squeezed the trigger. The gun clicked and she shuddered.

"Good girl. Do it again. This time with your eyes open."

A dozen more times she fired the bulletless gun. Each time she shook less.

"There now, that's good." Papa said. "When there are bullets inside, it will kick back a bit; be ready for that, Simone. But do just as I told you. Keep your arm steady and straight and your eyes open. Don't close your eyes."

She handed the gun back to him.

"Watch me now as I slip the bullets back inside." He spun the chamber and dropped them in one by one. When he was done, he put the gun back under the frayed polishing cloths.

"I don't want to have to shoot anyone," Simone said.

"I don't want you to, either. I will pray every day that you never have to."

"You said you showed Étienne how to shoot it."

"I did. But what if he and I are not here? What if something happens and we are not here for you?"

"Don't say that, Papa!"

Her father turned from the box to face her. "There is talk that the men will be sent to labor camps in Germany."

She didn't know what that meant. Her papa had done nothing wrong.

"Why? What men?'

"Men like Étienne and me, *ma chérie.*"

How could he even think of leaving her in Paris alone? And Étienne was only seventeen. She turned to leave the room. She would not have this conversation. But Papa took her arm and stopped her.

"Simone, I don't want that to happen. God knows I don't. I just need for you to know. In case—"

"In case what?"

"In case you come home from school one day and we are gone. It has happened to other men in the Seventh. If it does, I want you to take the gun, hide it in a traveling bag, and go to the address I am going to tell you. You must memorize the address, Simone. It's very important that you memorize it."

Tears were falling freely down her face now. Papa was speaking as if what he feared most was already happening. "Why must I memorize it?"

"Because it cannot be written down anywhere. Promise me you will memorize it. Don't write it down. Ever."

Up until that moment Simone had not known her father and brother had joined the fledgling underground Résistance. She thought their meetings with other men late at night were devoted to smoking their cigars and drinking all their brandy before the Germans did. And yet she'd overheard the boys at school whisper-

ing about a secret movement to oust the Germans and retake the
city . . .

"Where are you going at night with Étienne?" she whispered
now, as she began to understand what that kind of activity could
mean. The occupational forces had announced early on that any
opposition to their rule would not be tolerated. Rebels would be
shot.

Papa's eyes flashed dread and surprise at the same time. He had
no answer at the ready.

"I know what the boys are talking about at school," Simone
continued. "I know there are people who want to take back Paris."

Papa pulled her away from the door and the remote possibility
that anyone outside on the street could hear them.

"You must never, ever mention this to anyone. Ever." His whispered words were laced with anger and fear. "Do not talk to those
boys who are saying things that could get them killed. Swear you
will not!"

His gaze was tight on hers and his grip on her arms bit into her
flesh. Simone was surprised into silence by the violence of his reaction.

"Swear to me! Swear that you will not speak of that to anyone!"
he said.

"I swear I won't, Papa. You're hurting me."

His eyes widened in shock and he pulled his hands away. A
second later he drew Simone into his arms. "I am so sorry this is
the world we have created for you, *ma chérie*. So very sorry."

For several moments father and daughter stood in a tearful embrace in the cramped room.

"I just want you to be safe," her father finally said.

He released her and took a step back. He placed his hands back
on her shoulders, this time more gently. "The address you need to

remember is twenty-three Rue de Calais. You are to ask for Monsieur Jolicoeur. Say it back to me."

"Twenty-three Rue de Calais."

"And the name."

"Monsieur Jolicoeur."

"Say it again."

"Twenty-three Rue de Calais. Monsieur Jolicoeur."

"Say it to yourself every day so that you do not forget. I will remind you." He squeezed her shoulders.

"I will."

"And what did I tell you about the gun?"

"Keep my arm steady and my eyes open."

"Good girl."

He placed one hand under her chin and smiled at her. "You look so much like your mother, my Simone. I promised her I would take good care of you."

"You are taking good care of me, Papa."

He removed his hand. "One more thing about the gun. Tell no one we have it. And I mean no one. Not your friends, not your teacher. Not even the priest. No one can know. We aren't allowed to have them."

After returning to the shop, which Papa had closed for the day, they went into the back room, where Étienne was standing at the window in case a German soldier came by to demand his boots be shined, despite the *Closed* sign over the door.

He tipped his chin to Simone—a wordless affirmation that he knew all that she now knew.

And then her brother asked her what was for supper.

Six months later, when Papa and Étienne were told they were bound for a labor camp in northern Germany, Papa was able to convince the officer in charge that he and Étienne would much

better serve the Wehrmacht by staying in Paris and making sure
the officers had professionally polished boots for when Nazi digni-
taries and high-ranking officers came to call.

Simone had no need of the gun that first year of the occupation,
nor the second or third. Somehow the three of them found enough
food to eat and enough coal for the furnace. They endured muttered
insults and rebuffs from neighbors who begrudged them their now
strictly German clientele. But Simone knew her father gleaned
much information from the officers who spoke to each other while
having their shoes shined, never realizing that the proprietor who
pretended to speak only a little German actually knew quite a bit.
Her closest Catholic girlfriends from school had fled to southern
France with their families. The few Jewish friends in her neighborhood had been rounded up by the French police and sent to German
and Polish labor camps. Bertrand, the boy Simone liked, had already
been sent away with his father, who died of pneumonia after a year.
As far as Simone knew, Bertrand was still alive, building tanks and
bombs for the Germans.

As 1943 neared its end, Simone's existence had been reduced to
three activities: avoiding the shoe-repair shop during business hours,
keeping Étienne and Papa fed and their clothes mended, and counting the days until the war would be over.

The monotony she endured left her unprepared for surprises,
however. On the third of December 1943, at two in the afternoon
when she was alone in the flat, she'd heard angry shouting downstairs. She had been keeping up with her schoolwork on her own,
opting not to attend classes anymore—too dangerous—and she laid
her pen down to listen. The shouts were in German.

She had been instructed by Papa never to come downstairs when
the shop was open, but she cracked open the front door to the flat
and peered down the flight of steps that led to a frosted-glass door
and the back room of the shop. More shouts. Simone could not dis-

tinguish the voices, but she thought she heard her father's and Étienne's in the mix. She crept down the steps and listened at the glass door. The voices were sounding farther away and there was the sound of scuffling. The shop was quiet and the yelling seemed to be only coming from one man now, a German, outside on the street.

Simone listened for her father's voice and the rap on the wall that would let her know all was clear and she could come downstairs. But she heard neither. Slowly she opened the door and peeked into the back room. No one. Carefully, she tiptoed to the front of the shop, staying to the shadows. She could see just beyond the front door's glass that a crowd had gathered. A row of Gestapo officers stood in the street with rifles raised. In front of them stood four men—Papa, Étienne, and two men whom Simone did not know— with their hands raised over their heads.

Another German officer pushed each man to his knees. And then, before Simone could work out what was happening, the officers with the rifles fired, multiple times. Simone had no time to scream or cry or think. A moment later, Papa and Étienne lay dead in the street.

For the first few seconds she could only stand at the glass and whisper, "Wake up, wake up," for surely she had to be dreaming.

One of the Germans addressed the crowd in broken French. "This is happen when we find Résistance. This!" He pointed to the four dead men. And as he walked away with his comrades, he gave each of the bodies a swift kick with his polished boots.

When Simone at last found her voice and legs, she bolted out of the shop. "Papa!" she wailed.

But before she could step out into the street where the bodies of her father and brother lay, an arm shot out across her chest and held her fast.

She struggled, but the man who had her in his grasp was strong.

Simone looked up, ready to bite, scream, lash out with her fists, anything to get away, but she was helpless to break free.

The man leaned in close to her.

"Run, Simone. Now. They will come back for you. Some of them know your father has a daughter. Run."

She stared at the stranger. How did he know her name?

His gaze back on her was steel.

"Go! Now," he murmured. "Run!"

He pushed her away from the store—from her dead father and dead brother lying in the street, from the gun in the back room, from everything she knew—and she took off as fast as her legs could take her.

Five

NEAR SOUTHAMPTON, ENGLAND

FEBRUARY 1946

A teasing gust from the icy Atlantic thirty miles away tugged at the travel documents Annaliese clutched to her chest as the queue of war brides moved slowly forward. The ends of her wool scarf danced about her face, but she didn't dare tuck them back into her coat and compromise her hold on the papers. They'd be impossible to replace.

The other two dozen or so young women waiting to enter the registration building at Tidworth laughed and chattered despite the frosty chill. Some clasped the mittened hands of impatient toddlers whom they attempted to placate with promises of warm cocoa, very soon. Some held babies that cried, or cooed, or slept. Some stroked abdomens sweetly swollen with the unborn children of American servicemen. Some, like Annaliese, held nothing in their hands save their papers.

Ahead stood the brick-and-mortar edifice where each would begin the final stage of her transition from war bride to American wife. Here, at the army base known as Tidworth, their immigration papers would be processed, their health scrutinized, and their passports stamped. Within a few days, or so they had been told, they would board a bus that would take them to Southampton and one of a dozen vessels that had been commissioned to transport them to New York harbor.

Annaliese had never been across the Atlantic before and she wondered, as did nearly every woman in line, it seemed, if she would be seasick. Still, what was one more difficulty among so many others? The American husbands had first needed their commanders' permission to even marry a European girl. Then there had been the hasty ceremonies and the wedding dresses made of parachute material or lace tablecloths or fabric remnants bought with donated clothing coupons. Then there had been, for most of them, the waiting. British women who had fallen in love during the months of preparation before D-Day had had the longest time to worry and tarry while their beloved soldiers marched across Europe. After Germany's surrender in August, there had been more waiting, along with reams of paperwork to fill out and trips to the embassy in order to be reunited at last with their foreign husbands.

But now all that stood between them and their new lives as official immigrants to the United States was the processing camp at Tidworth and the voyage across the Atlantic.

A young woman in a red plaid coat just ahead turned to face Annaliese. She held on her hip a chubby-cheeked tot who had fallen asleep against her chest. "So, where's your husband from?" she said brightly, in English.

Annaliese thought maybe the woman had been speaking to someone else. The lady behind her, perhaps. She chanced a glance over her shoulder, hoping she was not the one being invited into a conversation in English. But the women directly behind her were engaged in their own chat. She turned back around.

"Yes, you!" the woman said happily.

"Oh." Annaliese had not spoken to anyone all morning. Her voice sounded weak and unsure. The English response she had been rehearsing tumbled awkwardly off her lips. "He's . . . he's from Boston."

The other chattering voices around her stilled.

The woman in plaid stared at her wide-eyed, a polite smile still plastered to her face. "Boston, did you say?"

"*Ja*—I mean yes!" Annaliese's cheeks instantly flamed hot, and she closed her eyes for a second. What a stupid mistake. She'd practiced speaking only French or English for days upon days. How could she have made such a blunder?

"You're German," another woman gasped, unmistakably shocked.

Annaliese shook her head. "No. Belgian. I'm from Belgium."

"But Belgians say *oui* for yes." This from another woman, in a blue peacoat. Annaliese tried to calm the fluttering of fear in her chest.

"I . . . I'm from Malmédy. Close to the border. Most speak German there. But we are Belgian. I . . . I am Belgian."

Her explanation was met with silent stares.

"Why are you even here?" said a tall woman from farther up the line, whose baby had been crying in her arms for the last fifteen minutes. "These ships are for British brides."

Annaliese was struggling to work out a response to that question when a woman spoke from behind her, the accent clearly French.

"No, they're not," the woman said.

"I wasn't talking to you!" the tall woman shouted over Annaliese's head.

Annaliese peered over her shoulder. The woman who had spoken up for her was petite and golden-haired. She looked to be Annaliese's age, twenty or so, but her countenance suggested otherwise. There was a hardness in her eyes and in the set of her mouth that reminded Annaliese of the gray-haired Red Cross matron who'd welcomed them off the bus minutes earlier.

The French woman fixed a challenging stare at the tall British lady before letting her gaze drift to Annaliese, who offered her a tiny smile of gratitude before she looked away.

"Neither one of you should be here," the tall woman continued. "I've got a flatmate who's been married to her GI longer than either of you, and she's still waitin' for her travel documents. It's people like you that are taking her place on these ships."

"It's people like you that make the world a sad place when it should be happy," the French woman tossed back.

The woman in plaid leaned toward Annaliese. "Those two got into a row on the bus from the railway station about this very thing. Guess they're still at it," she whispered.

Before Annaliese could nod, the woman in the peacoat spoke up. "So why *are* you here in England?" she asked.

"I . . . My grandfather is British. He lives outside London. I've been staying with him since the war ended. We . . . I couldn't stay in Malmédy. Our house was bombed."

"Welcome to the club," the tall woman grumbled.

"Was it bad where you were?" said the woman in plaid, compassion filling her eyes.

For a moment Annaliese felt as though she were teetering on the edge between two places—the private abyss from which she had just escaped and the tortured world of public war. In her mind's eye she saw Rolf on one side, smelled his tobacco and schnapps, felt his hand strike her face, his boot crack against her ribs. On the other side she saw the rubble and blood on the streets of Malmédy: a haven nonetheless.

"It was hell," she finally said.

"Did you get to see your husband before he went back to the States?" the woman in plaid said, clearly wanting to change the subject.

Annaliese pushed away the images in her mind and shook her head.

"Me neither. I haven't seen him since he shipped out for D-Day.

I'm half-afraid that when we get to New York I won't recognize him!"

The matron at the head of the line called out for their attention. "All right, ladies, we're ready for the next group to come inside. Keep your little ones close to you and have your papers ready. That's right. When it's your turn, step up to the first table and present your documents. Then you will proceed into the theater for the medical screening. We'll get you settled in the dormitory and then a hot dinner awaits you."

The line began to move forward. Annaliese was glad for the distraction. Perhaps she could blend back into the background now and attract no more attention. She had only one aim: to board the first ship to America without anyone else paying her any mind.

But the line moved slowly. Only a few women at a time were allowed to approach the table inside. The woman in plaid turned her direction.

"I'm Phoebe. Phoebe Rogers. My husband's name is Harold, but everyone calls him Hal." She smiled at her child, who had awakened and was now looking around. "And this is Douglas."

"It is nice to meet you," Annaliese said after a moment's pause.

Phoebe grinned. "Aren't you going to tell me your name?"

The line inched forward. Phoebe closed the distance to the next woman in line and then turned around again. "Come on," she said with a warm smile. "What's your name?"

Annaliese hadn't expected such kind attention from any of the brides. "You don't have to be nice to me. I know what I sound like to people."

Phoebe shrugged. "But you said it yourself. You're Belgian. Is Belgium pretty? I've heard it's very pretty."

Annaliese thought of the ballet studio, the hummingbirds in Madame's garden, the slippery sound of the satin when she and her best friend, Katrine, tied the ribbons around their ankles, and the way Katrine's laugh had sounded like music. "It's the most wonderful place in the world," she said.

"I've never been to the Continent. I've never been anywhere," Phoebe continued. "I'm scared to death of the open water. They're probably going to have to drug me to get me onto the ship!"

Annaliese smiled politely. Phoebe was kind, but Annaliese wished she would stop talking. She wanted to be invisible. She wanted no one to remember meeting her. They inched forward.

"So you must speak French, too, then. Yes?" Phoebe said.

"I do."

"And here you are speaking English, too! That's so remarkable."

"Some English. I struggle with the words."

"But your grandfather lives near London? Where?"

The stuffed pony Douglas was holding fell from his grasp. Annaliese bent to retrieve it, letting the woman's question fall away.

"He is a very handsome boy," Annaliese said as she handed him the toy.

Phoebe's smile broadened. "I can't wait for Hal to meet him!"

A burst of wind suddenly swept around them. Two of Annaliese's papers flew from her hand and swirled off in different directions. Other girls also found themselves chasing after their papers. Annaliese dashed after the precious marriage certificate and from the corner of her eye she saw Phoebe snatch from the air the other document: an affidavit that attested her husband had the means to care for her.

She and Phoebe returned to the queue as the menacing wind settled.

"Katrine," Phoebe said, glancing at the affidavit as she handed it back. "What a pretty name."

Annaliese thanked her and pressed the documents to her chest.

Six

⁂

The chilled breeze that had earlier in the day taunted every war bride waiting to register had matured by nightfall into a surly tyrant that now hurled itself against the bricks of the dormitory at Tidworth Camp. Annaliese lay on her bunk and tried to block out the whining of the wind outside. Phoebe had sweetly insisted that she take the one above hers so that they'd be able to talk to each other as they tried to fall asleep in damp and unfamiliar quarters.

The army had hastily converted Tidworth's footlockers into cots for infants and toddlers, but Douglas kept climbing out of his. Phoebe was singing lullabies to her son, and every now and then she'd ask Annaliese if she was all right.

Annaliese had no strength to fend off her new friend's unexpected care. The activities of the day had mentally exhausted her, as had every day since she'd left Germany.

She knew when she stepped up to the first registration table hours earlier that she had all the documentation needed to be processed into Tidworth; Katrine had had everything in order a week before she was to leave. But Annaliese hadn't been certain she'd be able to convince the man behind the table that she was Katrine. They had always favored each other in looks; their ballet teacher had mistaken one for the other all the time.

But that was when they were eight.

Of all the documents Annaliese was required to present, it was the passport that had worried her the most. She and Katrine had been roughly the same height and weight, they'd had the same eye and hair color, and their birthdays had only been four months apart. But the black-and-white photograph of Katrine on page three of her passport had been taken in Brussels in October with a very nice camera. The image was sharp and clear. Cutting her hair and styling it exactly as Katrine had hadn't diminished the fact that Annaliese's eyes were narrower and her lips thinner. She'd trampled on the photo with muddied feet the day after everything changed. It was the only thing she could think to do to alter the photograph so that the subtle facial differences between her and Katrine wouldn't be noticed. When the mud dried and Annaliese had scraped it away, the luster and crispness of the photo was gone. *I was in a car accident the day before I was to come here,* Annaliese had practiced saying. *My passport flew off the dash and was run over. I'm so sorry. I cleaned it off as best I could.*

She knew she could say those words convincingly. Most of them were true. Her passport *had* been inside the car when it careened off the icy road and tumbled down an embankment. Her purse had flown out the space where the front window had been. But she'd left its contents, including her passport, in a spray of broken glass.

When Phoebe stood in front of the registration table, Annaliese listened carefully to everything she'd been asked. But there were other conversations taking place next to her and behind her and at a second table to her right. She hadn't been able to catch everything being said. Phoebe's paperwork was processed quickly and she was soon moving off to the next station to be fingerprinted.

"Next," the official said.

Annaliese laid her papers before him.

"Name, please." His gaze was on the documents.

Annaliese took a breath and steeled herself for whatever would come next.

"Katrine Sawyer."

He'd looked up quickly and Annaliese half-expected him to respond with, "Katrine Sawyer is dead," and then shout for guards to come arrest her. But he didn't.

"You're not British," he said, his voice laced with equal parts annoyance and curiosity.

"I am Belgian," Annaliese said calmly, masking her immense relief. The ruse was apparently working. No one had figured out yet what she had done.

He began to flip through her papers. "And why are you seeking passage to America from England?"

"As you will see there"—she pointed at the document in front of him—"I have permission. My mother was British. She married a Belgian man and moved to Belgium before I was born. But I couldn't live in Belgium anymore. My home had been bombed."

The man seemed satisfied, with both her documents and her answer. Then he opened her passport and frowned.

"I was in a car accident the day before I was to come here, and my passport flew off the dash and was run over. I'm so sorry. I cleaned it off as best I could." The words flew off her lips in a rush, and the man raised his head to stare at her.

"A car accident?"

Her pulse pounded in her head. "Yes."

"Everyone all right, then?"

His question had summoned images that Annaliese couldn't stop from replaying in her mind: Katrine crumpled in the driver's seat next to her, blood trickling from her nose and mouth, her head bent back at an odd angle and her eyes vacant and unblinking.

"Yes," she managed to say. "A few bumps and bruises, that's all."

But the lie had tasted like bile on her tongue.

"Do you have a criminal record, Mrs. Sawyer?"

Annaliese's heart skipped a beat. "What?"

"We have to ask every one of you this question. Do you have a criminal record?"

Annaliese shook her head and her eyes immediately filled with unwanted tears. "No."

"Ever been arrested for prostitution?"

"No!" she'd gasped.

"Are you pregnant?"

She shook her head.

He stamped her documents and then handed them back to her.

Relief coursed through her, at least for the moment. She had gotten past the registration tables. She found herself in a dazedly euphoric state while being escorted to the base theater with the same group of women she had waited with in line. Once inside the theater, they were told to remove their clothes and proceed onto the stage, where army doctors in white coats waited.

Angry cries of protest had erupted from the group of women, setting off wails among many of the babies and toddlers. But there was no getting past the medical exam, the Red Cross nurses told them. They were required to take off their clothes. The nurses held the children while the shaken women stepped out of their dresses and undergarments and lined up at the stage stairs, with their arms over their breasts.

Annaliese watched in shock as the first three brides were called up and then instructed to stand with their legs apart so that the doctors could use flashlights to inspect them for genital diseases.

Not one of the three could have been older than twenty, from what Annaliese could tell, and each of them burst into tears.

"I can't do that!" cried one.

"If you want to go to America, then you'll have to. It's as simple as that," said one of the doctors.

Additional cries of protest had risen up from the other women.

"Can they really make us do that?" Phoebe had whispered to Annaliese as they stood next to each other, nude, in the queue.

But Annaliese scarcely heard her.

Her mind had slammed her back to her wedding night, when Rolf had demanded the same thing of her. She had stood naked before him while he, too, fully clothed, had inspected her. He had done the exact same thing these doctors wanted to do. He had done other things. Worse things.

"This is immoral," said the woman who had earlier been wearing the peacoat.

"It's indecent!" the tall woman said.

"If you all want to get on a ship bound for America, this is how it is!" insisted one of the doctors.

"You're only doing this because you're just cheesed off that we married Americans!" the tall woman yelled.

More shouting had ensued. More children had begun to cry.

"What are we going to do?" Phoebe said, as she'd looked from Annaliese to the doctors to the shouting women all around them.

Then from the young, golden-haired French woman came a louder cry of "Enough!" She was standing fourth in line, at the top of the little stairs.

The theater went silent.

"After all we have survived, what is one more cruelty?" she'd said to the women who gazed up at her. "What is one more?" Then she turned toward the stage, strode forward, and stood in front of the crying girl who was to have been the first inspected.

The French woman dropped her arms and stood resolute with her legs apart. Her body was petite but beautifully formed. A tiny mound rounded her abdomen; she was pregnant, but only by a few months. The rest of her curves were shapely, and her skin was smooth.

"Is this good enough for you, Doctor?" she said, sarcasm subtly threading together every word. "Is this what you require of us?"

The doctor said nothing but went about his task, shining his little flashlight on the most private parts of her body and asking her calmly how far along she was.

Afterward, she walked confidently down the other set of stairs and began to put her clothes back on.

One by one the women followed suit.

Annaliese kept her eyes screwed shut when it was her turn. *It is a dream,* she told herself, over and over. *Soon I will wake up.*

Rolf. The war. Malmédy. Katrine.

I am dreaming and soon I'll wake up.

I am dreaming and soon I'll wake up.

Even now, as she lay shivering on the bunk, she whispered it again.

"What was that, Katrine?" Phoebe said.

"Nothing."

"Are you all right?"

Phoebe had asked this question several times in the past hour, and Annaliese had said yes. But not this time.

"I don't know," she said.

"Are you still thinking about that awful medical inspection? Because I think we should just pretend it didn't happen. I'm just going to forget what they made us do. It's done now. Just pretend it didn't happen."

"Pretend it didn't happen," Annaliese echoed.

"All right, yes, it sounds silly. But those people will never be able to make us feel that way again. We'll be in America soon and they can just kiss our little bare bums then, can't they?"

They shared a quiet laugh and then were quiet.

"Are you afraid of getting on the ship, Katrine?" Phoebe said a few moments later.

Getting on that ship is all I can think about.

"No."

"I'm afraid of all that water. There's so much of it. And you can't see where it ends. What if we sink? What if we hit an iceberg?"

"That doesn't happen anymore, Phoebe."

"Do you want to see if we can share a cabin on the ship? I'd feel better about it if you did. Please?"

It hadn't been in the plan to make friends. To become known to someone else. The plan had been to blend in quietly and unnoticed, get on a ship, out of England, and as far from Europe as possible.

And yet Phoebe reminded Annaliese of Katrine in so many little ways. Her quick smile, talkative nature, compassionate leanings. She could be Phoebe's friend for a handful of days, for that was all she could give her. When their ship docked in New York, Annaliese would need to disappear into the crowd as the rest of the war brides ran to be reunited with their husbands. And, Annaliese reasoned, Phoebe would actually be of some help to her in that regard. She could leave a letter with Phoebe, hide it in her coat pocket or something. Inside the letter could be a note to be given to Katrine's husband that would explain why she had done what she'd done.

Annaliese couldn't bear to have him hate her.

And maybe if she explained it, he wouldn't.

"Katrine?"

"All right," Annaliese replied.

"Oh, good!" Phoebe exhaled heavily. "I'm so glad. We need to talk about something else now or I will dream about sinking ships. Tell me about your husband. What he's like?"

Phoebe wasn't asking about Rolf, of course. She meant Katrine's husband, John. And it was easy to tell Phoebe what John was like. He was a kind, gentle, nice-looking man. Had things been different, Annaliese might have wanted John to have fallen in love with her instead of with Katrine.

But for a sliver of a moment Annaliese wanted to tell Phoebe what her real husband was like. She wanted her new friend—her only friend—to know why she'd left her beloved Katrine dead in her car and stolen her identity to get away from him.

RMS *QUEEN MARY*
BOSTON HARBOR
FEBRUARY 1942

There are no more serene sunsets over the water or champagne toasts or silk ties or velvet gowns. No children in the nursery, no shows in the cinema, no gala dinners. The beautiful paintings and woodwork have been covered with leather, and the twinkling chandeliers, the miles of carpet, the tapestries and silver have been stored away, not to be returned until the war is over, so said one crew member to another.

A gun, massive and strange, sits on the bow with its barrel pointed toward the skyline. The men who stand around the weapon speak about it as if it were a girl they are anxious to impress. The hull of the ship and the stacks—everything—are gray now, just like the gun.

The decks teem with passengers, but they are dressed for battle, not shuffleboard and afternoon tea. We are being readied for departure. The passengers are soldiers going to war.

I swirl about the captain, a man I do not know, as he speaks to the others on the bridge. He announces that we are headed for South Africa, a place I have never been.

When the tugs pull us out, the passengers stand at the railing, watching the safe confines of land slip away.

"There'll be U-boats," one soldier says to another.

I wonder what a U-boat is, as the two soldiers shake their heads and flick cigarette ash over the railing. They watch the receding coastline as though it will be the last time they see it.

They do not respond to my touch.

Their gazes are fixed on the disappearing ribbon of land that is falling away.

Seven

There were few people Brette trusted with the knowledge that she could see into that strange bit of ethereal property that lingering souls defiantly occupied. She'd discovered that either people didn't believe that ghosts existed—and therefore she was delusional—or they were terrified by the possibility that they did exist—and therefore she was somehow an accomplice to that terror. The circle of people who knew was small, just as it had been when she was very young, when Aunt Ellen had offered one bit of advice to her parents that they'd been happy to follow.

Tell only who you need to.

After her great-aunt deposited six-year-old Brette in her room upon their return from the attic, Ellen told her to stay put until she or her mother came for her.

"Wait here on the bed and look at books," Ellen had said. "And don't listen to what I am going to tell your mommy and daddy." Ellen had closed the door behind her, but then she'd opened it slightly so that a thin line of space peeked at Brette as she sat on the bed. From the slim opening Ellen looked at her and then laid a finger to her lips.

Brette had waited only a second before scampering over to the door to eavesdrop on the hushed conversation taking place in the next room.

At Ellen's request, Nadine asked Cliff to come inside from trimming the hedges. She had something she needed to say to the both of them and it needed to be said while the other guests were out of the house.

"Brette has it," Aunt Ellen announced quietly a moment later, as though Brette had been handed something important and now held it in her grasp. She had looked down at her empty hands. What was it that she had? she wondered.

"Has what?" her mother had asked, and she sounded fearful. "What do you mean?"

"You know what I mean."

"Good God, Ellen!" Cliff said angrily. "What have you been telling her? She's just a kid."

"So was I when I saw my first ghost. Believe me, I wouldn't have wished this on her for a million dollars. I told her nothing, Cliff. Not a thing. But you and Nadine need to know. And so does Brette. She needs to know she has the Sight."

Brette's father had cursed then, voicing a string of words Brette knew she was not supposed to say. But she barely heard them. The word *ghost* was swirling about in her head. Ghosts were white-sheeted, floating wisps that moaned and groaned on Halloween. Aunt Ellen wasn't making any sense.

As Ellen recounted to Brette's parents what had just happened in the attic, she began to understand. The child on the windowsill, the boy who looked like mist and whose feet made no noise and who vanished in a blink, was a ghost.

And while Brette contemplated that revelation, her parents shouted at each other. *You should have listened to me,* her mother said to her father. *Aunt Ellen should never have come to visit,* he replied.

"Wishing isn't going to make this go away," Aunt Ellen said.

"You need to let me talk to Brette so that I can explain some things."

"Not a chance," Cliff said angrily.

Aunt Ellen's voice rose then, and Brette could hear her as if she were right in the room with them.

"The cruelest thing you can do," she said, her voice steely, "is to send me away without letting me talk to Brette. Do you want your daughter to be terrified of what she can see? Do you want her to grow up ostracized, or worse, institutionalized?"

Brette heard her mother admonish them to keep their voices down.

"We should never have allowed you to come," her father said again.

"You should thank God in heaven that I did!" Aunt Ellen said, just as loud as before. "Do you really want to imagine what it would have been like for Brette if this had happened when I wasn't here? Does Cliff know what became of Cousin Lucille? Does he know why your mother didn't want treatment for her cancer?"

Aunt Ellen must have said this part to Nadine because her mother said, "No."

"You have got to let me tell her the barest minimum, Cliff," Aunt Ellen said. "Just enough to keep her in the know until she's older. And then I need to tell her the rest."

Her mother started crying.

"The rest?" her father asked. But he didn't sound quite as angry as before. He sounded frustrated.

"She doesn't need to know everything right now." Aunt Ellen said this in a louder voice, almost as if she wanted Brette to plainly hear that there was more she needed to know just in case her parents tossed Aunt Ellen out of the house that very minute and she never saw her again.

"I don't even know if I believe any of this," her father said.

"It doesn't matter what you believe, Cliff. This isn't about you. Nadine, I have to speak to her. You know I do. You've seen what this can do to the women in our family."

"So you're telling us this house is haunted?" her father challenged.

"Maybe we should sell it. Move. Find another B and B somewhere else," Nadine offered in a trembling voice.

"Your house isn't haunted," Ellen answered. "There is just a thin place in this house where spirits can slide in. And you know as well as I do that moving won't change anything, Nadine. There are thin places everywhere."

In the end her parents had relented.

The four of them sat down in the living room. Cliff and Nadine were quiet while Aunt Ellen tried to explain that Brette might see someone like the boy in the attic in another place, another time. Or maybe even inside the house again. Someone who didn't seem quite all there, and whom other people could not see.

"You don't need to be afraid of them, Brette," Aunt Ellen said. "None of you need to be afraid." And then she looked at Cliff and Nadine. "They won't hurt anyone."

"Are they ghosts?" Brette asked, and she remembered feeling no fear.

"That is what some people call them. I call them Drifters because they kind of float in and out. Like birthday balloons. You don't need to call them anything, Brette. You don't need to do anything with them. Or for them. Do you hear me?"

Brette had nodded.

Aunt Ellen leaned forward then and took Brette's small hands in her wrinkled ones.

"I want you to listen carefully to me. It is very important that you remember what I tell you now. Are you listening?"

"Yes," Brette had said.

"You can see them, and I can see them. Your grandma could see them. There are very few people who can. It's something that some of the girls in our family can do, but not all. Your mommy can't."

Brette cast a glance at her mother. A tear had run down one of Nadine's cheeks, leaving a shiny trail. She smiled at Brette reassuringly.

"Brette, since most people can't see what you and I can see, this has to be our little secret," Ellen continued. "Yours, and mine, and your mommy's and daddy's. Okay? You can't tell anyone because they won't understand. This is our secret for the four of us. Just us four. Will you promise me that? Can you keep a secret?"

Even then, Brette didn't quite understand what the big deal was, but her parents were nodding encouragingly. "I can keep a secret," she'd said.

"That's my good girl. Now, one more thing. And this is the most important thing. Are you ready to hear it?"

She nodded.

"I want you to promise me you won't talk to them, Brette. I know you might want to. I did when I was your age. But it's not a good idea."

This seemed a silly request to Brette. "Why isn't it a good idea?" she'd asked.

"Because if you talk to them, they will come around more often. And you won't want that. You're going to have to trust me on this, Brette. If you were to talk to the little boy in the attic, he might want to stay here. But this is not his house. It's your house. Yours and Mommy's and Daddy's. If you start talking to him, he may never want to leave. And he needs to leave. He doesn't belong here. None of them belong here."

"Because they're dead," Brette said, and her mother shuddered. Her father had closed his eyes.

"Yes," Aunt Ellen replied.

"Why aren't they in heaven?"

"I don't know. I don't know why they didn't go on to where they were supposed to when they died, but that's not your problem, sweetie."

"Whose problem is it?"

"It's *their* problem. I think they know what they need to do. But they are afraid."

This concept fascinated Brette. "Ghosts are afraid?"

"Yes," Aunt Ellen answered. "They are afraid of what they can't see, just like us. It's as if there's a bridge they need to cross. And it's like crossing over the ocean, Brette. They can't see the other side. So they are afraid to cross it."

While Brette contemplated this, Aunt Ellen squeezed her hands again. "Can you remember the two things you need to do?"

Brette nodded. "Keep the secret. And . . ." The other request had floated away on her thoughts.

"And don't talk to them. Say it aloud."

"And don't talk to them."

"That's right. Pretend you can't see them, that's what I do when I want them to leave me alone. When you are older, you and your mother can come visit me in Phoenix, and we will talk about it again. All right? Can you promise to do those two things?"

It had seemed easy enough to say she would, and her parents had looked so relieved and happy.

So she had promised.

Ellen left the next day.

And that was the last time Brette saw her. Eleven months later, she died of a massive stroke. Since the episode in the attic, Brette had only seen one other ghost—a fleeting female image outside a Mexican restaurant in Old Town that hadn't even looked Brette's way. In the days after Aunt Ellen's death, Brette wondered if perhaps her great-aunt would come visit her in the attic, like the little boy had, and tell her the rest of what she needed to know.

But she didn't.

Instead, a letter addressed to Brette was found paper-clipped to Ellen's will, dated just two weeks after she'd left Willow House. It had been sent by registered mail to Nadine from a Twin Cities attorney's office. Her parents had read it first, and then her mother read it aloud while the three of them sat on the private patio, away from any B and B guests:

My dear Brette:

It is my hope that when you are older, I will be able to tell you myself what you need to know. But life is uncertain. I can't guarantee that in a few years' time I can share with you in person the fact that there is a dark side to the secret world you are able to see. If you are reading this letter, it means I have passed on, and you must be told earlier than I would have liked that there is a great responsibility attached to the gift you possess. Having the Sight means you can see into the thin places of the spirit world. It is a real world, just like ours, but it is not ours. Angels live there, but so do other beings. I think you know what I mean.

You will not see the angels. They do not wander, lost and confused, like the Drifters. The angels are good and they do good things. You might see the Others, though. And they are not angels. They are not to be trusted, Brette. They are not good. As you grow older, you may think you can tell which ones are ghosts and which ones are the Others. And maybe you will be able to do so. But trust me, it is not worth trying to see if you can. The Others will try to trick you, or harm you. People who chase after ghosts often encounter the Others instead and they do not even know it. The Others do nothing for your good. Nothing, Brette. But they can't hurt you unless you befriend them. So don't.

You may wonder if I will visit you after I have died to tell you these things, but if the choice is mine, I won't. I have no assurance that I could choose where I might wander or that I could prevent myself from crossing that bridge I told you about. I don't even know that I would remember why I stayed behind, if indeed I could do such a thing. An earthbound soul does not think the same way as when he or she was alive. It's like they are sleepwalking or just on the edge of waking up. They don't possess all the reasoning skills they had before. They will whisper the same questions, loiter in the same places, move the same objects from place to place. They do not make much progress at anything they attempt and they don't seem to understand that it's because they don't belong here. You may think you can help them. But it is dangerous, exhausting work, Brette. And it is not your responsibility. Remember that. You owe them nothing. Other women in our family who tried to help were overtaken by the weight of spending too much time in a dimension not meant for them. My cousin Lucille spent the first third of her life misunderstood and feared, the second third cavorting with entities on the other side, and the last third as a resident in a mental hospital, dying too young at fifty-three.

You are the last of the women in our family who has the Sight. It skips around the generations with no regular pattern. Right now, you are the only one. And you must not go looking for other people who can do what you do. You must be very careful who you tell.

Do not go looking for ghosts, Brette, even if people you care about ask you to. And do not talk to any Drifter that looks like me. Ever. Don't do it, dear Brette. I assure you, it won't be me.

The more time you spend interacting with the souls on the other side, the more attracted to you they will be. And you have your own life to live. Always remember, Brette: You dwell in the land of the living. This is where your life is. This is where you belong.

All my love,
Aunt Ellen

When her mother finished reading the letter, she and Brette's father gently demanded that Brette promise to heed all of Ellen's words of advice, adding that to do otherwise would be to disobey a direct instruction from them.

In her younger years, Brette kept her promise—for the most part. But there were times she failed. When she was nine years old, she couldn't resist talking to a spectral young woman who said her name was Marjorie, and who for more than a year sat on Willow House's back porch every night, staring at the surf. And when she was ten, she befriended the ghost of a man wearing a policeman's uniform, who wandered about the playground at school every noon recess. Just as Aunt Ellen had said in her letter, it was hard to have a meaningful conversation with ghosts. The two she'd encountered were so inwardly focused and seemingly only half-awake. She had eventually stopped talking with them.

Having a secret life made it hard to make and keep friends, though. Other girls found Brette strange, a bit of a daydreamer and hard to get close to. In junior high, she was befriended by a freckled redhead named Kacey, to whom she told everything, and who did not run home screaming. Kacey was a good friend, but she moved away at the end of eighth grade and stopped writing to her a year later.

In high school, Brette mostly kept to herself, almost preferring the odd company of a ghost now and then to the self-fixated girls in her classes, who clearly thought her freakishly peculiar.

She'd been able to keep the Sight a secret from everyone at school until her senior year, when, in a moment of weakness, she spilled it to ever-popular Kimberly Devane. Brette had mistaken Kimberly's patronizing kindness as a true overture to friendship, an error high school wallflowers too often tend to make. The fact that weird Brette Mason claimed she could see and talk to dead people had been the kind of secret that Kimberly Devane simply had to blab—in record time—to everyone she knew. Sixteen years later Brette could still see the repulsed and astonished looks of classmates—in the hallways, in class, and in the library—who'd been on the receiving end of Kimberly Devane's bit of hot gossip that day. Kimberly and every other high school classmate who'd heard that Brette Mason talked to ghosts dissolved into the thorny horizon of post–high school life. Brette went away to college, though she could have stayed in San Diego, choosing Arizona State University to get her psychology degree, mostly because Aunt Ellen had lived in nearby Phoenix, and there had been a time when she thought all of her questions would be answered if only Aunt Ellen had lived a little longer.

She did get some answers in Arizona, but they were not provided by Aunt Ellen.

A fellow ASU student, and the first true friend Brette had made since eighth grade, was keenly interested in all things supernatural. Heather was a Phoenix native and had a sizable group of friends in the area who shared her fascination with the paranormal. Within a few months of meeting Heather, Brette found herself the center of attention after her new friend told several of her chums what Brette could do. There had been no disbelieving eye rolls, no wide-eyed stares, no fearful uneasiness. On the contrary, the response from Heather and her friends had been near-reverent curiosity. To suddenly have peers genuinely impressed with her was a new and thrilling feeling for Brette.

She declined their initial requests to demonstrate her ability, but eventually Heather convinced her to let them witness her encountering a Drifter. The first ghost hunt had been tame and easy. One of Heather's longtime friends lived in an older house where unexplained things happened all the time. Objects went missing, strange noises were often heard, and lights and other appliances would switch on for no reason. Brette was able to easily make contact with the Drifter—a woman who had died during the influenza epidemic of 1918. Her name was Blanche, and she'd left behind a fiancé who went on to marry another. Nearly one hundred years later the Drifter was still pining after a love she'd not been able to fully experience in life.

The second hunt took place at a hotel known for its share of ghosts. Again, Brette had easily been able to wow her new friends with her talent. It wasn't until three or four encounters later that she remembered Aunt Ellen's warning that using the Sight would attract unwanted attention, and that dark forces residing in the spiritual realm would also begin to show interest.

The shadowy apparitions started first, then the sense of being continually followed, and then the outright stares from beings that looked like Drifters but seemed highly aware of their surroundings and intentional in their behavior. Then, late in her sophomore year, one of Heather's friends threw a party that included a séance, and Brette, against her better judgment, was prevailed upon to invite an audience from beyond the physical realm. The response had been swift and oppressive, a malevolent force so heavy and thick that Brette had screamed and then passed out under its weight. When she awoke, the lights had been turned back on, the candles blown out, and the curtains in the room pulled back. Festive music was playing, and all signs of the séance had been whisked away.

A shaken Heather was standing over Brette, holding a compress to her head while the other partygoers hovered nearby, equally stunned. For a few fleeting moments, Brette learned later, Heather thought she was going to have to call 911.

It had taken weeks for the sensation that demons were tracking her every move to dissipate, and even longer for the whispers of *We can help you* to fully fade. For months, vivid nightmares disturbed her sleep, blinding headaches interrupted her days, and a raw sense of foreboding shadowed her even after she returned home for the summer. Her parents had been worried about her, and the experience had so unnerved Brette that she opted not to return to Phoenix. She transferred to San Diego State, changed her major from psychology to public relations, and slowly learned how to ignore anything having to do with the Sight. Over the next few years she fell in and out of love and made new friends. But she told no one. Not the roommate she shared an apartment with in Pacific Beach. Not the boyfriend she met at a New Year's Eve party three years after graduation. Not the next boyfriend she met online a couple of years later. She even put off telling Keith until after he'd proposed and she'd accepted. And even then she shared with him only the barest minimum. *Ghosts exist, Keith. And I can see them.*

There were days she wished there were another female in the family whom she could talk to. Surely there must be someone among her second or third cousins who had the Sight. But she had never summoned the courage to locate and then reach out to any of them. What was she to have done? Send off a letter that began with, *Hi. You don't know me, but I'm your distant relative. Do you happen to be able to see ghosts?* The idea was laughable.

The circle of people who knew was as small as it had ever been.

Her parents and Keith. Just three people. Keith's parents and brother didn't know. Her friends at the hospital and in book club didn't know. The couple next door with whom she and Keith sometimes double-dated didn't know.

Most of the time the ghosts she saw didn't even know.

And that was the way she intended to keep it.

Eight

⁂

The days following the baby shower were challenging, but that came as no surprise to Brette. A physical encounter with a ghost always seemed to lay out a welcome mat to other nearby Drifters.

Brette was confident that the ghost anxious over the whereabouts of someone named Bess wouldn't trouble itself to follow her home twenty miles up the coast from downtown San Diego. Ghosts tended to stay in one place. But the little conversation in the bathroom had temporarily increased Brette's sensitivity to other Drifters and theirs to her. Like the floating dust motes from a shaken rug, the air around her needed to settle again, and that always took too long.

On Monday, there had been a ghost at the microbrewery where Keith wanted to have dinner. On Wednesday, a Drifter stared at Brette during her lunch hour at the hospital where she worked as an admissions counselor.

On Thursday, as she and Keith took an evening walk along the beach, an apparition of a skinny man with a ragged beard began to trail them. The timing couldn't have been worse. Keith wanted to have the "let's have a baby" discussion again, and he had no sooner mentioned it than the hair on the back of Brette's neck prickled. A quick glance back was all she needed to see that a ghost was now following them.

She'd mentioned that fact to Keith and suggested they walk a little faster. Keith immediately assumed she was just looking for reasons to talk about something else.

"Come on, Brette." His voice was tinged with disappointment.

"There's a Drifter. He's right behind us," she said softly.

Keith exhaled heavily, the sigh of a frustrated man.

"I'm not kidding. There really is one."

Keith had glanced back but she knew he wouldn't be able to see anything out of the ordinary. He said nothing when he swung his head back around, and the expression on his face was difficult to read. She actually hadn't had that many ghostly encounters since meeting Keith, and so few in his presence that he had begun to minimize the ability in a way that made her feel like she might one day outgrow it, even though she knew that was unlikely. Aunt Ellen had the Sight until the day she died. So did Cousin Lucille. So did the grandmother she had never met. Keith's being able to downplay that which had seemed to define her was one of the things that she'd liked best about him. A researcher for a biomedical firm, Keith was decidedly a man of science, but he had never made light of her gifting. There were plenty of things science couldn't explain, he'd told her on the night he proposed—a year after they met—and the same night she'd at last confessed what she could do.

"Are you saying we're not going to talk about this?" he asked now.

"I'm just saying I want to walk a little faster."

He had looked behind them again. "Because there's a ghost following us."

"Yes. Why would I lie to you?"

For a moment there were just the sounds of the lacy surf off to the right, the call of a gull, and the whirring of a cyclist moving past them in the bike lane.

"So we can talk about it then?" he asked.

She hesitated.

"You asked for some more time. I think I've been patient," Keith continued, when she said nothing.

"I know you have," she murmured.

He *had* been patient. The last time he'd brought up the topic of having a baby had been six months ago.

"I hate to be cliché, but we aren't getting any younger. We're both thirty-four. And we don't even know if you'll be able to get pregnant right away. What if it takes a while?"

They stopped and Brette looked out toward the indigo vastness of the Pacific Ocean. Ellen's words from long ago echoed in her mind for the first time in years. *They are afraid of what they can't see, just like us. It's as if there's a bridge they need to cross. And it's like crossing over the ocean, Brette. They can't see the other side. So they are afraid to cross it.*

"Brette."

She turned from the blue-gray seascape to face her husband.

"What is it you're afraid of?" Keith asked, almost as if he'd read her thoughts.

Brette paused a second before answering. "What if we have a girl?" She shuddered slightly as the words passed her lips.

"A girl?" Keith echoed.

"Yes." Brette turned to face him.

Keith was silent for only a moment. "*That's* what's bothering you?"

"Of course that's what's bothering me! Aren't you concerned about it?"

He put his arm around her. "No. I guess I'm not."

For the first time in their married life Brette wished she had shared more, told him more, opened Keith's eyes to what it was like to be able to see into the thin places where ghosts resided. The ragged Drifter hovered a few yards away, staring at her.

"You should be," she said gently. She had thought she was doing them both a favor by keeping him largely in the dark. "You don't know what it's like. It's nothing I would want to afflict a daughter with."

"Brette—"

"It only shows up in the women in my family, Keith!"

"Some of the women. You told me it was just some."

"There's no regularity to it! It just pops up without warning!"

Keith coaxed her to sit down on the cement wall that separated the sand of the beach from the sidewalk and the street.

"I hear what you're saying. But that didn't stop your parents from having you," he said.

"My mother doesn't have the Sight. I doubt she was even thinking that she could pass this on to me." Keith didn't appreciate the risk at all. And that was her fault.

"But how do you know that? She knew it skipped generations, right? She knew her mother had it and her aunt had it. So she probably did consider it."

This was a thought she hadn't pondered before. She was silent as she let this revelation wash over her. Her mother had to have known that if she gave birth to a girl, that child might end up with the Sight. Of course she had known.

"And maybe it's not really as bad as you think it is. Maybe . . ." Keith's voice trailed off.

She turned to face him. "Maybe what?"

"Maybe it's not that bad if you just ignore it. That's what you've told me you always do."

She laughed lightly at her naïveté in having shared so little with Keith. "You have no idea how incredibly bad it can be," she replied.

"And that's my fault. I never wanted you to know. I didn't want you to think I was crazy or delusional or for you to tire of dealing with it. With me. The sightings can be hard to ignore, Keith. Really hard. I've just always pretended to you that it's easy."

They were both quiet for a moment.

"Perhaps it's time you talk to someone about this," he finally said.

"What do you mean?"

"I mean perhaps you should see a professional." Keith did not look at her.

"A professional *what*?"

"A psychologist or something."

"And tell him or her that I see ghosts?" Brette felt a terrible tugging within the fabric of their faith in each other. Keith had always made it seem as though she had an unwanted ability, not a psychosis of some kind. "I'm not crazy, Keith."

"I didn't say you were."

"Well, what are you saying?"

He slowly turned to face her. His gaze was kind but full of uncertainty. "I'm saying maybe you should talk to a psychologist who understands what you can see."

Several seconds of silence passed between them.

"Do you believe I can see ghosts?" She kept his gaze, willing him to answer her truthfully.

He took a moment before answering. "If you say you see them, then I believe you."

They sat quietly for several long moments.

"I have that trip to Chicago coming up in a few days," he finally said.

"I know." Brette closed her eyes against what he might say next.

"Maybe you could do a couple things for me—for us—while I am gone."

She inhaled deep the evening sea air. "What do you want me to do?"

Please don't tell me to make an appointment with a shrink, she inwardly pleaded.

"Talk to your mom about this. Ask her if she had to do it all over again, would she still have had a child."

Brette already knew what her mother would say, that she could not imagine life without Brette. But she answered that yes, she would.

"And look into seeing if there's a professional of some kind who can help you. Not some nutcase or wacko. An expert. You've shouldered this on your own long enough. Find someone you trust who believes you and can help you handle this ability you've got. Will you do that while I'm gone?"

She started to answer that there was no one like that. But the truth was, she had never looked. Maybe there was. Maybe there was someone out there who could help her figure out how to live the full life Aunt Ellen had wished for her way back in the beginning. Maybe there was someone who understood what she could do, and had the answers to the questions she'd wanted to ask Ellen and had never had the opportunity to.

Brette leaned into her husband, and he slipped his arm over her shoulder.

"All right. I promise," she said.

The ragged Drifter slid in to sit beside her on the wall, and the three of them gazed silently at the rolling surf.

Nine

Keith left for his weeklong trip to Chicago late Sunday afternoon, and Brette found herself uncharacteristically glad to have the condo to herself for the next seven days. Since their walk on the beach she'd come to see with even more clarity that it had been a mistake to keep Keith in the dark about how often she saw the thin places and their mysterious occupants. She had deluded herself into thinking that she'd been shielding him, but now she knew it had really been an act of self-preservation.

He gave no hint that he was worried about her mental state when they got back to the condo after the walk, behaving as if what stood between them becoming parents were just a simple thing, easily fixed. They had spent the weekend organizing the garage, eating out with friends, kayaking in La Jolla Cove, reading the paper on the patio, and sipping cappuccinos. Keith hadn't mentioned again what they had talked about on the beach, but the unspoken mood between them all weekend was slightly artificial, as if they both knew there was unfinished business that wouldn't get taken care of until he left for Chicago and she made good on her two promises. Their parting at the airport was affectionate, but Brette felt the weight of his restlessness as he kissed her good-bye. She knew as she drove off and he waved a final farewell that he'd squelched his concerns from Thursday so that they could enjoy the three days before he left. But they hadn't been far from his mind.

When he texted her later that he'd made it to the hotel with no complications, he added that he was already looking forward to coming home. On Tuesday evening when he called, Keith asked if Brette had made any progress on what they'd talked about.

"I was thinking I'd call Mom later tonight," she'd replied hastily. The lie had flown off her lips before she could ponder why she didn't want to just tell him no, she hadn't.

"Glad to hear it," he'd said. "You don't mind if I ask how it went when I call on Friday, do you?"

"Of course I don't mind."

"I'm curious now. I'd like to know what she tells you."

Keith's interest in this masked extension of her life was strange and new. And almost comforting but not quite. "Um. Sure," Brette said, after a moment's pause.

They hung up after saying good-bye, and Brette refilled her wineglass. It was a few minutes after seven. Her parents were probably just sitting down to eat. She'd wait a bit. Maybe she'd ask if her mother wanted to get together for dinner later in the week so that she could ask her questions in person rather than over the phone. She was sure now that her mother had to have weighed the risks and opted to take her chances. But had she brooded over it first, like Brette was doing now? Did she have to be talked into trying to have a baby? Was her dad the one who'd said, *Are we really going to let fear dictate our decision here?* Or had it been Nadine who asked that question and then answered it with a decisive *No, we're not?* And then of course her maternal grandmother had the Sight as well. Had she wrestled with whether to have children? Did Nadine ever ask?

Brette sat down at her laptop and opened a web browser. While she waited to call her mom, she'd trawl the Internet to search for a paranormal professional. Keith had said maybe she needed to speak to a psychologist, but Brette didn't think that was the place to start. She needed an educated professional, but it had to be someone who had the practical expertise to advise her. Someone who didn't think she was nuts. Someone who was convinced death wasn't the end of it all. Someone who could appreciate the wonder and danger of having the Sight but who also had the wisdom to know how Brette could take charge of it.

The number of results for her search words, *professionals* plus *paranormal* plus *help*, was astonishing. Everything from how to work with a medium to how to schedule an exorcist to how to know if your house was haunted was instantly at her fingertips. Clicking through the dozens of pages of results would take far longer than one night. Brette had grudgingly browsed through the first set of largely unhelpful results when her cell phone rang. Seeing that it was her mother seemed almost providential.

"Hey, Mom. I was just going to call you."

"Something up?" Her mother spoke softly, as though calling from the inside of a library.

"No. I just . . . I thought maybe we'd grab a bite sometime this week. There's something I want to run by you."

There was a momentary pause.

"Mom? Is everything all right?"

"Yes. I was just trying to get to a quiet corner of the house so I could talk to you in private. We've a gentleman who's been here the better part of the afternoon waiting for your dad and me to get home from a funeral. He says he knows you. And he really wants to see you. He says he needs your help."

Brette looked up from her computer screen. "Who is it?"

"Some old friend of yours from high school."

A warning bell went off inside Brette's head. "I don't have any friends from high school."

"He said you and he had a number of the same classes. Trevor Prescott? I think he said he lives in Texas now."

Good Lord, Brette breathed. Trevor Prescott had been in Kimberly Devane's circle of friends. He had also been the only one in that group of highly popular students who had been nice to her. He'd always behaved toward her as if she were a member of his crowd, which she knew she was not. She had appreciated that about him, his way of making her feel accepted and of value. But on the day Kimberly broadcast Brette's secret, he'd looked at her with the same fear and revulsion as everyone else. She waited for the *I'm just kidding!* response that should follow something as ridiculous as what her mother had just said. But it didn't come.

"Brette? Do you know him?"

"Yes. I know him."

"He really wants to talk to you. And he won't say what it's about. He just said it was very important and that he's only in California for a few more days. I told him I'd call you to see if you'd allow me to give him your phone number. He seems very nice. I don't recall you ever mentioning him, though."

"That's because I never did."

A dozen thoughts raced in Brette's head, paired with a dozen images. Trevor in her freshman comp class picking up her pencil when she'd dropped it. Trevor sitting one chair away in American History and asking if she wanted a piece of gum. Trevor surrounded by jocks and cheerleaders but nodding hello to Brette as she walked by.

Trevor shocked and wide-eyed the day Kimberly Devane announced Brette's macabre talent.

That day was the last time he had made eye contact with her. Sixteen years had come and gone since their high school graduation. Brette had stayed in contact with no one from that time in her life.

"Well, what do you want me to tell him? He's out in the common room with your father," her mother said.

Brette twirled her finger on the base of her wineglass. What could Trevor Prescott possibly want from her?

"Brette?"

"Put him on."

"All right. Hold on a sec."

A few moments later, a voice that Brette had never expected to hear again spoke her name.

"Brette. Thanks for talking to me. I can't tell you how glad I am."

For a moment she could not speak.

"How did you find me?" she managed to say, even though she didn't care in the least how he'd located her. It was that he'd contacted her at all that was mind-boggling.

"I remember you told me once your parents owned this bed-and-breakfast. I tried to find you on Facebook and Instagram and LinkedIn. But you're not on any of those sites."

"What do you want?"

"I need to talk to you about something important. May I come over to your place? Or I could meet you somewhere. Please?"

"Trevor, what is this about? You and I haven't spoken a word to each other since high school."

"I know. I wouldn't have bothered you at all if it wasn't important. But I need your help. I don't know who else to turn to."

"You need my help."

"Yes."

Her more practical side kicked in at that moment. As fascinating as it was to hear Trevor Prescott speak to her this way, she knew she was no one to him. Whatever it was he wanted, she had probably been the last resource he'd tried.

"I haven't stayed in touch with anyone from high school, if that's what you are hoping. I don't know where any of your old friends are."

"Can we just meet somewhere?"

The subdued desperation in his voice was both off-putting and appealing. But she did not trust it. He was probably wondering where Kimberly Devane had ended up.

"I seriously doubt I can help you, Trevor. Sorry, but I need to go."

"Please! I'm not asking for me. I'm asking for my daughter."

"Your daughter?"

"She thinks her mother is on the *Queen Mary*! You know. The ship." Trevor's voice faltered. "We toured the ship on Saturday. It's all Emily will talk about now. She can't sleep. She won't eat. All she wants to do is go back there and be with her mother."

"Trevor, I—"

"Her mother is *dead*. My wife died in a car accident six months ago. Laura's dead, Brette. You've got to help me."

For several seconds silence hung between them.

"Help you do *what*?" Brette finally said.

"Was what Kimberly said about you all those years ago true? Can you see and talk to ghosts?"

Brette had no interest in ghost-chasing, but the tone of Trevor's voice was so childlike and earnest, hopeful and yet so afraid. In her mind's eye, she saw his grief-stricken daughter, grappling with such tremendous loss at so tender an age. Brette's dormant mother-heart awakened with a jolt, and she winced as though a splinter from what had been a protective shell had sliced into her. It had been on the tip of her tongue to tell Trevor it didn't matter if she could talk to ghosts, she could not help him. But those weren't the words that came out of her mouth.

Instead, she gave him her address.

Ten

After Sébastien left the wine cellar, Simone was alone with the wounded American.

The flashlight had been left with her but it was sitting atop a barrel to her right. Its meager light was illuminating only the back wall—a length of rock and wood that revealed that the hidden cellar was part cave. She wanted the light closer to her so that she could see the American's face, but she dared not lift her hand from the wound to crawl over the straw to get it.

Sébastien had pressed her for details on how she'd killed an officer of the Gestapo, but she had told him nothing, and he hadn't the time to convince her to reveal more. He'd seemed proud of her, envious maybe. His admiration for her—if that was what it was—unsettled her.

There had recently been moments when Simone had almost forgotten that she'd done what her father had told her to do: She had held the gun steady and she'd kept her eyes open when she'd fired it. Some mornings she would awaken and not instantly remember the German man with the gold tooth. She wouldn't remember the sound the gun made when she pulled the trigger or see the spray of blood. Sometimes she would wake up and for a moment she was in her own bed in the flat above the shoe-repair shop and she would wonder for just a second what was poking her. But then she'd open her eyes and she'd smell the barrels and the dirt and she'd feel the coarse straw she'd slept on and it would come back to her.

All of it.

But she'd told Sébastien only that she was not proud of what she had done, it had just seemed the only thing she could do. And he'd nodded once and then headed up the stairs to get the woman named Marie.

She was wondering if the American would die while everyone was out fetching things, when he suddenly spoke. She hadn't realized he was awake. The faint light cast by the flashlight was not strong enough to plainly show that his eyes were now open.

The words that came out of his mouth were masked by pain, a parched throat, and a language of which Simone only knew the elementals.

"I am American," he sputtered, almost proudly, and Simone supposed he had been told to say this if he was captured in occupied territory. He said other words, too, but most were lost on her. She heard the English words for *airplane* and *United States* but the rest of what he was saying was a mystery. He tried to get up and then cried out as he fell back onto the straw.

Simone repositioned her hand on his wound and he grimaced. She didn't know the English words for *Lie still. You have been shot. Do not worry. You are among allies. We will help you.* All she could remember from those long-ago English classes at school were useless conversational phrases like *I have a gray cat* and *Do you think it will rain?* and *The bus leaves at three o'clock.*

So she made a shushing sound, the kind a mother might make to a child who has awakened from a nightmare. She said the French phrases she wished she knew how to say in English, in as gentle a tone as she could.

He quieted. And then he spoke in halting French. "Where am I?"

"Do you speak French, *monsieur*?" Simone leaned closer to him to get a better glimpse of his face.

"Only little."

"You have been shot. Help is coming. Do you understand?"

The American hesitated only a moment before continuing. "My camera. Do you have?"

"*Oui*. Henri has your camera. It is safe."

"Henri?"

"This is Henri's wine cellar. A secret one. You are at a vineyard near Venelles. Henri and François and Sébastien brought you here."

"Who are . . . who are those?"

Simone pondered her answer a moment. "They are people who can help you."

"Résistance?"

Papa had told her never to mention the word, never to admit knowing anything about it.

"And you?" the American continued, when she said nothing.

"I am Simone."

Perhaps the American had been expecting her to say she was part of the underground movement as well. He seemed taken aback that she had said her name instead.

"I am Lieutenant Everett Robinson," he replied.

He had no sooner said his name than the cellar door opened and boots again were heard on the steps.

The man startled, and Simone used one hand to gently touch his arm. "Shhh."

Henri and Collette rounded the corner, laden with a basin of hot water, more blankets, strips of cloth, and the bottle of Armagnac. Henri had also brought a kerosene lantern that threw a stronger light about the room.

"He is awake?" Henri asked as he set the lantern down on the same barrel with the flashlight.

"Yes," Simone answered. "He knows some French. Not much. His name is Lieutenant Robinson and he knows we are here to help."

"You talked to him?" Henri frowned, unhappy that Simone had said anything to the American.

"He wanted to know where he was and who brought him here. He was agitated. I needed to assure him we were here to help him. And that's what I told him." She narrowed her gaze at Henri so that he would understand she had divulged nothing about who Henri was besides a simple vintner.

Henri knelt down to get a better look at the man and spoke directly to him. "We found the remains of your plane. You were found a mile from here unconscious in an abandoned barn. We are looking for your parachute to get rid of it."

"I told you he only speaks a little French! He's not going to understand all that," Simone gently scolded.

Collette, a sturdy brunette in her late thirties, leaned over Simone to peek at the wound. "Marie can't fix that!" she muttered to Henri. "She's just a midwife."

"She's all we have. There's no one else we can trust. It's either her or you."

Collette stood up straight. "I'm not touching it. And what are we going to do with him if he dies?"

Henri set the basin down on the straw and said nothing.

"You're going to need another lantern," she said, a light sigh escaping her.

"Simone's lantern is here. You go back to the house and make sure the children have not awakened." As Henri set the Armagnac on the dirt floor, he saw the teacup Simone had used earlier that day cradled in the straw at his bent knees. Simone felt the color drain from her face. She'd neglected to hide the cup for the night with her books, sketch pads, and lantern. If she was asleep and the Gestapo came, it would take longer to get into the barrel. She would not have time to awaken and stow away her things. No evidence that she was living in the cellar could be visible when she went to sleep. Henri picked up the cup and glared at her.

"Do you want to get us all killed?" he growled.

"I am so sorry, Henri!"

"It's no trouble to explain a teacup!" Collette said. "It's him I'm worried about." She pointed to the American. "There's no hiding him! He's the one who's going to get us all killed."

Henri drew his lips into a flat line. "Go back to the house, Collette. Stay with the children. Leave this to me."

Collette opened her mouth to say something else but then shut it. She turned for the stairs and was gone.

"I'm sorry about the cup," Simone said when Collette was gone.

Henri used a corner of the blanket to wipe out the teacup and poured some brandy into it. "Forget about it now. Hold that compress down tight while I try to get him to drink this."

The American moaned as Henri forced him to raise his head to drink the alcohol.

"*De l'eau s'il vous plait,*" the American murmured when he'd drunk some of the brandy.

"It's not water you're going to want when Marie gets here," Henri replied. "Drink up."

"*S'il vous plait. Eau.*"

"He just wants water," Simone said.

Henri poured more brandy. "He can have water later. This is what he's getting now."

The American sputtered through three more swallows before he fell back onto the straw, unable to drink any more.

Henri put the stopper in the bottle and set the cup down. "How many more are there of you?" he said to the man. "Are there more? Are the Allies going to attack here?"

The wounded man stared up at Henri with glassy eyes.

"He doesn't understand what you're asking him," Simone said.

Henri harrumphed. "How much English do you know?"

"Only a little."

"Ask him if there are other planes. Are there more? Are we safe here?"

Simone turned to the injured man. "More planes, *monsieur*? Should we . . . uh . . . run?"

The American shook his head, held up one finger, and said one word. "Reconnaissance."

"Reconnaissance!" Henri echoed. "For what? Are the Allies planning to invade? What is your camera for? What were you taking pictures of?"

But the man's eyes fluttered and closed.

Henri sucked in his breath. "Is . . . is he dead?"

Simone could see the rise and fall of the man's torso against the hand she held to his side. "He's still breathing."

The cellar door opened and seconds later Sébastien, carrying another lantern, was coming toward them. A woman with strands of gray at her temples was behind him, and she carried a basket and a wooden spatula. She was amply built with a kind face.

"He's reconnaissance, Sébastien," Henri said. "That's why he had the camera. The Allies must be planning something."

Sébastien turned to the woman. "Please, Marie. Do what you can for him."

The woman got to her knees beside Simone. "Bring the light close," she said to Sébastien.

When the lantern hung just above Simone's hands, Marie told her to lift the shirt.

"My God," Marie exclaimed when she saw the wound. "This man needs a doctor."

"There is no doctor. There is only you, Marie," Sébastien said.

"And you are sure the bullet is not inside?"

"There's an exit wound on his back."

Marie shook her head but opened her basket and took out a bottle of alcohol, strips of cloth, and a spatula.

"You brought nothing to stitch him up?" Sébastien said, frowning.

"I stitch a dirty wound like that, any infection will be sewn up inside him and he will die. Is that what you want?"

Sébastien said nothing and Marie handed the spatula to Henri. "Have him bite down on this. I have nothing to numb him. He will feel everything."

"And cover his mouth if he screams, Henri," Sébastien added.

Henri nodded and placed the flat end of the spatula near the American's mouth.

"Teeth to wood," Simone said to him in English. He opened his mouth and Henri slid the handle just over his gums.

"Hold the light right here, Sébastien." Marie turned to Simone. "And you. Who are you?"

"Simone Devereux."

"Hold him down. Don't let him thrash about. Keep his hands out of my way. Sébastien, you hold down his other arm. She can't be reaching across."

Simone placed one bloody hand over the man's knees and the other on top of his clenched right fist.

Marie made the sign of the cross and then doused the wound with alcohol.

Had Henri not been holding the man's mouth closed, the scream would have echoed off the rock wall. Even so, his voice would carry to the cellar door and the world beyond if he kept it up.

As she started to pack the wound with the strips of cloth, the American's body jerked and he thrashed his head from side to side.

"Hold him still!" Marie commanded.

"Talk to him in English, Simone. Say something to calm him!" Sébastien said.

"I don't know enough English!"

The American squirmed and Henri's hand faltered. A guttural wail erupted from the American, and Henri fumbled to get a better hold on the spatula and the man's jaw. "Simone, tell him to lie still!"

She opened the man's fingers so that she could hold his hand and not just cover it. It was the gesture of a friend, or a lover. He gripped her hand in kind.

She could not think of the English words to tell him to lie still, so she said the words that she did know, over and over, tenderly but loud enough for the man to hear.

"I have a gray cat. Do you think it will rain? The bus comes at three o'clock."

With each second he grew quieter, until the alcohol, pain, and exhaustion bore his consciousness away.

When she was done tending both wounds, Marie sprinkled a yellow powder over them and then bound the American's torso in layers of cloth.

"The turmeric will help keep the wounds clean," Marie said as she placed her belongings back into her basket. "If it looks like they are getting infected, mash up some onions into a paste and put it on. Leave it on for an hour. Don't touch the paste with bare hands afterward. Make sure you dispose of it so no one else will either. I've done all I can do for him. Pray that he lives." She got to her feet.

"But you're coming back, aren't you?" Henri asked, concern in his eyes. "You're coming back to check on him, right?"

"That's not a good idea, Henri," Sébastien answered before Marie could. "Everyone in Venelles knows that Marie is a midwife. Everyone in Venelles knows that Collette is not expecting. Marie can't come back here, not even in the middle of the night. We can't take the chance that someone might see her. We will have to care for the American ourselves and hope that he survives. Simone can help. She is already down here anyway. You can care for the American, can't you, Simone?"

Her gaze had been on the wounded man's face, peaceful and slack under the numbing bliss of unconsciousness. But she raised her head and looked at Sébastien.

"His name is Everett," she said.

Eleven

Dawn was approaching when Simone finally lay down to sleep on a new spread of straw, just a few feet away from the American. Or at least she imagined it was nearing dawn. Every hour in the cellar was the same. When Henri, Marie, and Sébastien left the cellar after tending the wounded man's injury, she'd thought she'd seen a peep of milky morning light spill onto the stairs, gently reminding her that in the world above a new day still arrived with every sunrise.

Simone was allowed to have several hours of lantern light a day—kerosene, like everything else, was in short supply—and she usually used her lantern time for reading in the evening when the tedium of the day was the most unbearable. Henri had reluctantly agreed to leave the cellar door cracked each day for a few hours so that a ribbon of sunlight could be enjoyed on the second step. It was a shaft of light just wide enough to bathe Simone's face in subtle radiance every day from noon to two. Collette had been the one to insist Simone have access to that bit of sunlight every day while they waited on instructions for getting her safely to Spain. Collette was clearly not happy about Simone hiding in the secret cellar where Henri had hidden his best wines from the Germans, but she was not without compassion. Somehow she knew that Simone had lost more than just her father and brother to a Gestapo firing squad.

The day that her courier had deposited her at Henri and Collette's vineyard, the last day of April, was the last time she'd seen the sun in its entirety. She'd arrived dressed as a Catholic novitiate, having crossed the checkpoint alone into what had been the Free Zone in southern France. She'd had in her hand a fake *Ausweis*: a travel pass that identified her as Sister Marie-Thérès. Simone had met the courier, whom she knew only as J, at a patisserie in Bellerive-sur-Allier, just outside Vichy. The four-hundred-kilometer trek to Venelles had taken them ten days: some of it on foot, some in a vehicle disguised as a medical relief van from Lyon, and all on poorly maintained back roads. They'd ditched the vehicle in Avignon and walked the rest of the way, at night, over the course of three days, arriving at the Maisson Mandarine Winery just before twilight. She'd promptly been escorted down into the secret cellar located several yards behind the winery's main barrel room, but not before she had seen Henri and Collette's three children playing with a ball in front of a white stucco house up a slightly elevated path. A trio of tangerine trees lined the stone pathway. Beyond the house and the children were rows of grapevines wired to wooden posts.

Until she had come, Henri had only allowed Résistance fighters and messengers from Marseille and Toulon to use the cellar for meetings and occasional overnight stays. No one had ever stayed more than a couple nights.

"How long?" Henri had asked J at the top of the cellar stairs. J had not followed them down.

"I don't know that. I was only tasked with getting her here safely." J had peeked down the stairs to look at Simone standing at the bottom of them. "Farewell, *mademoiselle*." He'd tipped his hat to her.

Simone had barely realized J was leaving that very moment when he'd turned from the opening and was gone from view.

"Wait!" Simone stumbled up the stairs, tripping twice.

But when she got to the top, Henri kept her from chasing after J, who had taken off in a gentle run and was now many yards away.

J, who had reminded her of Étienne in so many ways, had been with her every tense moment for the last ten days of her escape. He'd stolen food and gas for them, lied for them, passed the monotony of the days by telling her all about his life as the son of a Marseille fisherman, and had put his arm around her as they shivered in the dark in old barns and abandoned buildings. He had risked his life to get her to Henri's winery, and now he was gone. And she had not hugged him good-bye or even thanked him.

Her life had morphed into an existence defined always by losses.

"Wait . . ." Simone whimpered as the tears began to fall.

Henri's tight hold on her loosened somewhat. "It's better for him that he leaves right away."

"But I didn't even say thank you!" she murmured.

"He knows you are grateful. You need to get into the cellar, Miss Devereux. I can't have my children seeing you."

Simone had turned and headed back down the stairs, the image of those three innocent children propelling her each step. When she got to the bottom, she stepped past the wall of barrels that hid the rest of the room from the vantage point of the stairs. Stacked barrels lined all three sides, their tops scrawled with batch numbers and dates in charcoal pencil. Two stood on their ends by a pile of straw where a folded blanket rested.

"My wife, Collette, wanted you to have a proper mattress, but I'm afraid that is not possible, *mademoiselle*. If the Germans suspect I am hiding someone here and come storming down those stairs, you will not have time to hide a mattress."

"Yes," Simone replied numbly.

"One of those barrels is for your lantern and any dishes or books or clothes that have been brought down to you. At night when you sleep, you must put it all away. Only you and the blanket can be out. If you hear the cellar door open and it's not me or Collette, you must take the blanket and climb into the other barrel. Make sure you hold on to the lid when you crawl in. Practice it so that you know you can do it."

"How will I know it is you or Collette?" Simone's voice sounded faraway in her ears, like it was someone else asking for these details.

"We will knock three times. I am certain if it is the Germans, you will know."

She nodded silently.

"I'll go get a lantern for you and I'll tell Collette you are here. She'll bring you some food, some different clothes, and a pot for your . . . your—"

"I know what the pot will be for, Monsieur Pierron."

He'd smiled weakly. "Please just call me Henri."

"And I am Simone."

"Do you know how long you will be here before the next courier comes to take you to Spain? I was told you would only be here a few days."

Henri was nervous about her being there; Simone had sensed his apprehension.

"I don't know," she'd answered. "I was told I would not be given that information so that I could not be persuaded to provide it. I did not even know your name until today, *monsieur*."

"Henri."

"Henri."

When she and J had arrived a few minutes earlier, Simone had thought Henri Pierron was like every other Résistance fighter she'd met since she started running, including the gruff man outside the shoe-repair shop who'd told her to flee. But the moment Henri asked how long she'd be staying, he looked like merely an ordinary husband and father, worried about the safety of those he loved. He was someone's papa. Someone's beloved. A sliver of sorrow had slid through her as she stood there looking at him in the semidarkness.

"Do you want to know why the SS is looking for me?" she'd asked him.

"You are Thierry Devereux's daughter."

"I killed a Gestapo officer."

Henri had said nothing for a moment. "It's no concern of mine why you're here. I'd kill them all if I could," he finally said.

"He raped me and I killed him," Simone said, and it was as if someone else were speaking for her.

Henri Pierron had looked away. When he'd turned back, he had the same look that the woman at 23 Rue de Calais had. Revulsion, pity, and the clear desire to turn back the hands of time covered his face like a mask.

"I'm sorry," he said, as though to apologize for just being a man.

"Do you want me to leave?" she asked. She suddenly was very tired of running.

Henri inhaled a deep breath, strengthening his resolve to stay the course, it seemed. "You leave now and they will find you. And all who have helped you will have risked their lives for nothing."

Tears of exhaustion and sorrow had started to trickle down her face. "I hadn't thought of it that way."

Henri reached out a hand, work worn and rough, and laid it on her shoulder.

"Don't give up, Simone. We can't give up. Don't let them have everything."

A sob escaped her and she stifled a second one. "They already have taken everything from me," she said, the words thick in her throat.

"No," Henri had replied quickly. "No, they haven't. Do you hear me? They haven't."

He had lingered until she nodded in agreement. Then he ascended the cellar stairs to get his wife, leaving her in total darkness.

She'd been in the cellar for more than a month. Henri had

learned that the network that was working to get her safely to Spain had been discovered and several of its members arrested. A new network was being formed to get downed Allied pilots and wanted Résistance fighters from their area out of France, but it was going to take some time. No one could guess how long.

After a week, she'd begged to be given something to do, and Collette had reluctantly given her the family's darning and mending baskets.

She was almost happy to suddenly have a new responsibility now: that of minding Everett's bandages, keeping him still, keeping him quiet, keeping him alive.

But when the others left and Simone found herself alone with the wounded man, a deep sorrow had slowly come over her. Hers was a life marked by defeat. She didn't want this man to die.

Even as she pleaded with God silently to let him live, the American stirred. She'd been allowed to keep a lantern burning low and she could see that his eyes were open.

"*Eau?*" he rasped.

Simone reached for a flask of water that Henri had left with her and helped the man drink. When he lay back down on the straw, he reached for the bandages around his middle.

"No, no, *monsieur*. No touch."

"*Mademoiselle?*"

"Simone."

"Simone. See leg." He patted his knee. "See? Medicine. Sulfa. Sulfa." He reached again for his middle and pointed to the bandage.

Simone felt the man's leg and noticed a pouch strapped to his uniform pant leg. She opened it and saw a red tin. "This is medicine, *monsieur?*"

"*Oui.* Sulfa." He pointed to his wound.

Simone opened the tin. It was full of a white powder.

"Sulfa," Everett said.

Simone carefully unwound the bandage, trying very hard to not hurt him, but he grimaced and moaned nonetheless.

"Shhh, *monsieur*," she said, as the wound lay open before her.

Sweat was running down his face. "Sulfa!" he said again, his voice almost a cry. He motioned to the tin.

"All right. I see. Shhh. You must be quiet." Simone shook the powder onto the wound as Everett writhed, his jaw clenched and his hands balled into fists.

"I will save some for tomorrow." She placed the lid back on the tin and set it down on the straw. When she turned back to Everett, he had slipped again into unconsciousness.

She covered the wound as best she could and lay down next to him, watching the rise and fall of his chest in the dim light.

Rest, when it finally came, was dreamless.

The German with the gold tooth did not visit her in her sleep.

Twelve

Annaliese slept fitfully the first night at Tidworth; every loud noise in the hallway sounded like policemen ready to burst into the room and haul her away. First to jail, and then back to Germany. Perhaps the other women and their children slept as poorly, but not from dread of discovery.

As she dressed for the day she prayed that God would be merciful and put her on the first available vessel if indeed she could beg for such favor. Was it a very bad trespass to pretend to be someone you were not? She wasn't sure. She was fairly certain it was a crime. Katrine had told her weeks ago that she should do whatever was necessary to get away from Rolf. Rolf was the criminal. Annaliese was the innocent one. But that had been before the accident, back when Katrine had been searching for a way for Annaliese to stay in hiding in England after she left for America.

Katrine.

Hearing that name all day yesterday had left Annaliese aching for the numbing silence of slumber. And even though sleep had eluded her, she hadn't had to hear Katrine's name over and over. Once Phoebe had fallen asleep, she'd enjoyed a sweet respite that lasted until her bunkmate awoke and asked her how she'd slept.

She'd really had no private moment to grieve Katrine's death. Annaliese had spent the night of the accident crouched in the St. Albans train station ladies' room, fearful of making a sound and alerting the night watchman. The next day, with nowhere else to go, she'd made her way to Waterloo Station, moving from bench to bench during the day and again sleeping on cold tiles until daybreak, when she could use Katrine's railway ticket to Tidworth. Even the moment of Katrine's death she'd kept at a mental distance, though it replayed itself in her mind every time she glanced at the travel documents that were not hers.

Annaliese had extricated herself from the wrecked car and limped back to the house where they'd been staying so that she could call for an ambulance even though she knew Katrine was dead. She hadn't known what else to do. Through a veil of tears she'd seen the tidy collection of papers on the telephone table: Katrine's birth certificate, her marriage license and passport, John's affidavit that he could financially support her, the certified letter from the U.S. Army, her train ticket to the coast. Annaliese had been only a second away from picking up the phone when Katrine's words from a few days earlier had suddenly echoed in her head.

If only there were a way I could help you after I leave for America, Annaliese. I wish I knew of some place where you could hide where Rolf could never find you . . .

She'd taken her hand off the phone at that moment and placed it on the little stack of documents. Blood from where window glass had cut her hand had spattered onto the table.

If only there were a way.

She had looked down at her feet and the purse that she had grabbed from the car. Katrine's purse. Hers had been nowhere in sight and its contents were scattered in the brush in every direction. But she had for some reason taken Katrine's purse when she staggered back to the house in the gathering dark, weeping.

If only there were a way.

When the car was discovered with the body inside, the only identifying factors would be Annaliese's passport and purse. The car would be traced back to this house and Katrine's grandfather, who was in India on business.

Eventually the police would figure out that it was Katrine's body they'd found in the car, which meant the woman who'd checked into Tidworth and boarded a ship for America couldn't possibly be Katrine. Perhaps it wouldn't be until Rolf arrived to identify the body that her little ruse would end. How long would that take? If the car wasn't discovered right away, it could take several days at least. They would have to find Rolf first. And then they would have to find Katrine's grandfather somewhere in Calcutta.

If only there were a way.

The next second Annaliese was stuffing her suitcase with her belongings.

BREAKFAST AT TIDWORTH WAS A PLATE OF WATERY EGGS, PALE sausage, and toast. The servers at supper the evening before had been Italian prisoners of war, but that morning when the war brides sat down at the long tables, fair-haired German captives, most of them teenagers with only fuzz for whiskers, waited on them. Annaliese knew Hitler had been desperate for fresh troops at the close of the war; he hadn't cared how old they were. She kept her voice low when she spoke, but it didn't take long for one of the servers who was refilling coffee cups to hear the German inflection in her English words. The young man leaned toward her, his whispered voice tense with anxiety and his gaze pleading for pity.

"*Bitte helf mir. Bitte?*" he begged. "*Ich wollte nicht kaempfen. Ich wurde gezwungen. Ich hatte keine Wahl. Bitte? Ich will zu meiner Familie!*"

In an instant the other conversations at the table stilled. Women who had been eating or spooning food into their children's mouths stopped to gape at them both. At the far end of the table the French woman stared, an eyebrow crooked in displeasure.

Annaliese looked away from the young man as an army officer strode forward from the corner of the room where he'd been observing the prisoners at their tasks.

"You!" the officer yelled. "Back away from that woman!"

"Bitte!" the boy continued to plead at her side. *"Ich hatte keine Wahl! Ich will meine Mutter!"*

"I can't help you," Annaliese murmured in English, without looking at him.

"She's Belgian!" Phoebe said to the German man, pointing to Annaliese with her butter knife.

"Ich will meine Mutter!" the young man yelled as the officer gripped him by the shoulders and pulled him away from Annaliese.

"You'd think they'd put those Germans where we couldn't see them after all they'd done!" a red-haired woman said to her tablemate.

"How hard would it have been to give that job to a poor East Ender rather than the likes of 'im," said another as the German man was dragged away, tears now streaming down his face.

Annaliese couldn't keep herself from watching as the German lad was taken from the room. A woman in a Red Cross uniform asked Annaliese if she was all right. Had the prisoner hurt her? Said anything that upset her? Did she need to speak to someone about it?

"I'm fine. Thank you," she answered. The Red Cross woman patted her shoulder and moved away. Several seconds ticked by before the women around them began eating again.

Phoebe tore off a piece of toast and handed it to Douglas, who sat on her lap. "What did he want?" she asked softly.

"He just wants to go home." Annaliese took a bite of eggs so that she couldn't answer any more questions.

Minutes later the dishes were cleared away and the women were told to remain at the tables for an important announcement about their upcoming sailing date. Animated conversations popped up around the room, and a sense of excitement permeated the air.

Let it be soon, let it be soon, Annaliese whispered to herself.

A Red Cross matron with a clipboard in her hand stepped to a microphone at the head of the hall. She touched it lightly and the sound of her tapping echoed in the room.

"All right, if I could have your attention, please, ladies." She waited as the chattering at the tables quieted. "With just a couple of exceptions here, you're all cleared for departure tomorrow morning."

Cheers and applause erupted all around the tables.

Phoebe turned to Annaliese. "Isn't that splendid! We're leaving tomorrow!"

But Annaliese could only smile wanly. The woman had mentioned there were a few exceptions. Exceptions.

"I am pleased to tell you that at ten o'clock tomorrow morning you will be boarding the RMS *Queen Mary* for your passage to America."

A deafening peal of delighted shrieks exploded in the hall.

"The *Queen Mary*, Katrine!" Phoebe said, squeezing Douglas tight. "We're going on the *Queen Mary*!"

Annaliese nodded absently. She knew of the *Queen Mary*. She knew it was England's gem cruise liner, bigger and more opulent than even the *Titanic* had been. But that did not matter to her.

Who were the exceptions? She willed the woman at the microphone to tell her.

But the matron read off a list of instructions about luggage and baby cots and telegrams to husbands.

Who are the exceptions?

The woman at last finished reading off the many details, and she turned the page on her clipboard. "Now if these three ladies could please stay behind a moment. I need a word with you. The rest of you are dismissed."

Annaliese closed her eyes.

"Molly Templeton, Frannie Belinsky, and Eleanor DiMarco, if you could please come see me at the lectern, please."

She snapped her eyes open. The woman had stepped away from the microphone. She was done reading names.

Annaliese wasn't one of the exceptions.

"Come on, Katrine! Let's go see if we can room together on the ship!" Phoebe tugged at her arm.

She rose from the table relieved, but her heart was thumping in her chest.

Thirteen

※

From the time she was seven Annaliese had only ever wanted to be a ballerina.

She fell in love with the way dancers made a story come alive while watching Tchaikovsky's *Swan Lake*. It was a concession of sorts, taking a seven-year-old to the ballet for her birthday. Her father, Gunter Lange, hadn't minded his daughter's interest in so rich a cultural distinction as the ballet if that fascination eventually led to higher pursuits. Annaliese was Gunter and Louisa Lange's sole child, whom they'd had later in life. Gunter believed his daughter should grow up making financially astute choices. There surely was no monetary security in a dancing career, but wealthy people were often generous patrons of the arts and frequently attended what they supported monetarily. Annaliese's birthday wish to see a ballet had been an opportunity to mingle with Cologne's affluent. If their daughter's interest in dance continued, that was something that could possibly be used to their favor as well as hers.

The Langes lived in a town called Prüm, just minutes away from the Belgian border and an hour and a half by train to Cologne. Her father was a banker, as all his family had been, and her mother kept the house, socialized with the other wives of influential men in Prüm, shopped for pretty things, and insisted that Annaliese endeavor to be just what Louisa was—comfortably married to a man of means who was respected, if not envied, by his peers.

Gunter wanted all that and more for Annaliese. To be comfortably wealthy was not enough for his daughter. He wanted her to be in Frankfurt or Munich or Hamburg, not in some quiet little hamlet near the Belgian border. The Great War had left most of Germany in economic ruin; only the already rich could survive another financial crisis were one to come. And wealth tended to be found in the cities.

Annaliese returned home from *Swan Lake* transfixed by all things ballet. Louisa promptly enrolled her in a dance class taught by a retired prima ballerina—despite the studio being half an hour's drive away in Winterspelt—because the instructor came so highly recommended. Madame Nardin had danced for twenty-five years with a prestigious company in Vienna. The woman had connections, even though she'd been out of the circuit for more than a decade. If the lessons were going to pay off in the long run, it had made sense to Louisa to make the once-a-week drive.

Katrine Dumont had been the first and only friend Annaliese made in ballet class and not just because the two girls looked like they could be sisters: both had the same honey-brown hair, hazel eyes, slender nose, and rosebud mouth. The others in the class had been taking lessons since they were four and five, including Katrine, who lived with her grandparents over the Belgian border in St. Vith. The steps and exercises didn't come easy to Annaliese, and while the other girls snickered when Madame *tsk*ed and forcibly placed Annaliese's clumsy limbs into the correct positions, Katrine watched with tender concern. She showed Annaliese how to do what Madame wanted when their teacher wasn't looking. Madame joked from the very beginning that the only way she could tell the two girls apart was when they were at the barre, and then it was painfully obvious which one was which.

After every class, Annaliese's mother would ask Madame how

her daughter was getting along, and when Madame would answer that Annaliese needed to practice at home or concentrate more or stop biting her nails or eat less strudel, Louisa would spend the half-hour ride home reminding her daughter how important it was that she try harder and that there was no reason to pay for the lessons if she wasn't going to take them seriously.

Ballet was harder than she thought it would be. Still, Annaliese loved it, and she loved having a friend who looked so much like her to be so good at it, and so willing to help. The first time Annaliese was invited to Katrine's house, Louisa had said no, partly because Katrine lived across the border—albeit in the German-speaking part of Belgium—partly because she was an orphan living with grandparents, and partly because the girl was half-British. Katrine had been just a toddler when her English mother and Belgian father had been killed in a disastrous train derailment outside Cambridge. Her father's grieving parents, André and Helene Dumont, took her in, since Katrine's maternal grandfather traveled too much to raise his granddaughter. She spoke both French and German as well as some self-taught English. Katrine had wanted to connect with her mother's British roots, and her grandparents had bought recordings of English lessons to satisfy that curiosity.

Annaliese believed all of these details about Katrine's life to be tragically fascinating, but her mother was disconcerted by her daughter's enthrallment with the look-alike girl in her ballet class. There was nothing to be gained by encouraging a friendship with the orphaned half-Belgian, half-English classmate. But Katrine persisted in inviting Annaliese over to her house, and Annaliese persisted in asking for permission to go. Katrine eventually figured out that Louisa desperately wanted Annaliese to do well in ballet class. When at last Katrine said that Annaliese could come home with her and practice their dances, Louisa relented somewhat. She allowed the girls to get together after class, but at Annaliese's house, not Katrine's. Class was on Saturday mornings, and often after that, Katrine would stay overnight and her grandfather would come for her the next day.

It wasn't hard for Louisa to see that despite Katrine's unfortunate circumstances, the girl was a natural on the dance floor, and Annaliese responded well to her mentoring. In time, she allowed Annaliese to visit Katrine's house, but never overnight. They were soon best friends, despite the border that separated their two countries and the disparate aspirations of the people raising them. While the Langes wanted wealth and stability for their daughter, André and Helene merely wished for Katrine a future without heartache in it.

As the years went on and the girls matured both in age and technique, they performed in the same shows, attended the same dance camps, and auditioned for the same roles. Annaliese was never the natural that Katrine was, but she had a disciplined style that occasionally won her roles that Katrine was not offered.

Katrine never begrudged Annaliese's successes over hers, something Louisa found odd.

"How does Katrine feel about you having won that role over her?" Louisa asked when the girls were fourteen and Annaliese was chosen for the lead in a Bonn production of *Hansel and Gretel*.

"She's happy for me," Annaliese answered.

Her mother had murmured something about how ridiculous it was for Katrine's grandparents to have spent all that money on lessons if the girl didn't care whether she won a part or not.

"But she did want that role," Annaliese had insisted. "She did want it. That doesn't mean she's not happy that I got it. I would've been happy for her if she got the role instead of me."

That same year, Germany invaded Poland, and two days later

England and France responded by declaring war. Annaliese was unsure what those events meant; it didn't feel like Germany was at war, but she could tell that her father was suddenly very worried about the future. She overheard a hushed conversation between her parents in which her father declared that the new president, Adolf Hitler, didn't like the rich. His Nazi political party, which was gaining ground in terms of popularity, influence, and power, consisted mainly of lower- and middle-class individuals with a bone to pick with the wealthy. It would be prudent for a banker like himself to keep a low profile. Annaliese had heard of the Nazi attack on Jews in Munich the year before—anyone in earshot of a radio had heard about the Night of Broken Glass, when hundreds of Jewish homes, businesses, and synagogues were destroyed or set on fire. She knew the word *Nazi* was a word to fear if you were Jewish. Her father's concern about their own welfare had surprised her.

A month later, in October, Madame said there would be no more lessons for a while, and Annaliese and Katrine had cried when they said good-bye. They only lived twenty-seven kilometers from each other, but tensions were tight between Belgium and Germany. Louisa insisted there would be no more visits to Katrine's house either, nor would she allow Katrine to come visit Annaliese.

"I will write to you!" Katrine said as her grandfather drove away from the studio on the last day of class. With tears in her eyes, Annaliese promised to write back.

The months went by as the girls wrote their letters and the Nazi regime continued its march across Europe, gobbling nations. In the span of just two weeks in the spring of 1940, Holland, Belgium, and Norway all surrendered to Germany. And on the fourteenth of June, German forces entered Paris.

There would be no more letters from Katrine, even though much of German-speaking Belgium was reannexed to Germany. Gunter and Louisa didn't allow Annaliese to maintain contact with Katrine for fear of arousing suspicions that they were sympathetic to the Belgians' plight. Annaliese could only hope that the war would be over soon and she and Katrine could go back to the way things were.

Annaliese's parents were on edge sitting in what had been a quiet town near the Belgian border. Gunter made inquiries among his colleagues in Bonn and learned of an opening as the chief accountant at a large industrial company. Louisa bristled at the thought of leaving the prestige of the bank in Prüm for an office in a factory, but Gunter assured her the position would pay him nearly as much. The difference was he would seem more of a sympathizer to the Nazi Party's ideals rather than an elitist outsider who had no compassion for the common man.

"We have to appear to be more than just compliant," he'd said. "We have to look like we're supportive."

Annaliese hadn't wanted to move; she liked Prüm, and she liked the idea that Katrine was close, even though she was allowed no contact with her. But her father accepted the job and they took just what they needed from the house in Prüm, leaving most of its furnishings covered in bedsheets, and settled into a furnished flat in Bonn. Annaliese would have found the entire situation intolerable except for the fact that in Bonn, ballet lessons were still being given at various studios throughout the city. Louisa enrolled Annaliese in lessons and it was at the barre that Annaliese could forget that the whole world seemed to be at war.

Three years later, in the spring of 1943, and just days after Annaliese celebrated her eighteenth birthday, she won the lead role in a production of *Sleeping Beauty*. Despite the Allied bombings over Berlin, Hamburg, and even nearby Cologne, the ballet companies still performed, concerts were still held, galleries were still open. The Reich Ministry for Public Enlightenment and Propaganda contained a division devoted to art, music, and theater. Control and manipulation of the fine arts was a part of the reshaping of culture as much as the removal of the Jews. Cologne's residents continued to flee to safer places, but tens of thousands still lived in both the damaged and undamaged parts of the city.

Annaliese didn't care about any of that. She only wanted to dance and take her mind off how much she missed Katrine's friendship and the carefree days of their youth.

For her, ballet was an escape, a retreat from reality. When she danced, she put her heart and soul into every movement, drawing from deep within remembrances of life at a simpler time, when she and Katrine would practice in toe shoes and braid each other's hair and giggle about boys.

She performed on opening night to a decent-sized audience, but the number of filled seats didn't interest her. Only the swell of the orchestra, the shimmer of the lights, the sheen of the ribbons that crisscrossed her ankles, and the movement of her body mattered to her.

Annaliese danced with exquisite grace that evening, completely unaware that in the third row, a Nazi named Rolf Kurtz sat enthralled with her performance. He was the son of a highly placed ministry official who was following along in his father's footsteps. He had come to the ballet to report on its cultural contributions—or lack thereof—to the Third Reich's new world order.

When the performance concluded, he turned to his assistant, a ferrety wisp of a man, and said, "I want to meet the ballerina. Make it happen."

Pleased to have played a part in impressing a ministry official, the stage manager escorted Herr Kurtz backstage to meet Annaliese. She had just changed into street clothes, and her parents were in her dressing room with her, telling her how wonderfully she had danced, when a knock sounded.

"Annaliese, this is Herr Kurtz from the Ministry of Public Enlightenment and Propaganda," the stage manager said when she opened the door. "He enjoyed your performance tonight and wished to meet you." Annaliese could only stare back in stunned amazement. No one had ever come backstage to meet her before. The man stepped into the room and held out his hand.

"Fräulein Lange, it's a pleasure to meet you."

She hesitated a second before taking his hand. He pulled hers to his lips and kissed it. A tremor of delight coursed through her.

He was of average height, in his mid- to late twenties, she thought, with an angular build, penetrating blue eyes, and wavy blond hair that had been slicked into submission.

"Thank you for coming to the show, Herr Kurtz," she said.

"Please, call me Rolf."

Annaliese withdrew her hand, smiled, and said nothing. Her heart had begun to beat a little faster at his flattering words and the charming style with which he'd uttered them.

"You dance like an angel, Annaliese. May I call you Annaliese?"

She glanced at her father, but his tight gaze was on Rolf Kurtz, a nervous smile plastered to his face. It was obvious to Annaliese that her father's heart was beating faster, too. "Thank you, *mein Herr*," she replied.

"Rolf, please. I would like very much to take you out to dinner, *Fräulein*. The skies are beautiful and quiet tonight." He referred to Allied bombing, which hadn't taken place in force over Cologne since February. "That is, if it is all right with your parents."

Equal parts amazement and trepidation somersaulted inside her. The man was a Nazi Party official and here he was, resplendent in his uniform, asking her to dinner.

Her father nodded, wide-eyed, and said, "Of course, *mein Herr*." Annaliese could not tell if he was pleased or perplexed.

"I promise to have her home at a decent hour," Rolf said with a laugh, as he took Annaliese's arm to lead her to the stage door. "Even angels need their rest."

Annaliese had not been out to dinner with a man before. Her experience with the opposite sex had consisted of what she had seen in romantic movies at the cinema with Katrine, secret high school infatuations, and practicing the art of kissing on her bed pillow. She didn't know what to say to Rolf as his driver took them to a restaurant—the assistant had been summarily dismissed—and she was grateful that he carried the conversation, not just in the car but at the restaurant, too. He seemed quite at ease being in complete control, and content to talk about himself when he wasn't asking her questions about her so that he "could get to know her better."

He was keenly interested in all her answers, especially when he asked her how many boyfriends a beautiful girl like her had had and she'd replied—red-faced, she knew—that she'd had none. He grinned at her and jokingly accused her of lying to him.

"I haven't had a boyfriend!" She attempted a playful tone. "There have been boys I liked, but they were never . . . I never let them know I liked them."

Rolf's grin widened and he leaned forward. "So. There were boys you liked, then? Who were they?"

His continued interest thrilled her. "Just boys at school. No one special."

"You've never been with a man, then?" he murmured.

Annaliese was poised to take a bite of food and her hand holding the fork froze. Words failed her as fresh heat rose to her cheeks. Rolf Kurtz was still smiling congenially but there was a hardness in his eyes, as though he was prepared at that very moment to execute whoever might have robbed Annaliese of her innocence. That look both scared and mesmerized her and she could not speak.

After a moment he cocked his head and nodded; a happy nod.

"I can see by your face that you have not, my dear. You really are an angel, aren't you?"

"I . . . I am just me," she finally said.

"And a delightful one at that." He raised his wineglass as if to toast her beauty, talent, and poise, but Annaliese would realize much later that he was congratulating himself for having found her.

The helmsman zigs the bow toward the sun one moment and then zags it away the next. Over and over, he does this. "We are being hunted," the captain says. Fear and dread are as thick as mist. Thousands of soldiers crowd the decks like anxious schoolboys, always looking out over the water.

An escort ship that sails in our wake hovers close. I see what will happen before anyone else and I can do nothing to stop it. The escort is too near, the zigzagging is too abrupt.

I hear the cries, the shouts, and the long moans of the escort cruiser being ripped in two. Our helmsman has driven us like a spear into the other ship. Everyone on the bridge is scrambling or shouting or cursing. I can only hover over them to see what they will do.

There is blood and oil in the water and those who felt the collision are running to the decks to see what has happened. "Have we been torpe-doed?" one man asks. He is so young; he is but a boy. "No," says another. "We hit the Curacoa.*"*

Men are streaming to the railings, and their mouths drop open when they see the riven escort ship spilling her contents into the sea. Our captain has not given the order to stop, to turn about, to pull up the living from the debris or the dead before they sink. He mustn't stop. Enemy subma-rines are looking for the Queen, *they are searching for her, he says. His orders are to continue. His hand trembles as he motions to the men at the instruments to hold steady the forward course.*

"Why aren't we stopping?" yells a soldier at the railing. "We can't," says another. "Orders."

Lost souls are calling out as we sail past them, and with all the force I can muster I bid whoever is willing to come join me.

I will do what the captain will not.

Fourteen

—✳—

Brette used the fifteen minutes Trevor Prescott needed to drive from Solana Beach to her Carmel Valley condo to tidy up the living room, run a brush through her hair, and put on a pot of decaf. Wine was for intimate conversation between close friends; coffee was the better choice for two acquaintances who hadn't seen each other in more than a decade. While the coffeemaker sputtered and dripped, Brette used her phone to Google the RMS *Queen Mary* coupled with ghost sightings and was surprised by the number of results. She had barely glanced at the first batch of hits when the doorbell rang. She stopped at the hall mirror for one last look at herself. Keith had always said that her splash of freckles made him smile, and her pixie haircut framed her face perfectly. She had worn her hair long in high school. As she reached for the doorknob, she idly wondered if her old high school classmate would remember that.

She swung the door wide and the man standing on her welcome mat smiled.

Trevor looked relatively unchanged. Underneath the conservative haircut, the fifteen or so extra pounds, and the Oxford button-down shirt was the same man from high school. The only discernible difference was that his youthful charm had been replaced with a more mature bearing, and there was a lingering sorrow in his mocha-brown eyes that had not been there all those years ago.

"Brette," he said as he stepped in. He leaned forward and kissed her on the cheek. "You look great," he said warmly. Believably.

"Come inside," she said. "We can sit in the living room. I've made some decaf if you'd like a cup."

"That sounds great." He smiled appreciatively. It was clear he was already banking on her coming to his rescue when all she'd said was that he could come over and they'd talk.

When she came back into the living room a few minutes later with mugs, Trevor was standing at the fireplace, looking at her wedding portrait.

"Beautiful photo. What's his name?"

Brette set the mugs down on the coffee table and took a seat in an armchair. "Keith. He works for a biotech firm. He's in Chicago this week. I'm sorry you missed him."

Trevor turned away from the photograph. The sadness in his facial features had subtly intensified.

"I'm sorry, too." He sat down on the sofa across from her. "And where are you working these days?"

"I'm an admissions counselor at a hospital. You?"

"Sales. Electrical components. I'm based out of Austin. I was in LA for a long while, though."

"Oh."

He reached for his cup and sipped from it. "No kids?" he said when he set the mug back down.

"No. We've, uh, only been married two years. So. You know."

He reached into his pocket and pulled out his cell phone. He swiped the screen and handed the phone across the coffee table. A cherub-faced little girl with sunny-blond curls smiled at Brette.

"That's Emily," he said.

"She's adorable." Brette handed the phone back.

"Spitting image of her mother," Trevor said, a tight smile on his face.

"I'm so very sorry, Trevor."

He nodded and silently slipped the phone back inside his coat pocket. "We had just sold our house in Los Angeles and were getting ready to move to Texas when it happened. A guy in a truck going sixty fell asleep at the wheel. Caused a four-car pileup on the 405. Laura was the only one who didn't survive. The coroner didn't think she suffered, though. She was already gone when the first responders got there." He blinked back the threat of tears.

Emotion gathered at the back of Brette's throat. "I really am so very sorry. I can't imagine what it must have been like."

"It was getting better for Emily and me. Time had been helping," Trevor said with a tender shrug. "We eventually made the move anyway and I started the new job a few months late. My mother thinks maybe I should have found a way to stay in LA, but I honestly thought the change would help Emily. I worried that if she was constantly around places that reminded her of Laura, it would be too difficult. And she was . . . she was starting to come around, I think, but then we came out here to visit my mother before school started up and we visited the *Queen Mary*. Emily thinks she heard Laura speak her name and felt her arms around her while we were on the ship. I didn't know the *Queen Mary* is rumored to be crawling with ghosts. I just decided to take my mom and Emily to see the Princess Diana exhibit and then have lunch. I've never been okay with the idea of ghosts, to tell you the truth. The idea that they could be real freaks me out a little."

Brette stiffened slightly. "Yes. I remember that about you."

He had been staring into his coffee cup, but now he raised his head to look at her. "Hey. I've always felt bad about how we all treated you. I didn't know what to say to you after Kimberly said what she did."

"You wouldn't even look at me after that day."

"I was an ass. I'm sorry. The whole thing just took me by surprise. You had always seemed to be the one person in school who wasn't putting on a show. You know, you were authentic, down-to-earth, normal. You were different from everyone else in my group of friends, but in a good way. But then—"

"But then you found out my little secret and you realized just how truly different I was." The collective rejection of her high school peers still hurt, she realized. They had shunned her for something she'd had no control over, and it still stung.

"Like I said. I was an ass. I was young and stupid. I didn't know what to make of what Kimberly had said. I thought maybe you were . . ."

"Crazy?"

Trevor met her challenging gaze. "Maybe. Is that why you kept it a secret? Because you knew people wouldn't know what to make of it? Isn't that why you still keep it a secret?"

"How do you know I still keep it a secret?"

"You're practically invisible on social media. You've written no books, you're not on TV. If it weren't a secret, I wouldn't have had so much trouble trying to find you."

"So then it won't surprise you when I say that I am the wrong person to seek help from. I can list on one hand the number of people in my life now that know I can see ghosts. I don't exercise that ability. I tolerate it. I can't help you. And I can't help Emily."

Trevor frowned. "But of course you can help Emily. You can tell her it's not true. That her mother isn't on that ship. If I tell her you can see people who have died, she'll believe me. And if you come to the *Queen Mary* and look for Laura, and you don't find her, you can tell Emily she's not there. You're the only one who can tell her she's not there."

"I'm not the only one. There are—"

"You're the only one I trust to do this. We used to be friends once. Won't you do this for me? This one little thing?"

"What you are asking isn't just a little thing," she said. "I make myself known to whatever might be on that ship and I open myself up to all kinds of attention. I get by in life unnoticed because the Drifters don't know I see them."

"The what?"

"The ghosts. They are real, whether you think they are or not. If I poke about that ship looking for your deceased wife, I will have to deal with whatever else is there. If there are ghosts there, they will know I can see them. I look different to them than other people do. It's like . . . like I will have a glow about me while I am actively looking for Laura and it will hang around me when I leave. And that means when I come back home, I will still have it. I don't want that kind of attention. You don't know what it's like."

"What *what* is like?" Trevor's eyebrows were knitted into a frown.

"Having them following me around, hovering over me, disrupting me, asking me questions I can't answer. They don't belong here, and the longer they hang around, the more they lose their ability to think rationally. I can't reason with them. It's terrible."

Trevor stared at her. She couldn't tell what he was thinking.

"I know all about terrible," he finally said. "It's terrible to bury your wife and to have to tell your little girl her mother is never coming home. It's terrible for your six-year-old daughter to suddenly think her daddy has it all wrong, that her mother isn't gone forever, she's on an old boat in Long Beach harbor. It's terrible when your daughter cries every day for you to take her back to that ship."

Brette had not expected such a response and had no words at the ready. She stared back at Trevor openmouthed.

"You're right," Trevor went on. "I don't know what it is like to experience what you do, but it can't be worse than what I am going through right now. We were supposed to be on a plane back to Texas today. But Emily doesn't want to leave LA. All she wants is to get back on that ship."

His eyes held her gaze, willing her to not look away from him.

"What is it you want me to do?" she asked.

"Just come to the ship. Walk the length of it. Tell Emily whatever you want. Tell her you see other Dwindlers, or whatever you call them, but that you don't see Laura."

"Drifters. And what if I get on that ship and she *is* there? What am I supposed to do then?"

Trevor frowned. "She died in a car crash on the 405. I told you that. You're not listening."

"No. You're not listening. The ones that stay, drift. They look for places to hover where the membrane between this world and the next is thin. If there are ghosts on the *Queen Mary*, it's probably because that ship is located in a thin place. Long Beach is just a few miles off the 405."

He rubbed a hand across his forehead as if to scrub away the notions he didn't know how to make sense of.

"I need to know if things were all right between you when . . . when Laura died," Brette said.

"Yes," Trevor replied, his voice terse with emotion.

"Did you ever get the impression she was afraid of what happens to us when we die? Was she overly anxious about that?"

Trevor shook his head. "No more than any of us."

"I can only see the ones who don't cross over," Brette said. "If Laura's on the other side, she won't be on that ship."

"All I am asking you to do is tell that to Emily. Assure her that her mother is . . . that she's not here anymore. And that if she were, she'd want Emily to go on with her life."

"She may not believe me."

"She already doesn't believe me. If anyone can convince her that her mother isn't a ghost on that ship, it's you."

Fifteen

※

Thursday morning dawned sultry and still. It would likely be warm on the ship, Brette thought, as she lay in bed after turning off the alarm on her cell phone. Drifters didn't seem to care what the temperature was, but she'd found they were easier to see when the air was damp or chilly. A warm environment usually meant a more transparent appearance. She would have to be more intent about looking for them, which in turn would draw more attention to herself. Not the best way to keep a low profile.

Brette breathed in deeply to steady herself before rising and looking again at the photo of Laura that Trevor had texted to her. She'd had to convince Trevor that she needed to be alone when she went to the *Queen Mary* to look for Laura. Having Emily with her before she'd had a chance to check it out was definitely a bad idea, and having Trevor there wasn't the best situation either. She wanted some time to acclimate to the ship. If there was a thin place on board—and with all that she had read about it, she was fairly convinced there was—she needed to assess it without a skeptic like Trevor asking a million questions.

She'd asked for a personal day, telling her supervisor she needed to visit a grieving friend. Trevor was only too happy for her to go as quickly as she could, but Brette had her own reasons for visiting the ship on a weekday. The smaller the crowds on the decks, the more easily she would be able to do what she had to do and the sooner she'd be done with it.

She'd also decided to forgo explaining to Keith in detail her impromptu decision to drive up to Los Angeles to see a former high school classmate. She sent a simple text to that effect the night before. Calling to tell him the scope of that visit would be making it a big deal. And it wasn't a big deal. Keith was going to call Friday night anyway and she could tell him then.

Brette rose from bed and showered, choosing a pale pink cotton dress that she usually felt pretty and confident in. She needed that boost. She had spent the evening prior reading up on the *Queen Mary*'s history and its reputation for being haunted.

She had learned that the British luxury ocean liner made its maiden voyage across the Atlantic in 1936, that kings and queens and movie stars had walked its decks. During World War II, it had been commissioned as a troop carrier, painted gray, and nicknamed the Grey Ghost. In 1946, via many crossings, the ship transported twenty-two thousand GI war brides and their children from England to the United States and Canada. By 1967, air travel was the preferred mode of passage across the Atlantic. The *Queen* was sold to the City of Long Beach in California. Too big for the Panama Canal, the ship sailed around Cape Horn and up the coast of South America before permanently docking in Long Beach. It had been a floating hotel and museum ever since.

Of the most concern to Brette were the multiple claims that more than one hundred fifty spirits lurked on the ship, including a little girl in the long-emptied second-class swimming pool, a beautiful woman often seen dancing alone in the Queen's Salon, and a dark-haired man roaming about in what had been the first-class staterooms. There had been multiple accounts over the years of water running and lights turning on in the middle of the night, phones ringing in the early morning with no one on the other end of the line, a piano playing on its own, doors slamming, and the lingering fragrance of things long since passed. Brette had wondered if perhaps a Drifter who'd once been a mother saw Emily and broke the barrier between spiritual and physical to touch the child and comfort her. How else could Emily have experienced what she claimed she had? Trevor had said neither he nor his mother had mentioned to Emily that ghosts apparently frequented the ship.

During the ship's years at sea, only forty-nine deaths had been reported aboard. If there were more than a hundred Drifters on the *Queen Mary*, where had they come from and why were they there? What if some of them weren't Drifters at all, but malevolent pranksters, enjoying the attention that paranormal activity elicited and pleased to entice the naïve into believing they could be trusted?

She did not want to attract the attention of even one of those.

As she sipped a cup of coffee at breakfast and ruminated on what she had gleaned in her research, it was clear that she would need to step aboard the *Queen* on full alert. If there was even half that amount of transcendent activity on the ship, she needed to make the first pass alone. Brette hurried through the rest of her morning routine and was out the door by seven fifteen.

Traffic was ample but smooth heading north out of San Diego on Interstate 5, and except for a few stretches of stop-and-go, she made good time. By ten twenty-five, Brette was taking the Queen's Highway exit and the black-and-white ocean liner was suddenly in view, its red smokestacks piercing the blue sky. The ship looked old and yet timeless as Brette parked her car and then began to walk toward the ticket office. She purchased a passport for the day, was apprised of the numerous tours she could take, and made her way through the entrance and to the dockside elevator that would take her to the promenade deck.

She could sense the electrical pull of something—or many things—charging the air around her, and the fine hairs on her arms and neck began to tingle as her ticket was scanned and she stepped into the elevator. A moment later she was standing on a permanent gangplank that linked the present with the past. The wood of the promenade deck seemed to welcome her as she stepped onto it, and the oxygen in the air immediately seemed thinner somehow. The deck was weathered to a warm patina from eighty years of footsteps across it, and it looked like the edge of a portal, as though if she walked across it in either direction, she would be borne away to another time. Brette paused for a moment before taking another step forward. There was something very different about the ship, different than what she had expected, even with its famed notoriety. At once, she could tell there was veiled truth to the unexplained stories that sold tickets and kept paranormal enthusiasts interested. Under the sensationalism, the mystery, the entertainment value of the ship being hailed as haunted, there was weight here, and she knew within the depths of her being that there was no way she could continue farther onto the deck without being noticed.

A shiver ran up her back at that same moment.

And she knew she had already been spotted.

"I mean you no harm," she whispered, and a mother and father with their two young children stared at her as they walked past.

She stood still as a trembling breeze caught her in its gauzy grip, swept up around her, lifting wisps of hair off her neck.

Brette was being scrutinized, but she could not tell by whom. Most Drifters, when they realized she had the Sight, concentrated their energy on being seen. She was an anomaly to them, and they were usually curious. But not this one. She didn't know if it was male or female. Young or old. Hostile or welcoming. Alone or with others.

Brette stood still and let the breeze swirl into nothingness as whatever Drifter had taken notice completed its examination.

"I mean you no harm," she said again, this time louder. A man wearing a headset and studying the map of the self-guided tour looked up for a moment and then continued on.

"I'm just here for a friend," Brette murmured, thankful that the other people around her were many feet away, looking at ship brochures, taking selfies, or strolling the deck.

The air grew very still, and Brette wondered for a moment if the invisible Drifter had been satisfied with her and left. But the hairs on her body were still fully charged with electricity. The Drifter was hovering over her as if deep in thought about what to do with her next.

"Please," Brette whispered, closing her eyes. "I promise you I am only here to help. I promise you. I want no trouble with anyone. I'm just . . . looking for Laura. If she's here, she is new."

The breeze swept over her again, knocking a ball cap off a man's head as he walked past Brette and sending him chasing after it. A tour guide and his entourage were a few feet away and a handful of the ticket stubs he held fluttered out of his grasp.

"What in the world?" the guide said, as he and several of his guests chased after the pieces of paper.

Brette said nothing as the breeze swirled again into stillness. The tour guide and his people moved on.

But the Drifter remained. Was it convinced she was not there to exploit or demand anything of it? Was she free to continue? Brette didn't know.

"Will you help me?" Brette murmured, attempting a different approach.

And a tiny gust of warm air fluttered at her ear.

Come, it seemed to say.

And she felt pressure at her back, gentle but firm, prodding her forward

She wasn't just being welcomed, she was being drawn in with a surprising force, and yet she did not pick up on malicious intent. It was rather a sense of urgency, as if this Drifter that refused to materialize wanted her to see something or do something. Maybe both.

"Laura?" Brette whispered the name as she moved forward into the interior of the ship. She hoped that the Drifter would show itself now, but as she stood in the beautifully appointed main hall with its wide central staircase and art deco features, she found herself amid a clutch of mere mortals readying for tours or stepping out of the gift shop.

"What is your name?" Brette said softly to the air around her.

An older woman with blue-gray hair smiled at her as she walked past. "Why, my name's Mabel!" she said brightly. "What's yours?"

"Um . . . Brette."

"Nice to meet you." The woman walked away.

The Drifter that had ushered Brette inside was now gently pushing her toward the central staircase. Trevor had told Brette that Emily had felt Laura's arms around her when they were on the bridge, which Brette knew was in the opposite direction of the steps. She tried to turn toward the bow but was met with an invisible wall of resistance.

"Look. I don't know what you want," Brette whispered.

Come . . .

The command was not audible but Brette heard it nonetheless. The Drifter pressed her toward the staircase leading to the lower decks. Brette had never been at the will of a Drifter before. Unease rippled through her. She almost wished she had asked Trevor to join her.

"I mean you no harm," she said for the third time as she took the first stair.

The Drifter said nothing in return but continued to push her downward, past the M deck and down to the A deck, where the ship's hotel lobby was located. The Drifter pulled her gently toward the starboard side and down the paneled, carpeted hall that stretched from one end of the ship to the other. Stateroom doors of richly burnished wood gleamed on either side. A transparent wisp seemed to hover for a moment at the farthest end and then disappear, leaving Brette to believe a second Drifter had darted away upon seeing her or the Drifter that accompanied her.

She was propelled at a gentle but insistent pace down the hall, passing doors and little alcoves right and left. There was no one else in the hallway.

"Please, tell me your name," Brette said, but there was no response from the Drifter.

She was about to ask again when the Drifter pulled her to a stop in front of a little hallway that led to two staterooms. The doorknob of A-152 suddenly turned and Brette stepped back to make room for whoever was coming out of the room. But there was no one at the door. It swung open and she felt the Drifter press her in.

"I'm not going in there," Brette said sternly. "That's someone's hotel room."

But the force at her back propelled her forward and a second later she was standing just inside the cabin. A new king-size bed dominated the room, and there was a flat-screen TV attached to a wall, but other than those evidences of modern-day life, the rest of the room had the look of a 1940s movie set, from the light fixtures to the cupboards to the faucets in the little bathroom just visible at the door.

"I don't need to go in," Brette said, although it appeared no hotel guest had been assigned that room.

But the Drifter urged her inside. It occurred to Brette that perhaps the Drifter had once been a passenger. Perhaps a young passenger. Maybe it was a child that was tugging her forward. She felt a strange compassion for the Drifter that would not show itself.

"Was this your room? Is that why you brought me here?" Brette found herself asking, hoping that if she showed interest, the Drifter would become visible so that she could gauge its age and intentions.

But the Drifter said nothing. Instead, a cabinet door on the far wall opened slowly. Brette stepped forward and bent down to look inside it, her heart pounding. It was empty.

"Whatever was there is gone now." Brette straightened, and as gently as she could, she said, "You can go, too, you know. You don't have to stay here. You can—"

The Drifter pushed Brette back toward the open door and pressed her outside. As soon as Brette was standing in the little hallway, the door slammed shut.

"I am not trying to tell you what to do," Brette began, but the Drifter pushed her back into the main hallway and toward the staircase and the main hall. Brette wondered for only a moment if the Drifter was done with her, but once on the promenade, she was led to the stern and outside at the back of the ship. She stopped to get her bearings as she emerged into sunlight again. Clutches of people wearing earbuds and listening to the audio tour were scattered here and there, but the Drifter urged Brette down one flight of exterior stairs after another until she was standing in front of a doorway that led back inside the ship. A sign on the outside with an arrow pointing down read *TO THE ISOLATION WARD*. The Drifter nudged her. Brette shaded her eyes and stepped inside the darkened opening. A set of stairs met her and a second sign cautioned her to watch her step. She took the steps carefully and wound her way to the right, the only direction available. The area that had been the ship's sick bay now lay before her, and a few self-guided tourists were taking pictures and reading placards. Brette was nudged forward with an elevated sense of urgency. Something had happened to this Drifter on the ship. It hadn't happened in the stateroom, though there had been something in the little cupboard that had mattered at the time. She was led into a little anteroom where historical records hung on the walls. A couple was looking at one of the framed documents. The Drifter swirled about Brette, and the hair on her neck stood on end. The man looked up. He had felt the electrical charge, too, but didn't know why. He seemed to think Brette had somehow been responsible for it, and he put his arm protectively around the woman as they moved away. Brette smiled politely and they smiled, too, but warily. As soon as the couple was gone, the Drifter propelled Brette toward the document they had been looking at.

It was a chronological list of those who had died aboard the ship, from first to last.

The Drifter pressed Brette forward with renewed force.

"It might help if you just let me see you and then you can just tell me your name," Brette said as she nearly stumbled forward, closer to the document on the wall.

But the Drifter remained invisible.

"Is your name on this list? Is that why we're here? You're not Laura, are you? Just tell me. I can't help you if you don't tell me."

Look.

"Look at what?" Brette said. "What do you want me to see? Your name? Is your name here?"

Brette peered at the list.

Look, the Drifter seemed to say, and Brette felt it gently push her line of sight toward one date, February 12, 1946. One of the war brides crossings.

Look, the Drifter seemed to whisper, a third time.

Brette read the first name aloud even as the Drifter seemed to murmur it in her ear.

Annaliese.

Sixteen

※

Papa had told Simone to memorize the address on Rue de Calais but to never, ever go there until he told her to. He had shown her on the street map where it was and he'd even walked with her as far as two streets away. But he'd told her that some French people would do anything to keep themselves and the people they loved safe, and that meant even telling a German soldier that a neighbor whom they had known all their lives was engaging in suspicious activity and visiting places they didn't usually visit.

"You could unknowingly lead the Gestapo right to it by going by there," he'd told her. "They would arrest those they found. Maybe torture them for information."

Simone had honored that request. For three years she had walked past the side street that led to Rue de Calais but had never gone down it.

She had always imagined number 23 to be just another indiscriminate brick three-story building with iron grillework on the windows and maybe a brass knocker wanting polish. There might be a pot on the front step sporting pale geraniums, and the front door—blue or green—would need a bit of fresh paint. It would be a house that looked like all the others so that no one would ever suspect it was a place of safety.

But as Simone ran from the scene of her father and brother's execution, that halcyon image escaped her and all she could think about was that she didn't have the gun. She didn't have anything. Papa and Étienne were dead. She couldn't go back to the shoe-repair shop and get her sketchbooks or her mother's photo album or her grandmother's cameo or her favorite pajamas. Or the gun. She had nothing but the clothes she was wearing and her fear. The sun was starting to set and the light all around her was failing.

She scampered down one block of Rue de Cler, cutting down a side alley to deflect notice, and continued on to Rue de Grenelle. A voice inside her urged her to slow down and stop crying; she was attracting too much attention. A running girl with tears streaming down her face would be remembered by anyone she passed. Simone forced herself to relax and slowed her pace to that of a young woman merely late for an appointment or about to miss a bus, and she willed the tears to ebb. She could not think about Papa and Étienne. Not now.

From her previous walks on streets near Rue de Calais, she knew it would take fifteen minutes to reach the house, maybe longer, since Papa had told her if anything should happen and she needed to flee to it, he wanted her to take side streets. Instinct bid her check over her shoulder to see if she was being watched or followed.

It seemed that everyone was looking in her direction when she turned around; every eye was fixed on her. If she was not careful, she would expose not only Monsieur Jolicoeur but anyone else at 23 Rue de Calais. She decided to take another alley and wait until the sun had finished its descent so that she could approach the safe house under the cover of darkness. She turned into a narrow side street empty of people where she knew a Jewish clinic had been. The clinic, vacant for the last two years, was a ruin of broken windows, crumbling stucco, and a kicked-in door. She could slip inside and wait for nightfall. Simone made her way to the abandoned building, her worn shoes crunching on broken glass. She had no sooner crossed the threshold inside when she heard the sound of someone else stepping on the shards behind her. Simone turned and there in the doorway was a man in a Gestapo uniform, smiling at her. A gold tooth winked in the scant light of the setting sun. Her stomach lurched.

"Mademoiselle Devereux!" He grinned in mock delight. "You easy I catch!"

His French was piecemeal, like so many of the Gestapo who knew no French at the beginning of the occupation and had learned what they could from those they had come to oppress.

Simone backed up a step. Her gaze darted to the right and left as she looked for a way out, since the front doorway was completely blocked by the Gestapo officer.

"You want more to run?" he said, also taking another step inside. "You want hide in building and I come find you? You want play games, *mademoiselle*? Go, run! Find place you hide. See if I find you!" He came closer.

"Please . . ." she said. "Please let me go."

"You think you hide from Gestapo? Here? In Jewish pig barn?" His tone was more sinister now and yet he still smiled.

She backed up a few more steps, and through the haze of semi-darkness she saw a hallway and a trio of doors.

"You think your father clever spying while shine our shoes?"

"No . . . I . . . Please." One of the doors was ajar just a few feet away. If she could just get to it and slam it shut. Maybe it had a lock. Maybe there would be a window to the outside. Maybe—

"Please, what, *mademoiselle*?"

She sprang into action and sprinted across the broken floor-boards. Her hand was on the doorknob, wrenching it open, when the man grabbed her arm. She swung at him and missed, yanking free of him as she whirled into the room. He lunged in after her. There was no window in the room. There was no lock on the door. There were only the remnants of a wheeled stool and a shattered sink.

She saw all of this as he knocked her to the ground. Her cheek and right temple hit broken tiles and gravel with a cracking thud, and for several seconds she could see only twinkling stars, and then the sparkle of his tooth as he tore at her clothes. She screamed and he hit her, yelling in German words she did not know.

The blow stunned her for a moment, giving him time to unbuckle his pants and lower his zipper.

"Very pretty, very clever *mademoiselle*. So very clever. I show you clever."

She screamed again but he did not care. And then there was fire between her legs as he pushed himself inside her—a searing, tearing, wrenching away of anything good left to her. She cried out in agony and he grunted. She felt his pistol still in its holder bumping against her leg, and through her anguish she heard her father tell her how to hold the gun, how to pull back the lever, how to hold it steady and straight. She reached for the weapon, fumbled it out of its holster, and pointed the barrel against the German's rocking torso. She opened her eyes and screamed Papa's name as she pulled the trigger.

For several seconds the only sound she could hear was a ringing, like an alarm, reverberating in her head. The clanging subsided and she heard next the sound of the man who had violated her gasping for breath as blood and foam rimmed his mouth. He was staring at her in disbelief, still on top of her, his eyes wide and the gold tooth glistening crimson.

She pushed him off her, turned to the side, and vomited.

Simone knew she needed to get to her feet and run as far away from the man as she could. But she could only lie on the broken tile as the Gestapo officer struggled to breathe. A moment later he was still.

They would be coming for her now. She had only to wait and they would come. They would find her and they would find the dead Gestapo officer. They would pull her out of the building, drag her to the street, and do to her what they had done to Papa and Étienne. She only had to just lie there and they would come and then it would be over. Soon she would be in heaven with Mama. And Papa and Étienne. They would all be together again. She only had to lie there.

A bit of time passed and there was no sound of rushing boots.

"I am here," Simone called out in a raspy whisper. "I am here."

But several more minutes went by and no one came, and she knew Papa would have her get up. She could feel him tugging at her torn sleeve, urging her to get to her feet.

"No," she said aloud, fresh tears spilling down her cheeks.

Yes. Yes, Simone!

Slowly she rose from the dirt and fragmented tiles. The Gestapo officer was on his side, his vacant eyes fixed in her direction. Blood pooled all around the buttons of his uniform. The gun lay between them, pointed toward the wall where Simone now noticed a picture of the human body, stripped of its skin and tissue, and its amazing organs all tucked in neatly.

Go, Simone!

She pulled her torn dress tight around her middle and staggered away, the pain where her legs met making her feel like she'd been sliced in two.

She walked to the battered front door. No one was rushing toward the little alleyway. She was only a block or two from Rue de Calais and night had nearly fallen. Simone rubbed her face with her hands to wipe away the stains of her tears.

Just stay to the shadows, do not run, the voice in her head whispered to her.

There were a few people on the street, but they seemed disinterested in her and the way she walked, a bit hunched and with her arms crossed firmly across her chest and her dress torn and dirty. The occupation had been one long and terrible stretch of deprivation. One more street urchin was nothing new.

She at last rounded the corner onto Rue de Calais, a tiny passage off a characterless street lined with tired-looking buildings. Simone found number 23, a locksmith and key-making shop, two buildings in.

She had pictured the safe house as a home, not a run-down retailer that appeared to be on the verge of closure. She looked again at the number on the building to make sure it was number 23 and then went in. Keys of all sizes and shapes hung on the facing wall. A waiting bench sat along another wall. An older woman sat behind the counter, grinding a key on a spinning disc.

"We're closed," she said gruffly, not looking up.

Simone stepped up to the counter. "I am . . . I am here to see Monsieur Jolicoeur, *madame*," she said, not much more than a whisper.

The woman lifted the key off the grinder for the barest second. Her hand twitched before she returned the key to the disc. "We are not hiring, *mademoiselle*. Good day." The woman nodded toward the door without looking up.

Simone could only remain where she stood, stunned into silence.

The woman raised her head then, noted Simone's condition, and raised an eyebrow. But then the shock dissipated as quickly as it had appeared. "Did you not hear? We are not hiring."

"I was told to ask for Monsieur Jolicoeur," Simone replied, her voice and body trembling. "And I am not leaving until I speak with him."

The woman stood and studied her with a frown. "What do you want?"

"I will only speak to Monsieur Jolicoeur." Tears that she fought to keep at bay began to stream down her face. This was not how Papa had said it would be. He'd assured her that she could find help at 23 Rue de Calais. Her legs threatened to give out underneath her.

"Who are you?" the woman said, with no trace of courtesy.

"I will only speak with Monsieur Jolicoeur."

"You will speak to no one unless you tell me your name!"

A sob escaped Simone. She felt like no one. She wanted to die there in the locksmith shop and become nothing.

"I am Simone Devereux," she replied as another sob erupted from deep within her.

The woman came out from behind the counter, brushed past Simone, and looked out the shop's front-door glass. She locked the door and drew down the shades over the door and front windows. Then she turned to Simone and her gaze was intense.

"Where are your father and brother?"

"I must speak with Monsieur Jolicoeur!"

The woman put her hands on Simone's shoulders. "*I* am Monsieur Jolicoeur! It is just a code name! It means nothing. Where are your father and brother?!"

"They are dead!" Simone cried, and the room felt like it was spinning.

"My God!" The woman's angry gaze instantly became one of horrified astonishment. "Are you sure?"

Simone nodded and her body swayed. "I saw them get shot."

"Sweet Jesus," the woman said. She took a peep out one of the front windows, and then she drew Simone into her arms. "My name is Celeste Didion. This is my husband's shop. Come tell me what happened."

The woman led Simone up a flight of narrow stairs to a flat above the shop. After settling her onto a sofa with a cup of hot cider mixed with brandy and seeing to the needs of her ailing husband, Monsieur Didion, the woman told Simone to tell her everything.

So she did.

She told Madame Didion about the firing squad in the street and the man who had told her to run. She told her about how she took side streets, and how she went to the old Jewish clinic to hide until nightfall so that she would not unknowingly lead anyone to the safe house. She told her about the Gestapo officer with the gold tooth and what he had done to her.

And then she told the woman what she had done to him.

Seventeen

When Rolf asked her to marry him eight weeks after having met her, Annaliese knew that she did not love him.

She was entranced by his devotion to her, attracted to him physically, charmed by his extravagant gifts and compliments, and in awe of his strength and control. She never felt unsafe when she was with him, not even when air-raid sirens sounded and they had to seek cover. Others would fly about in a panic, but he would calmly usher her into whatever shelter was closest and assure her that all would be well.

He was attentive, but not romantic. Polite, but not thoughtful. He was kind to her, and a gentleman in every way, but he did not seem to be captivated by her. And she was likewise not captivated by him.

She liked him, but she was not in love with him.

He proposed one evening in late June when he was at the Lange home in Bonn. There had been aerial bombings an hour away the previous night, and when Rolf asked if he might join them for dinner to discuss something important, Annaliese's father assumed he was going to say it would be wise for the Langes to return to Prüm, where there were no munitions factories or airfields. The bombings in and around Cologne were becoming more intense and more frequent. Annaliese had been sad to think of leaving the ballet studio in Bonn and even Rolf's affections, but the thought of going home at last, and perhaps being able to sneak in a visit to Katrine, had filled her with hope.

That hope had been momentary. Rolf had no sooner finished his meal, which he thanked Louisa for, when he announced he was being transferred to Frankfurt and he wanted Annaliese to come with him as his wife.

He said it so swiftly that Annaliese could only sit at the table in mute astonishment.

"Our Annaliese?" her father said, his tone a mix of wonder and dread.

Rolf reached across the table for Annaliese's hand and covered it with his own. "Your daughter has made quite the impression on me and I've grown very fond of her. You have raised her well. She is all that a man like me could want in a wife. She will want for nothing, I can assure you. She will be well cared for."

There was no asking of permission, no declaration of ardent love. His words were more a proclamation of intent. Annaliese had been staring wide-eyed at Rolf, but now she turned to her parents and her gaze begged a single entreaty. *Please, don't make me marry him, please, don't make me!*

Her mother glanced at Annaliese and then quickly looked away. "What a surprise, Herr Kurtz," she said with slightly feigned exuberance. "You've only known each other for a few weeks."

"Yes, but when you meet the right girl, you know it. Isn't that right, Gunter?"

Annaliese's father nodded numbly.

"I don't have to tell you we live in uncertain times, but I will keep your daughter safe and she will always have a strong roof over her head. You have my word."

"Well, I . . . Annaliese, what do you say to your proposal of marriage?" Gunter said, turning to his daughter with eyes as wide as hers.

Gratitude filled her soul. She could tell he was as bewildered as she was. She opened her mouth to respond that she was grateful but stunned and not ready to answer. But she waited too long for those words to form on her tongue.

Rolf filled the momentary silence. "She's my little angel." He squeezed her hand and then turned to face her. His sapphire eyes glittered with calm resolve. "She came from heaven to be mine. We both know that, don't we, *liebchen*?" He turned his head to face her parents again. "It's important for a ministry official such as myself to have someone like Annaliese at my side. I am a man of influence. As is my father."

The connotation was lost on no one.

To deny Rolf Kurtz was to tangle with the Nazi Party.

Annaliese and her parents had seen what happened to those the Nazi Party deemed problematic to its intentions. Labor camps all across Germany and Poland were full of prisoners who didn't line up with the Nazi ideal. There were rumors of mass executions at those camps.

"When are you leaving for Frankfurt?" Louisa said, her voice calm but strained.

"In five days. I would like us to marry on Sunday."

Annaliese felt as though she were suddenly underwater and unable to breathe. The room began to sway, and she closed her eyes to let the water envelop her so that she could merely float away and never wake up.

She felt Rolf squeeze her hand again. Harder this time. He was trying to keep her from sinking.

"That's . . . that's in two days!" Louisa replied, and it was hard to tell if she was appalled at the notion of planning a wedding in forty-eight hours or that Annaliese would be the wife of a Nazi official and on her way to Frankfurt in that amount of time.

Rolf raised Annaliese's hand to his lips and kissed it. "I've arranged for everything, Frau Lange. You have nothing to worry about."

Annaliese opened her eyes and her gaze met Rolf's. His stare was controlled, victorious, content.

Rolf knew she didn't love him.

He didn't care.

It only mattered to him that she feared and respected him, and surely the return look in her eyes confirmed that she did.

When he left the house, Annaliese at last found her voice. "I don't love him!" she cried to her parents. "I can't marry him. Please don't make me!"

"He's a man of means, Annaliese," her father said, looking her in the eye. "You will be well cared for."

"But I don't love him."

"Love is for fairy tales, Annaliese," her mother snapped, unnerved by the evening's events. Her voice lacked confidence. She stacked the dinner plates and they clattered against each other.

"I don't believe that. And you don't believe that either."

"But you like him. That is enough. You will learn to love him." Her mother rose with the dishes in her hands. Her father, who never helped in the kitchen, grabbed the wineglasses to follow her into the kitchen.

"I want the person I marry to be in love with *me*. Rolf doesn't love me," Annaliese said, chasing after them.

"He's fond of you. He said it himself." Louisa set the dishes in the sink. Her hands were trembling.

"But why would he want to marry me if he's only fond of me?" she persisted.

"Annaliese." Her father said her name with an odd tugging that seemed to come from the back of his throat, as though he could barely push the air past his vocal cords.

"What, Papa?"

Gunter Lange placed the goblets on the kitchen counter. The glass clinked on the tile. "The man is a Nazi official. We are at war. What would you have us do?"

His voice broke on the last sentence. He would not look at her.

"You'll like Frankfurt," her mother said as she scraped a dish with unusual vehemence.

Her parents said nothing else. They didn't look at each other, nor did they look at her. Louisa continued to scrub the dish past its need for it, and Gunter, eyes closed, leaned against the kitchen counter as if to keep it from crumbling into ruin.

ANNALIESE MARRIED ROLF KURTZ AT A CHAPEL IN BONN AT NOON on Sunday. She wore a pale pink linen suit, pearls, and a tangy-sweet perfume—all items that Rolf had somehow procured. The labels on all three were in French. She had no idea how he had gotten them. His parents in Berlin did not attend. Indeed, only a handful of his friends from the ministry came. Annaliese told a few of her friends in the ballet company that she was marrying the enigmatic young officer she'd been dating, and a couple of them attended, along with her director and a few of her parents' friends. A dinner reception was held at a restaurant that had been provided with enough sugar and butter to make a stunning cake, although it was so deathly sweet Annaliese could not eat it.

They left Bonn at three in the afternoon and drove to Lahnstein, a quaint town on the Rhine halfway to Frankfurt that the aerial attackers hadn't troubled.

Her mother had attempted to prepare Annaliese for her wedding night, but her advice was minimal.

"It hurts for the first week or so, and then it doesn't," was Louisa's sage advice to a daughter who knew only the basics of what a husband and wife did in their bedroom.

Annaliese had imagined that she would don the peignoir set that frothed with lace and satin ribbons—which her mother had given her out of her own closet—and then she and Rolf would slip under the covers with the lights off and somehow he would find his way past all that material. She was surprised, when they arrived at a hotel with a peaceful view of the river, that her body was yearning for Rolf in an almost visceral way. Perhaps if they made love, they'd find love, she thought. She for him, and vice versa. She knew she would not be Rolf's first lover—he had hinted as much—but he'd told her plenty of times that she would be his first "angel," and for some reason, he was thrilled about Annaliese being a virgin.

When they got to their room, however, her yearning quickly morphed into apprehension.

Rolf had no sooner closed the door and set the latch when he took her into his arms and began to kiss her, plunging his tongue into her mouth. He used one hand to hold her trembling body steady and the other to explore her through her clothes. She couldn't breathe, and she felt like she might vomit into his mouth. She broke away, gasping for breath.

Annaliese wanted to tell him to go slow, give her time, allow her to put on the negligee. Couldn't they just sit for a moment and let the sun set first? But the words would not come. Instead she could only say his name in desperation. He seemed to greatly enjoy the tenor of her shaking voice.

"My little *liebchen* is nervous," he said coyly, his hand inside her shirt.

"Yes," she admitted.

He laughed and stepped away. Relief flooded her and she opened her mouth to say thank you. But before she could, he told her to take off her clothes while he watched.

"What?" she whispered.

He took another step back so he could see her fully. "You heard me." He laughed.

Annaliese swallowed hard as she fought back tears. "Rolf. If I could just . . . In my suitcase I have—"

"Take off your clothes."

"I want to put on the peignoir my mother gave me. It's very pretty, and—"

"But that's not what I want." The smile on his face disappeared.

"Please, Rolf." Two tears slid down her cheeks.

"Do it." The playful tone was gone. "You will obey, Annaliese. You are my wife now. This is how it works. Take off your clothes. And stop crying."

She closed her eyes so that she could pretend she was merely getting ready to go on stage and dance, and that instead of taking her clothes off, she was putting on a tutu of softest tulle.

When her clothes lay in a heap at her feet, Rolf commanded her to open her eyes. She would realize later that he wanted her to know that he was in control. He had always been in control. He then inspected her naked body as though she were a new car he had just bought and was immensely proud of, turning her this way and that, and touching places on her body that had never been touched by anyone.

Something was being awakened in her even as something was dying.

Then he pushed her onto the bed.

What had been awakened was snuffed out in seconds, never to return.

And what was dying continued to swirl down into the darkest depths of human misery as Rolf did whatever he wanted.

Eighteen

PRESENT DAY

The air around Brette felt stiff and cool, even though the day's heat had those milling about in the ship's former sick bay fanning themselves with deck maps. The unseen force that bid her look at the placard listing those who'd died aboard the *Queen Mary* had loosened its hold on her, but she could sense that the ghost still hovered just at her shoulder, making sure that she took careful note of the name.

Annaliese Kurtz.

"I can't help you. Honestly. I can't." Brette spoke the words just above a whisper, and still a couple of tourists just a few yards away stared at her before moving off.

She pulled her cell phone out of her pocket and put it up to her ear, feigning a conversation with a person on the other end.

"Did you hear what I said, Annaliese? I'm not the person who can change anything for you, okay? So I'd like to go now."

She started to move away, but the ghost blocked her, like a mighty wind, from taking another step forward.

Brette whirled around and whispered harshly into her phone. "Look. You're not playing fair. I told you I can't help you. I can't. I am really sorry if something terrible happened to you. Life is hard sometimes. We don't always get treated fairly. If I were you,

I'd just head on out of here. Nobody can change the past. Not even you."

The air around her stilled.

"Did you hear what I said?"

Nothing. Not a sound. Not a breath of movement.

"I'm leaving now."

Brette took a cautionary step forward and encountered no resistance. But the tingling of the hairs on the back of her neck told her the Drifter was still with her. She walked out of the sick bay and up the stairs to the deck outside, the presence of the ghost all around her. Whoever it was wasn't finished with her, and yet remained invisible.

"Great," she mumbled as she shoved her phone back in her pocket. Brette climbed another set of stairs back up to the promenade deck and began to walk the length of the port side, hoping the Drifter would tire of her and leave. She closed the distance to the ship's bridge, all the while sensing that other opalescent Drifters spirited themselves away at her approach, almost as if they'd been told to leave her alone; she'd already been claimed by the Drifter that had found her when she first stepped aboard.

Brette returned the phone to her ear. "I just want to know if there's someone here who is new. That's all. Her name is Laura."

The Drifter that followed made no sound.

"Fine," Brette mumbled, and climbed the steps that led to the bridge, the place where Trevor's daughter had said she'd felt her mother's arms around her. The ship's instruments, little towers of shining brass and gleaming wood, stood on the other side of a thick rope held aloft by stanchions. Tourists were taking photos with the instruments behind them as a backdrop. A shimmer of gauzy light lingered at the starboard-side door. It was another Drifter, a young woman in a flowing gown, with long hair that looked amber in the late-morning light. Definitely not Laura. Annaliese perhaps? It started to move away and Brette closed the distance between them.

"Don't go," Brette whispered.

The vaporous spirit hung back and Brette waited until the tourists had left by the portside door.

"Please," Brette said. "Are you Annaliese?"

The Drifter shook her head slowly.

"Is there . . . one like you here named Laura? She misses her daughter. Do you know her?"

Again the Drifter shook its head. Its face was expressionless.

Brette didn't even know if the ghost understood what she was asking.

"What is your name? Can you tell me?" Brette hoped to make some kind of personal connection that would coax the Drifter into trusting her.

The ghost cocked its head to one side, almost as if it were considering the benefit of answering.

"I'm not here to cause trouble for you. I just want to know if there's someone like you named Laura. Someone who misses her daughter, Emily."

The ghost began to drift upward, clearly indifferent to Brette's questions.

"Wait!"

The apparition looked down on her, its appearance languid. Brette could feel the first Drifter pressing in all around her, wanting to reclaim her attention.

"What is it you all want here? What does Annaliese want?" Brette asked.

The Drifter in front of her blinked dreamily.

"Why are you all here? Please tell me."

In a split second the Drifter was at eye level, its face inches from her own. The ghost had had blue eyes when she was alive. *She lets us come.*

The whispered words floated across the air between them, and then the apparition was gone, like a snuffed candle flame.

But Brette wasn't alone on the bridge. The Drifter she surmised to be Annaliese enveloped her, desperate for her attention.

"I said I was never going to do this," Brette muttered, more to herself than to the ghost. The Drifter seemed to caress her then, as if it could sense Brette's unease. The touch felt like a gentle half embrace, meant to soothe and reassure.

"I'm not the one you want," Brette said to the invisible presence.

You are, it seemed to say in response.

A gentle tugging pulled her down a flight of stairs and out onto the sun deck. She could feel the Drifter pressing from behind, directing her back to the promenade deck, back toward the rear of the ship and the sick ward where the placard hung with the names of the dead.

"Okay! I'll do it!" Brette said sharply. A ship's employee walking past eyed her curiously.

"Everything all right, miss?" he said. He looked to be in his late twenties, with close-cropped hair and wearing ear gauges the size of dimes. The name tag on his uniform read *Shane.*

"Yes. No!" Brette exclaimed. "I mean, yes, I'm all right. But I have a question."

"Sure. How can I help you?"

"I . . . uh. So how could I find out more about one of the names listed on the tally of people who died aboard this ship?"

"More about what?"

"You know. That placard in the old isolation ward that lists all the names and dates of the people who died while aboard this ship."

"Oh. That list." The young man pointed back toward the middle of the promenade. "I'd start in the gift shop, I guess. There are several books in there about the ship's history."

Brette thanked him and then turned to walk back the way she'd come, thankful the Drifter seemed to approve. She headed down the deck and into the ship's gift shop, making a beeline for the bookshelves. She thumbed through several books before finding the name "Annaliese Kurtz" in the index of a book detailing the history of the *Queen Mary's* three lives: first as ocean liner, then as troop carrier, and finally as floating hotel. She flipped to the page the index referenced and found the chapter on the many voyages the *Queen* undertook to bring twenty thousand war brides and their children to their new homes in America.

The crossings were made beginning in February 1946 and ended in September, and each voyage lasted approximately five to six days. A complement of army nurses and Red Cross workers accompanied the brides, along with a full crew, and while the weather wasn't always amenable, every voyage was made without major incident save for one.

Brette continued to read:

Annaliese Kurtz, a German citizen pretending to be an American war bride, committed suicide by jumping overboard the night before the ship was to dock in New York. Mrs. Kurtz had stolen a passport and travel documents belonging to Belgian war bride Katrine Sawyer, a friend of Mrs. Kurtz's who had died in a tragic accident a few days prior to the sailing. Kurtz, who was the wife of a German Nazi official and who favored Mrs. Sawyer in appearance, had boarded the ship claiming to be Katrine Sawyer and was planning to disappear once the ship docked in America, according to her roommates, Phoebe Rogers and Simone Robinson. It is believed Mrs. Kurtz heard that the ship's commodore had received a telegraph message alerting him to the presence of the German woman posing as an American war bride, and that law enforcement would board the *Queen* when it docked to take Mrs. Kurtz into custody. Mrs. Rogers said she and Mrs. Robinson had learned of Mrs. Kurtz's true identity only minutes prior to Mrs. Kurtz's suicide. "She'd been forced to marry a Nazi who beat her," Mrs. Rogers told reporters clamoring for news of the stowaway's death. "She told us she'd rather die than go back to him." Her roommates, who saw her jump, were unable to reach her in time to pull her back over the railing.

There was nothing else in any of the books in the gift shop about Annaliese Kurtz.

Brette bought the book with its minimal information and returned to the promenade deck, wondering what the Drifter wanted her to do.

She strolled away from other people, exiting the promenade deck and stepping out on the sun-drenched stern.

The Drifter was still with her.

"I don't know what you want me to do about this," she said.

A breeze that seemed to only exist around her ruffled her hair and the skirt of her dress.

"I'm really sorry you felt like you had no way out but to jump, Annaliese. I—" But her breath was cut short as a solid weight pressed into her chest. The Drifter was practically shoving Brette's words back down her throat.

"Why don't you just show yourself and tell me what you want!" Brette spun around, searching for a snatch of the Drifter's spiritual body. "I'm not a mind reader!"

The book she'd just bought was suddenly out of its bag and on the wooden deck, landing with a *thwap*. Brette watched in astonishment as the pages flew open and then stopped at the part about Annaliese's suicide.

Aunt Ellen had told Brette years before that some souls lingered in the in-between because they were afraid of what awaited them on the other side. But Brette had figured out that others remained because the manner in which their mortal lives ended was undeserved, and they were afraid if they crossed over they would never see justice.

Those Drifters were waiting for the wrong done to them to be made right.

Brette bent down to pick up the book. "You didn't jump, did you?" she said.

The open pages fluttered slightly in her hands, a gentle nod of paper and ink.

No, they seemed to say.

Nineteen

❋

Brette stayed on the ship for two more hours, using the self-guided audio tour to familiarize herself with the ship's storied history. The Drifter hovered all around her, shooing away shadows of other Drifters as though to give Brette space and quiet to study the ship. She took the paranormal tour only for the chance to ask the guide if there had ever been a sighting of the ghost of Annaliese Kurtz, the German woman who died in 1946. The guide, a middle-aged man who'd worked on the *Queen Mary* for a decade, told her that some ghost hunters had supposed that she was one of the dozens of earthbound souls that haunt the ship simply because there are so many reports of paranormal activity and her story is so tragic. But no one had actually "talked" to the ghost of Annaliese Kurtz or captured her shadow or image on film. She'd left no electromagnetic bread crumbs, so to speak. Not like the ghost of the little girl in the second-class swimming pool named Jackie, or the woman in white who appeared from time to time in the Queen's Salon, or the angry apparition in the only remaining engine room who didn't like guests poking about his corner of the ship, far belowdecks.

Another woman taking the tour was listening in on their conversation.

"So do you really think there are ghosts on this ship?" the woman asked the guide. Her slight grin suggested she believed the ship's paranormal tour to be more for entertainment value and that the tour guide was paid to behave as if the ghosts were real.

The guide appeared unfazed by her question; he'd obviously been asked it before. "I can only say there are things that happen on this ship that defy logic. I've heard noises and seen things that have no explanation."

"Other than your imagination," the woman quickly countered. "The human mind can conjure up all kinds of things that aren't real."

"But my imagination can't make *you* see or hear something. It only works for me," the guide said. "If my mind conjures a sound for me to hear, you're not going to hear it, too."

"Unless you suggest I hear it," the woman said.

"Exactly," the guide said, smiling as if she'd just proven his point. "Unless I suggest it. Which means if I say nothing and you and I both hear the same sound, I'm not imagining it, and neither are you."

Their conversation had attracted a couple more people on the tour.

"But why would the ghosts come here? It's not like they all died on the ship. And why so many?" said another woman.

"It would appear they like the ship," the guide said. "Maybe they feel safe here."

"Safe from what?" said a man wearing a Dodgers T-shirt. "What have they got to be afraid of? They're ghosts!" He laughed at his little joke.

The guide smiled and motioned for the rest of the group to follow him. The tour was moving on. "I guess just because you're a ghost doesn't mean you don't have worries."

The group continued to ask questions as they walked down the long aisle of staterooms on the A deck. Brette had learned all she could from the tour, so she left it and returned to the stern. She took the steps to the lowest deck, stepped outside, and stood by the railing in the sunshine.

"Show me where it happened," she whispered, knowing the Drifter was still at her side.

Brette sensed no movement. She asked again.

Several seconds ticked by before Brette felt a slight tugging. She moved along the railing until she was on the starboard side of the back of the ship. Below her, on the other side of the railing, was the rippling blue ribbon that was the Long Beach harbor.

Brette put her hands on the rail and pictured herself standing there in 1946 on a chilly night lit by starlight. Below would be the freezing Atlantic. Annaliese Kurtz had stood here after learning she'd been found out. The commodore had been told she was a stowaway pretending to be a Belgian war bride named Katrine Sawyer. He'd been advised that Annaliese Kurtz, who looked like her childhood friend Katrine, had switched passports and identity documents and boarded the ship bound for America. But while the *Queen Mary* sailed, the identity of the dead woman in the car had been confirmed as that of Sawyer, not Annaliese Kurtz. The ruse was up. She was going to be arrested when they docked in New York and then sent back.

"You stood here," Brette said, pondering what would have happened next. "You knew you were going to be sent back in handcuffs. So maybe you climbed the railing and then . . . then you changed your mind. You decided you wanted to live. So you were about to come back over and then . . . you fell. A bit of rough water?"

The Drifter swirled about her unseen.

No.

"Were you pushed, Annaliese? Did someone push you?"

The movement was more erratic now, pulsing and intense.

"Can't you just tell me?"

The Drifter pulled away in one powerful, swift movement and for the first time since she boarded the ship, Brette felt alone.

"Annaliese?" She looked about her but there was no indication of any kind that the Drifter was still with her.

It seemed she had her answer. The Drifter couldn't tell her what had happened. Maybe Annaliese didn't know how she ended up in the water. All she knew was that she hadn't jumped. She had changed her mind and wanted to live.

But she went overboard anyway and a knife-slice of icy water had welcomed her into the deep. It had greedily pulled her down, filling her lungs with its heaviness.

Annaliese's roommates, Phoebe Rogers and Simone Robinson, had told reporters they saw her jump, which meant either they had lied or the nighttime visibility had obscured their vision and they could not see what or who pushed Annaliese over the railing, only that one second she was there and the next she was gone.

They'd surely run to the spot where she fell, screaming her name. No, perhaps one ran to the spot and the other ran for help. The ship had been traveling at cruising speed to make its New York arrival on time. How long had it taken for the man-overboard siren to clang? How long had it taken for a life preserver to be thrown over, and the ship's engines to stop, and a lifeboat to be lowered for a search that would prove useless? Too long. The water had been too dark, too cold, and the ship traveling too fast. Annaliese's body had slipped under the satin blackness, never to be recovered. Eventually the commodore had ordered the engines to be started up again and the ship sailed on to New York. Those waiting to arrest Annaliese Kurtz were told she had taken her life the night before.

All these years Annaliese must have been biding her time on the *Queen Mary* waiting for someone like Brette to help her understand what had really happened. Perhaps Annaliese's ghost had appealed to other people with gifts like Brette's, but they'd been unable to communicate with her. Or they had missed her altogether.

Brette, being a reluctant visitor, had been unlike the many other paranormal enthusiasts and researchers and hunters eagerly boarding the *Queen* for the chance to encounter a ghost.

Brette would have seemed very different.

She knew what she needed to do next if she was going to attempt what she'd always said she would never do: assist a ghost.

If those two war brides who said they saw Annaliese jump were still alive, they alone knew the truth. Brette would have to locate them and then somehow convince them to tell her what really happened.

If she did find them and they agreed to talk with her, they were surely going to want to know why Brette believed Annaliese hadn't jumped.

"They'll think I'm crazy," Brette muttered as she walked away from the railing.

Even though the Drifter wasn't at her side anymore, Brette still felt its presence, like a cloud above her, watching over her almost protectively. For the first time in her life she knew she wanted to help a Drifter. She wanted to help this one.

This one was different somehow.

"I'll be back," Brette whispered as a moment later she stepped off the ship and the wide embrace of the Drifter lifted.

As she walked back to her car, deep in thought about how to proceed and how to explain to Keith everything that had happened, her phone vibrated in her pocket.

Trevor.

"I can't wait any longer," he said when she answered. "Are you still on the ship? Have you been there all this time? Did you see Laura?"

"I'm just now leaving. And no. I was all over the ship and I didn't see her."

"But you saw other . . . ghosts."

"Yes."

He paused for a moment. "How many others?"

Brette had reached her car and clicked the remote to unlock it. Trevor sounded doubtful. "Do you really want to know how many ghosts I saw?" she replied.

"I just want Emily to know you saw some but you didn't see her mother."

She slid into her car. The interior was hot and oppressive. "I saw a sufficient number of others."

"And did you talk to them? I remember you saying you could talk to them."

"I did."

"You asked them about Laura, right? And they said she wasn't there."

His tone and questions were tight and deliberate, like he wasn't interested in anything but lining up answers for his little girl.

"She's not there."

He hesitated again. "And why would she think she did feel her mother there on that ship? Was a ghost maybe trying to trick her? Play games with her?"

"Drifters aren't like that."

Another second passed as he thought on this. "It doesn't matter to me what they might be like, Brette. I just need to know why Emily thinks she felt her mother there."

"So you can explain it all away."

"God, yes! I want her to forget all about this!"

She heard the desperation in his voice and the cry of father-love in his words. "All right. Maybe Emily ran into a ghost who had been a mother when alive and that ghost reached out to your daughter because it sensed Emily's sorrow and wanted to comfort her."

"Is that what you think happened?"

It was remotely possible and as good an explanation as any. "Sure."

Trevor exhaled heavily. "I told her what you were doing this morning. She knows you are at the ship right now. She's mad I didn't bring her over there."

Thank God you didn't, Brette wanted to say. "If you and she had tagged along, it would have changed nothing. Laura's not here."

"I'm going to tell her you didn't see Laura. But if she doesn't believe me, will you talk to her?"

"I will if you think it will help. But it might not, Trevor. I'm no one to her."

"You're my friend who talks to ghosts. That's who you are."

Brette smiled. "That's what you told her?"

"It's true, isn't it?"

"So now you think I *can* talk to ghosts?"

"If there are ghosts, you'd be a great person for them to talk to."

"Okay. Very funny. I'm going to hang up now and head back to San Diego."

"I owe you one."

"No, you don't."

"But you drove up all this way to find nothing."

She could have said he was way off the truth, but she merely told him she'd been glad to help and hoped he could soon get back to the life he and Emily had waiting for them in Texas.

THE DRIVE HOME FROM LOS ANGELES SEEMED LONGER THAN usual as Brette itched to get on the Internet and follow up with what she had learned on the ship.

She made it home by five, changed into yoga pants and one of Keith's old T-shirts, and got comfortable with her laptop.

Annaliese Kurtz's roommates, Phoebe Rogers and Simone Robinson, were both listed on websites dedicated to archiving information about GI war brides from World War II. Both had been interviewed over the years for newspaper articles. Phoebe and her husband, Hal, had retired in Missouri, and he'd passed away in 2005. A St. Louis newspaper had done a story on her in 2016 for the seventieth anniversary of the war brides' arrival in the United States. The story mentioned the suicide of Annaliese Kurtz, but the main thrust of the article was how Phoebe and her American husband met, how difficult the war years were, how exciting it had been to travel to the States on the RMS *Queen Mary*, and what it had been like to live as an American for the last seventy years. Brette skipped to the paragraph about Phoebe's roommate, Annaliese.

"She must have had it terrible back home in Germany to have done what she did," Phoebe was quoted as saying. "I could tell something was bothering her before we even got on the ship. She was in the queue behind me when we registered at the camp at Tidworth. Everyone who heard her speak thought she was German, and you can imagine the looks she got after everything Hitler and the Nazis had done. They'd killed the boy I loved before I met my Hal, and bombed my house, and you know what they did to all those Jews. Everybody in that queue had suffered in some way, so to hear Annaliese's voice was to be reminded of all that. She said her name was Katrine and that she was Belgian and grew up close to the border where lots of people spoke German. And I felt sorry for her because everyone seemed to mistrust her. I tried to be nice to her. But in the end she got found out. And I guess she just decided she'd rather be dead than go back to Germany. I try not to think about it much."

The article included a photo of Phoebe and her husband as newlyweds in England, a family photo of her with her three children, eleven grandchildren, and eight great-grandchildren, as well as a single shot of her sitting on the balcony of her assisted-living condo in St. Louis.

Brette found less information on Simone Robinson, who seemed to have lived a quieter life as an American. She was listed in 2010 as living in New Mexico. Simone had been part of a larger story on her husband, Everett, who'd been interviewed in 1995 for the fiftieth anniversary of V-E Day. A reconnaissance pilot, he had been shot down over southeastern France during scouting missions for Operation Dragoon, an offensive that would later be known as the Other D-Day, when Allied troops landed on the Mediterranean coast of France and marched upward into Germany. Everett, who had been rescued by local villagers after he'd bailed out of his plane, had been hidden in a wine cellar where Simone, a Parisian wanted by the Germans for her work with the Résistance, was also in hiding. Simone had nursed his wounds while Everett waited for the opportunity to rejoin his battalion. They had fallen in love while he taught her English and she taught him French, as there was nothing else to do in the concealed wine cellar while they waited. After the Allies landed on the beaches in Provence, Everett had gone on to fight in the Ardennes and advanced into Germany. They'd married in Paris right after the war.

The interviewer had apparently asked about Simone's eventful voyage on the *Queen Mary* and the death of her German cabinmate, but Simone had declined to comment on that.

"She doesn't like to talk about what happened on the ship," Everett was quoted as saying.

No other news article was found about Simone. The only other Google hits were related to stories about Everett. The couple apparently still lived in the Albuquerque area. A white pages link offered an address that appeared to be current.

Brette looked down at her notes. She had a phone number for the administrator's office for Phoebe Rogers's assisted-living complex in St. Louis and an address for Simone Robinson's New Mexico home. The easiest next step would be to try calling Phoebe. It was just a few minutes before six, nearly eight o'clock in St. Louis. The office would be closed. She'd have to wait and call the following day at work, perhaps on her lunch break. She didn't have a number for Simone, and a Google search didn't immediately locate one.

There was just one more thing to check before going for an evening jog before dark.

She Googled *Annaliese Kurtz*.

She paged through the results, looking for any new information. It seemed the woman was a mere footnote in the annals of history. Every news account or historical archive confirmed what Brette already knew about her, with only a couple of exceptions. The body in the car, originally thought to have been Annaliese Kurtz, had been identified as Katrine Sawyer by Katrine's maternal grandfather, a British exports trader who had been in India at the time of the accident. A second news account mentioned that Annaliese's German husband, a former Nazi Party member named Rolf Kurtz, remarried two years after Annaliese's death. He had never commented to reporters about why his first wife had left him. His second wife died young, at thirty-seven, the result of a fall down a flight of stairs. Investigators had said the details of the fall were suspicious, but no charges were ever filed against anyone.

Brette was about to close out the browser when she saw that one of the results for Annaliese Kurtz included an image. She scrolled down and clicked on it.

Her breath stilled in her throat. The image was a photo from a Cologne ballet company's production of *Sleeping Beauty*, dated 1943. The dancer was identified as Annaliese Lange. She would marry Rolf Kurtz not long after the photo had been taken.

The pose was an exquisitely beautiful bend of body and limbs as Annaliese mimicked death's graceful but solemn slumber.

Twenty

For the first few days Henri and Collette did not think the American would survive. He spiked a fever even after Simone applied the rest of the sulfa powder. Collette made the poultice of mashed onions to draw out the infection as Marie had suggested, and Simone was tasked with changing the dressings every few hours and laying cool compresses across him to lower his body temperature. The pilot seemed to be in a continual nightmare state, near as Simone could tell, but now and then he would stretch out his arm as if reaching for something. She would take his hand and murmur to him in French that he was all right, among allies, and safe.

Every noise outside the cellar took on new meaning. In the past, if Simone heard a strange noise from above, she immediately crouched into position to jump into the barrel. Henri told her she still needed to do that if the cellar door opened without the signature three knocks. If the American was found and dragged up the cellar stairs to be hauled off as a prisoner of war or shot there on the spot, there was no need for the same fate to befall her, he'd said. But Simone knew she would not leave the wounded American to that kind of end. If the Gestapo came storming down the steps, they would find them both, and the thought of meeting their end together, even though she barely knew Everett, filled her with a strange sense of calm.

Caring for Everett became Simone's only focus. After five weeks of having nothing to do except ponder the circumstances that had brought her to a wine cellar in the south of France, she found herself suddenly energized with a sacred purpose. Keeping the American alive quickly morphed from a simple request of Henri and Sébastien and the other local Résistance fighters to a solemn and holy duty. They wanted him alive so they could ask him what the Allies were preparing. She just wanted him to live. As she nursed his wounds and cooled his brow, she was reminded of the time she was seven and had a severe case of influenza. Her *maman* had cared for her with such tenderness, gently massaging her aching limbs, telling her stories, singing lullabies to her. She did these same things now for Everett, talking to him as if he were a child who could hear her instead of a grown man suffering from delirium.

His fever broke in the middle of the night, four days after he arrived. Simone had extinguished the lantern early and had only a candle at the ready for light. She was lying a few inches away when she felt Everett stir beside her.

"Is anyone there?" he said in English. He sounded weak but in his right mind.

"Here, *monsieur*." Simone sat up and moved closer to him. She lit the candle and put her palm against his forehead. It was cool.

"Simone?"

He remembered her name. "Yes."

"How long I am here?" he said in broken French.

"Four days, *monsieur*."

"Everett. Please, Everett."

"You had a fever, Monsieur Everett. But I think you are better now."

"*Comment?*" he replied, apparently not having understood what she said.

"You sick. Hot," Simone said in English.

He replied with a string of English words she did not know. When she said nothing, he said, "Monsieur Pierron?"

"Henri sleeps. It is night," she said in English.

"Oh. Is there water?"

Simone reached for a flask and poured water into a cup by the light of the candle. She placed Everett's head in her lap and helped him take small sips.

"Not fast, Monsieur Everett. Only slow."

Simone put the cup down and settled him back on the straw. She lifted the candle and brought it close to the bandage on his chest, checking to see if it needed changing. It looked dry.

"Sleep now, Monsieur Everett. Morning later."

"Everett," he said.

"Everett. No candle now. For tomorrow. Yes?"

He nodded and she blew out the candle. The cellar was instantly black as pitch.

Simone stretched out on the straw next to Everett, with just inches between them.

She heard him turn his head toward her.

"Simone?"

"*Oui?*"

"What day? What date?" he said in French.

"Oh. I think it is Sunday."

"June fourth?"

"Yes."

Several seconds of silence followed before he spoke again.

"Simone?"

"*Oui?*"

"Merci pour tout."

She would look back later on that moment and realize that was when she started to fall in love with him. And he with her.

OVER THE NEXT TWO DAYS SÉBASTIEN AND FRANÇOIS VISITED Everett twice to ascertain from him what the Allies were planning and how the local Résistance could assist.

At first Everett was too weak for a lengthy conversation with men who barely spoke any English. When they came back the second day, they brought with them a man from Aix-en-Provence who had studied at Oxford and was sympathetic to the Résistance. He wanted to help and he knew English. He looked to be about Papa's age, with a silvery mustache and slightly receding hairline.

Simone helped Everett raise himself to a slight sitting position when the men arrived with several lit lanterns. Henri trailed them, carrying Everett's camera.

Sébastien crouched down by Everett. He began to speak.

"I am Sébastien, this is François," he said in French. "We saw your plane go down and we brought you here. This is our friend, Monsieur Vallot. He speaks English."

Monsieur Vallot translated.

Everett spoke and then Monsieur Vallot turned to Sébastien. "He says his name is Lieutenant Everett P. Robinson from the 111th Reconnaissance Squadron, Texas National Guard. He is very grateful for what you did and are still doing for him. He wants to know if you have news from the west."

"News? News from the west of what?" Sébastien asked.

Monsieur Vallot and Everett exchanged some words. "He wants to know if you've heard anything today regarding activity on France's western coast."

"We've no radio in this village! Ask him why he wants to know."

"He says he is not at liberty to say why."

Sébastien frowned. "We are fighting the same damn enemy! Doesn't he know that? Ask him what he was doing flying over Provence. Ask him if an invasion is being planned. Ask him why he was taking photographs." Sébastien pointed to the camera.

When Monsieur Vallot translated for Sébastien, Everett looked to Simone, seemingly searching her eyes for some kind of affirmation. Then he said something in English.

"He is not at liberty to say," Monsieur Vallot translated, "but he would very much appreciate your helping him get to Spain or Italy as soon as he can travel."

Sébastien cursed under his breath.

"He wants to trust us but he's not supposed to say anything," Simone suddenly said.

"And how would you know that?" Sébastien replied.

"Because. I just do. I've been taking care of him for the last six days."

"You don't speak English!" Sébastien barked.

"That doesn't mean I can't see how this is for him. He doesn't know us. We're not military. He's not supposed to say."

"She's right," François said. "He won't tell us anything."

Sébastien leaned over and put his face close to Everett's. "We know you are Recon. We know you were taking pictures!"

"Then you have your answer, don't you?" was Everett's translated reply.

Sébastien smiled a half grin. "When? When is the invasion? Can you not even tell us that?"

"He cannot tell you when!" Simone exclaimed.

"We can help you!" Sébastien continued, ignoring her. "We can provide the intelligence! We have the spies. Let us help you! Tell us when!"

Everett responded.

"He wants to know where the nearest radio is," Monsieur Vallot said. "He knows someone has one in the vicinity. He's heard it."

Sébastien snickered. "Tell him we're not at liberty to say."

Everett tried to sit up and grimaced. Simone gently pressed him back down.

"You will reopen the wound. Lie still," she said in French, knowing he would not understand.

Everett closed his eyes as waves of pain washed over him. He muttered something to Monsieur Vallot.

"He said he will tell you more if you go to where the radio is and listen for news from the west and then come back and tell him what you heard."

Sébastien cocked his head. "You are telling us something happened today, aren't you, friend?"

But Everett did not answer when Monsieur Vallot translated this.

"He's tired," Simone said. "I think you should let him rest."

Sébastien stood up. "I think you should let us decide what happens next, little girl." Then he turned to François. "Tell Denis we need the manure truck again. We need to get to Éguilles. Don't tell him why." He turned to face the reclining American. "We'll be back."

Everett popped open one eye. *"Bien."*

The three men left, forgetting one of their lanterns. Simone reached for it as soon as they were gone, nearly giddy at the thought of more light. She set it between them.

"You. Never go out?" Everett said in French and motioned to the world above.

"No."

"Jewish?"

She shook her head, leaning forward a moment to stuff more straw under his head.

"Résistance?"

She settled back on her bent knees. "My papa. Yes. He was Résistance. And my brother."

"In Provence?"

"In Paris."

"Where are father and brother?"

Simone hesitated only a moment. "They are dead. The Gestapo."

"And your *maman*?"

"Dead many years, *monsieur*."

Everett said nothing for a moment, but his gaze never left hers. "I do not know word I want."

And Simone did not know which word he was searching for.

He pointed to his uniform jacket, which Simone had folded and placed on the top of her hiding barrel. She rose and retrieved it for him. He pointed to an inside pocket.

"*Merci?*" he said.

Simone unzipped the pocket and withdrew a slim Bible.

"My *maman*. She gave me. Look."

She opened the little book. The whisper-thin pages were printed in English.

"You have Bible?" he asked.

She didn't know how to tell him she had nothing; not even the clothes she wore were hers. She just shook her head.

"Henri has Bible?"

Simone supposed he did. "*Oui.*"

Everett placed his hands side by side, palms up, simulating a book. "You and me. Two Bibles. I learn French. You learn English." She understood. The same book, two translations. The empty hours that stretched before them were instantly infused with purpose.

When Collette brought down their lunch, Simone asked if she could borrow a Bible, and Collette, surprised for a brief moment, said she'd bring one down at suppertime.

Two hours later Sébastien returned. He came flying down the stairs into the cellar, scaring Simone, who was reading by candlelight, and waking Everett, who was napping.

Sébastien carried Henri's bottle of Armagnac and two glasses. Monsieur Vallot was not with him.

He crouched next to Everett, who had risen with help from Simone and now rested his upper body on one elbow.

Sébastien poured the brandy into the two glasses and handed one to Everett. "*À votre santé!*" He saluted the American with the glass and then downed its contents.

Everett was still holding his glass when Sébastien set his down on the dirt floor.

"*À Sainte-Mère-Église!*" Sébastien said, smiling wide.

Everett looked to Simone.

"Sainte-Mère-Église is um . . . town in Normandy," she said in English.

"The Allies landed at dawn. All up and down the coast!" Sébastien said excitedly. "They've taken the beaches, Simone. Sainte-Mère-Église was the first village liberated early this morning. The Allies are advancing into France."

Simone turned to Everett, unable to think of one English word to describe what Sébastien was saying.

But he seemed to understand nonetheless. She could tell he had known this day had been planned. He just hadn't known if the plan had been executed or had met with success.

Everett looked both relieved and troubled, as though it was too early to celebrate anything and the real battle was only just beginning. But he tipped his head back, drank the brandy, and handed the glass back to Sébastien. "*À votre santé,*" he said.

"There is more!" Sébastien said, pouring more into each of their glasses. "Rome was retaken. Yesterday. The Axis is crumbling!" He handed Everett the glass.

Everett offered his to Simone but she didn't like the taste of brandy. And she could tell Everett was guardedly happy with the news Sébastien had brought.

"And now, my American friend, you can tell me what is in store for us here in Provence, eh?"

Everett nodded but said nothing.

"He doesn't know what you said," Simone interjected.

"Oh, yes, he does. Tomorrow, my friend. Tomorrow, I bring Monsieur Vallot back, and you and I will get to work."

He grabbed the glasses and the bottle and left. The cellar door closed. And Simone and Everett were again surrounded on all sides by shadows.

Twenty-one

There were many meetings between Everett, the local Résistance, and Monsieur Vallot after news of the Allied invasion of Normandy had spread throughout the village. The Germans in place in Provence were placed on high alert, and rather than it becoming easier for Simone and Everett in the cellar, their situation became more precarious. Simone had hoped the Allied presence in France meant she and Everett could crawl out of the cellar, but the opposite was true. She was told it was even more important now that she stay hidden and care for the injured American. Sébastien had heard through his intelligence channels that German forces in Marseille were looking for an American pilot who'd survived the downing of his plane by antiaircraft gunfire over Aix-en-Provence. A bounty had been placed on Everett's head despite the attention that was now riveted to reports of Allied troops marching across Upper Normandy.

When the men had their meetings in the cellar, Simone would scoot to the far wall to stay out of their way and pretend to read. But she listened to everything Everett told Henri and Sébastien and the others.

Everett told them the photos in his camera were to help identify the best places for an airborne landing prior to an invasion of the southern ports of Marseille and Toulon. It had to be a place without Wehrmacht-controlled high ground. He also said a bombing campaign was imminent to destroy several key bridges and cut the

Germans off from reinforcement once the invasion started. Then there would be the landing at the coast, at several beaches, but Everett did not know which ones. And he didn't know when the invasion would take place. All of that was to have been decided after he returned and his film was developed.

"The invasion hasn't been authorized by the Allied Combined Chiefs of Staff," Everett had said on the first day of their meetings. "Nothing will happen until they sign off on it."

Then there had been much talk of what the Résistance fighters could do to sabotage German operations and weaken their response. Everett asked them to get word to Résistance fighters who had communication with Allied forces that he was alive, and they said they would try.

After the meetings there was nothing left for Everett to do except heal and wait and learn how to speak French.

He and Simone started with the gospel of Luke and slowly and methodically taught each other line by line, word by word, their respective languages. After a few hours of Bible translation, they would draw pictures with a stick on the dirt floor to learn the words that weren't in the scriptures, like *refrigerator*, *giraffe*, and *mailbox*. At night when the cellar was completely dark, they would take turns telling their favorite childhood bedtime stories in the new languages.

Everett's wound continued to heal, as did his other injuries. He and Simone would get exercise every afternoon by walking around the cellar, he slowly at first, as they quizzed each other on verb conjugations and tenses.

Their favorite part of the day was the two hours of slanted sunlight that they shared on the stairs from noon to two.

On one sultry afternoon in late July, the cellar, normally cool and dry, was warm and moist. Simone and Everett were sitting on the third and second stair from the top, letting the sun bathe their faces in its audacious heat and brilliance.

Henri had opened one of the casks earlier that day and had brought them a bottle. They sipped the citrus-hinted rosé from teacups.

"How did you end up here, Simone?" Everett spoke in English, as they had agreed that during stair time they would alternate each day which language they would speak.

She laughed lightly. "Sometimes I still ask myself that question."

He waited.

"I came in disguise as a Catholic novitiate. A courier brought me."

"A courier? Also Résistance?"

"He was Résistance, yes."

"You came all the way from Paris? By train?"

"No, no." Simone shook her head. "No trains. We had a truck for a little while. And some of it we walked. It took many days. Many. It was . . . difficult. It was hard to know who to trust."

"And where did you sleep? In churches?"

"No. I was dressed as a novitiate but I am not one. I did not want to attract attention. It was better to sleep in the truck or in barns or abandoned houses. Sometimes other Résistance would put us up."

Everett sipped his wine and Simone wondered if he was done asking questions. She found herself strangely hoping he was not. They had grown close in the last seven weeks as they struggled to learn each other's languages. They had shared the details of their childhoods, where they were born, the names of their siblings and family members, their favorite foods and music, the books they liked and the books they'd hated. She had learned everything about him all in the name of vocabulary building, and he had learned the same about her. She knew he was four years older at twenty-two, the oldest of three sons, a native of Texas, that he'd studied aeronautical engineering in college, that he had a dog back home named Beau. His mother was a schoolteacher and his father sold cars. She knew he liked baseball and Italian food and that he'd played the trombone in high school. She had told him everything about herself as well but had always stopped short of telling him about the day Papa and Étienne died and what happened in the ruined Jewish clinic afterward. She hadn't told him about the woman at the locksmith shop who'd cared for her broken body and then taken her down to the basement where five others waited—including two young Jewish children—for assistance out of the city. She had known at that moment that she had indeed saved the lives of those people and Monsieur and Madame Didion by ducking into the old Jewish clinic. Had the Gestapo officer followed her all the way to 23 Rue de Calais, everyone in the house would have been arrested and Madame shot or tortured to reveal her sources. She had not told him about the nun at the Saint François Xavier Catholic Church who had tutored her on how to be a believable novitiate and provided her the clothes to wear.

She wanted to tell Everett all these things, and yet she didn't want him to know what the German with the gold tooth had done. Simone was already in love with Everett, and it was different than any teenage crush she'd had. Far different than the infatuation with Bernard. She could not imagine her life outside the cellar, where there was no war, and him not a part of it.

"What is wrong, Simone?" he asked.

His question startled her and she realized that two tears were now sliding down her cheek. She could not answer him.

"Why can't you leave this cellar?" he asked, gently.

She shrugged a shoulder, wanting to tell him everything, wanting to tell him nothing. "I told you. The Gestapo wants me."

"No, I know that. But why?"

"Because of what I did."

He paused a moment before asking her to explain. And when he did ask, it was as if he were her oldest, truest friend inviting her to share her most troubling secret so that he might help her carry it.

She spilled it all then, telling him everything that had happened, from the time she heard the shouting in the shoe-repair shop to when she arrived at the wine cellar disguised as a would-be nun. She was afraid to look at him when she was done, now that he knew she had been violated in the worst possible way, and that she had killed the man who had done it. When she finally did, his eyes were glistening and he reached out to touch her face and catch the tears that were sliding down her cheeks.

She tipped her head to lean into his palm and closed her eyes. His gentle touch was almost too much to bear after everything that had happened.

"I didn't mean to kill him," she whispered. "I just wanted him to stop."

"What he did to you was wrong," Everett said, his voice intense but tender.

Simone turned her head toward him to look into his eyes. "I am a murderer."

He took his hand and placed it under her chin so that she could not look away again. "You are not a murderer. This is war, Simone. That man was not only a criminal and a beast, he was your enemy, the enemy of France, and the enemy of all things good and right."

"He . . . he made me want to die."

"But you are here. You are not dead. You are alive. The world will be a beautiful place again. I promise you, Simone."

As Everett spoke, the sun was falling across his face in brilliant strands of light, so bright that Simone found she could believe he was right.

She slept in his arms that night.

It was the first time since Papa and Étienne had died that she had been in the embrace of someone she loved and who loved her.

TWO WEEKS LATER, ON TUESDAY, AUGUST 15, THE 551ST PARA-chute Infantry Battalion landed in Valbourges and liberated Draguignan, a city located just one hundred kilometers from Henri's wine cellar. Navy ships that had approached the coast during the night were in position when aerial bombardment began shortly before six A.M. Landing Craft Infantry fired rockets to explode mines on the beaches so that troops could come ashore at the coastal cities of Cavalaire-sur-Mer, Saint-Tropez, and Saint-Raphaël, and begin the Allied takeover of Provence. The Other D-Day would eventually lead to the liberation of Marseille on August 28, three days after Paris was retaken by the Allies.

Everett was gone by then, though.

As soon as Sébastien brought word to the cellar that the southern invasion had begun, he was on his way to rendezvous with the American troops making their way up through Provence.

But he made a pledge to Simone before he left.

"I am coming back to you," he said as they stood fully in the sunlight for the first time since they had met. "I am coming back *for* you."

He'd kissed her, told her he loved her, and then sped away with Sébastien, promising to write to her as often as he could.

RMS *QUEEN MARY*
ONE THOUSAND KILOMETERS OFF
THE COAST OF SCOTLAND
DECEMBER 1942

The decks are crowded with so many soldiers they are sleeping in the galley, in the empty swimming pool, on the promenade, the staircases, in the bar, the lounges. Everywhere. They must take turns closing their eyes and dreaming of home because there are so many of them. The decks groan with the sheer weight of so many. They wear buttons—red, blue, and white—to indicate when they can eat and when they can sleep and when they may not do either.

I don't know what it is they must accomplish in this war they talk about. But when they aren't laughing or sleeping or lining up in great long queues to eat, they are looking off to the misted horizon. In a few days we will step off at the harbor that welcomes us and I won't see them again. I will never know if they were able to do what they crowded aboard these decks to do.

They think these isolated days at sea will be a time to rest and wait. But I can feel the storm coming. I can feel it all around me. I want to tell the soldiers to be brave, to hold on, to stay away from the rails. But they sleep and play cards and smoke their cigarettes and pay no attention to me. Not even when I slam doors or send a coffee cup flying. What they need is a soft whisper to break into their relentless cycle of sleeping and eating and playing cards and writing letters home. But no whisper of mine can be heard above the din of so many men.

And then it comes. The great ocean begins to swell and sway, and it is as if the core of the earth wishes to toy with us. At first the men laugh and point fingers at those who've been swept off their feet. But then the bell sounds as the storm unleashes its rage. The thousands upon thousands of men are driven inside to cower and crouch, to hold on to anything that won't move. Soon we are tipping wildly, tossed about as if the sea were turning itself inside out. A great wall of water is gathering itself off the starboard side, like a man filling his lungs with air. The massive wave is reaching for us. It has its eye on us. It wants to send us end over end so that what was up will be down. The men are praying, cursing, shouting. They huddle in groups, some with their eyes closed tight, and some with them wide open, as though they want to see for themselves what the world looks like when it's upside down. I reach for those crying out for their mothers; some respond to my feather touch, some brush me away, too afraid to trust that anything good is happening at this moment. If this is where it ends, I and the others shall go with them to the deep. This thought fills me with an overwhelming sadness.

And then, just when it seems there is no way to rise up against so formidable a foe, the mighty sea takes back its boundaries, and the great wall of water flattens outward, grasping haphazardly as though to take a souvenir: a deck chair, a flag, or a curious looker who has no business being outside at the railing. As the men raise their heads to glance at one another, the sea beneath us begins to slowly fold back under like a blanket. The rain continues to fall but it is gentle now, as though apologizing for what the unruly waves had done. Some of the men laugh and whoop and holler. Some wipe the sweat from their brows or the vomit from their chins.

Some lean back against whatever hard surface is behind them and close their eyes and murmur their thanks to God. These are the ones I go to first, so that I might catch a wisp of that holy association. When the passengers pray, I am as close to them as I can ever be. The plane between us thins to gossamer and for a moment we are in the same dimension— in that space between flesh and spirit, light and shadow.

Twenty-two

To the outsider, Annaliese and Rolf appeared to be a devoted couple, content as two newlyweds could be in the throes of a devastating war that was getting more intense by the day. Rolf was supremely attentive to Annaliese, such that people would remark how clearly he loved her. She was never out of his sight; indeed, he had his arm on the small of her back every minute they were together in public. He appeared to be a man head-over-heels in love with his new bride and afraid she might disappear into thin air if he lost physical contact with her.

Annaliese quickly learned, however, that his hand on her back meant just one thing. *You are mine.* At home and when they were alone, Rolf was kind and cordial as long as she was compliant. He was happy when she did what he wanted and didn't do what he didn't want. Annaliese had made the mistake of telling him no only once. He'd asked her playfully to serve him his breakfast in the nude one morning. When she'd declined, his backhanded slap had sent her to the floor and raised a welt on her face that lasted for five days. Whether he wanted sex or a cup of tea or the newspaper or a neck massage or his shoes shined or conversation, she was to provide it. She was his wife. It was her duty.

When she complied with his various requests without a hint of hesitation or complaint, he was happy. Annaliese was free to write to her mother or anyone else, but Rolf read every letter she sent before it was posted, so her notes were short and full of generalities about her new life as Mrs. Rolf Kurtz. While he was at work, she was to stay in the flat and wait for him to come home. This was for her own safety, Rolf had said. Frankfurt had been bombed the year before and was still considered a prime target. He'd secured a nicely appointed apartment twenty-five kilometers away on the eastern edge of Weisbaden, a city that had largely been ignored by Allied forces. Aside from her oppressive marriage, she felt safe there, especially when she learned three weeks after moving to Wiesbaden that Cologne had been heavily bombed and four thousand people had died. She was glad her parents had decided to return to Prüm.

But despite Wiesbaden's relative safety, Rolf didn't allow her to be on her own. The first time she'd gone out while Rolf was at work was merely to take a stroll and see if there were any ballet studios downtown. Rolf had been livid when he'd come home from work to find a brochure for a dance class sitting on the kitchen table.

"You were to wait for me here in the apartment," he'd said. He hadn't raised his voice. He usually didn't. That was a sign of being out of control. And Rolf was never out of control.

But he was angry.

"I . . . I was waiting for you here!" Annaliese had replied, fear rippling her words like she was speaking into wind. "I was right here when you got home, just like you asked."

"What I *said* was you were to stay in the flat until I got home. There was no asking. I was very clear on that! I don't want anything happening to you. It's not safe."

"But there is nothing for me to do here in the flat and—"

Annaliese had not seen the blow coming. One second she was standing there talking to her husband and the next she was on the floor, the right side of her face on fire.

"How dare you tell me I am not providing for you. Do you know how much this flat is costing me? Do you know how many girls would love to trade places with you and live where you live? What an ungrateful thing to say."

"I'm sorry, Rolf," she'd whispered.

"And I was going to take you out tonight. I was in a good mood when I came home. And now you've ruined it." He'd turned to fill a tumbler with brandy.

Annaliese had risen, trembling, to make amends. Rolf was much easier to take if he wasn't angry. She'd walked over to him and put her arms around his middle, laying her head against his back. He liked contrition almost as much as he liked submission.

"Forgive me? Please?" she begged. "I don't know what I was thinking."

He'd hesitated and then placed his hand over hers. "Don't let it happen again, Annaliese. You are not to so much as touch that front door unless it's to go into the basement if there's an air raid. Do you understand?"

She told him she did.

Annaliese tried to keep the swelling on her face at bay, but the blow had been too intense. The black eye disgusted Rolf. For the next five days she was instructed to come to bed with a pillowcase over her head so that he didn't have to look at it.

A month into their marriage, she worked up the courage to ask him if he might allow her to take a ballet class to keep up with her skills. Annaliese had figured he had been so enchanted by her performance in *Sleeping Beauty*, he'd surely think this was a good idea. If she could just get him back to the place where he'd been when he first met her, maybe he would treat her the way he did then. She was itching to dance. The war, her marriage, and her separation from Katrine and home were suffocating her. If she could escape onto the ballet floor, perhaps she would survive her terrible isolation.

"Ballet class?" Rolf frowned. They were sitting at the dining table finishing supper. His tone suggested it was the strangest idea she could've come up with.

"Yes. I know how much you love it when I dance."

The frown disappeared and Rolf laughed. Annaliese smiled nervously, unsure why he found this funny.

"You're joking, right?" he said.

"Well . . . no."

Rolf set down his fork and began to speak to her as if she were a child. "Do you really think I would want you to dance for other people again?"

"Other people?"

"Honestly, Annaliese. Why would I want anyone else looking at you the way I was looking at you when I saw you at the ballet?"

"But—"

"You want to dance? Is that what you want?"

"Um. Yes."

Rolf sat back in his chair and put his napkin on the table. "You can dance for me. Go put your things on and then come out here and dance for me. Go on."

"What? Now?"

"Of course now. You said you want to dance. Dance. Dance for me. Go on. Put on your things."

"I . . . I didn't mean I wanted to dance right now."

"So you *don't* want to dance?" he asked, his tone mocking.

"Not right now, Rolf."

"So you want to dance for other people, but not for me."

"No! That's not what I meant!"

"Go get your ballet things. All of them. Go get them."

"Rolf—"

He slammed his open palm onto the table. The dishes shook and Annaliese jumped in her seat.

"Go get them."

Annaliese rose from her chair, went into their bedroom, and came back a few minutes later with her leotards, ballet slippers, and toe shoes in her arms. Rolf stood and swept them out of her hands and into his own. He strode past her, into the kitchen, and tossed everything into the kitchen garbage.

Then he turned to her. "You take those out of the trash and I'll break your arm."

He left the room and Annaliese just stood there, staring at the tangle of satin ribbons and pink leather and black fabric. For a moment she was willing to risk the broken arm just to have them back. But then she realized that it was the ballet that had led Rolf to her. If she hadn't been in *Sleeping Beauty*, he never would've met her. If she had never known ballet, she would be home in Prüm right now and this nightmare of a life wouldn't exist.

And yet, if she had never known ballet, she would never have met Katrine.

She slumped to the floor next to the garbage and wept without making a sound.

Rolf hated it when she cried.

The next day when she went into the kitchen, the trash had been emptied. She made Rolf his breakfast; he kissed her good-bye and then reminded her that she was not permitted to touch the handle of the front door unless there was an air-raid siren. He would know if there was one.

For the next two months Annaliese spent every weekday alone in the flat, sometimes dancing in her bare feet for hours to keep herself occupied. One morning as she stood outside the balcony of their second-floor apartment, she suddenly remembered how she and Katrine had once climbed out her second-story bedroom window and used the neighbor's tree to get to the ground. They had snuck off to the bakery to buy sweets, even though Madame had told Louisa that Annaliese was not to have any more fattening desserts of any kind.

Annaliese now eyed the railings, the eaves, and the position of the neighbors' iron trellis. Before she could talk herself out of it, she was on the other side of the railing, and onto the ground, her lithe dancer's body making it easy. She was outside without so much as having looked at the front door. For the first time in weeks she laughed. The sound of her own happiness brought tears next and she sank to her knees on the bit of grass between the building and the pathway that led to the street, missing ordinary things like sun on her face, birdsong, and a kind voice.

That first day she just walked around the block once. The following day she walked two blocks. The third day she went to a bakery and bought the sweetest thing wartime rations would allow—a cruller with a scattering of powdered sugar on top. The bakery owner hadn't seen her in his shop before and asked her name.

She told him it was Katrine.

After a month of successfully sneaking away from the flat, Annaliese began to wonder what else she could do to get away from her prison of a marriage.

Five days before Christmas, the RAF flew six hundred fifty aircraft over Frankfurt and dropped two thousand pounds of explosives on the city. Annaliese spent the night in the apartment building's basement along with a dozen other residents, waiting for the all-clear siren to sound. At the bakery the next day, there was talk among other customers that the damage in Frankfurt was extensive and many people had been killed. For four days, Rolf didn't come home from work, and Annaliese found herself woozy with a strange mix of apprehension and relief that he might be dead.

On Christmas morning, he returned bandaged and limping and angry that she had not come to see if he was all right. His offices had been flattened in the bombings and he'd suffered a broken arm, bruised ribs, and several lacerations. His driver had brought him home after four days in the hospital.

"You told me not to leave the apartment, Rolf. So I didn't," she answered, unable to mask the edge of impertinence in her voice.

Annaliese could tell he wanted to hit her then, but with his injuries, it would've hurt too much.

Rolf spent the holidays recuperating at home, and there were no more escapes for Annaliese via the balcony. When they did leave the flat, it was because Rolf wanted out, and they left together. He kept in contact with his superiors in Berlin by courier and telegrams. He was a terrible patient, but he needed her in a different way while he was mending, and his broken arm and ribs kept him from striking her, which was a welcome reprieve.

New Year's Day dawned quiet. Annaliese lay in her bed as snow fell silently outside the window, contemplating what 1944 might hold in store. Perhaps another bomb on another day would kill Rolf. Or maybe the next bombing spree would be over Wiesbaden and they'd both be killed. Either scenario was one she would welcome. Unless . . . unless there might be a day in 1944 when she would climb down the trellis and she wouldn't come back. Unless she just kept walking west. Out of the neighborhood, out of Wiesbaden, out of hell. She could keep walking until she got to Prüm. No, she'd keep walking until she got to St. Vith. Damn whatever patrol she'd have to get through to get into occupied Belgium. She would see Katrine or die trying. Dying on her way to see Katrine was preferable to dying slowly day by day in Rolf's viselike grip.

She would need money, though. Money for transportation. Money for bribes, if necessary. It would take some time to collect it without Rolf figuring it out. And she'd have to hide the money somewhere he'd never look. Her empty ballet bag, perhaps . . .

She heard Rolf grunt in his sleep as she contemplated all of this. She rose from the bed quietly and withdrew a deutschmark from his coin purse, unzipped her deflated ballet bag, and slipped it inside.

The months ticked by and Annaliese bided her time, pilfering pfennigs and marks and enduring Rolf's daily abuses. And all the while, the bombs continued to fall. On Berlin, Hamburg, Leipzig, Stuttgart, Frankfurt, and elsewhere. Rolf became even more difficult to please, and he no longer began sentences with *when we win the war.* Work was becoming increasingly stressful as the ministry's propaganda machine struggled to convince the German populace that the Third Reich would triumph over all its foes.

Finally, one day in early June, Rolf came home late from work, after Annaliese had gone to bed, and went back early the next day. Something significant had happened, but when she asked him at breakfast, he wouldn't tell her what it was. She found out a few hours later by eavesdropping on conversations on the street. Several days earlier, Allied Forces by the thousands had landed on the western coast of Normandy and were now marching across France. Thousands upon thousands of them.

This was the distraction she needed.

This.

And right now.

Today.

Annaliese hurried home, changed into traveling clothes, and grabbed her ballet bag and identification papers. It was only nine thirty in the morning. She had ten hours of daylight ahead of her, the weather was warm, and the skies were quiet. She wasn't afraid to beg for a ride or buy one or steal one. Somehow she would keep moving—and she wouldn't stop until she crossed the border into Belgium. She considered for a moment leaving the front door un-locked and ajar so that when Rolf got home he could see that she had defied him outright, but in the end she left by the trellis after tossing the bag to the ground, so that when he found her gone he might think, just for a few seconds, that his angel had sprung wings and flown back to heaven.

Twenty-three

※

Had Annaliese been able to rely on public transportation to get to Prüm, the three-hundred-kilometer journey would have taken only half a day on a combination of different trains. It would have been a scenic trip with time for coffee and *kuchen* in the dining car. But the trains were unreliable in the summer of 1944 and some railway stations had been bombed, which meant getting anywhere required patience, flexibility, and a stroke of good luck. As Annaliese left the flat for good, she was fairly certain the train station in Wiesbaden was the second place Rolf would look for her. She had taken a map she had bought on the sly, the pilfered money, a flashlight, a flask of water, a few *brotchen*, and very little else. He would not see an empty wardrobe and rifled bureau drawers and think she had left him, not immediately. The first place he would check would most likely be the ballet studio she'd found when they first arrived in Wiesbaden. He might return to the flat after that to furiously await her return, thinking she'd gone out shopping or on some other fool's errand. But after an hour or so he would begin to grow concerned: not that harm might've come to her, but that she'd had the audacity to leave him.

At that point he'd head to the train station in Wiesbaden. He would ask if anyone had seen her or sold her a ticket. And there would be no one who could say that they had. Annaliese purposely avoided that train station for that reason.

Instead she walked thirteen kilometers to the town of Eltville, avoiding main roads whenever possible. Three hours after fleeing the flat she was on a train headed north to Koblenz. It was the only train operating that day and she had no trouble boarding it when she told the ticket agent that she was the wife of a ministry official attending to important matters. She slept in the train station that night to save her precious deutschmarks, and the next morning she paid a man on his way to deliver coal to the village of Kaisersesch forty kilometers away to let her ride with him. For the next two days she made her way, in roundabout fashion, as far as she could go, making only one purchase outside transportation costs—a black leotard. When she was only a few kilometers from Prüm, she realized with a start that she could not set foot in the city where she'd been born and raised; she'd be too easily recognized. She could not stop to see her parents to tell them what Rolf was really like. When Rolf realized she'd left him, he'd likely head for Prüm, just as soon as his superiors let him. He might even be there now, waiting for her. She was grateful that she had never mentioned Katrine to him, and her parents had certainly long forgotten her childhood friend. She was counting on them to have forgotten about her.

Still, the thought of perhaps not being able to see her parents filled her with a strange sadness, and she found herself wishing she cared more that she might get shot crossing the border than that she'd never see them again. By late afternoon she had walked as far as the outskirts of Winterspelt, sneaking into a farmer's barn to grab a few hours' sleep. When darkness fell, she made her way off the main road by a couple kilometers using the map and flashlight. Her hope was that the Gestapo would only have bridge checkpoints on the roads that crossed the Our River, the natural former border between Belgium and Germany. If she could just get to the shores undetected and far from any bridges, she would swim across.

The evening was fair and warm and no Allied planes flew overhead. She found the river by moonlight and walked for a little while on its shore to find the narrowest stretch across. When she located a spot that appeared to be only a kilometer wide, she stripped off her clothes and put on the black leotard. Then she stuffed her clothes in the ballet bag and filled it with rocks so that it would sink and never resurface. For a second she considered putting her identification papers inside as well so that she could become a nameless no one when she stepped onto the Belgian shore, but there was no way she could continue to travel without them. And if she was to keep moving and stay ahead of Rolf, she needed her papers. She tucked them deep inside a leather billfold she'd brought along, and slipped the package inside the leotard to rest against her abdomen.

Annaliese knelt in the mud and asked God to be merciful and forgiving. Then she stepped in.

Having danced every day in the apartment for nearly a year gave her stamina that surprised her. The water was bracing but also invigorating, and the more she put one arm in front of the other, the more she tasted freedom. As she neared the shore of the other side, about twenty-five minutes later, she slowed her pace to make sure there was no one watching her swim across. The Belgian side was covered in trees and lined with a bank too muddy and steep to cross without the light of the sun to guide her. She swam upriver a little ways, though by this time she was growing weary, until she found a place she could climb out. Once on shore, she rested only until her breathing was normal, and then she was on her feet, shivering and muddy. She kept near the river, always in earshot of it as she moved north and west. She knew if she could find the town of Auel on the river, she would also find Luxemburger Strasse, a paved road that led to St. Vith. If she stayed to the shadows and hid from any approaching headlights, she could make it to Katrine's house in under three hours.

Though the day had been warm, the night air was damp and

cool and her wet leotard clung to her body like a sheath made of ice. She tried to jog to increase her body heat, but her bare feet were soon cut and bleeding from stones and the times she had to conceal herself in the brush when a late-night traveler drove past. By the time she reached St. Vith, Annaliese had neared exhaustion. She made her way as stealthily as she could through the sleeping city, letting herself into Katrine's grandparents' back garden so that she could knock lightly on the door and rouse Katrine without anyone on the street seeing her. A light rain began to fall as she rapped her hand against the wood.

She wanted to awaken only Katrine, but no one came in response to her gentle knocking. As the rain began to fall in earnest, she started beating harder on the door, desperate for someone to let her in, wrap her in warmth, and tell her she was safe. Annaliese had almost begun to believe that the war had chased Katrine and her grandparents away and the house was empty, when at last, through a tiny opening in the blackout curtain of the door's window, a seam of light appeared. The lock clicked, the handle turned, and the door opened an inch and stopped.

"Katrine! It's me! It's Annaliese!" she cried out.

The door opened wider and there on the threshold was André Dumont, Katrine's grandfather. He looked old and haggard, as though twenty years had passed since she had last seen him, and not five. "Annaliese?"

"Please tell Katrine I'm here! Please! Tell her I'm here."

"How . . . Why are you here?" He looked as if he believed himself dreaming.

She was weeping now and the rain was falling in sheets. She was so tired and so cold. "Please tell Katrine I'm here! Please."

André Dumont shook his head. "Katrine doesn't live here anymore."

Annaliese stood still and silent for a moment as his words fell on her like blows from a hammer. Then she pitched forward and collapsed, half in his arms and half on the muddied doorstep.

SHE DREAMED SHE WAS ON A BOAT ON A VAST OCEAN. THE SURFACE of the sea was smooth like glass and there was no wind, but somehow the boat moved, slicing through the water like a knife. The sun above was brilliant and warm on her skin. She looked down at her body and saw that she wore a gauzy gown that shimmered and yet was soft to the touch.

This is heaven, she thought, and was not afraid.

"You are safe, rest now," said a voice, sweet and gentle and without human form.

The gauzy dress billowed all around her and the boat sailed on and she closed her eyes.

Sometime later she realized that the boat had been a dream.

The last thing Annaliese remembered was being told by André Dumont that Katrine no longer lived in St. Vith. She'd been cold and wet and weary and alone and broken. Now she lay on a feather bed and she could feel under the blanket on top of her that her torn and bloody feet had been bandaged. She struggled to open her eyes, but her lids were so heavy and the room seemed dark.

There was movement beside her, the sound of a chair being scraped against the floor, and for a second she thought perhaps Rolf had found her and she was back in the bed at the flat in Wiesbaden.

She had no sooner startled when a light was brought near to her and she saw that hovering over her was not Rolf, but the dearest person she'd ever known in her life.

"Katrine?" she said, her voice raspy and unsure.

"Hush, my sweet. All is well." Katrine's face was close to hers.

Her friend's hair was darker and shorter than it had been five years ago, but everything else about Katrine was the same.

"Is this real? Am I awake?"

Katrine smiled. "Yes. You are with me. And you are safe now."

Her tears of relief came in wracked sobs, and Katrine lay down next to her to soothe her as best she could. Annaliese wanted so badly to tell Katrine everything, but every tear that Rolf had forbid her to cry was now spilling out of her. She fell asleep with Katrine's arms around her.

When she awoke again, morning sun was filtering through blackout curtains that had been shoved aside.

She was in a tiny A-frame bedroom with a narrow, pitched roof. She was wearing a nightgown she did not recognize. She sat up in bed and gingerly set her feet to the floor, wincing as her cuts and scrapes reminded her of the harrowing journey.

Katrine appeared in the doorway with a breakfast tray. "You don't have to get up, Annaliese. Just let your feet heal and your body rest."

Her friend set the tray down and helped her arrange the pillows so that she could sit in the bed.

"I keep thinking I am going to wake up and be back where I was," Annaliese murmured.

Katrine handed her a cup of tea. "You are here with me. And you can stay as long as you want."

Annaliese sipped the tea. Its warmth spread through her limbs. "Are we in St. Vith?"

Katrine sat in the chair next to the bed. "You are in Malmédy now. I teach school here. My grandfather brought you to me in his horse cart the night you arrived. He was so scared that you had died right there on the back step!" She laughed lightly.

"I thought I had died right there, too." Annaliese set the cup down on the bedside table.

Katrine's smile ebbed a bit. She nodded toward Annaliese's left hand. "You are married now?"

Annaliese looked down at the wedding ring Rolf had placed on her hand. She'd meant to toss it into the ballet bag so that it could sink to the bottom of the river with everything else. "I suppose I am." She looked up at Katrine as a sudden terrible thought fell across her. "What if Rolf comes here? What if my parents tell him about you? What if your grandfather tells him where I am?"

"Shhh," Katrine said, taking Annaliese's hand. "My grandfather will say nothing. He will say nothing at all. I told him that whatever made you come to us the way you did, it was nothing you should be made to return to. If anyone asks about you, he will say he hasn't seen you in years and that I am living in Brussels now."

"Brussels?"

Katrine smiled and shrugged. "I did live there for a little while when I was in school. I came back this direction when my grandmother died. Grandfather doesn't do well on his own and with me so far away."

Annaliese stared at the band of gold around her finger. "I didn't think I would make it this far, Katrine. I thought I'd be shot trying to get to you. I don't know what to do with myself now. I don't know where to go."

"You don't have to go anywhere."

She looked up at her friend. "I can't go back to him, Katrine. I can't. He's not . . . He's not what we used to daydream our husbands would be like."

"Tell me everything, Annaliese."

Annaliese started with her family's move to Bonn and the night Rolf saw her dance in *Sleeping Beauty*. When she was done, her breakfast was cold and Katrine took it downstairs to warm up. When Katrine returned a few minutes later with the tray, she set it down with purpose.

"You are staying here with me. I will tell anyone nosey enough to ask about you that you're my very shy cousin from Lontzen. We will find a way to keep you from having to go back to Germany. I don't know how, but we will figure it out, Annaliese. Don't worry. The war can't last forever. And when it's over, we'll find someone who can help you stay here with me."

"Who? Who can help me?"

"I don't know. Someone. For right now you are Anna, not Annaliese. And you're from Lontzen. And you're shy."

"Because . . . ?"

"Because the less you say to anyone, the better."

For the first time in nearly a year, Annaliese felt hope. Katrine was smiling back at her, and it was as if she were looking at a reflection of herself, happy and whole and free.

Twenty-four

PARIS

OCTOBER 1944

Simone returned to a Paris still getting used to its freedom. The shoe-repair shop had been boarded up and the flat emptied. No one could tell her where her father and brother had been buried, or if the flat's furnishings had been taken by the Gestapo and either destroyed or distributed among them. Not knowing where else to go, she returned to the locksmith shop and Celeste Didion, hoping for just a place to stay until she could make other arrangements. Celeste invited Simone to live with her in exchange for taking care of Monsieur Didion, who was now bedridden. With the ousting of the Nazis and the return of Parisians who had fled the city, there had been a flurry of key-making and locksmithing and she was doing it all herself. The grandson who was supposed to come home from the war and take over the business had died in a German labor camp.

Food was still scarce in the city, and tensions were still high, but the Nazis were no longer in power and no longer the enemy. Celeste told Simone that no one would care that she had shot and killed the Gestapo officer who had attacked her. It was old news that had mattered only to the German officials who'd been in power in the seventh arrondissement, and they were gone.

Simone had wondered what it would be like to come back home after so many months away. She was not the same woman she had been when she left, and she didn't know if Paris would be the same either. It cheered her to see the spire of the Eiffel Tower, the two towers of Notre Dame, and, off in the distance, the sparkling dome of Sacré Coeur, but she could sense that Paris had lost its innocence, just like she had. Paris had its ruins both physical and internal, and she had hers. The abandoned clinic was still only a few blocks away from the locksmith shop, and the street where she had grown up—and where Papa and Étienne had been shot as she watched—only a few blocks farther still. She and the city were like two sisters who had shared the same devastating losses, and now they were supposed to shake off the dust of their grief and move on.

But they would never forget what had been taken from them. Or done to them.

Weeks would go by in between letters from Everett. Each one had been read and censored before finding its way to her such that most said the same things: he missed her, he loved her, and he was counting the days until he could come back for her.

"Has he asked you to marry him, then?" Celeste said one bleak evening in February 1945. She and Simone had been sitting in Celeste's tiny living room and Simone had read part of Everett's letter to the old locksmith's wife.

Simone had not known how to answer. Everett had not asked her in so many words. But she knew she would marry him. It was as if she and Everett both knew he didn't need to ask a question he already knew the answer to.

"He will," she had finally said.

"It might be best to be prepared in case he doesn't," Celeste said, her tone maternal. "He'll be going back to the States when this war is at last over. He might even have a girl back home. Have you thought about that?"

Simone wanted to say she knew everything about Everett Robinson. She knew the name of his childhood best friend, and why he had a scar on his chin, and his favorite flavor of ice cream, and his shoe size. She knew he had no girl waiting for him in Texas.

"He is coming back for me and we are getting married," she said instead.

Celeste shrugged. "You don't want to be another French girl hurt by an American soldier who is only interested in one thing."

"Everett isn't like that."

Celeste rose from her chair, teacup in hand. "I just don't want to see you get hurt, Simone. Not after everything you've suffered."

Simone didn't fear losing Everett to another woman. She knew only one force could keep them apart: the German Wehrmacht. Everett had reunited with his squadron and was again in the cockpit of an airplane flying reconnaissance missions and therefore ever a target for German antiaircraft guns.

As the weeks passed, word eventually reached Simone that Everett had helped the Seventh Army eliminate the Colmar Pocket and provided the intelligence needed for the recapturing of Strasbourg. He and his comrades reached the Rhine during the first week of March and then moved on to capture Nuremberg and then Munich.

As April eased into May, all of Paris seemed poised to hear the announcement that the Wehrmacht had been defeated. Finally, on the eighth day of May, the bells of every cathedral in Paris began to chime, ringing out the news that the Germans' surrender had been unconditional. The war was over.

Several days passed before Everett got word to Simone that he was coming back to France to serve with the Allied occupational forces, photo-mapping the devastation spread across the country. He'd already turned in his request to his squadron commander to be given permission to marry her.

"You do want to marry me, don't you?" he had written on a wafer-thin V-mail.

Simone had rushed up the stairs to the bedroom where Celeste was having lunch with Monsieur Didion. She thrust the letter in front of her.

"See?" Simone said. "We're getting married."

Everett arrived in Paris in August, and while he was busy flying missions, sometimes for several days at a time, he and Simone found the time to reconnect after nearly a year's separation. They took long walks, waited for approval from the army to marry, and made their plans for a life together in the States.

On November 23, 1945, they stood before a magistrate and pledged their vows. Simone did not care what she wore, but Celeste insisted on something bridal. There was no organza or taffeta to be had for a decent price in postwar France, but there was parachute silk. Yards and yards of it. So Celeste fashioned a stylish but simple dress out of snow-white parachute material. The couple honeymooned in Versailles, and eight days later Everett was billeted back to the States.

Before he left, he made arrangements for Simone to stay with Londoners he'd befriended during the year of preparation for D-Day, believing it would be faster for Simone to get to America if his friends helped her. There were thousands of British war brides who would be getting transported to the States; he'd heard plans were already in the works.

On her last day in Paris, Simone surveyed the city where Maman's physical memory dwelled. The horrible sickness that had ravaged her mother's lungs had taken her from Simone when she was only nine, and the tenuous hold she'd had on her mother had been tied to every dish, every piece of linen, every nook and trinket in the flat above the shoe-repair shop. She hadn't even a photograph of her mother. All she owned of Maman now was what she saw when she looked in a mirror. The color of her eyes, the set of her brow, the fullness of her lips were her mother's. Papa always said she looked so much like Maman . . .

Simone was now the wife of an American man who lived thousands of kilometers and a sea away from Rue de Cler and all of its beautiful, horrible memories. When she sailed away to the United States, she knew it was possible she might never see Paris again.

But the part of Paris she loved most was gone already.

At dawn on the second of January, she boarded a bus bound for Calais, and then a ferry at noon that took her across the English Channel to the coast of Kent. By the time she arrived at St. Pancras Station in London, the sun was setting. Everett's British friends, an older couple whose only son had died at Dunkirk more than five years before, and who had found purpose in mothering Everett when he was stationed in England, met her on the platform, even though the airfield they lived near was another hour and a half away by train.

Over the next month Charles and Eloise gave Simone what she needed most during the strange pause between her old life and the new one that awaited her. Charles was good company on the long trips back to London to take care of immigration details at the American embassy, and Eloise provided a warm and loving home to rest in. Not only that, Eloise helped Simone realize that her exhaustion and nausea throughout the day weren't caused by a virus she'd picked up while traveling but because she was carrying Everett's child inside her body.

Though she had only known Charles and Eloise for a short while, she cried when all of her travel documents were in place and they took her to the train station for the last time.

They, and Celeste and Monsieur Didion, and Henri and Collette, had stood in as parent figures at the most difficult times in her life, times when she had felt like a child lost in the woods, scared and alone.

As Charles and Eloise waved good-bye, Simone realized she wanted to make them proud of her. All of them. She wanted them all to know that the sacrifices they had made for her had been worth it. She wasn't the broken child who had been tossed to them by unkind fates. She had survived what had been done to her and taken from her. She was strong. She was alive. Simone placed her hand on her stomach, feeling the tiniest rounded bump that rested there, and she knew Everett had been right. The world was becoming beautiful again.

Twenty-five

❋

BELGIUM

1944

For the first few weeks after arriving in Malmédy, Annaliese stayed inside Katrine's half of her rented two-story duplex. The building was owned by an older couple who'd lived in the other half but had long ago fled to Spain when the war began. Katrine had a key to her neighbors' place and would check on the pipes, locks, and such as had been requested of her in lieu of rental payments. She showed Annaliese where she kept the key. If at any time Annaliese felt like she needed to hide, she was to take the key, go next door, and secure herself inside. German troop presence was light in the town, but Katrine didn't want Annaliese to take any chances. The war was intensifying with Allied troops on the ground in France. Local occupation forces were thankfully distracted by the possibility that the Allies would be marching into Belgium next.

When June ended with no indication that Rolf had figured out where she was, Annaliese began to cautiously relax. She was fairly certain he wouldn't have been granted extended leave during the height of war to pursue her. He might have been allowed a day or two off, but if her parents had said nothing about her having an old friend across the river in what had been Belgium, it would not occur to him that that was where she had gone. He'd no doubt been wanted back in Frankfurt straightaway. His little domestic troubles would have to wait until the war was over. She had some time to figure out what her next move would be.

Annaliese spent the remaining summer months reconnecting with Katrine and her own sense of well-being. During the day, when Katrine was working at the school, Annaliese read, mended their clothes (Katrine had given her half her wardrobe), maintained a little vegetable garden, and listened to Katrine's English phonographs in the cellar with the volume on low—no recordings or printed matter in English were allowed. In the evenings, Katrine taught her French or they played cards or simply talked about the dreams they still carried deep within them. Katrine no longer danced, but she still loved the ballet and the big city. She wanted to go back to London and spend some time with her maternal grandfather, whom she had not seen since Britain declared war, and she still wanted to visit America to see Niagara Falls and the Grand Canyon. Annaliese didn't know what she wanted to do with her life after the war. She only knew she didn't want to go back to what she had been doing. And Katrine assured her that she would remember how to dream again.

At the end of August, word came to Malmédy that Paris had at last been liberated by Allied forces. The commander of the German garrison had been directed to burn the city to the ground before surrendering, but he defied that order. On August 26, General Charles de Gaulle led a jubilant march down the Champs-Élysées. On everyone's mind in Malmédy was how long it would take before the Allies marched into Belgium. Whispered conversations overheard by Katrine in the faculty lunchroom suggested it wouldn't be long. If the Allies reclaimed Belgium, all that would stand between them and an advance into Germany were all the little border towns. Things might get worse before they got better. The good news that Allied troops had entered Brussels on the third of September was slightly tempered by concern that fresh German ground troops would likely be dispatched to meet the Allies as they continued east. Reports that the retreating Germans were burning homes and businesses and telegraph wires as they fled was also cause for worry.

Over the next three months the Allies worked their way eastward. The Nazi propaganda ministry dropped leaflets over their German border towns, including Malmédy, warning their citizens that American troops were using riding whips on German women, and that everyone, in uniform or out, was expected to defend Germany to the last man. Katrine and Annaliese spent many nights in the cellar as the far-off boomings of artillery echoed in the distance. As October eased into November and the first snow fell, the first American troops arrived in the village to map its contours, study its position, and gauge the mood of its historically Belgian but heavily German-speaking populace. A hushed sense of expectation seemed to creep across the village.

The day that the American first lieutenant knocked on the door of the duplex, Annaliese stayed in the kitchen out of sight while Katrine talked to him.

Annaliese could only make out some of the English words. Katrine was not fluent, but she knew far more English than the majority of villagers in Malmédy. They talked for several minutes and then Katrine invited the man in and closed the door. She called for Annaliese to come out.

When Annaliese rounded the corner, she saw a soldier of average height, slim build with wavy brown hair cropped short. He was attractive, but in a different way than Rolf. This man had a kind face and gentle gaze.

"This is my cousin Anna," Katrine said in English. "She knows only a little English." Then she turned to Annaliese. "This is Lieutenant John Sawyer with the . . ." Katrine turned back to the man, a quizzical look on her face.

Lieutenant Sawyer smiled and put out his hand. "The 285th

Field Artillery Observation Battalion. A pleasure to meet you, ma'am. I would have thought you were sisters."

Annaliese shook his hand numbly as he said the word *sisters* in English. He had taken them for siblings, like most people did.

"The lieutenant and a few of his men need a place to stay until the rest of their battalion gets here in a few weeks."

"Here?" Annaliese echoed. "In Malmédy?"

"The war is coming to our village, Lieutenant?" Katrine asked.

He said something to Katrine in English. Annaliese only caught half of the words. Intent. Village safe. Women and children. Battle. Away.

Katrine turned to Annaliese. "They hope to avoid staging any battles here, but if the Germans counterattack, they must be ready. The city may be instructed to evacuate at some point. They are taking control of Malmédy."

The lieutenant said something else and Katrine answered him. Then she retrieved the key for the other side of the duplex.

"I'm going to open the rooms next door. I told him we'd be able to give them a hot meal tonight. There will be four of them. We will need to add more vegetables to the soup."

"Four of them?" Annaliese didn't hide her surprise. Food was in short supply.

"They are here to end the war, Anna," Katrine said simply.

For the next three weeks, the lieutenant and his men used the duplex to sleep and shower in and Katrine not only gave them a hot meal at night, she and Annaliese took a warm breakfast to them every morning. Katrine had many long conversations with the lieutenant, of which Annaliese could only understand the barest minimum.

At night when they were alone again in Katrine's bedroom, she would tell Annaliese all she'd learned from him, about the progress of the war and what was happening in the other parts of the world—

details that had been denied them by the Ministry since the war began—and about life in the United States.

"Teach me more English," Annaliese said one night after Katrine returned to their room. She'd spent two hours talking with the lieutenant about America.

"All right, I will. But you have to promise not to say much around the lieutenant or any of the other Americans, Anna. You have a German accent when you speak."

"So do you!"

"But not like yours. You don't want them to find out who you are married to."

Annaliese had almost forgotten that she was still married. Almost.

The second week in December, the lieutenant, whom Katrine called John now, and his men left to join the convoy that was the rest of the 285th. The mapping and study of the city was complete. If the enemy was to be engaged there, the occupying Americans would have the advantage. Annaliese watched from the open front door as Katrine and John said good-bye at the side of the road.

"Will I see you again?" Katrine asked.

"I'm counting on it," the lieutenant replied. And then he leaned in and kissed Katrine on the cheek. The gesture was so gentle and painfully beautiful that Annaliese felt an immediate ache in her gut.

"Write me!" John Sawyer said as he got into his vehicle with the rest of his men. He drove off with a cheery honking of the horn. A feather-light snow began to fall as his jeep grew smaller in the distance.

"You've only known him three weeks," Annaliese said when Katrine joined her at the threshold.

"It seems like longer." Katrine shrugged, as if to suggest Annaliese surely knew that love didn't take note of calendar pages.

It might have been many long months before Katrine would have seen John Sawyer again had the Germans not mounted a fortified attack up and down the Belgian border. On the afternoon of the seventeenth of December, the local officials in Malmédy, knowing that a clash between the Allies and Germans was imminent, recommended evacuation.

Since it was a Sunday afternoon, Katrine was not at the school when she and Annaliese saw through the front window civilians and Allied soldiers alike racing about to escape or prepare for what was headed their way. They did not know that a few kilometers south in St. Vith, a battle for control had already begun and the little village was being pummeled by artillery on both sides. Katrine's childhood home was already gone; her grandfather had escaped with other villagers to a nearby slate quarry.

"I don't know where we would go," Katrine said to Annaliese as the sound of multiple artillery rocked the air from somewhere close by and much of the town fled west.

Annaliese pulled her sweater tighter around her. "I am fine with us staying here. I don't want to run, Katrine."

"Let's get the cellar ready." Katrine pulled the front door shut and they gathered food and water and extra blankets to take with them. At a little after four thirty, they were just about to descend the stairs when a pounding sounded at the back door, loud and fierce.

The two women froze at the entrance to the cellar.

"Katrine!" A voice from outside the kitchen door called out.

"It's John!" Katrine ran to the back door and yanked it open. The lieutenant stood on the step covered in blood. He carried in his arms one of the men who'd also slept at the duplex, his olive-drab uniform jacket awash in crimson.

The attack on John's battalion that afternoon would later be known as the Malmédy Massacre. His convoy, traveling on the road between Malmédy and Baugnez, had been fired upon by an SS tank division that quickly outpowered them. The Americans surrendered, but instead of taking the nearly one hundred men prisoner, the SS officers had marched the Americans into a field and then begun to shoot them execution-style. Those who fell but showed signs of life were shot again. The bodies of those already dead were riddled with more bullets. Some of the Americans fled into a nearby café, but the Germans set the building on fire and then shot those who ran out. John had survived because dead comrades lay on top of him and their blood had spilled onto him. He'd held his breath until his lungs stung as the SS officers laughed and picked off those whose labored breathing sent puffs of white into the frozen air.

The SS officers finally had no one left to kill. John waited until they began to return to their tanks and vehicles before crawling out from under the dead to see if any of his comrades were still alive. He'd found only one man with a pulse, a young sergeant named Warren, who'd been shot three times in the chest. Blood from his wounds had run past his neck and up underneath his helmet, making it look like he'd been shot in the head as well. As John staggered away with Warren in his arms, more than eighty Americans lay dead in the snow behind him.

He'd made it back to Katrine's house using anything he could for cover, a house, a stand of trees, a barn, all the while telling the young man named Warren to hold on, hold on.

John told Katrine and Annaliese what had happened as the women rushed about the kitchen to get towels to stanch the young sergeant's bleeding until they could get him to the local hospital. Annaliese understood enough of what John said to know SS officers had killed unarmed prisoners of war in cold blood. It wasn't until Katrine turned the wounded man over to take off his coat that she saw that his eyes were open and vacant.

"He's gone, John," Katrine said, softly, laying her hand on his arm.

"No! He was alive when I found him!" John placed his fingers against the man's slickened throat, feeling for a pulse. He grabbed the man by the shoulders. "Warren! Warren!"

John shook the dead man harder and continued to shout his name. Warren stared back at him, his face slack, his eyes unblinking. The lieutenant pulled the body into his lap and cradled the man's head and torso in his arms as he softly cried. Katrine sidled up to him and put her arms around him, folding John in close to her bosom.

"You did all you could, John. You did everything right." Katrine said other soft words to him, but Annaliese did not know what they meant.

She sat on the floor across from them and watched her best friend comfort the grieving man, marveling at the depth of their newfound devotion to each other in the midst of horrific circumstances. She wanted with all her being to step into Katrine's body and experience that kind of love.

Four days after the massacre, and while John was still in the city, Malmédy was attacked by German troops that were repelled by American forces. On Christmas Eve and Christmas Day, the city was bombed repeatedly by American artillery in friendly fire meant to halt the German advance. Two hundred civilians were killed. Katrine and Annaliese emerged from the cellar to find the duplex leveled and much of the town destroyed. They met up with Katrine's grandfather in Verviers with other evacuees, and from there made their way to Brussels, where John said he would meet up with her again when the war was at last over.

Katrine wrote to John twice a week, whether she heard from him or not. As the weeks wore on she would sometimes get five V-mails from him at once and then a month would pass with no word at all. The cruelest of winters eased into spring as the Allies moved steadily east into the interior of Germany. As much as Annaliese wanted the world to be at peace again, she was afraid for the war to end. At some point she would need to move on with her life, and there seemed to be only a wide, dark sea ahead of her with no way to cross it. As long as there was a war, that vast unknown existed for everyone.

On the seventh of May, Germany at last surrendered. In Brussels, as in every city in league with the Allies, joyful revelers took to the streets. Katrine began to count the days until John would meet up with her again in Brussels. While she waited, she took a job translating at Allied Forces headquarters, known as SHAEF. Annaliese made a modest income caring for an invalid neighbor across the street from the little house they rented. She earned enough to pay her share of the expenses, and the job didn't require her to divulge that she was a German citizen. Katrine's grandfather went back to St. Vith to rebuild the house he had lived in since he was a boy, after extracting a promise from Katrine that he would one day see her again.

By the time John and Katrine were reunited in Brussels in August, it had been fourteen months since Annaliese had left Rolf. She wondered if he had been arrested or imprisoned as an enemy of the occupying forces. She lay in bed every night trying not to nurse the hope that he was sitting in a cell somewhere and learning what it was like to be trapped and forgotten. But he was a noncombatant Nazi who wore a uniform because he liked it. Had individuals like Rolf who hadn't killed all those people at the camps been made prisoners of war? Surely he'd known all along what Hitler was doing to the Jews who had been rounded up all over Europe and sent away to the labor camps. Had they arrested him for knowing? Even if they had, she supposed that eventually he'd be released. Rolf was adept at smooth talk. It was why he had been assigned to the Ministry of Propaganda.

As Annaliese had expected, Katrine married John Sawyer as

soon as permission from his commander was granted. The ceremony was a rushed civil affair, since John was due to be billeted back to the States in September, and yet Annaliese could see how happy and at peace they both were. Katrine wore a blue silk suit borrowed from a coworker and carried a nosegay of white roses. After the courthouse ceremony, a party was held at a restaurant popular with American servicemen. Annaliese kept as low a profile as she could, keeping her wedding ring in view so that none of John's American friends would ask her to dance or strike up a conversation with her and find out she was German. Katrine had already told John who she really was and why she'd run away from her marriage, and while he seemed genuinely moved by her predicament, she could see the conflict in his eyes at the thought of her being married to a Nazi official after all he'd seen the Nazis do. Annaliese wanted no one else to know.

Katrine insisted Annaliese stay with her and John in Brussels for as long as she wanted. But both women knew the time was soon coming when John would be transferred back to the States and that Katrine would eventually follow him. What Annaliese would do then was a prospect neither woman wanted to imagine.

When John suggested Katrine stay with her British grandfather after he returned to the States and until her own travel to America was secured, she came up with an idea.

"Come with me to London," she said to Annaliese. "We'll go to the American embassy to plead your case so that you can join John and me in America. You can make a new life for yourself there and you can stay with us until you get on your feet. We will tell the people at the embassy what your husband did to you. It was wrong what he did, Annaliese."

"I could never . . . To come live with you is asking too much," Annaliese said.

"It's not too much. It wouldn't be for forever, just until you can make your own way. I will help you. John and I both will," Katrine assured her. "And if it takes a while to get you to the States, at least Rolf will have a harder time trying to find you if you're in England."

That had been the plan.

It had started out just as they had hoped. There had been minimal interest in Annaliese's German passport in Bruges, where the two women boarded a ferry to cross the Channel, and even less curiosity at customs in Felixstowe. They were met at London's Paddington Station by Katrine's maternal grandfather, a genial man obviously grateful that his granddaughter wanted to spend her last few months this side of the Atlantic with him.

Wallace Goodwin lived in a quiet, woodsy suburb south of Windsor, and for the first week of their stay, he spent every minute he could catching up with Katrine. His job as an exporter eventually pulled him away, though, and as autumn fell over London, he was at home less often. The war had virtually stopped all trade with other nations and there was still much work to be done to reestablish lost economic ties. The trips to the U.S. embassy began not just for Katrine but for Annaliese as well. Katrine's embassy visits were always long but relatively uncomplicated affairs. Annaliese's singular woes were of little importance by comparison. After three months of quiet inquiry—she had to beg embassy officials not to try to contact the husband she was estranged from—she'd yet to find a compassionate soul willing to try to bend the rules of immigration for her.

Katrine's extensive travel arrangements began to come through just before Christmas, and by the first week of 1946, everything was in order. Wallace left for an extended trip to India a week before Katrine was to report to the army base at Tidworth, a detail that he was almost glad about since he'd already be gone when Katrine left for America. Wallace told Annaliese she could stay at his house while he was away, and if she happened to still be there when he returned in April, he'd help her find a room to rent. She looked so much like Katrine, he'd told her, it would be almost like having his granddaughter still there.

Two evenings before Katrine was to leave for the first leg of her trip to America, she and Annaliese had taken Wallace's car and gone to the cemetery to visit the graves of Katrine's parents. The day had been bitter cold. A biting, freezing rain had started to fall when they got back in the car to head home so that Katrine could finish packing.

Annaliese wanted to be happy for her best friend and what lay ahead, but her thoughts turned melancholy as Katrine drove on slick roads frosted with rain that had turned to ice.

"Don't despair, Annaliese," Katrine had said, just before the world turned upside down. "There is always a place somewhere in the world where the sun is shining."

"Not for me," Annaliese had replied, gloomily.

Katrine had turned then, reached over with one hand, and touched Annaliese's arm. "Especially for you."

Their gazes met and for a second there was only that shared moment of purest affection between them.

And then suddenly the car was spinning, turning, tumbling off the road into an icy, brambled ditch, already dark with twilight's first tendrils of shadow.

Twenty-six

⁂

RMS *QUEEN MARY*

1946

The luxury liner that had sported black and crimson paint before the war was still wearing its battle-gray camouflage when the war brides stepped off the bus that had transported them from Tidworth to the pier at Southampton.

It was easy to see why the RMS *Queen Mary* had been nicknamed the Grey Ghost during her time as a troop carrier. The ship seemed almost on the verge of disappearing into its surroundings, its image melding into the colorless sky and water.

"She was much prettier before the war," Phoebe assured Annaliese as they walked across the macadam to gangplanks and more registration tables.

She's lovely, was all Annaliese wanted to say. The ship was her means to a new life without Rolf. She could sense, even as she stood gazing up at the smokestacks pointed toward the clouds, that the ship was a safe place. It was a temporary haven between two worlds—the one she was desperate to escape and the one far away that she knew nothing about.

"Did you know there was one crossing during the war when sixteen thousand soldiers were aboard the *Queen Mary*? Sixteen thousand people on a ship built for three thousand. Can you imagine?"

Annaliese shook her head.

"I read about it in the *Telegraph*. The men had to take turns sleeping. And they slept wherever they could. On the deck, in the empty swimming pool, in the kitchen. Everywhere!"

Annaliese smiled politely and gave no comment. She was itching to get aboard and be enveloped by the aura of welcome that seemed to be emanating from the immense ship. Douglas toddled between them, babbling and pointing and walking at far too slow a pace.

"I suppose all the pretty furniture and paintings are still in storage. All of that was removed when she was made a troop carrier." Phoebe seemed to sense Annaliese's impatience and scooped up Douglas so that they could walk faster. "But still. It's the *Queen Mary*! The Duke and Duchess of Windsor have sailed her many times. And Winston Churchill. And Hollywood movie stars. I can't believe how lucky we are!"

They arrived at the first of several checkpoints to pass through before crossing the gangplanks. Annaliese again had to show Katrine's documents and again offer an explanation as to why her passport was in such terrible shape. And again she held her breath as each official scrutinized her documents and compared them with paperwork they had been provided with.

Finally the women arrived at the last table, where cabin assignments and keys were being handed out alphabetically by last name.

Phoebe grabbed Annaliese's arm and pulled her toward the front of the table. "Please, can't my friend Katrine room with me?" Phoebe implored. "She's Belgian and doesn't speak English very well."

The woman in the Red Cross uniform who was handing out room assignments smiled cordially but shook her head. "I'm sorry. Stateroom assignments have already been made, my dear. I am sure she will be just fine in the room she's been given. You can arrange to meet each other after meals and such."

"No!" Phoebe exclaimed. "She really doesn't manage well without me. She needs me. Please?"

Phoebe's begging was drawing attention that Annaliese did not want thrust on her. She yearned to be as invisible as the ship against the gray February sky. "I will be all right," she murmured.

Phoebe turned on her and admonished Annaliese with her eyes to be quiet.

But the Red Cross official had heard Annaliese speak.

"She sounds able enough to speak English," the woman said, a knowing smile on her lips.

Phoebe leaned forward. "Please let her room with me. I'm afraid of the water. Terribly afraid. I'd feel much better if she were with me."

The matron consulted her list. "Well, there's actually one empty bunk in the room you've been assigned, Mrs. Rogers. If you want to see about getting Mrs. Sawyer another key for the cabin, I suppose she can sleep there as well as anywhere. That's up to her, though, if she wants to move."

Phoebe squeezed Annaliese's arm. "You'll switch, won't you?"

Annaliese nodded. "I don't mind. Please, let's just get aboard."

"You'll have to go to her original room assignment to get her luggage when it's brought up," the matron called after them as they moved away. "B-24."

They moved away from the table toward a gangplank, every step feeling like both a gift and a stripping away. Seconds later Annaliese crossed from the walkway to the tea-brown planks of the promenade deck, Phoebe chattering all the while. Her heart ached with longing for Katrine and she had to steel herself against collapsing into tears. They found their cabin, A-152, down a carpeted hallway on the starboard side, after ascending a brass-railed central staircase. The room, like the hallway, was paneled in wood that needed polish, but it was beautiful nonetheless. Twin bunks on either side of the room had been made up with flowered sheets and blankets.

"Dougie and I will take these two bottom ones." Phoebe happily plopped her son onto the mattress of the left-side bunk and tossed her purse and travel bag on the one just across from it. "You can take that one above Douglas maybe? That way whoever has to room with us can sleep above me. You know. Just in case they don't want to sleep above my little tot. You don't mind, do you?"

"Not at all." Annaliese placed Katrine's purse and overnight bag on the cot above Douglas.

Phoebe ran to one of two side-by-side portholes on the other side of the little room. "Look! We'll be able to watch the world go by!"

Her son climbed off his bed and toddled over to her. Phoebe gathered him up to show him the view outside the glass.

The cabin door opened then, and Annaliese and Phoebe both turned.

There at the threshold was the French woman from Tidworth who had gone first when the officials had insisted the women strip off their clothes.

"Well, hello there!" Phoebe said happily. "Are you our roommate, then?"

"I suppose I am," the woman said in heavily accented English, looking from Phoebe to Annaliese and back again.

"Come on in!" With Douglas in her arms, Phoebe strode over to the French woman to welcome her. "I'm Phoebe Rogers, this is my little Douglas, and that's Katrine Sawyer. She's Belgian."

The French woman turned to look at Annaliese. "Yes. So I heard you say earlier back at the camp."

"Well, everyone thinks she's German but she's not. She's from a little place in eastern Belgium where they speak German. Isn't that right, Katrine?"

"Yes," Annaliese answered.

"I thought our roommates were assigned alphabetically," the French woman said, her eyes still on Annaliese.

"Yes, but I didn't want Katrine having to stay with strangers and Dougie likes her, and I'm awful afraid of the water. I tend to babble when I'm nervous and Katrine here doesn't seem to mind! And what's your name?"

Simone turned back to Phoebe. "Simone Robinson. Pleasure to meet you." Then she turned to Annaliese. "And you."

Annaliese smiled and nodded but said nothing. Simone Robinson's gaze was penetrating and a bit intimidating.

"You speak French as well?"

"Yes," Annaliese answered in English. "Some."

"Oh, now don't you two go speaking in French!" Phoebe exclaimed with a pout. "Please don't. It won't be fair!"

"I prefer English on the ship," Annaliese said.

Simone's brow crinkled in consternation as Annaliese spoke. "Forgive me," Simone said a second later. "It is very hard for me to hear the German accent in your voice and not think of the war. I . . . Much was taken from me."

Annaliese heard buried anguish in the French woman's voice. She opened her mouth to say that no apology was needed, that she wished she didn't have to say anything to anyone for the duration of the voyage, but she wasn't sure of all the right words. Tears stung her eyes and she shut her mouth.

Phoebe plopped Douglas down onto the floor and pulled Simone farther into the room. "Let's not talk about the war anymore! Simone, you want to sleep above me? Katrine doesn't mind bunking over Douglas, and then I can be near him if he cries during the night."

"I do not mind," Simone said as she placed a travel bag on the mattress above Phoebe's.

"We're going to have the best time ever!" Phoebe said happily as she took off her coat. "Five days of being treated like queens."

Simone and Annaliese unbuttoned their outer things as well.

"You're expecting, aren't you?" Phoebe said knowingly as Simone draped her coat over her bunk.

"You can see?" Simone said, looking down at her middle.

"Not really! I just saw the little bump the other day when . . . when you . . . when we had to . . ."

"When we had to parade naked across a stage?" Simone unwound a scarf from her neck and laid it across her coat.

"Oh, my, yes! Wasn't that the worst thing in the world?"

Simone laughed, but it was a weak chuckle. "I would say there are worse things in the world."

Annaliese found herself nodding in agreement. Simone noticed but said nothing.

"That was very brave, what you did," Phoebe said.

"What? Going first before the doctor?" Simone asked.

"Well, no, not that. Just how you did it. What you said. You reminded us that we were all survivors. We'd made it through hell. And we'd found love! Right, Katrine?"

Annaliese, lost in a pocket of grief, didn't look up. Didn't respond to the name.

"Katrine?"

And then Phoebe's hand was on her arm in a gentle squeeze. "Are you all right?"

Annaliese realized with a start that she'd missed answering as Katrine. "I . . . yes, I'm fine."

Phoebe looked at her with concern. "Well, shall we all go to the salon for our orientation?" she said a second later. "I hear there's going to be wonderful refreshments!"

They left the cabin to head back down two decks to the Queen's Salon. Even without its artwork and chandeliers, the expansive ballroom was still beautifully appointed. Long serving tables covered with starched white linens had been laid out with tea, coffee, and hot cocoa, as well as silver trays of éclairs and tarts, and slices of fresh fruit. Some of the women began to softly weep at the sight of citrus, bananas, and other luxuries they hadn't seen in five years, and that their children had never tasted.

Annaliese wanted to enjoy the thrill of such decadent food, but every new moment on the ship seemed to remind her that she didn't belong there. *Katrine* did. *Katrine* should be the one eating an orange slice and licking chocolate off her fingers and rooming with Phoebe and Simone on the stunning ship.

"You're not hungry?" Phoebe asked as Annaliese followed her and Simone to a table, her hands empty except for a cup of tea.

She shook her head and said nothing, not wanting her German accent to be heard above the din of chattering women.

They took their seats and minutes later a Red Cross matron stepped up to the stage microphone to welcome the war brides and to advise them of what the next five days would be like.

Meals would take place in the main dining room, they were told, and seating was by cabin and was to stay by cabin. They were not to exchange seating arrangements or to queue up at the doors before their set meal time. Nursery care was available for mothers needing a little break, but only for one hour at a time, unless it was to attend the ship's nightly cinema, and then only by reservation. Children's story hour would take place every evening from five to six P.M. Dispensaries would be available for medical care for a set number of hours per day, as would the ship's retail shops. Knitting and leather craft classes would take place in the afternoons, and cards and Ping-Pong and bingo would be available into the late hours every day. Every afternoon in the Grand Salon, classes on what life would be like in the United States would take place and every war bride was strongly encouraged to attend them.

After a welcome from the ship's commandant, the women were told that the ship would be pulling up anchor and setting out to sea. If they wanted to bid farewell to England, they could don their coats and scarves and head up to the sun deck to watch the ship set sail.

Some minutes later, Annaliese stood next to Phoebe and Simone and hundreds of other women as the *Queen Mary* was tugged out of the harbor. Annaliese could feel the weight of solid ground falling away as the ocean liner slowly steamed forward.

Only a few onlookers had gathered to watch the *Queen* leave the harbor, but dozens of the war brides waved and threw them kisses as if they were family.

"Good-bye, England!" Phoebe said, as she pumped one of Douglas's chubby arms up and down. "Good-bye!"

Simone, like Annaliese, kept her gaze on the vista ahead of them, not behind.

Five more days, and all that lay behind her would be too far away to chase her back.

She didn't know exactly how she was going to make her way in America. Perhaps she could find a way to amend Katrine's documents so that she could be Katherine Dumont, using Katrine's maiden name. She could pretend to be mute so that no one would hear her voice and identify her as German. She could make her way to California or Canada or Mexico. Surely there were still wide-open places in the world. . . .

Annaliese shook her head. Thinking of what awaited her on the other side of the Atlantic was too much to consider.

Right now, there were only five days.

Just five days.

Twenty-seven

Brette awoke to the sound of her phone vibrating at her bedside. Keith was calling.

She sat up and rubbed sleep from her eyes.

"Hi, honey," she said sleepily.

"I woke you, didn't I? Sorry."

"My alarm was going to go off in a few minutes anyway. Everything okay?"

"Just missed you and wanted to know how your trip to Long Beach was. I know we weren't going to talk until tonight, but I just found out I am supposed to go to some corporate dinner."

"Sounds like fun."

"Sounds like not fun. So how was your day with your high school friend?"

She considered how much to say. That she had agreed to do a little ghost hunting was going to be enough of a surprise to Keith, especially in light of their conversation on the beach. "I actually didn't see him. What he wanted was a favor."

"Really? What kind?"

Brette described Trevor Prescott's dilemma in as relaxed a tone as she could, and that she had only agreed to visit the *Queen Mary* because she felt such pity for him and his daughter.

"It's actually a pretty cool ship," she said, still faking a light tone as she swung her legs over the side of the bed.

"So did you find his wife's ghost?" Keith said evenly, after a moment's pause.

"No. I didn't think she was there to begin with, actually. I don't know why. I just didn't."

"I guess it was nice of you then to drive all that way to put that notion to rest for his kid. Hope he appreciated it."

"He did. He does. Although I don't know if his daughter's going to believe the word of someone she doesn't know."

"Not your problem, though."

"No, but . . ." Her voice trailed away as she pondered what to say next.

"But what? It's not."

"No, I know. It's just that . . . We can talk about it later. You're probably on your way to somewhere important." She padded out to the kitchen to switch on the Keurig.

"I've got a few minutes. What were you going to say?"

She hesitated before answering. "Well, while I was there, I came across something that interests me."

"Oh?"

"There were other Drifters there, Keith."

A moment of silence hung between them.

"Okay," he finally said.

"I was approached by one. I think I might want to check into how she died."

Another pause. "What for?"

"Well, this Drifter supposedly killed herself in 1946 by jumping overboard." Brette dropped a K-cup into the coffeemaker and slipped a clean mug under the spout. "She was a German ballet dancer trying to escape an abusive marriage by pretending to be a Belgian war bride. She'd switched her passport with that of her best friend, who actually *was* a GI bride but who'd just died in a car accident. They looked like each other. This German woman tried to come to America on the *Queen Mary* using her friend's identity, but the authorities caught on to her before the ship got to New York." The coffee dripped noisily into her cup. "It's always been believed she committed suicide when she found out she'd been discovered. But I don't think she did."

Silence hung on the other end. She'd said too much too soon. *Idiot.*

"Brette, what does all this have to do with you?"

"I can just tell you when you get home," she said, faking a nonchalant tone and picking up her mug.

"Tell me *what* when I get home?"

"Just why I want to look into it, that's all."

"Look into it." It was a question and not a question.

"I don't think she jumped."

"And how do you know that?"

Because she told me.

"Can't we just talk about this when you get home?" she said instead. "It's actually kind of interesting."

A long moment passed.

"I don't know what to say, Brette. This isn't like you. You've never wanted to get involved before. When I left for Chicago, you were going to look into getting professional advice about this . . . ability you have."

"I know. But this situation . . . this one's different."

"You also promised me you'd talk to your mom. Have you?"

"And I will. But I want to do this first. I feel like I'm supposed to. Like maybe . . ."

"Maybe what?"

"Maybe it's all related," she said, thinking out loud, and realizing at just that moment that solving the mystery for the ghost on the ship *was* somehow linked to figuring out how to make peace with having the Sight. The new concept sent her thoughts spinning. She needed time to ponder. "Can we just wait to talk about this when you get home? It's nothing you need to worry over. Honestly. It's just a little research project."

"But it doesn't sound like just a little research project, hon. You just said you think it's all related. You mean related to you and me and our starting a family? Is that what you mean?"

"I . . . I don't know. Maybe. I know that sounds crazy, but I think I'm making progress on what we talked about. I really do. Please, Keith. I need you to trust me on this."

"I wish you'd wait to go any further with this until I get home. I'm worried about you."

"But even if you were home, *I'd* have to be the one to figure it out. This is my dilemma. Do I have your trust, Keith? Please tell me I do."

"You have everything that's mine, Brette. You've always had it."

Despite a dozen thoughts ricocheting across her brain, she sensed a new layer of calm within. Keith's faith in her was still intact.

"I can't tell you how much that means to me. I love you and I miss you," she said, emotion thick in her throat.

"I love you, too. Promise me you won't make any big decisions until I get back."

"I promise."

They hung up and Brette hurried to get ready for work, her thoughts in a tussle but her heart calm as an ocean with no wind.

THE MORNING'S HOSPITAL ADMISSIONS WERE PLENTIFUL AND kept Brette busy until well after noon. She finally broke away a bit before one o'clock to step outside and make the call to the assisted-care facility in St. Louis. Brette got through to the administrator's office at the Somerset Village and asked if she'd be able to speak with Phoebe Rogers.

"And what is the nature of your call?" the administrator asked. "If you're a salesperson of any kind, I'm afraid I won't be passing along your information."

"I just want to talk with her about her time on the *Queen Mary* when she was a war bride," Brette said. "I'm doing some research. I promise I'm not selling a thing."

"I'll give her the message, but it's up to Mrs. Rogers if she'd like to return your call."

"May I ask what you think is the likelihood of that happening?" Brette replied.

"Well, if you've called to talk about the *Queen Mary*, I'd say you can count on it. I'll ring her room and see if she's willing to call you back."

Brette hung up and took a seat on a shaded bench. The day was balmy but a welcome breeze riffled the queen palms all around her. She had taken only a few bites of the lunch she'd packed that morning when her cell phone rang.

"Hello. This is Phoebe Rogers. Are you the young lady who called for me?" Phoebe's voice had the timbre and tone of a long-ago English childhood, mellowed now to the faintest hint of a British accent.

"Mrs. Rogers. Thanks so much for calling me back."

They exchanged pleasantries. Brette told her she'd found her story online and had recently been to the *Queen Mary*.

"She's a beautiful old girl, isn't she? The *Queen*?" Phoebe began to tell Brette all about the ship's beauty and charm and the five days she'd been aboard it as a war bride.

"It is indeed a wonderful ship," Brette broke in when Phoebe stopped to take a breath. "The thing is, and I hope you don't mind my asking, I'm very interested in what happened to your roommate, Annaliese Kurtz."

"Oh. Do we have to talk about that? It's very sad, you know, what happened to her."

"Yes, I know. But I have reason to believe that maybe . . . maybe she didn't actually jump."

"But I was there. I was on the deck."

"You and your other roommate?"

"Yes, Simone and I were both there."

"And you saw her go over? You actually saw her go over the railing?"

A second of silence passed.

"Why are you asking about this? It was such a long time ago." Phoebe's voice sounded thick with sadness. And something else. Regret, maybe?

"I know it was a long time ago. But I'm pretty sure she didn't commit suicide. She may have wanted to kill herself when she first found out that she was going to be arrested, but I think maybe she changed her mind. I think she changed her mind when she was on the railing and started to climb back over, and then something happened."

"What? What happened?" Phoebe sounded agitated, fearful. But also curious.

"You didn't actually see her go over the railing, did you?"

Phoebe said nothing.

"I promise I am not trying to get anyone in trouble, least of all you, Mrs. Rogers. You can tell me what really happened and I won't tell anyone."

"Well, of course you will tell someone! Why ask if you're not planning to tell someone!" The woman sounded close to tears.

"I won't tell the police or the newspapers or any other living soul," Brette replied, knowing it was a promise she could keep. The Drifter was not a living soul.

"Then why do you want to know?"

"Because . . . because I am one of those people who can sense things in the spiritual world. I don't say that to frighten you. It's something I have always been able to do. I was on the *Queen Mary* yesterday. I stood where Annaliese Kurtz would have stood. Something is not right. Her soul hovers on the ship, Mrs. Rogers. She didn't jump. I know she didn't."

God, please don't let her hang up! Brette inwardly begged. She hadn't planned on telling Phoebe Rogers about the Sight. It had just worked its way out.

"You can what?"

"I can sense things. See things. It's an ability that some women in my family have. I don't usually do anything about it. I actually prefer never to do anything about it. But this time, it seems like maybe I'm supposed to."

"So what are you saying? Are you saying Annaliese is a *ghost?*"

"I . . . yes, Mrs. Rogers. A ghost on that ship tried to tell me something yesterday. I think it was her."

"Tried to tell you what?" Phoebe said, not much more than a whisper.

"I think her soul is still here because she doesn't know what happened, either. It was dark that night, wasn't it?"

A weak sob sounded on the other side. "What will you do if I tell you what I saw?"

"Well, what do you think I should do?"

The woman sniffled into the phone. "Can you tell her I'm sorry I didn't get there in time?"

"In time for what?"

Another sob. "In time to help her! When she ran from our room, I could see she was at her wit's end. I was afraid for her. I would have run after her myself, but I couldn't leave Douglas!"

"Please tell me what happened, Mrs. Rogers."

Phoebe inhaled heavily. "I had just come back from the variety show. They had lovely entertainment for us on the ship. Katrine—I mean, Annaliese—had stayed behind in the stateroom to put Dougie to bed and sit with him. That's what she liked to do. Annaliese didn't want to be out at night. She was a quiet little thing and kept to herself for the whole five days on the ship. Everyone assumed she was German, and in the end I guess she was, although I kept telling everyone she was Belgian. But still. People would do a double take when they heard her speak. The war had been so hard on everyone, you know."

"Yes. So Annaliese was in your room when you got back? With Simone Robinson."

"No, Simone came in a few minutes later. She . . . she was very angry. She'd just overheard a conversation outside the telegraph room. They'd received a wire about a German woman named Annaliese Kurtz pretending to be a war bride named Katrine Sawyer. The wire included instructions about allowing the harbor police to arrest Annaliese when we docked the next day. Well, Simone . . . Simone had suffered so much at the hands of the Germans. And when she found out Annaliese's secret, she came to the cabin to confront her, telling her she'd known all along she was a dirty German and that she was glad she was going to be sent back. It was terrible, the things Simone said.

"Annaliese ran off in tears and I wanted to go after her, but both of them had awakened Douglas with their shouting. I told Simone she needed to go after her, and eventually she did. But I knew Simone would only make things worse, so I stood in the hallway until I saw someone I knew and I asked her to come watch Douglas for a moment while I went to find them. I asked several people who were still out and about if they'd seen either of my roommates, and one said she thought she'd seen Simone hurrying toward the back of the ship. When I got there and stepped out onto the deck, I heard a yell and a splash, and I saw Simone leaning far over the railing. I called her name and she turned with a frightful look on her face. 'For God's sake, get help, Phoebe,' she yelled to me. 'The damned fool has jumped.'"

Phoebe paused for a moment. Brette was fairly certain the woman had kept secret for seventy years what she had just shared.

"The ship's crew tried to find her," Phoebe went on. "They looked for well over two hours. But we all knew a drop like that into icy water was just too much for the human body. They only ever found her little cardigan. When the commodore questioned us, Simone was as shaken as I was. She told him we both saw her jump, and I went along with it because everyone wanted to talk to us and Anna-liese had been my friend, not Simone's. Simone didn't even like her. So I just got caught up with being someone that all the reporters wanted to talk to the next day. I never told anyone that I didn't actually see her jump."

Phoebe was now crying softly.

"I am so very sorry, Mrs. Rogers. I know this must be very hard to talk about, even all these years later."

"It is, it is!" Phoebe replied, sniffling. "What that girl did was wrong, but I think she suffered as much as or more than the rest of us. She was married to a Nazi who beat her and kept her locked up in their apartment. Did you know that?"

"Yes, I'd read that." Brette took a breath. "Mrs. Rogers, I need to ask you a difficult question. Do you think Simone Robinson might have pushed Annaliese? Does that seem possible to you?"

Phoebe exhaled heavily into the phone. "I don't know, I don't know! Simone lost so much in the war. I don't even know all the terrible things the Nazis did to her. I know the Gestapo shot her father and brother right in front of her. I think they might have done other things, too."

"Did you stay in touch with Simone? Do you know if she's still living in New Mexico?"

"She wasn't keen on staying in touch." Phoebe sniffed. "I was, but Simone . . . I think she just wanted to forget all about the life she led before she emigrated to America. She's never come to any of the reunions on the *Queen Mary*. I haven't seen or heard from her in years."

Phoebe was quiet for a second. "I was there on the ship twenty years ago for a reunion," she said. "Do you think Annaliese saw me?"

"I don't know."

"Is . . . is she a frightful thing with a terrible wail?"

"Not at all. She is as kind and humble a ghost as I've ever met."

"Oh! I've never heard of ghosts being like that. But oh, my. That sounds like her, Mrs. Caslake!"

"I'm glad to hear you say that."

"Do you think she knows I wish I had saved her?"

"I am sure she does."

Phoebe took a deep breath. "Are you going to try to find Simone?"

"I think I must."

"Mrs. Caslake?"

"Yes?"

"If Simone did push her, it was an accident. It had to be. Tell her I said that. I know she didn't mean it. It was an accident. Tell her that."

"You have my word, Mrs. Rogers."

When she hung up after they said good-bye, she saw that she had a text message from Trevor.

Emily didn't buy it.

Sorry to hear that, Brette texted back. Does that mean you want me to talk to her?

She won't talk to you. I already asked.

Give her time, Trevor.

I don't want it to be like this.

I know.

No, you don't. But someday you will. When your kid hurts, you hurt.

Brette's fingers hovered motionless over the screen.

Let me know if she changes her mind, she finally wrote.

She finished her salad and then headed back inside to ask for Monday and Tuesday off to visit an old friend in New Mexico.

The children's whimpers draw me as much as their laughter did earlier in the day. I long for the ocean beneath us to be at peace, to be still, but it is in one of its rollicking moods. The littlest ones do not mind, but the older children cling to ashen-faced mothers who wonder if the entire crossing will be like this.

They put the youngest to bed in little cots made of net attached to their bunks and now they hope that the rocking sea will hasten sleep. And for most, it does. I hover over them, watching as they drift into slumber, first the children, then their mothers.

These passengers are not like the men in uniforms. There are no more U-boats looking for us, no more zigzag crossings. No one stands by the gun.

Dream of our new home in America! *one of the mothers says to a child who refuses to shut his eyes.* Dream of all the things we will do there. *She kisses him and sings a song about lavender blue. Her voice is so beautiful.*

I wish the mothers and their children would stay forever.

Twenty-eight

RMS *QUEEN MARY*

1946

The first night on the ship found many of the war brides unable to enjoy the evening meal of crème Argenteuil, halibut en souchet, and steamed cauliflower with mousseline, and not just because the menu was so highbrow. The undulating swells off the southern coast of Ireland made for a tipsy ride that sent many of the women to their cabins to writhe and moan on the bunks.

The pitch and sway of the ship didn't bother Simone overly much, nor did it seem to affect the quiet Belgian named Katrine, but chatty Phoebe kept tossing down her fork to ask their steward, Marc, if it was time to head down to the lifeboats.

Simone had made a fast friend in the young man who'd been assigned to wait their table. Marc was newly seventeen, and while he'd been born in Britain, he was the son of French-born parents. The opportunity to speak French while he served Simone was obviously a thrill for him, and all three women noticed the schoolboy crush he had on her from the moment she spoke his parents' language back to him. He was particularly interested in the Résistance and whether Simone knew anyone who'd been a part of it. When she replied that she did, he made her promise that she'd meet with him for a few minutes after he got off-duty to tell him more.

"He has been told we're war *brides*, hasn't he?" Phoebe said when Marc left their table to wait on another. "You're married. And pregnant!"

Simone watched the young man leave, shaking her head when he looked back also. "He's just a child who had to grow up during someone else's war. The Résistance probably sounds like something exciting and dangerous."

"Was it?" Phoebe asked.

Simone speared a tiny cauliflower bouquet on the tines of her fork. "It was very dangerous, yes."

"But not exciting?"

She swirled the fork in a shimmer of mousseline sauce on her plate. "Not the way he probably thinks."

"Were you in the Résistance, Simone?" Phoebe asked, wide-eyed. Katrine was also looking at her with the same fretful curiosity.

Simone had lately been wondering that herself. Perhaps she had been an unofficial member when she cared for Everett in the secret wine cellar. But before that, she had been just the daughter of a Résistance member, a shattered daughter who had fired a gun. She didn't know what that made her.

"No," she answered, and then brought the fork to her mouth.

Phoebe looked like she wanted to ask something else, but at that moment the ship leaned into an unseen valley and a chorus of "Oh!" erupted around the room.

"That just doesn't seem normal!" Phoebe exclaimed, white-faced, as Douglas laughed on her lap.

Then the ship eased back into a steadier stride and the topic of Simone's role in the war fell away.

When the meal was over, Phoebe stood to take Douglas up to bed, and Katrine rose to follow her.

Marc swept by the table with a tray of dishes in his hand and told Simone he got off in twenty minutes and would she meet him on the promenade deck for a cigarette? He wasn't allowed in any of the lounges or game rooms.

"Make sure he sees your wedding ring!" Phoebe murmured as she and Katrine walked away.

Simone sat at the table, lingering over her coffee until she was the last in the dining room. A few minutes later she was on the promenade deck. Even with the windows shut to keep out the elements, the deck was chilly and damp. She wouldn't be staying for more than a few minutes and one cigarette.

When Marc finally arrived, she was sufficiently chilled and told him he could have five minutes to ask his questions and then she was leaving.

She looked at his empty hands. "Where are your cigarettes?" she said in French.

His eyes grew wide. "I thought you would have some!"

"When you ask a girl to join you for conversation and a cigarette, you're supposed to bring the cigarettes."

"Oh! I'll go find some!" He started to turn to go back inside, but she put out her arm to stop him.

"It's too cold out here for me to wait for you to do that. Just remember that the next time you ask a lady to have a cigarette with you, it's your job to offer her one. What do you want to know?"

"Who did you know in the Résistance? Were you in Paris? Did you see them fight?"

Even in the dim light Simone could see the excitement in his eyes. "I knew several people in the Résistance. And yes, I was in Paris for most of the war."

"Who did you know?" he asked again. "Did you have to keep secrets for them?"

"My father and brother were in the Résistance. And they did not tell me what they did because they did not want me to be tortured at some point for that information."

The young man's mouth fell open a bit. "Did they . . . Were they . . ." Marc did not finish.

"They were shot to death in front of me."

"They got caught? Or someone snitched on them?"

"I never knew how it happened. One afternoon the Gestapo figured out that my father and brother only pretended not to understand what the Germans were saying when they came into our shoe-repair shop. Somehow they suddenly knew that Papa and Étienne passed on to other Résistance members what they overheard while they shined the Nazis' boots. My father and brother were executed on the street outside our store."

Marc's eyes went wide. "You saw it happen?"

"I did."

"And then . . . And what happened to you? Did they hurt you?"

Simone thought of the officer with the gold tooth. She closed her eyes for a moment to let the rocking ship scoot that memory back to the black corner where it belonged. "I had to run after that," she said a moment later. "It took me ten days with false identity papers to get to Résistance members in southern France. I spent four months in a hidden wine cellar and didn't see the sun for weeks."

The young man's countenance had changed from one of eagerness to empathy. "The Germans killed my brother, too," he said softly, his eyes glassy in the spill of moonlight on the deck. "He was trying to get to Dunkirk. They shot him in the back five times as he was retreating. It about destroyed my mother. It's been nearly six years and she still cries out his name in her sleep."

Simone understood then that the young man's interest was not the intrigue of espionage that wowed him so much as the opportunity for revenge that the Résistance had offered the French people.

"I'm sorry," she said.

The young man tipped his head toward the inside of the ship. "How can you room with that woman who speaks German? I hear her voice and I just want to tell her to shut up."

"She is Belgian, Marc."

"She sounds like one of them."

"But she's not. Belgium suffered just like France did. Just like England did. She is also half-British, if you must know. Her mother was born and raised in London. She is more British than you are."

"Still," he insisted. "How can you listen to her?"

Simone rubbed her shoulders. She was freezing. "She barely says anything. You heard her at dinner. The only time she talked was when you asked her a question."

"I *have* to ask her questions! I have to ask her if I may take her soup bowl and would she like the fish or the beef and could I refill her coffee cup. I have to!"

"It's just for five days. Surely you and I both can handle hearing her say a word here and there for five little days. I'm going in."

"May I walk you to your cabin, Simone?"

"I am Mrs. Robinson to you, and no, you may not. Good night."

"Can we meet again tomorrow night? I'll bring the cigarettes."

She pushed open the door to go back inside. "I don't think that's a good idea."

Marc followed her inside.

"Why isn't it a good idea?" he asked, trailing after her.

"Why is it a good one?"

"I like talking to you. I never get to speak French with anyone." She kept walking. "I'll think about it."

"I'll see you at breakfast!" he called after her as she turned to head up the grand staircase.

Simone made her way to the room. Phoebe and Katrine were already in their pajamas. Phoebe was pacing the floor with Douglas in her arms, trying to get him to fall asleep. Katrine was standing at one of the portholes, her arms crossed loosely across her chest as she gazed at the deep violet sky beyond the glass.

"Well?" Phoebe whispered to Simone.

"Well, what?"

"He didn't try to kiss you, did he?"

"Oh, yes. But first I kissed him," Simone answered, as she slipped her room key into her handbag and hung the bag up on a peg.

"You didn't!" Phoebe gasped and ceased her pacing.

"And then we went up to the sun deck and made love on a chaise lounge," Simone continued, enjoying herself.

"All the saints!" Phoebe whispered, eyes as wide as saucers.

"She is teasing you, Phoebe," the Belgian said from the window.

"But . . . but . . ." Phoebe stammered.

"I am kidding," Simone said, setting the latch on their door.

"Ohhhh, you!" Phoebe laughed and commenced to pacing again, lightly patting her child on the back to hasten sleep.

Simone had toyed with going to the cinema or maybe to the game room but she didn't want to go alone, and Phoebe certainly couldn't with Douglas. She had no desire to ask the quiet Belgian if she wanted to go. And she was strangely tired, a side effect of being pregnant, she'd heard.

The little bathroom was available, so Simone got into her own pajamas, stroked the little mound that was Everett's child, and brushed her teeth.

When she emerged from the bathroom, little Douglas was asleep in his bunk. Phoebe got out a deck of cards and asked if the three of them could play a few games to get her mind off the fact that they were bobbing on the North Atlantic on a freezing night in February.

They arranged their bed pillows on the square space below the two portholes, covered now by a curtain that Katrine had drawn so that Phoebe didn't have to look out at the black nothingness of the open sea.

"How about gin? Shall we play gin?" Phoebe began to shuffle the cards. The ship rolled beneath them and several cards fluttered out of the deck. "Why does it have to keep doing that!"

"Here." Simone held out her hand and Phoebe gave her the deck. She counted out ten cards apiece and then set the rest of the deck in the middle of their circle of pillows.

They played for a few minutes, Phoebe chattering about nothing and everything and making a clucking sound every time the ship leaned or rocked.

Katrine was particularly quiet, playing her hand with little interest. Even jabbering Phoebe noticed that Katrine seemed unhappy.

"Goodness, Katrine. Are you homesick already? Aren't you excited about seeing your husband?" Phoebe said.

The Belgian looked up from her cards. "What?"

"You didn't hear anything I said?"

"I . . . No. I'm sorry."

Phoebe folded her cards into her hand. "What is the matter? You seem so sad. The rest of us can't wait to get to America. You want to go back to Belgium? Is that it?"

"No!" The answer was swift and loud.

Little Douglas stirred on his bunk and then settled again.

"No," Katrine said again, more softly this time. She looked from Phoebe to Simone and her bottom lip trembled slightly. "I . . . I want very much to go to America."

"But you seem so sad," Phoebe persisted.

Tears rimmed Katrine's eyes and she blinked them away. "I lost someone dear to me a few days ago. Sometimes I start thinking about her and I cannot stop."

"Oh! Oh, my!" Phoebe instantly teared up as well. "Who was she?"

"She was my best friend. We met at a ballet school when we

were both seven. She was like a sister to me." Tears slipped down her cheeks.

The depth of the woman's sorrow somehow softened her German accent. It still unnerved Simone to hear it, but compassion for the woman was outweighing her aversion. "I'm so sorry, Katrine," Simone said.

"What happened to her?" Phoebe pressed.

"We were in . . . in my grandfather's car, coming back from visiting my parents' graves. It was my last day in England. There was ice everywhere but we did not see it. The car slid off the road and tumbled over and over into a ditch. When I came awake, she was dead beside me."

"Oh, Katrine! That is so very sad!" Phoebe blotted her eyes with the sleeves of her bathrobe.

That explained the little bruise above Katrine's right eye and the curious limp she had, Simone thought. "And she came to England to see you off to America?" she asked.

"She came to England with me to escape her husband. He . . . he is a Nazi. And a monster to her."

"What did he do?" Phoebe whispered.

Katrine hesitated a moment. "Whatever he wanted."

The three women were quiet. Simone noticed that her own cheeks were now wet.

"She hadn't wanted to marry him," Katrine finally continued. "But he didn't care. And he was a ministry official, so her parents told her she had to marry him when he said he wanted her for his wife. He made her do things she did not want to do. And if she told him no, he beat her. He wouldn't let her out of their apartment. Some days she would sneak out anyway."

Phoebe stared at the Belgian woman, openmouthed.

"And you could do nothing, could you?" Simone said.

Katrine shook her head. "I didn't even know. The war kept us apart. Her parents moved away and they didn't want Annaliese having any contact with me."

"That was her name? Annaliese?" Phoebe asked.

"Yes. I didn't know what had become of her until she showed up in the middle of the night at my house in Belgium. She had run away from her husband, and swum across the river that bordered the two countries in nothing but a ballet leotard. She spent the rest of the war with me, hiding from him. I brought her with me to England after the war was over because I didn't want him to find her."

"And now she's dead?" Phoebe shook her head sadly.

"Yes." Katrine covered her face with her hands.

Phoebe scooted over to her and pulled her into an embrace.

"But she'd want you to be happy now, wouldn't she? You did your best to protect her. Your very best. She'd want you to think about the new life you will have in America with your sweet husband. What is his name again?"

"John," Katrine answered, her voice barely a whisper.

"Yes, with John. And that terrible brute can't hurt your friend anymore now, can he?"

Katrine shook her head slowly from side to side.

"So tell us how you and John fell in love, eh, Katrine? Tell us that!"

Katrine leaned in to Phoebe. "I don't know how it happened. It just did. He and some of his men stayed next door to Annaliese and me. They were scouting out our village. They knew the Germans would be coming. Then one day the Germans did arrive. And nearly every man in his battalion was massacred in a field after they'd surrendered. The SS thought John was dead, too, because he was lying in that field covered in bodies and blood. He brought the only man he found alive back to the house, but that man died on my kitchen floor."

Simone reached out to the Belgian woman and placed her hand on her knee in a wordless sign of solidarity.

Phoebe turned her head to face Simone, her expression one of dazed shock. "Do you, um, want to tell us how you fell in love with your American, Simone?"

"Everett and I fell in love while waiting, and let's just leave it at that, shall we?" Simone answered, after a moment.

The Belgian held her gaze for just a moment before looking away.

Twenty-nine

For the next couple of days, Annaliese kept to herself as much as possible, declining offers to walk the sun deck with Phoebe and Douglas and only attending the afternoon classes on what the war brides could expect life to be like in America. In the evenings, Phoebe wanted to go to the cinema and play bingo and chat with the other mothers about the cute or funny or exasperating things their children were doing. Annaliese offered to mind Douglas after dinner so that she could have a reason to stay in the cabin and maintain an inconspicuous presence on the ship.

She did not mind the many hours in relative seclusion. The ship had settled into a gentle agreement with the North Atlantic, and the undulant movement now felt more like a mother rocking a child to sleep. Simone, like Annaliese, seemed to also prefer to be on her own or chatting with the few other French-speaking people on board—including the moon-eyed dining room steward. When the three roommates were in the stateroom at the same time or together in the dining salon at meals, Annaliese would catch the French woman sneaking glances at her. Annaliese's German-accented English unnerved Simone, that much was obvious, and Annaliese wondered what she'd suffered in the war to have such an aversion to even the sound of a German voice.

Annaliese spent the quiet evening hours with Douglas rehearsing in her mind her vanishing act. The women had been told that
when they docked in New York, the few non–war bride passengers
and military personnel would get off first. Then the war brides
whose husbands were meeting them in New York would disembark
in groups of fifty to board buses bound for a nearby armory. The
brides who would be traveling by train to other destinations would
get off last. They would board different buses that would take them
to Grand Central Station. Katrine's husband, John, would be one
of those at the armory waiting for his wife. Annaliese had his last
letter in Katrine's purse.

Her plan was to get on the bus to the armory as expected, but
then to pretend to be so nervous and excited that she'd need to use
the ladies' room as soon as they got off the bus and before they
entered the big meeting room where all the husbands would be
waiting. She'd duck away to use the restroom, popping in for just
a moment to leave the letter she had already written to John, which
explained why she had impersonated Katrine and how desperately
sorry she was. She'd leave the letter, with his name on the envelope,
sitting on the countertop. When someone came to see what was
taking her so long, probably a Red Cross worker, the matron would
see the letter but not her. The matron would check all the stalls,
calling out Katrine's name. She would exit the restroom with the
letter in hand, looking every which way for Katrine Sawyer.

With all those brides and all the husbands and all the crying
children, there would be enough chaos to be able to slip away unnoticed. Annaliese was counting on it. She didn't know where in
Manhattan the armory was—likely not very far from the harbor,
and therefore not far away from a taxi rank. She would hail one and
get to the train station. Then she would buy a ticket that would get
her as far south or west as she could go.

She would never use the name Annaliese again.

And she would be free.

Annaliese had just imagined the entire escape plan from start to finish as she sat atop her bunk when Phoebe returned from the cinema clutching a little bag of caramel corn, which she handed to Annaliese. Simone followed a few minutes later, smelling of cigarette smoke. It was late, and the other two women got into their pajamas and were in bed minutes later.

"So did you spend the evening with that dining room waiter?" Phoebe asked Simone above her, in a low voice so as not to wake Douglas.

"It was only a few minutes, Mama," Simone said.

"Go ahead and laugh!" Phoebe replied with a hushed chuckle. "That boy is positively smitten with you. You're going to break his heart when we dock. Isn't she, Katrine?"

"He will forget about me in a day," Simone answered before Annaliese could say anything.

"What the devil does he want to talk about anyway?" Phoebe went on. "Still the Résistance? For pity's sake, the war is over!"

"The war is, yes, but not what it did to us, *mon ami*. Marc lost a brother to the Germans. He was only eleven when it happened."

Phoebe sighed. "Yes, but that was before. Isn't life supposed to get better now?"

"Of course it is better now," Simone replied. "You ate strawberries and cream today. You saw a cinema. You put sugar in your tea at lunch. There are no U-boats chasing us across the Atlantic. It *is* better. But better doesn't mean that we forget what happened. I don't know that we will ever forget."

"Well, I plan to forget how terrible it was sleeping in a Tube station night after night and eating tripe at every meal and wearing the same pair of worn-out shoes for five years. Right, Katrine?"

Annaliese didn't know how to answer. She wanted to forget everything. She wanted to forget nothing. "I don't think you can choose what you get to forget," she said.

Simone yawned. "Katrine's right. How can you choose to forget something? You'd have to think about it to keep choosing to forget it. Impossible not to remember it then."

"Well, the first thing I am going to do in America is buy a whole crate of oranges," Phoebe said. "And bedroom slippers with rhinestones on them. And bath salts. And a new hat. What about you, Katrine? What's the first thing you want to do?"

Run.

"I don't know," Annaliese said, unable to think of a believable lie.

"For heaven's sake. We need to help you come up with some ideas, then!"

"Maybe just being reunited with her husband is enough," Simone ventured.

Annaliese looked over at the bunk across from hers. In the dim light provided by a peep of moonlight beyond the porthole curtain she saw Simone staring up at the ceiling, her arms crossed loosely over her head.

"Yes, but after the kisses and hugs, there must be something you gals are looking forward to," Phoebe said.

Simone peered over the bunk to peek at her bunkmate. "Having someone else to sleep with besides you seems pretty nice."

Phoebe giggled. The women curled up under their covers.

Within ten minutes Annaliese heard the steady, relaxed breathing of her roommates. She lay on her bed for a long while, going over her escape plan several times before slumber finally claimed her.

She had no idea how long she'd been asleep when she was awakened by whimpering in the bunk across from hers.

The French woman was writhing under the blankets, crying out, "No! No!" in a muffled voice laced with anguish.

"Simone?" Annaliese murmured.

But the woman only thrashed more.

Annaliese climbed out of her bunk and approached Simone's elevated cot above Phoebe. She reached for her, hoping that Simone was not being chased in her nightmare and that a hand on her arm would not have her think she'd been caught.

"Noooo!" Simone moaned.

Annaliese gently shook her. "Simone!" she whispered as loud as she dared. "Wake up. You're dreaming," she said in French.

Simone sat up in bed with a start, her covers clutched to her chest as if they were her clothes.

"You were dreaming!" Annaliese said again, patting her leg.

Simone jolted and turned to Annaliese, unable, it seemed, to remember where she was and who stood by her bunk. Her breath was expelled in a short gasp.

"You had a nightmare," Annaliese continued, in French.

Simone lowered herself back to her pillow. "I'm sorry I woke you, Katrine."

"It is all right." Annaliese climbed back onto her bunk. Below them Phoebe gently snored.

"No. I really am sorry."

Annaliese pulled up her covers. Simone was a mere shadow now in the darkness. "I have bad dreams, too, sometimes."

"God, I hope none of yours are like this one." Simone turned on her mattress to face Annaliese.

"Is it about your father and brother? Is that what you dream?" Annaliese asked.

Simone didn't immediately answer.

"I am sorry. You don't have to say," Annaliese quickly added.

"I dream about something else. Something that happened to me. And something I did."

Annaliese waited to see if Simone would continue. "I also dream about things that have happened. And things I did," she said when the French woman said nothing.

"Do you believe there are some actions that can't ever be forgiven, Katrine?" Simone asked a moment later.

Annaliese thought of Katrine's lifeless body, which she'd abandoned in an unforgiving ditch. She thought of the letter she had written to Katrine's husband, and the stolen identity papers she carried, and all those times she wished Rolf was dead. There had to be as much mercy in the world as there was anguish. There had to be compassion for those who did wrong because they had been wronged. "No, I don't," she said.

"How do you know?" Simone murmured.

"I just do."

"I shot a man, Katrine. I killed him."

The air in the little room seemed to still. Somehow Annaliese knew the man Simone killed had hurt her in the worst way a man could hurt a woman. She knew that pain.

"He shouldn't have hurt you," Annaliese replied.

Simone paused, surprised but grateful, perhaps, that Annaliese had correctly assumed the details. "But I killed him."

"You wanted him to stop."

"Yes." Simone's voice was barely audible.

"If you had not shot him, what would he have done?"

Simone hesitated only a moment. "I think he might have killed me. Or shared me with his friends. He was Gestapo. He was one of the officers who shot my father and brother. He thought I was Résistance, too."

"It was war, Simone."

"And that makes it not a crime?"

"That makes it survival. That is what you do in war. You find a way to survive."

They were quiet for a moment.

"You sound less like a German when you speak French," Simone whispered with a tired laugh.

"I would speak French all the time, then, but Phoebe wouldn't like it."

Simone chuckled. "Good night, Katrine."

"Sweet dreams," Annaliese replied.

She lay awake the remainder of the night, unable to surrender to rest while she pondered all that she still had to do. All the lies she still had to tell. All the forgiveness she would have to beg from heaven.

Annaliese would not kill to escape Rolf, she knew that. But she would die to escape him.

Yes, she would.

She would not go back. Ever.

She would be free of him one way or another.

Thirty

※

The sun deck was empty of people.

A late-afternoon sun had dipped into the bottommost part of the daytime sky, and a bank of clouds prevented any low-lying trails of radiance from bathing the ship in any real warmth. The last night on the *Queen Mary* would be a wickedly cold one, and the ship seemed to lean into the approaching twilight with a desire to hold its occupants close.

Simone pulled her coat more tightly around her torso and fished in a pocket for a cigarette. She'd spent most of the day contemplating the conversation she'd had with Katrine the night before, and the brisk air felt good against her warring thoughts.

It had been a while since she had dreamed of the man with the gold tooth. She had begun to think maybe he was someone who no longer mattered, that perhaps finding love and safety in Everett's arms and in his bed had chased that demon away for good.

But all of Phoebe's talk the night before about what they'd be able to forget when they got to America had no doubt dredged the Gestapo officer out of the buried place where he'd been flung, a jab from a conscience that didn't know how to live with what she had done.

Everett had assured her that in war, good people must do things they would never do in times of peace, to preserve the good. Katrine had said something similar: To kill in a time of war is to survive.

But where was the joy in surviving if the soul was tortured by the desperate acts of the will?

What bothered Simone the most was not that she had shot the man who had participated in the killing of her father and brother and then raped her, but that she would do it again. And again. And again. If the day were to replay itself and she woke up tomorrow morning in that destroyed clinic with that man chasing her, she would kill him a second time. A third. As many times as she opened her eyes and she was there and he was there, she would grab his gun and pull the trigger.

She would pull it for every Jewish person in her neighborhood who was there one day and on a train to Auschwitz the next. She would pull it for all the fathers and brothers in the Résistance who had risked so much and paid with their lives. She would pull it for every girl like her who didn't have a gun when her innocence was torn from her.

There had been a time when the man with the gold tooth had been a little boy who loved playing with his dog and fishing with his grandfather and eating ice cream on hot summer days. Back then he didn't have a gold tooth, or the uniform, or the desire to kill and steal and destroy. He had been like her. Young and curious and hopeful.

Something had happened to that little boy.

He became someone different.

Did he even remember what he had been like before? When he was following her, sneaking into the ruined clinic behind her, tackling her to the ground, reaching for his zipper, wanting her to know there would be others who would want to do to her what he was doing, was there an echo of a voice inside his mind, whispering to him, *This is not who you are?*

When Everett had taken her into his arms the first time they'd made love, he'd been so gentle. He had kissed her everywhere first, showing her that physical intimacy begins with the sweetest of touches. There was nothing about Everett's body that was like the man with the gold tooth, and nothing Everett did was like what that other man had done. But still she could sense the man that she'd killed hovering at the periphery of everything good in her life.

What we did in the war will not define who we are, Everett had said.

But then what would?

Simone put the cigarette to her mouth. She attempted to light it, but the wind on the deck was too fierce. She ducked into a covered area just outside the telegraph office and tried again. The flame caught and she inhaled, slipping the lighter back in her pocket.

Her hand went to the rounded bump at her middle, the tangible evidence that life goes on after the dust of war settles.

Katrine had said survival was the only goal of war for those who had no desire to fight in the first place.

But perhaps survival was only half of it. Perhaps the other half was hanging on to who you were before the guns were drawn.

She leaned back against the wall of the telegraph office, only half-aware of voices inside.

She would have tuned them out completely if she'd not heard a name that made her turn her head to listen more intently.

"Get this, mate. There's a stowaway on board traveling under someone else's name. Katrine Sawyer," said one of the men inside. "She's one of the war brides. Real name's Annaliese Kurtz. A *German.*"

"You're kiddin' me," said another.

"I got the wire right here. She stole the passport and tickets off a dead friend and took her place on the ship. The friend *was* a war bride. Belgian, though. And died in a car accident a week ago."

"That so? Where'd that wire come from?" said another.

"The Port Authority in Southampton. They want the commodore to detain her when we tie up in the morning."

"Crikey. How do you suppose she managed to get aboard?"

"Beats the hell out of me. Best get that telegram right up to the bridge. Southampton wants a reply that we've received it and are ready to comply."

"Right."

Simone dashed around the corner and back out into the elements on the sun deck as the man fully opened the door to the telegraph office.

Her thoughts were flying in all directions.

Katrine's real name was Annaliese.

She was married to a Nazi, not an American serviceman.

She was German.

She had lied to Simone. Lied to them all.

Lied about everything.

Thirty-one

※

Brette spent Saturday morning doing laundry and tidying up the condo for Keith's return. His conference had ended at noon and he'd managed to snag an earlier flight home for that evening.

She had yet to accomplish either of the two things she'd promised to do while he was gone, and yet she was still convinced that helping the Drifter on the *Queen Mary* was part of coming to terms with her own predicament. She didn't have an explanation for that hunch, only a sense of quiet urgency that finding out what had happened to Annaliese Kurtz that wintry night in 1946 somehow mattered. It was the "somehow" part that she wished she had a better answer for because then it would be easier to convince Keith, if he was going to need convincing, that going to Albuquerque was a good idea.

When Brette wasn't contemplating how to explain the upcoming trip to Keith, she was pondering her visit with Simone Robinson, assuming the woman was still alive and able to have a conversation. Phoebe had retained all her mental faculties, but there was no guarantee that Simone Robinson had. On the other hand, if she was still able to recall everything about that night, then she would remember her part in Annaliese Kurtz's death, and surely she'd played a role. If that was the case, it might mean she'd have no desire to talk to Brette.

If confession was good for the soul, Brette hoped Simone's conscience was hungry for absolution, and that Brette's ethereal connection with the German woman Simone had hated would compel her to spill the details in exchange for Annaliese's forgiveness. If Simone was dead, the most Brette could do for the Drifter was return and offer assurance that her death had to have been an accident, and that there was no point hovering for an ironclad answer that no one could provide.

SHE WAITED FOR KEITH'S PLANE AT THE AIRPORT'S CELL PHONE lot and swung by arrivals after he'd texted that he had his luggage and was outside waiting for her.

The minute he got into the car and they kissed, Brette was overcome by how much she needed Keith to fully get behind the new task she'd undertaken. He'd always been her rock, her steady voice of reason. His solidarity with her was suddenly what she wanted more than anything.

"I'm so glad you're home," she said as she eased the car into the outgoing lanes. "It seems like longer than a week that you've been away."

"I've missed you, too. I wish we'd worked it out so that you could've come with me. You would love Chicago. I had plenty of downtime."

"Next time, maybe?" she said, with little inflection. "You hungry? Want to stop and get a bite somewhere?"

"Let's just get home and make sandwiches or something. I just want to hear about the rest of your week."

She gripped the wheel a little tighter as she merged onto Harbor Drive. "I'm anxious to tell you about it. But let's wait until we get home. Tell me about Chicago."

Keith filled the drive home with highlights from his trip and conference, but Brette could tell he was only minimally interested in telling her what his week had been like.

They made turkey, prosciutto, and avocado sandwiches when they got to the condo, and while they ate, Brette told Keith in detail about her experience on the *Queen Mary*, leaving nothing out. She also told him about the phone call to Phoebe Rogers and the flight she'd booked for Monday to Albuquerque.

He ate and listened in silence, his expression difficult to read. He did not look pleased, especially about the impromptu trip to New Mexico.

"You really think that's a good idea?" he said at last, as he pushed his plate away and sat back in his chair. "Running off to New Mexico without even knowing if this woman is there? She might not even be alive."

"I know it's possible she doesn't live there anymore, but I feel like I have to try. I have to meet with her. In person."

Her husband stared at her for a second. "And tell her what? That you think she killed this German girl?"

"I'm not going to accuse her of anything. I just want to know what really happened."

"But why would she tell you, hon?" Keith said. "If I were her and had done what you think she's done, I'd say it was none of your business. I'm just being realistic here. There's no reason for her to tell you anything."

"But what if she's lived her life carrying this terrible secret? What if she'll welcome the chance to confess at last? Or maybe what happened to Annaliese Kurtz was just an accident."

"Or maybe she really did jump."

Brette stiffened. "She didn't. I know she didn't. I'm probably the only one besides Simone Robinson who knows."

"Because her . . . ghost told you she didn't?"

He'd said it gently, but the implication still stung.

"You're saying I made it all up?"

"No. That's not what I said."

"You think I didn't talk with her ghost?"

"How do you know for sure that you did? You didn't actually see her."

An ache was starting to bloom deep in her gut. The idea that she could've been lied to by the Drifter sliced into her like a knife. She said nothing.

"What if you were just taken in by the surroundings and the aura of the place. You went there looking for a particular Drifter, whom you didn't find, right? So maybe . . ."

His voice dropped away but she knew what he was implying. "Maybe I imagined the whole thing? Is that what you're saying?"

"That is not what I'm saying. I'm saying this—all of this—is not like you. You've never wanted to get involved with them before. You've told me your Drifters are illogical and impossible to reason with."

"This one is different," Brette said, and the minute the words were out of her mouth, she knew they were true. Annaliese's ghost *was* different. It was almost as if this Drifter still had the ability to be aware of someone else's desires and fears, not just her own. She still knew how to care.

Keith, deep in thought, said nothing.

"What are you thinking?" Brette asked.

He hesitated before answering. "Just that this wasn't what I thought you were going to be doing when I left for Chicago."

"It's not like I planned it."

"You did what you said you would do for your old high school friend. You don't have to do anything else."

"But I feel like I do. I made a promise, Keith."

"To a ghost."

"Yes."

Keith reached for her hand across the table. "What about the promises you made to me?" he said gently. "You said you would talk to your mother. And that you'd find a professional to help you deal with . . . *this*."

He hadn't meant for the comment to sting, she knew that. But his one-word summation at the end of his comment made it sound like everything she'd experienced on the *Queen Mary* was just another wild flight of fancy meant to further delay the decision to have children.

"What happened to me on that ship was real. You weren't there. You didn't see that book I bought come flying out of the bag and open by itself to the page about Annaliese's death."

"I'm not saying it didn't happen. That's not my point, Brette. Whatever did or didn't happen to this woman all those years ago has nothing to do with us."

But it does, Brette wanted to say. Somehow it was all linked. She needed Keith to allow her the freedom to do what she needed to do even though he didn't—and couldn't—fully understand it.

He was staring at his empty plate, probably feeling as isolated as she was.

"I love you, Keith. And I want to have children with you, I really do. But this is part of my journey to understanding who I am, not just as your wife and perhaps someone's mother, but who I already was when I met you. You told me I had your trust, remember?"

He stroked her thumb with his, indicating that he'd heard her, but he said nothing for several seconds.

"I know you feel alone in this because so do I," he finally said, looking up at her. "You promised me you'd talk to your mother—"

"I know. And I will."

"But you haven't, because you are keeping those who know what you can do out of the loop, Brette. You always have. You feel alone in this because you are alone. By choice."

The realization that he was right fell over her like a crashing wave. It suddenly made no sense at all that she and her mother hardly ever talked about the life-defining talent that had been passed on to Brette. The Sight came from her mother, a carrier, but their scattered conversations about it never lasted more than a few minutes.

They had talked about Brette likely also being a carrier only once before, when Nadine sat her down at the age of eleven and gave her the facts-of-life talk. Brette hadn't brought it up again, by choice.

"I'll go see her tomorrow." She squeezed his hand. "All right? I'll talk to her tomorrow."

Thirty-two

Weekends at the B and B were usually busy in late August. When the summer days of leisure started to thin, the urgency to get in one last getaway usually kept Willow House at *No Vacancy* status until after Labor Day.

Brette had reached out to her mother, as she'd promised Keith.

Mind if I swing by sometime tomorrow afternoon? she'd texted. Want to ask you something.

The reply came a few minutes later. Sure. You want to bring Keith and stay for dinner?

Brette and Keith arrived Sunday afternoon at the agreed-upon time of four o'clock to find the makeshift lobby brimming with newly arrived guests. While Keith helped Cliff with luggage and parking, Brette pitched in getting extra bath towels and bed pillows, assisting with Wi-Fi login, and recommending restaurants. By five, all the guests had left to seek out dinner or a show or a walk along the beach, and the big house was quiet. Nadine sent Cliff and Keith to the grocery store for artichokes and heavy whipping cream, leaving her alone with her daughter.

The two women went into the kitchen, where Nadine began to clean and devein two pounds of jumbo prawns that sat in a colander in the sink. Brette offered to help, but her mother handed her a glass of Chardonnay and told her to relax and keep her company while she got the meal ready.

"Keith had a good trip to Chicago?" Nadine asked, as Brette took a seat on a stool next to the counter.

"As good as those conferences can be." Brette didn't want to waste the time the men would be away talking about Keith's business trip, and while she was eager to finally have the conversation she and her mother should have had long ago, she was still unsure how to start it.

Nadine peeled away an outer shell and tail from a shrimp and tossed its waste into a paper towel spread on the countertop. "So, what did that old friend of yours from high school want the other day? That Trevor . . . What's his last name?"

"Prescott."

"Yes. Did I do the wrong thing in calling you while he was here? Is that why you wanted to talk to me?"

Brette suddenly thought of a way to begin. Telling her mother the details of Trevor's request would easily segue into a conversation about herself.

"No, I'm glad you did call me. He needed my help with something."

"Oh?" Nadine said.

"He lost his wife in a car accident six months ago, when he was still living in LA. He and his little girl moved to Texas not long after that."

"Oh, how sad for him."

"Yes. Very. His daughter, Emily, is only six."

"And so what did he need your help with?" Nadine, who had paused a moment in her messy task, picked up another prawn.

"He and Emily came back to LA to visit his mom before school starts, and they went to the *Queen Mary* to see the Princess Diana exhibit. While they were there, Emily said she heard her mother speak her name. She felt her put her arms around her."

Nadine fumbled the shrimp in her hands and it tumbled to the sink. "She what?"

"Emily's convinced she felt her mother's presence on that ship. I don't know if you've heard, but it's one of the more celebrated haunted locations on the West Coast. Ghost hunters love that ship."

Nadine turned her head slowly to face her. "So what did your friend want?" Her tone was cautiously curious.

"He wanted to me to come to the ship, make a sweep, and then tell his daughter that her dead mother was not on board."

"But how . . . how did he know . . . Why did he ask you?"

"Because he was one of the people at high school who knew. You remember when I came home crying because someone who was pretending to be my friend blabbed to everyone she knew that I could see ghosts?"

Nadine closed her eyes for a second. "I remember that day."

"Trevor apparently does, too. He didn't know who else to call. Emily didn't want to go back to Texas and he was desperate."

"Couldn't he have called a grief counselor or something? I mean, why involve you? You don't even do that kind of thing. You're not going to go, are you?" Nadine locked eyes with Brette.

Brette took a sip of her wine to steady her courage. "I already went," she said calmly as she set down her wineglass.

"You what?"

"I already went."

Her mother blinked and her facial expression gave away nothing. Brette couldn't tell if her mother was appalled or fascinated. "Why?" Nadine said. "You've always been so careful."

"I know. I surprised myself by agreeing to go. But I felt sorry for him. And his little girl. I went Thursday. His wife wasn't there, just so you know. At least, I didn't see her there."

Nadine turned from her daughter, grabbed the shrimp she had dropped, and stripped it of its legs and shell in one swift yank. "Well, thank God that's over with, then."

"Except it's not over."

"Of course it is. You said yourself she wasn't there."

"Yes, but there *are* Drifters on that ship. I met one. Or rather, she met me. I think she's been looking for someone like me for a long time."

Nadine paused with the clean shrimp in her hand and stared at Brette. "She?"

"I think she's the ghost of a German woman who supposedly committed suicide by jumping overboard in 1946. But she has me convinced she didn't jump. I think maybe she was pushed. She was posing as a Belgian war bride and she got found out the day before the ship was to dock in New York."

"But even if she didn't jump, that has nothing to do with you."

"I think maybe it does. This time everything feels different. *She's* different. She's not like other Drifters. I want to help her."

Nadine tossed the clean shrimp into a bowl. "Are you sure that's a good idea? Who knows what you might find if you go poking about."

"I'm hoping I'll find the truth."

"And then what?"

Brette said nothing. She didn't know what she thought might happen next.

"I'm just surprised, Brette," her mother continued when she still said nothing. "Considering what happened at the baby shower, I thought you were still keeping all of this hidden away. You told me you had gotten very good at ignoring it."

"I know. But I've been thinking about . . . things. About why I have this gift. I just want to help this one. I feel like I am meant to."

"But you could be making a terrible mistake. What if you're wrong? Aunt Ellen said—"

"Aunt Ellen is of no help to me now!" Brette said, louder than she meant to. "There's no one else to talk to and I need to figure this all out. That's the real reason I wanted to talk to you today, actually. I need to know something. And I need you to be honest with me."

"Of course, Brette."

"I need to know if you and Dad talked about what it might mean to have a daughter when you decided to have kids."

Nadine's face was again expressionless. She said nothing, but Brette could see she was contemplating something.

"Keith wants us to have a baby," Brette went on. "He's aware of the risk I pose, but he says he's okay with it. I'm not sure I am."

"A baby," Nadine whispered.

"Yes, a baby. I need to know if you and Dad talked about it before you had me. I need to know how you decided. Did you have to convince Dad or did he convince you? And how did you know you would be comfortable with whatever the outcome was? Did you talk to Grandma about it? Did you go to her like I've come to you right now?"

Nadine turned her head to look out the window above the sink. A blue band of ocean was visible in the distance. "I did. I did go to her." Her mother's voice sounded far away, as if she'd floated back to another time and place.

Brette waited for her mother to continue.

"And I was worried, just like you are right now," Nadine went on. "Maybe worse than you are because she *had* it. She had the Sight. And I saw what it did to her."

"What? What did it do?"

Nadine paused a moment and then shrugged. "It wearied her. She had compassion for every one of those lost souls she saw. Every one. She wanted to help them, but Ellen told her they had to find their own way to where they belonged. Ellen was older and my mother looked up to her, so she did what Ellen said. It's very hard to be able to see something that makes you sad and be unable to do anything about it."

"Is it true that Grandma opted out of treatment for her cancer because of the Sight?"

Nadine swiveled her head slowly around. "Where did you hear that?"

"That day I saw the little boy in the attic, Aunt Ellen left my bedroom door ajar when she went to tell you about him. I think she wanted me to hear what she was saying in case you tossed her out of the house."

"Aunt Ellen thought that was why she didn't want the chemo. Maybe she's right. I don't think we can know for sure. When the doctors found the cancer it was already advanced. But yes, I think maybe my mother was ready to be set free of everything here on earth that caused her pain."

The two women were quiet for a moment.

"What did Grandma tell you when you asked her about whether to have a baby?" Brette asked.

Nadine inhaled deeply. "She told me that the lost souls had taught her better than anything else that life is precious and worth having. She said that if your dad and I wanted to bring new life into the world, that was always a good thing and could never be bad."

Brette let this elevated notion settle about her, noting how warm it made her feel inside. And yet, still she sensed caution. "You waited a long time to have me," she finally said.

A slight smile curved Nadine's lips. "I did. I had to be sure I'd be okay with whatever happened. Your father wasn't convinced the Sight was real at that point. I think he thought my mother and Ellen were just overly imaginative. But he understood that I was worried about it. We both wanted to be sure we were ready for whatever was in store for us. Prospective parents should be prepared for any kind of outcome when they decide to have a child. I would advise you of that even if the Sight didn't run in our family."

"And when the doctor said *it's a girl*, what did you think?"

The smile on Nadine's face widened. "You know, all I thought was how beautiful and perfect and wonderful you were." She turned to Brette. "I still think that."

Brette smiled now, too. "Why don't we ever talk about this?"

"Because for a long time I didn't want to, and then when I thought maybe we should, you didn't want to."

The light moment stretched thin and wafted away.

"But I'm realizing that I have to talk about it," Brette said. "It's part of my life. I've got to figure out how to live with this. Especially if I am going to be a parent."

"I know you do."

"If you had to do it all over again, would you still have me?"

"A thousand times yes."

"Even if you knew I'd be born this way?"

"But we don't ever get to know those kinds of things about our unborn children, Brette. That's the beauty and burden of having a child. You don't pick and choose the one you think you want, you are handed the one God gives you."

The sound of a car pulling into the driveway caused the women to turn their heads toward the open front windows.

"They're back," Brette said.

"Does Keith know you and I are having this conversation?"

Brette laughed. "Keith insisted we have this conversation."

Nadine reached out to her daughter and squeezed her arm. "You and Keith will be wonderful parents."

"I'm glad you think so."

Nadine hesitated a moment before picking up a shrimp. "Are

you still going to try to figure out what happened to that German woman?"

"I am. I need to know what I am meant to do with this ability if I am going to take the risk of passing it on to a child. I'm having to figure this out on my own. There's no one to ask. Pardon me for saying it, but I am all alone in this. There's no one else to go to for advice."

Nadine held the shrimp's pale gray body in her hands. "That's not exactly true."

Brette had started to pick up her wineglass, but she stopped. "What do you mean?"

Her mother didn't look at her. "I mean there's someone else."

"Someone else?"

"Cousin Lucille had a daughter."

"What?"

"Aunt Ellen didn't want you to know about her. She didn't think she was safe to be around, and I promised her I wouldn't tell you. And then when you got older, I felt I had to respect the distance you wanted to keep around it."

Brette stared at her mother, openmouthed.

"She lives in Oregon," Nadine said, finally looking at her daughter. "At least, she did."

"And she has the Sight?"

Nadine exhaled heavily, and Brette could feel the weight of guilt mixed with mother-love in that breath. "Yes."

Thirty-three

⁎

Brette had grown up believing Aunt Ellen's cousin Lucille was the perfect example of what would happen if she indulged in the Sight. While Brette was acclimating her six-year-old mind to the reality that she could see ghosts, what had troubled her most after Aunt Ellen left Willow House were the remembered snippets of the conversation on the other side of the nearly closed door. Ellen had been talking the way adults did when they were upset, saying her words like each one ached a little when spoken. Cousin Lucille's name had come up for the first time in those tense sentences, as did the words *ostracized* and *institutionalized*—chilling words she did not know—and *terrified*, which she did. Ellen's tone, as well as her parents', had been quite different when the three of them came into her room a few minutes later with their cotton-soft voices and tender assurances. Lucille hadn't been mentioned then.

The second time Lucille's name came up was when Aunt Ellen died and Brette was given the letter. Ellen had written that Cousin Lucille involved herself too much with the Drifters she encountered. It was the reason that Lucille was committed to a mental hospital and died young at fifty-three.

Lucille was the unmentioned, token family black sheep, whose strange life and early death were never spoken of at extended family get-togethers, events that Nadine and Cliff rarely attended because they were always held in the Midwest or farther east. Cliff's side of the family knew nothing at all about the Sight, and Nadine's family now consisted of just one brother, two nephews, and a scattering of second cousins whom Nadine wasn't close to, most of whom—including the brother—thought the so-called family gift was just the stuff of legend. Lucille was the cousin who went crazy, not the cousin who'd been able to see into the spiritual dimension and who let it get the best of her.

It had never occurred to Brette that Lucille might have had a child, and a daughter, no less.

Now as she stood in the kitchen with her mother, she was filled with equal parts relief that she wasn't the only one in the family with the Sight and astonishment that Nadine had kept this knowledge from her.

Cliff and Keith were standing in the kitchen now, too, looking from one woman to the other.

"Everything okay in here?" her father said.

"Does he know?" Brette said to Nadine.

"Do I know what?" Cliff set the grocery bag on the counter. One artichoke rolled out. Its pointed leaves made it zigzag toward the shrimp cleanings before it came to a wobbly stop.

When Nadine didn't immediately answer, Brette filled in the blank. "Cousin Lucille had a daughter."

Cliff looked from Brette to Nadine. "What brought that up?"

"So you knew, too?"

"I promised Ellen a long time ago I wouldn't say anything," Nadine said. "When you were young it seemed to both your dad and me the right thing to do."

"Who's Lucille?" Keith said.

"My great-aunt Ellen's second cousin," Brette answered. "She had a daughter that is apparently like me."

"No. Not like you," Nadine said quickly. "Maura is nothing like you."

A few seconds of silence hovered in the room. A sense of quiet betrayal clung to Brette. She wanted to shake it off but didn't know how.

"Ellen told us it was best you didn't know about Maura. And she didn't want Maura knowing about you," Nadine said. "How were we to know otherwise, Brette? We weren't given an instruction manual, either."

Brette felt Keith move closer to her. "Why didn't you tell me?" she asked.

"The same reason you never asked if Ellen was correct when she said there was no one else. You stopped asking questions, Brette. We weren't going to ask them if you weren't."

"Did she try to contact Brette or something?" Cliff said, his brow furrowed.

"No. I just mentioned it now because Brette seemed distressed about having no one in the family to talk to about it." Nadine turned again to Brette. "We've tried to do our best, Brette. We didn't know that what you can do was affecting you and—" Nadine cast a quick glance at Keith. "And your decisions."

All the years Brette had thrust the Sight to the furthest recesses of her consciousness had come with a cost, she now realized. What she didn't want to talk about, her parents weren't going to bring up in conversation.

"Where is she?" Brette said. "Why didn't Ellen want me knowing about her?"

Nadine paused a moment before answering. "I don't know where she is. Twenty years ago she lived in Oregon, that's the last place I knew of. I think Maura was born when Lucille was in one of her homeless stages. Ellen told me Maura was just like Lucille. She had the gift and she liked having it. She was taken away from Lucille when she was ten or eleven and spent the rest of her childhood in foster care. Maura was apparently as reckless with the Sight as Lucille had been. Ellen assured me Maura would only be a danger to you, Brette. We trusted Ellen because we had to. I have had no one to talk to, either. I really thought I was doing right by you."

As her mother spoke, Brette's resentment diminished. It wasn't her parents' fault that she had spent the last dozen years pretending she was just like everyone else.

"It's okay, Mom," Brette said. "I'm sorry if I sounded like I was angry. I just . . . It would be really nice to talk to someone who knows what it's like."

"I'm sorry if I should have told you sooner, Brette. I've only ever wanted to protect you from harm. I've never known for sure what was safe and what wasn't. And it has killed me that I haven't."

Nadine seemed on the verge of tears, and Brette got off the stool and folded her mother in her arms.

"No, I'm the one who's sorry. I know it can't have been easy."

"We thought we were doing the right thing," Nadine said, as they broke away. "I can try to find her if you want."

"Sure, Mom. That'd be great."

"Okay. Can we change the subject now?" her father said. "Maybe talk about something happy?"

Brette and her mother shared a smile as Keith and her father grabbed beers from the fridge.

Brette turned to her mother. "I'm not going to do anything stupid with this situation on the *Queen Mary*. I just want some clarity. You don't need to worry about me."

Nadine laughed lightly. "That's like telling the sun it doesn't need to shine," she said.

ON THE DRIVE HOME A FEW HOURS LATER, KEITH ASKED IF BRETTE and her mother had a good conversation up to the point of Nadine's surprise revelation.

Brette told him what her mother shared about deciding to have a child.

"She had fears about getting pregnant, just like I do, but in the end she believed that her mother was right, that having a baby is being a part of life renewing itself," she said. "I just don't want to burden a child unnecessarily, Keith. I really don't."

"But we could have a boy. Or we could have a girl who won't have it."

"And if we do have a girl and she does?"

Keith was quiet for a moment. He kept his eyes on the road ahead as he formulated his answer. "We will love her. And she won't have to grow up feeling alone like you did. She will have you to help her understand how it works. And how it doesn't."

"But I don't even understand it."

"That's not true, Brette. Not anymore. I think you've pushed this ability aside because you had no one to come alongside to help you manage it. But now you're figuring it out. I don't know what it's like to see what you can see and I don't understand it, not scientifically or any other way, but I do know I love you, every part of you, even that part. I want you to make peace with it, Brette. And if you think finding this woman in New Mexico will bring you the answers you're looking for, then I want you to go. And I'll gladly take off tomorrow and go with you."

Immense relief flooded Brette for the first time in she couldn't remember how long. She didn't mind going alone, but it was gratifying that Keith would so willingly drop everything, especially after being gone from his office for a week, to accompany her.

"You don't have to come," she said.

"And you don't have to go. Let me come with you." He took her hand from across the seat. "Stop making this such a solo thing, Brette."

To suddenly have Keith at her side as she was dealing with what she had always managed on her own was both wonderful and odd. She didn't quite know how to share so openly this shielded niche of her life. She also wasn't sure she wanted Keith along for what might be a fruitless endeavor.

"I don't mind trying to find this woman on my own, especially since I'm only assuming she's still alive," she said. "But I'd like you to come back with me to the ship when and if I finally figure this out. I told that Drifter I would be back. I think she is the kind to remember that I said I would return. I think I'd really like it if you came then."

KEITH DROPPED BRETTE OFF AT THE AIRPORT BEFORE THE SUN rose for her six thirty A.M. flight to Albuquerque. She used the hour and forty minutes in the air to rehearse what she would say if Simone Robinson was indeed at the address listed in the white pages. The worst-case scenario was that Brette would discover the woman had died, even though her obituary hadn't popped up in any search engine. Or perhaps, worse still, she'd be alive but would refuse to speak to Brette. If that was the case, Brette would return to the *Queen Mary* and share with the Drifter what Phoebe Rogers had told her—that the fall into the water surely had to have been an accident—and then hope that the Drifter would find enough peace in that to leave the physical realm, with all its imperfections, behind. Brette had allowed herself two days in Albuquerque to find the answers she sought, but she'd also made a mental note of evening flights back to San Diego in case she found out quickly that Simone Robinson would be of no help.

As soon as she was behind the wheel of a rental car and had cranked on the air conditioning to counter the eighty-nine-degree heat, she punched in the address she'd found on the white pages website into the car's GPS. The address was in an area known as

Paradise Hills, located eighteen miles from the airport and not far from the Rio Grande.

Brette met with moderately busy pre–lunch hour traffic. Twenty-five minutes later she was pulling into the parking lot of a semi-independent living facility boasting rows of freestanding casitas—stucco, one-level, single-dwelling bungalows—as well as a multistoried high-rise consisting of apartments. The GPS directed Brette to one of the casitas, and she was glad there would be no lobby attendant to prevent access to the doorbell at number 14.

As Brette parked her car in front of what was hopefully Simone Robinson's house, a trim, elderly woman holding a watering can opened the door and stepped out onto the porch. She began to sprinkle the succulents and cacti arranged in terra-cotta pots to the left and right of the front door.

The woman's short white hair was cropped close, and her capris and cotton blouse hung loose on her slight frame. Her hand holding the watering can shook a little from the weight of the water. A marmalade-striped cat that had followed her outside was rubbing against her ankles. White espadrilles covered her slender feet. She didn't notice Brette approach and startled a bit when Brette cleared her throat and said, "Pardon me?" from a few feet away.

"Oh!" the woman said.

"Sorry. Didn't mean to frighten you," Brette said quickly.

"Quite all right," the woman said, and Brette detected the faintest melodic lilt to her voice. "Can I help you?"

The woman looked to be in her late eighties perhaps; her weathered face, though still pretty, was textured with lines and wrinkles, the result, no doubt, of decades in the Southwest's ample sun.

"I am looking for Simone Robinson." Brette took another step forward. "Might you be her?"

The woman blinked, but her facial expression did not change. "I might."

Brette took a breath to steady herself and call to mind the words she had practiced on the plane. "My name is Brette Caslake. I'm sort of a friend of Phoebe Rogers."

The woman cocked her head. "Sort of?"

"We've only just met. And only by phone. I was hoping I might talk to you for just a few minutes about your time as a war bride on the *Queen Mary*."

"I don't give media interviews, Miss . . . I'm sorry. I've forgotten what your name is. If you had called first, I could have told you that."

"I am not with any media. And I would have called first but your number is unlisted. I asked Phoebe for it, actually. But she didn't have it either."

Simone stared at Brette for a moment. "Like I said, I don't give interviews, Miss . . ."

"It's Mrs. Caslake. But please just call me Brette. And I don't want to interview you. I just have a couple of questions."

One, really.

"That sounds like an interview to me. And I don't give them. Good-bye." Simone turned to head back inside her little house.

"Wait, Mrs. Robinson. I've come a long way to talk to you. Please? I am not here for myself. I am here for someone else."

Simone turned around with her hand on the doorknob. "Who could you possibly be here for?"

"It's . . . a bit complicated. Might I come inside and explain? Please?"

"Young lady, I do not know you. And I am not going to invite you inside my house so you can rob me blind."

Simone opened her door and Brette rushed forward to lay a hand gently on her arm.

"It's about Annaliese Kurtz!" Brette said.

Simone paused in midstep over her threshold and looked back. The cat scooted inside. "What about her?"

"I know she didn't commit suicide."

Brette had not known what kind of reaction to expect when she made this rehearsed pronouncement. The old woman seemed to have turned to stone for a second, neither blinking nor saying a word.

"And how would you know that?" Simone finally said a moment later, in a tone that did not reveal what she was thinking.

"I'd like to tell you how I know. I really would."

The old woman's eyes widened a fraction and she seemed to contemplate a dozen different thoughts in the span of just a few seconds.

"Please, may I come in?" Brette said. "I promise I mean you no harm."

Simone studied Brette for a moment and then pushed the door open, motioning with the watering can for her to go inside.

The casita's front door opened to a small living room tiled in terrazzo and decorated in a Southwest theme. Lithographs of hot-air balloons and the Grand Canyon hung on the walls. Rainbow-hued Navajo blankets covered the backs of a sofa and two chocolate-brown armchairs. The ambience of the room was warm and inviting and decidedly American. Down the hallway, where Brette assumed the bedroom was, she could hear gentle snores.

"My husband is resting and he's not well, so I'd appreciate it if you said quietly what it is you have to say," Simone said as she sat down in one of armchairs. "Please. Have a seat." Simone motioned to the sofa as the cat jumped up onto her lap.

Brette took a seat on the couch. "You have a lovely place here, Mrs. Robinson."

"You're already inside. You don't need to ply me with small talk, Mrs. . . ."

"Caslake," Brette said again. "But please call me Brette. And I really do like how you've decorated your home."

"Why are you here, Mrs. Caslake?"

The get-to-know-you conversation Brette had hoped to have clearly was not going to take place. Brette knew the next words out of her mouth could get her ushered right out of the house. "I've come about Annaliese Kurtz . . ." Her voice dwindled away.

"So you've already said."

Brette inhaled deeply to steady her voice. "The thing is, Mrs. Robinson, I know she didn't jump overboard because she . . . she told me."

Simone registered neither dread nor astonishment. "Is that so?"

"Doesn't . . . doesn't that surprise you?"

"Should it?"

"Well, Mrs. Robinson, you said you saw her jump all those years ago. You told the harbor police and a reporter from the *New York Times* that you saw her jump."

Simone Robinson merely blinked and said nothing.

"And I asked Phoebe Rogers about this. She told me she didn't actually see Annaliese go over. She pretended she did when you told the authorities and the press that you both saw her jump. But Phoebe was too far away. She didn't see it happen."

"Continue," Simone said evenly.

"Phoebe said you didn't get along with Annaliese Kurtz, that you'd found out she was an impostor and was going to be arrested and you confronted her. Mrs. Rogers said you and Annaliese had words. Annaliese ran off and Phoebe told you to go after her."

"And?" Simone said, as though Brette's comments hinted of no moral consequence.

"Mrs. Robinson, Annaliese Kurtz was pushed. Either on purpose or by accident. You were there. You know which one it was."

Simone's eyes finally widened in surprise. And something else. Annoyance?

"Pushed? You told me she spoke to you," Simone said, with a half laugh.

"She . . . This will be hard to explain, but please just hear me out. I was born with an extrasensory ability. It's a gifting that shows up now and then in the women in my family. I can see into the dimension that lies between our world and where we go when we die. There's a place in between the two that some people linger in after they've died. I can see these earthbound souls. I can hear them. And they can see and hear me."

A slight smile curved Simone's lips. Brette had seen that look before. It was the amused grin of unbelief. "You see ghosts, Mrs. Caslake? Is that what you're telling me?"

"Yes," Brette said with as much confidence as she could muster. "I was aboard the *Queen Mary* last week on another matter. I was approached by one of these souls. I believe it was the ghost of Annaliese Kurtz."

Simone Robinson narrowed her eyes. "Oh, really?"

"Yes, really. She doesn't know how she ended up in the water. She doesn't know if she was pushed or if someone tried to pull her back from the railing and the opposite occurred. But not knowing the truth has kept her stuck on the ship all these years. She needs to know. You're the only one who knows what really happened, Mrs. Robinson."

Simone sat back in her chair and stared at Brette for a moment. "What is it you want?" she finally said, her voice iced with disdain. "Money? Is that it?"

"I don't want anything but the truth," Brette said. "I'm not going to blackmail you or notify the police or anything. I just—"

"Notify the police!?" Simone echoed abruptly.

"I said, I'm *not* going to! I just need to know the truth so that I can tell her! So that she can be at rest."

Simone glared at Brette. "If anyone should be calling the police, it should be me."

"What . . . what do you mean?"

Simone leaned forward in her chair. She raised her hand and pointed an accusing finger. "I mean, *you* are a fraud."

The air in the room seemed to thin to nothing for several seconds. Brette had been called a freak and a weirdo in times past, but never a fraud. "I assure you I am not a fake," she said, surprised by the tears that had so quickly sprung to her eyes. "I see and hear ghosts. And I know what I heard on that ship. Annaliese Kurtz did not jump. She was pushed! She showed me your cabin. A-152. She showed me the little cabinet in that room. Something had been in that cabinet that belonged to her. And she showed me the place at the bow where she fell in. I *know* what I saw and heard."

Simone relaxed back in her chair, studying Brette intently and saying nothing.

"I'm not a fraud," Brette said a second later.

"Then you are terribly misguided," Simone finally said. "Annaliese Kurtz is very much alive."

Thirty-four

Simone found the woman who for the last week had been calling herself Katrine standing at the stern's railing, looking out over the water and the pale horizon of the ending day. There were a few other people on the deck: a handful of war brides, a couple of civilians, a man in a military uniform. The dinner bell would be sounding soon and the deck would clear, but not for many minutes yet.

Her resolve was complete now. She approached her roommate, whose real name was Annaliese Kurtz, with a steady stride. The story that Annaliese had shared with Simone and Phoebe about the best friend she'd loved and hidden was true, only *she* had been the one hiding from the man she'd been forced to marry, and who had abused her. This woman at the railing had known in an instant what Simone had dreamed of the evening of her nightmare because she had experienced it another way, multiple times over. She was German, yes, but she was not Simone's enemy. The enemy was someone else entirely and it always had been. Everett had told her it is complicated fighting for freedom and justice, but necessary if they were to hold on to what made them human and not beasts.

The woman looked up when Simone reached her, and her eyes were filled with sadness and hope, longing and regret. Annaliese was no doubt contemplating all that she would have to accomplish when they docked. An escape of some kind was surely on her mind. Simone wondered for a moment how Annaliese Kurtz planned to go ashore and get away when the ship made harbor. What was she planning to do for money, for a job, for a place to live? Had she really thought she could simply disappear into America with such a pronounced German accent and rudimentary English skills?

"I need to talk to you," Simone said softly in French.

"*Oui?*" Annaliese said, curious but also concerned.

"It is very important that you do nothing but stand there and pretend I am just telling you what is on the menu for dinner."

"What?" Annaliese's eyes grew round and the color drained from her face.

"Do not raise your voice, do not back away from me. Do nothing except stand there and listen to me. Do you understand?"

The woman's eyes immediately shone with fear.

"There has just been a wire message from Southampton. I was on the sun deck just now and I overheard the radio operators talking about it. They've only had it in their hands for a few minutes."

"From Southampton?" Annaliese echoed, her voice trembling.

"It's a wire for the commodore with instructions for when we arrive in New York tomorrow."

Annaliese shook her head. "I don't understand what this has to do with me."

Simone put her hand firmly on Annaliese's arm. "They know. They know who you are. They are going to arrest you when we dock."

"Oh, God!" Annaliese swayed and Simone reached out to steady her.

"You promised you would stand there and just listen to me!" Simone said between her teeth as she glanced behind them to see if anyone was taking note of them. No one was. "Don't you dare faint or get sick or scream."

"I can't . . . I can't . . ." Annaliese whispered, her breath coming out in short gasps.

"Shut up and listen to me."

A sob threatened to erupt and Annaliese slapped a gloved hand to her mouth to keep from making a sound.

"Just look out over the water, just like you had been before," Simone murmured.

Annaliese removed her hand so that she could grip the railing. She nodded, blinking back dozens of tears.

"I know you're Annaliese Kurtz. I know you're the one married to a Nazi official and I know he hurt you. I know you were the one your best friend, Katrine, was trying to help, not the other way around. I know you're German."

"I'm sorry, I'm sorry—" Annaliese said, biting back a sob.

"Be quiet. I want to help you."

The woman shook her head. "I can't go back to him. I can't!"

"Then don't."

Annaliese cast a glance toward Simone. "But you said they are going to arrest me!"

"And they will if you're in the stateroom when we dock."

"So what should I—"

"Don't be in our stateroom."

"I don't understand."

"What are you willing to do to avoid being sent back?" Simone asked.

Annaliese blinked and swallowed hard. "I won't go back to Germany. I won't. I'll die before I go back to him."

Simone nodded. "You need to do exactly what I say. Exactly."

Annaliese stared at her. Simone could see the question forming even before Annaliese spoke the words.

"Why are you helping me?" Annaliese said.

Simone had thought about this for several long minutes after overhearing the conversation in the telegraph room. She knew she'd had three options. She could've said nothing and simply let the officials come for Annaliese in the morning. She could have told every bride she'd met on the ship who her roommate really was and let the rumor mill have its way among the seventeen hundred war brides aboard. Annaliese's last few hours on the ship would have been hell. Or she could do what she was doing now: helping a young woman much like herself escape a life of misery.

"It's not our fault what happened to us, Annaliese. We didn't ask for any of this. And we didn't cause it. Before the war we were just young girls spinning dreams for the future. If I do nothing when I know I can help you, I can never again be the girl that I was; I will only ever be that other girl, the one the war tried to make of me."

Annaliese seemed to need a moment to internalize those words and realize they were true for her as well. "What should I do?"

"The dinner bell will ring soon. You need to go down to the salon and sit at our table and eat whatever is put in front of you."

"I couldn't possibly eat!"

"You must. You must pretend that everything is just as it was when you woke up this morning."

Annaliese nodded slowly.

"When the meal is over, go up to our stateroom like you have all the other nights to sit with Douglas," Simone continued. "Phoebe will want to be out and about. It's our last night. I will come in later like I usually do. Don't go to bed. Don't put your nightgown on. Stay up reading or something. When I come in, I am going to be angry. I am going to say that I just overheard that the telegraph room received that wire. I am going to accuse you of being a lying, dirty German who left her best friend dead in a car and stole her identity. I'm going to say terrible things, Anna-liese. And when I say these things, you need to react like you had wanted to just now. Phoebe can't ever think that I helped you. When she's asked she will say that I didn't get along with you, and that I was very angry about what you had done. I will be shouting, you will be crying, and Phoebe will no doubt be panicking. We will wake Douglas. You will run from the stateroom in tears. Phoebe will want to run after you but Douglas will be wailing, if we've done our job right, and she will want to hand him over to me. I will refuse. She will beg me to go after you. She will say it wasn't your fault and that you did what you did because you were desperate. I will finally relent and go looking for you. Now, when you run from the stateroom, you need to come to the back of the ship. To this place right here. Make sure at least one person sees you but don't let them stay to ask what is the matter. Tell them you want to be alone. And then when you are sure no one is taking note of you, take off your cardigan and leave it right here for me. I won't be far behind. That's how I will know that no one saw you when you left. And then you need to go belowdecks using the staff stairwell. No one can see you, Annaliese. You must make sure no one sees you."

"But where will I go then?"

Simone was fairly certain that she could count on Marc to help her. But she wasn't sure that Annaliese's true predicament would matter to him. What did matter to him were deeds of bravery and risk undertaken by those who'd been oppressed but had risen up to resist. She would tell him that her roommate with the Ger-man accent was actually a counterspy attempting to escape a Nazi who would stop at nothing to find her. It was mostly true. She would tell him it would mean the world to her if he would help her and it would be his own contribution to the courageous acts of the Résistance.

"I shall persuade Marc to help us," Simone said. "He will do it for me. I know he will."

"But . . . but if I go belowdecks and am not in my stateroom, won't the commodore search the ship for me?"

"Not if he thinks you are dead."

HALF AN HOUR LATER, SIMONE, PHOEBE, AND ANNALIESE WERE at their table in the dining room. Phoebe chatted without ceasing about everything and nothing, stopping only once to ask Katrine why she was merely picking at her food.

Simone had glared at Annaliese surreptitiously, and the German woman had speared a piece of chicken and said she was too excited about seeing her husband tomorrow to eat. This happy comment set Phoebe up for fifteen additional minutes of chatter about the life that awaited them in America.

Marc was attentive but nervously so. He'd taken to Simone's request as if he were being asked to dig for buried treasure that was assured of being found. She had cornered him before dinner just outside the staff entrance to the dining room. She'd told him she had a favor to ask that was as important as any act of resistance during the war that she or her father or brother had undertaken.

"If you get caught, you will probably lose your job," she'd said. "You might even be arrested."

He'd said yes before even hearing what it was Simone wanted him to do.

When he served them their coffee, he lingered at the table, making small talk. It seemed to Simone that he was trying too hard to appear normal. She caught his gaze and tipped her head to indicate he needed to move on. Annaliese watched him leave with interest, and Simone kicked her lightly under the table.

"Please come with me to the variety show tonight, Katrine," Phoebe said as Marc walked away. "It's going to be such fun. I can bring Dougie to that, I think. And we can sit near the back in case he gets fussy."

Simone reached for her coffee cup, hoping Annaliese could come up with a convincing reason for why she didn't want to go.

"I don't think so, Phoebe. I like the quiet of our room after dinner. And I don't mind watching Douglas while you go to the show. It will be my last night with him. I . . . I am going to miss him."

Well done, Simone thought.

"Oh, you're such a dearie. He's going to miss you, too. We must all be sure to exchange our addresses before we get off the ship tomorrow."

"Yes," Annaliese said numbly.

"How about you, Simone? You want to come with me to the show?"

Simone set her cup down on its saucer. "I'm not one for variety shows. Besides, I already have plans."

"You're not rendezvousing with that steward, are you?" Phoebe frowned.

Simone laughed like it was a silly assumption. "I have better things to do on our last night than smoke a cigarette with a boy. I am playing Barbu with some of the other French war brides. It will be the last time we shall all play it for a while, since no one in America will likely know how to play."

Phoebe shook her head. "I don't even know what a Barbu is. All right, then. I guess I will just go by myself. And I'll let you put Dougie to bed, Katrine, if you're sure you don't mind."

"Not at all," Annaliese said with a convincing smile.

Phoebe scooped up Douglas from the high chair he was sitting in, and Annaliese rose as well.

"Don't be too late, Simone," Phoebe said. "We'll want to have some girl-talk time before we turn the lights out. Don't you think, Katrine?"

"Um. Yes."

"I'll try to keep an eye on the clock," Simone answered casually. Annaliese walked away without a backward glance.

The plan was in motion.

SIMONE WAITED UNTIL THE VARIETY SHOW LET OUT.

She watched from behind a pillar as Phoebe laughed and chatted with another war bride as she came out of the theater, said good night, and headed up the staircase along with many others to the A deck. Simone followed at a safe distance and waited for five minutes after Phoebe entered the stateroom before inserting her key into the lock.

She took a deep breath, fixed a frown on her face, and opened the door.

Annaliese was sitting in one of the armchairs under the portholes with a book open on her lap, still in her clothes. Douglas was asleep in his bunk. Phoebe was standing in front of Annaliese, telling her all about the show, no doubt. Annaliese's gaze flitted to Simone, and Phoebe turned.

Simone pushed the door closed, hard.

"What the devil?" Phoebe said, with a quick glance toward her son's bed. Douglas did not stir.

Simone ignored Phoebe and strode purposefully toward Annaliese. "You damned, dirty German," she said.

Annaliese flinched.

"Simone!" Phoebe exclaimed.

"You're not going to get away with it," Simone continued, injecting as much venom into her tone as she could. "They know what you've done. You're going to be arrested when we dock tomorrow."

"What the . . ." Phoebe could not finish.

Annaliese looked stricken but appeared frozen to her chair.

Say something, Simone silently begged her.

"What . . . what are you talking about?" Annaliese finally said, her voice thick with dread.

"You know exactly what I'm talking about, you conniving liar."

"Simone!" Phoebe glanced back at Douglas again. He moved a pudgy arm.

"What are you saying?" Annaliese whimpered.

"There was a wire today from Southampton," Simone went on. "I heard them talking about it in the radio room while I was having a cigarette after my card game. I was right outside. You are to be detained when we dock tomorrow and then the police will come and arrest you. And they'll send you straight back to Germany, where I hope you rot."

"Katrine! What is she talking about?" Phoebe said.

Simone turned to Phoebe "Her name isn't Katrine. It's Annaliese. Katrine is dead. She left that poor girl dead in her car, stole her passport and identity papers so that she could board this ship under someone else's name. She's a German, Phoebe."

Phoebe, dazed but ever compassionate, knelt before Annaliese. "Is this true? Is what she is saying true?"

Tears were streaming down Annaliese's face. "I'm sorry," she whispered.

"But why?" Phoebe murmured.

"Because she wanted a quick way out of Germany and into America, that's why," Simone replied.

"All those things you told us about the girl named Annaliese. They happened to you?" Phoebe asked.

Annaliese opened her mouth, but Simone filled the second of silence. "I bet you lied about that, too, didn't you? Didn't you?"

Annaliese stood and Phoebe followed suit. "I . . . I can't go back. I can't go back there," she said, her voice quivering.

"You should have thought of that before," Simone shouted.

Douglas, at last, woke up.

Phoebe rose and crossed the stateroom to kneel at his bunk. "Shhh, sweetheart," she crooned, her voice breaking. She patted his back as he continued to howl. "There must be some mistake!" she said, turning back toward Simone.

"There's no mistake," Simone said. "She lied about everything."

"I can't go back!" Annaliese wailed, her most convincing response yet.

"You disgust me," Simone said. Their gazes met. It was time for the second phase.

Annaliese brushed past her, flung open the stateroom door, and ran out.

"Katrine!" Phoebe yelled, pulling Douglas into her arms and dashing to the door.

"Her name's Annaliese!" Simone shouted, more toward the retreating form of the German woman than to Phoebe.

"You have to go after her!" Phoebe said.

"I certainly do not."

Phoebe turned to watch Annaliese round the corner to the central staircase. "Then take Douglas, please? I will go after her."

"No."

Phoebe swung back around. "Simone! Whatever it is she has done, she must have had her reasons! What if she was telling the truth about the girl named Annaliese? What if she *was* forced to marry a man she didn't love and who did all those terrible things to her?"

"And what if she wasn't telling the truth? She's a German. Married to a Nazi. The Nazis killed my family, stole everything from me, and I mean everything, and made my life hell."

"But *she* isn't a Nazi, Simone! She didn't kill your family! She didn't steal anything from you!"

Simone let a few seconds of contemplation pass. "I don't know where she went."

"It's a ship! How many places could she have gone?"

She pretended to think on it.

"Please, Simone. Go after her. Or take Douglas and let me go after her."

"I'll do it," Simone said, feigning a reluctant tone.

She started to move away from the door.

"Tell her we'll vouch for her."

"I'm not vouching for her!" Simone called out over her shoulder.

"Then tell her I will."

Simone huffed and then started down the hallway toward the central staircase. When she was out of Phoebe's view, she quickened her steps.

It did not take long to get to the promenade deck and head outside to make her way to the stern. It was near freezing outside, and there was no one taking air at ten o'clock at night. She walked to the far end and opened the door to the little storage cabinet where a bevy of deck cushions were lined up for warmer days.

The promised thirty-pound bag of potatoes was leaning up against the inner wall.

Marc had come through with his first assignment. She hoped he'd already been able to make good on his second. She made sure she was still alone on the deck before hoisting out the sack. She hefted the heavy bag into her arms and peeked out of the double doors that led to the outer decks of the back of the ship. There was no one out and about. Simone pushed her way through and made her way to the white-railed steps that would take her to the last accessible outside deck.

She wanted to see no one, not a soul, on that deck. There could be no one watching her lug a sack of potatoes down three sets of metal stairs. Simone peered into the dimly illuminated stern. She saw a fluttering at the rail.

Annaliese's cardigan.

She stepped out fully and winced at the razorlike aggression of the wind off the freezing water. Her hands began to feel stiff and numb, and she feared she would lose her hold on the sack. Simone willed herself to hang on tight. Just a few more stairs. Just a few more.

Then she was at the bottom and scurrying to the port side where the cardigan was tied. She set her bag down and reached for the sweater; the weave still bore a remnant of the warmth of having just been taken off. Simone pulled up the bag and balanced it on the railing with one hand as she held Annaliese's cardigan in the other. She was so cold. But she wanted to wait until she saw the shadow or form of just one other person out for a bracing walk or a look at the stars. Just one person to notice movement at the back of the ship and to hear her call out Annaliese's name or shout the word, "No!" and to hear the splash of something heavy hitting the water below.

Her fingers were stinging with cold and her legs were numb. She would not be able to hold on to the potatoes much longer. And then, from the port side of the deck, she saw a figure in the semi-darkness. A woman who called out Simone's name.

Phoebe.

Phoebe started running toward her.

"No!" Simone yelled as she let the sack fall.

Four seconds later she let the cardigan go, too, and it floated down like a butterfly, alighting gracefully on the water just as Phoebe reached the railing and screamed Annaliese's name.

Thirty-five

※

It was nearly one in the morning before Simone and Phoebe returned to their stateroom after Annaliese Kurtz's apparent suicide.

The search and rescue for the impostor war bride had proved fruitless. By the time the alarm had sounded, the ship's engines had been ordered stopped, and the great vessel had stopped moving, the spot in the water where Simone said the woman had jumped was hundreds of yards behind them. A lowered lifeboat found no trace of Annaliese Kurtz, not even the cardigan that both Simone and Phoebe reported they'd seen in the water.

Phoebe had been nearly hysterical at the loss of the woman she still kept calling Katrine. The ship's command staff, the Red Cross matrons, and the other military officials on board all wanted statements from both women, and each time they explained what happened, Phoebe wept with increased sorrow and guilt. Simone had guided them back to their room, assuring Phoebe that it was no one's fault, least of all hers, that Annaliese had jumped.

"You were too hard on her, Simone!" Phoebe had said, as they'd made their way back to the room with Red Cross blankets wrapped around their shoulders.

"I did her a favor telling her that her secret was out," Simone had replied with little compassion. "You heard what Annaliese said. She'd rather die than go back."

"She can't have meant it!"

"How do you know she didn't mean it? I said nothing to her that wasn't true."

"But the way you said it was so hateful!"

"I tried to stop her, if you must know. She willingly went over the rail, Phoebe. She did what she wanted to do."

When they arrived at the stateroom, the war bride from across the hall who'd agreed to stay with Douglas went back to her own cabin and the two women went wearily to bed.

Phoebe fell asleep quickly from emotional exhaustion, but Simone lay awake for an hour or more, wondering, praying, and hoping that Marc would be able to pull off the second half of their plan. The man was young and impulsive, and so much was riding on his being clever and cautious from here on out. She would want to check in the morning to make sure everything was still in place for Annaliese's grand escape, but she knew she could not seek him out to confirm he had all the details in hand. Simone placed her hand on the tiny mound at her waist, wishing she could feel the child inside her move so that she would be assured that love and life is always stronger than fear and death.

She slept for a few hours and then awoke with a start a few minutes after sunrise when Douglas began to babble. She peered over the bunk. Phoebe was awake, and her cheeks were streaked with last night's tears.

"Can you sit with him while I do something with my face?" Phoebe said. "I must look a fright. I don't want Hal thinking he married a troll."

"You do look a fright. Go. I will play with him." Simone sat up in bed and put her legs over the side. Her gaze fell on Annaliese's bunk; the flowered blanket was pulled up tight and neat.

Phoebe was also looking at the empty bed across from them. "I can't believe she's gone."

"We can't think about that now, Phoebe. We are reuniting with our husbands today. It's supposed to be a happy time. We can't let what she did ruin this day for us."

"I suppose you're right." Phoebe rose with a sigh, grabbed her cosmetic bag, and headed for the bathroom.

Simone climbed down off the bunk and picked up Douglas to take him to the porthole. There was still nothing outside the window but a vast expanse of blue. The ship was supposed to dock in New York harbor at seven in the morning, but the situation the previous night had put them behind schedule. Every extra hour on the ship would no doubt seem an eternity as Simone waited to see if the plan had been compromised and Annaliese discovered.

An hour later, as the women prepared to head downstairs for breakfast, a knock sounded at their door. The ship's purser and a Red Cross matron were there to collect Annaliese Kurtz's things. Simone and Phoebe showed them the clothes Annaliese had brought, the purse that had been Katrine's with her passport and travel documents, the suitcase and travel bag in the cabinet. The items were placed in a cardboard box and the purser took them away.

The Red Cross matron lingered for a moment. "Are you both all right this morning? I know it must have been a terrible night. Do you need anything? Is there anything we can do for you?"

Phoebe opened her mouth to speak, but tears welled and she just shook her head.

"We'll be fine," Simone answered for them. "Thank you."

As they made their way down to the salon for breakfast, Simone looked casually about for Marc to make sure he was on duty as usual. She saw him at a nearby table, serving eggs and chatting with the diners.

Several minutes later he was at their table, pouring coffee. Annaliese's place was noticeably empty, and Simone hoped Marc would say something. She had forgotten to tell him that to be silent about the suicide would be odd.

"I was so very sorry to hear about the death of your roommate last night," he said gently and convincingly. "You have my sincerest condolences, ladies."

"Oh, thank you!" Phoebe said, with a tight smile and glistening eyes.

"Yes, thank you. It was quite a shock," Simone replied.

Marc leaned in especially close to pour Simone's coffee and, with his free hand, dropped a folded piece of paper on her lap under the table.

Simone had admonished both Marc and Annaliese not to contact her unless it was urgent. She crumpled the note into her fist as Marc walked away.

"I just need to use the ladies' room," Simone said to Phoebe. She rose to her feet. "I'll be right back."

In the restroom off the dining salon, Simone chose a stall and closed and latched the door. Then she uncrumpled the note in her hand. The words were written in French.

Inside the lining of your friend's suitcase is a letter for someone named John. She said you would know who that is and that you could tell him you found it among her things. She said it was important.

Marc

Simone pressed her head against the stall door. There was no way she could honor this request. Annaliese's belongings were gone. The suitcase would likely be tossed out and her clothes with it. Only the documents that had belonged to Katrine Sawyer would be kept to return to her grieving husband. Simone tore the note into confetti, dropped the pieces into the toilet, and flushed it.

There was nothing she could do about that letter or John Sawyer. She went back to the dining room.

A few minutes later Marc returned to offer her orange juice. Phoebe was in conversation with several other war brides who'd heard what had happened and had come to their table to hear the details.

"Tell her that the suitcase is gone. They took it this morning," Simone whispered as Marc poured. "And no more notes."

He nodded once and moved away.

She finished her breakfast and did her best to tuck away any worry that Annaliese would be discovered. She focused her thoughts on finally seeing Everett, and feeling his arms around her and his kisses on her neck and hair and his voice whispering in her ear that he loved her.

They made their way back to the A deck to get their coats since all the war brides wanted to watch from the deck as the ship was tugged to Pier 90 in New York harbor and to greet the waiting media. The rails were soon crowded with women and children bundled against the bitter cold to catch their first glimpse of America. When the Statue of Liberty came into view, the women cheered.

The *Queen Mary* was met just outside the harbor by a white Army Transportation Corps vessel. On its decks a band played "Here Comes the Bride," and more cheers broke out on the deck. Simone found it easier to push away concerns for Annaliese as the excitement of coming into port enveloped the ship. A female voice from the army vessel called out from a loudspeaker, "Welcome to America, girls!"

Simone stood by Phoebe and Douglas, marveling at the shining Manhattan skyline and how different it looked from London or Paris. Nothing about the urban horizon looked familiar.

"Isn't New York beautiful?" Phoebe exclaimed, and Simone merely nodded.

From the moment she'd spoken her wedding vows, Simone had thought she was ready to leave France and its memories behind, but as she stared at the welcoming edge of America, she sensed a profound sadness just underneath the wild joy. Her new life as a wife and mother in America was about to begin, and everything about her old life would soon be shut away inside the folds of her mind. She'd be speaking English every day, not French. She would have dollars in her wallet, not francs, and there would be no corner *boulangerie* or long walks in the Tuileries or gazing up at the lattices of the Eiffel Tower. Everett and the baby would be her whole world, perhaps for a long while. The punishing years of the war had taught her to be cautious about giving her heart over to the people she loved. She would have to unlearn that caution.

She was glad Everett had made the trip from Texas to New York to collect her. Some of the brides had to get on trains after docking and travel farther west before reuniting with their husbands. And she was strangely glad that Phoebe's husband would also be meeting them at the armory. Her roommate's incessant chatter distracted her from thoughts about the transition as well as from worries about Marc being able to pull off the harder part of the plan without implicating them both.

The only way she would know if the plan was a success was if she heard nothing. If the police came looking for her, she'd know it hadn't worked.

After docking, and waiting for what seemed like too long a stretch of time, the brides who were to be met by their husbands were finally told to queue up for their dismissal off the ship. Rows of newspaper reporters and photographers had gathered at the pier, eager to talk to the "Petticoat Pilgrims," as the London media had called them when they'd left Southampton. A Red Cross matron who signed Phoebe and Simone off the passenger manifest told them that reporters were waiting to speak to them about the suicide of their roommate, but that they weren't obligated to say anything. Brides who had gotten off before them had identified them to the waiting journalists.

"Should we?" Phoebe asked as they started across the wide gangway.

Simone wanted nothing more than to get on the bus and get to the armory and Everett, but talking to the newspaper men would give her one last chance to solidify the notion that Annaliese Kurtz was dead.

"We can just tell them very quickly what happened and then be on our way," Simone suggested, knowing that Phoebe wasn't opposed to the attention or having her picture in the American newspapers. As soon as they were on solid ground, an influx of reporters surrounded them. An army private stepped forward to escort them to the bus, but Simone put up a hand, letting him know they would answer a few questions. The reporters wanted to know who saw the woman jump (they said they both did), why she jumped (she couldn't face going back to Germany and her abusive husband), and what it was like being her roommate. They posed for a few pictures and then Simone nodded to the army private and he guided the two women past the rows of reporters and photographers to the waiting bus.

Half an hour later they were pulling up to the armory, where more reporters were waiting, but this time they declined interviews and she and Phoebe were ushered inside.

The large room was brimming with men both in uniform and plain clothes. Some husbands had brought with them parents and siblings eager to meet their new daughters- and sisters-in-law. Names of the brides were read individually over a loudspeaker so that couples could find each other in all the chaos. For some of the brides, Phoebe's fear had been true—they didn't recognize the men they'd married, who looked different after nearly a year apart, especially those who were no longer in the military and now wore civilian clothes.

"Do you see him? Do you see your Everett?" Phoebe said, as she craned her neck to look for Hal.

"No." Simone stood on tiptoes and scanned the sea of faces.

A few minutes passed before Phoebe's name was called and she turned to Simone in delight.

"Oh, my! That's me! Come find us after your name is called, Simone. We must stay in touch!" Phoebe wrapped her arms around Simone with Douglas squished between them. "I wish it were all three of us reuniting with our husbands today," she added in a whisper.

"You know that was never going to happen, Phoebe. Annaliese wasn't a war bride. Katrine's husband isn't even here. I am sure he knows now what happened."

"I know. But I can still wish it."

They broke apart. "Go on." Simone nodded toward the lectern. "Your husband's waiting for you."

Simone watched as Phoebe made her way with Douglas in tow to the front table where record keepers sat. A man with reddish brown curls and a plaid cap in his hands was emerging from the crowd of men to stand at the table. Phoebe ran to him. Simone could not hear the sound of her happy sobs, but she could see Phoebe erupting into tears of elation as Hal ran to meet her as well.

And then, over the din of happy voices and laughter and cries from tired babies, Simone heard her own name, not over the loudspeaker, but from across the room. She turned toward the sound. Everett, looking resplendent in his dress uniform, had spotted her and pushed forward through the ranks of waiting men. Simone instinctively placed a hand over the rounded swell that was her child and hiked her skirt to step over the stanchion rope. Everett was moving toward her, smiling wide, the tiniest hitch in his step from his old wound. The doubts she'd had earlier that morning fell away like autumn leaves. She ran to her husband and fell into his outstretched arms. For several seconds, there was no one else in the room—no officials wanting to check off her name, no other joyful couples embracing, no toddlers and babies laughing and shrieking, no Red Cross nurses or military police or reporters or newsreel photographers. There was only Everett and her, just like in the wine cellar, holding each other amid chaos.

"You are so beautiful," he said in French, whispering it as though they truly were alone in the room.

"I've missed you so much," she replied in English, nuzzling his chest.

He placed his hand on her abdomen. "And she is beautiful, too."

"She?" Simone said with a laugh.

"I already know she's a girl."

Everett hugged her tighter. Simone closed her eyes and relished the sensation of warmth and strength. When she opened her eyes a moment later, she saw a pair of military policemen walking toward them.

A different kind of heat suddenly cloaked her as the men closed the distance.

The plan had surely failed. Annaliese had been discovered. Arrested. Marc, too.

And now they were coming for her.

She began to tremble and Everett loosened his arms to look at her.

The police were just a few yards away.

"You there," one of them said in a gruff voice.

In that instant Simone realized she had no regrets. None at all.

She'd let them take her, question her, charge her with whatever offense they wanted. She didn't care that she'd been caught helping a fugitive fake her death, nor even that it had been her idea, not Marc's, not Annaliese's. It had been her plan and she was proud of it. It had been an act of resistance but also an act of mercy, and if she'd learned anything the last six years it was that war wasn't just about ideas and land and control. It was first and foremost about people. Annaliese Kurtz was neither offender nor defender, she was just a girl from a little town near Belgium who had a best friend named Katrine and who had liked to dance.

Helping her had been the right thing to do.

Simone eased herself out of Everett's embrace, ready to answer for her actions.

When the policemen were only a few feet away, one of them pointed a finger at her. "You need to follow the protocol just like everyone else. You can't just hop the ropes like that. There are records to be maintained. Forms to sign."

Relief, nearly stinging in its clarity, rushed over her.

"It's my fault," Everett said quickly. "We'll take care of it right now." He put his arm around her waist to usher her toward the lectern. "Don't want you to get into trouble on your first day in America!" he murmured with a laugh.

Simone smiled but had no words at the ready. Annaliese was safe, she had to be. Only one detail remained—a telegram to Paris—and she could take care of that at a nearby telegraph office.

Everett took care of the necessary paperwork, then retrieved her suitcase.

"Shall we?" he said a few minutes later as he offered her his arm. "I want to hear all about your voyage. Our train doesn't leave until five and I'm starving."

A sense of fullness fell over her at the joy of her new life finding its footing. She took Everett's arm. They had taken a few steps toward the exit when Simone suddenly remembered Phoebe's request that she find her. She paused for a moment.

"You forget something?" Everett asked.

Simone scanned the room, saw Phoebe in a clutch of Hal's extended family, all laughing and smiling and talking at once.

Perhaps it was best for them both to just move on from here, she thought. The dark days of deprivation were over, and the long wait to be reunited had also ended. More importantly, the man with the golden tooth was a fading memory and Annaliese Kurtz was on her way to freedom, God willing.

She had magnificently crossed the bridge into her second life with Everett.

"Is that woman a friend of yours?" Everett had followed her gaze.

"She was one of my roommates."

"Oh. Want to say good-bye?"

Simone moved closer to him. "I already did."

They headed for the open doors.

RMS *QUEEN MARY*
CAPE HORN, SOUTH AMERICA
NOVEMBER 1967

The water is warm and wide and strange to me. Everything about this voyage is unsettling and different.

Passengers are sitting on a red, two-story bus stored in the forward hold, honking the horn and laughing. "We're at the bottom of the world in a double-decker!" one of them yells, and the rest of the people on the bus cheer.

I don't know where we are. The others want to know what is happening, and I've no answer for them other than we are at the bottom of the world.

Above on the sun deck, the captain says to one of the passengers that California's weather will be good for the ship. It will be easy to keep her beautiful there.

"No regrets about the sale, then?" asks the passenger.

"No," the captain says, and then he adds how sad it was to pilot the Mauritania *to her demolition site. "I couldn't turn around for one last look at her," he says.*

I don't know what this means.

I don't know where we are.

The others with me are restless.

I tell them not to worry, all is well.

The revelers get off the bus to head upstairs to change into party clothes. Later, they will dance under stars whose glittering places I do not recognize.

Thirty-six

Brette stared at the elderly woman seated across from her. Words of protest formed in her head but seemed to flutter away when she opened her mouth to speak. It was impossible that Annaliese Kurtz was alive. Impossible.

"I think it's time for you to go," Simone Robinson said with little inflection.

"What you're saying can't be true," Brette finally said. "I know what I heard on that ship. I know what I saw."

Simone regarded Brette coldly for a moment and then a look of pity replaced the one of annoyance. "I assure you, Mrs. Caslake, Annaliese Kurtz left that ship very much alive."

"But . . . her body went into the water," Brette whispered.

"Her body did *not* go into the water, not that it's any of your business. She walked off that ship in a maid's uniform. Now, I've already told you more than you deserve to know. I'd like you to leave."

"No. There is a ghost on that ship that showed me your cabin, Mrs. Robinson," Brette said, anger and fear coating her words. Her voice sounded like a child's in her ears. "It showed me the place at the back of the ship where it happened!'

"Any archived passenger manifest can alert you or anyone else to our stateroom number, and every newspaper that covered the story mentioned where Annaliese supposedly jumped. It's time for you to go."

Nausea roiled in Brette's stomach. It just couldn't be. A ghost had communicated with her. Pressed on her. Led her down stairs and hallways. Revealed things to her. What had happened on the ship had been real.

"I know what I saw," Brette said again, and a tear slid down her cheek.

"You are mistaken, Mrs. Caslake."

"Tell me then how Annaliese got off that ship! How did she get away?"

"I owe you no explanation of any kind. You need professional help. That's what you need. And now I really must insist that you leave." Simone stood.

Brette made no move to do the same. "Please. Please tell me how you know she left that ship alive."

Simone walked over to the front door and opened it. She turned to face Brette, a silent summons on her face.

Brette slowly rose from the couch, shaken and numb at the same time. She made her way to the door. "Please? How do you know she isn't dead? How do you know she got off that ship alive?"

"Because I helped her," Simone said evenly.

Brette waited for Simone to tell her more, but the woman stared at her, silent.

"But I was led to your stateroom. I was shown that little cabinet. The doors opened and closed on their own . . ." Brette said, as if she needed the old woman's validation that she wasn't going crazy like Lucille had.

A flash of unease—or something like it—flickered across Simone's face and then was gone. She said nothing.

"Maybe she left the ship like you said but something terrible happened to her," Brette continued. "And now she haunts that ship. Maybe—"

"No," Simone said, her tone flat.

Simone Robinson knew far more about Annaliese Kurtz beyond what had happened on the *Queen Mary*, of that Brette was sure. But it was also obvious the woman would tell her nothing more today. Brette could only hope that in the days or weeks to come, she'd have a change of heart. Only Simone Robinson could tell Brette what she needed to know. There was no point in going back to the ship until the old woman told her what had become of Annaliese Kurtz. She reached into her purse and pulled out a Walgreens receipt and a pen. She wrote down her phone number and address on the back and extended the piece of paper to Simone.

"Please. If you change your mind, would you contact me?"

Simone stared at the piece of paper. "Change my mind about what?"

"About telling me what happened to Annaliese Kurtz. You know more than you are telling me. Something had been in that little cabinet in your stateroom. There is a ghost on the *Queen Mary* that is troubled by what happened on your sailing and by what happened to Annaliese. I just need to know for myself now, Mrs. Robinson. I need to know what or who was leading me around that ship."

The two women stood still and quiet, with Brette's outstretched arm between them. Simone made no move to take the receipt. Brette laid it on the entry table next to her and then stepped outside into the afternoon sun.

She listened for the sound of the front door closing behind her but did not hear it. When she got into her rental car a moment later, Simone Robinson was staring at her from just inside her little house.

Brette wanted to call Keith so that she could hear his voice and hide away for a few moments in his love and affirmation, but she didn't want to make the call with Simone standing on her threshold. She started the car and drove away, pulling into the first shopping area on her way back to the airport. The call to Keith went to voice mail and for a just a moment fresh tears welled in her eyes. She blinked them away. Perhaps it was just as well. She didn't know how to tell him how wrong she had been about Annaliese Kurtz. She left a message saying Simone Robinson had been no help and that she was taking the 5:03 P.M. flight back to San Diego if there was room on it. She'd text him if she was able to get a seat.

She held the phone in her hand after she'd hung up and stared out the windshield. A lost soul had wanted her to know that Annaliese Kurtz hadn't jumped. The Drifter had been real. Brette wasn't like Lucille. Couldn't be like Lucille. As she sat there, the phone vibrated in her hand and she flipped it over to see if Keith was calling her back. But the caller was Trevor.

Trevor would be contacting her about only one thing. She let it ring and go to messaging. Then she tossed the phone onto the passenger seat and set the GPS for the airport.

There was only one seat left on the flight back to San Diego and for the one-hundred-fifty-dollar change fee, it was Brette's. She didn't care that it had been an expensive day. She wanted answers, not her spent money back in her wallet. The cost of the rental car and the airfare seemed inconsequential compared to the deeper issues she was wrestling with.

She pulled out her phone when she got to her gate to text Keith her flight number. As she was typing the words, an incoming message arrived from Trevor.

Call me. I need you.

"No, you don't," she mumbled, and tapped the icon to hear his earlier voice mail:

"Brette, it's Trevor. I need you to call me as soon as you get this. I'm in a bind. I'm getting nowhere with Emily. We're still in LA and I'm at my wit's end. Please call me back."

Brette deleted the voice mail and opened a web browser to absently prowl home decorating sites while she waited for her flight. She couldn't help Trevor or his daughter or even herself. She had no idea how to manage the Sight, and the best thing she could do—the smartest thing she could do—would be to let it die with her. She and Keith could adopt a child. It made the most sense. The Sight was fickle, untrustworthy, and nothing that should be passed on to another person.

She was never going to hear from Simone Robinson again, and even if she did, even if Simone told her that she'd helped Annaliese create a new life for herself in America, it didn't change the fact that Brette had been duped on the *Queen Mary*, or worse, carried away by her own imagination.

Trevor texted her twice while she waited. She ignored the first and answered the second.

I've done all I can do for you, she wrote.

When she boarded, she turned the phone off well before being instructed to do so by the airline attendants. And when she turned her phone back on after the plane landed in San Diego, she ignored Trevor's return message, deleting it unread.

Keith wanted to hear all about her visit with Simone Robinson. Brette told him it had been a wasted trip and wanted to leave it at that. It wasn't until he pressed for more details that she told him Annaliese Kurtz was apparently alive and well somewhere, having faked her death seventy years ago with Simone Robinson's help.

"Then . . . who did you . . . Who was talking with you on the ship?" he'd asked, and she could hear the concern in his voice.

"Apparently not Annaliese Kurtz," Brette snapped, and then immediately wished she hadn't. "Sorry," she said a second later, surprised to feel tears of frustration and anger on her cheeks.

"Brette."

"I don't know what's happening to me," she whispered to the window glass next to her and the shimmering lights on the other side of it.

Keith reached across her seat to take her hand. He squeezed it and said nothing for a moment. "Maybe it was another Drifter who just wanted you to know Annaliese Kurtz hadn't jumped," he finally said.

Brette had been wrestling with that same thought for the last couple of hours. "They aren't like that. Drifters don't care about other people. And I don't mean that in a bad way. They just . . . they are only focused on themselves. That's their biggest problem."

"So, what are you saying, then?"

She had no answer for him. She had no answers for herself. Brette said nothing.

"Let's go back to the ship," Keith said. "You and me. Let's find out who it was you met. You told me before this Drifter was different."

The thought of going back to the *Queen Mary*, exposing herself to the strength and will of that lost soul, filled her with a sense of exhaustion. She hadn't the strength to tangle with that Drifter again.

"I'm tired, Keith."

He laughed lightly. "I don't mean right now. In a couple days. Maybe this weekend."

"No, I mean, I'm tired. I'm tired of it. All of it. I just want to go back to pretending I'm normal."

He squeezed her hand and said nothing. But she heard the echo of her own words and even his unspoken thoughts in her head.

Pretending was no way to live.

Her phone vibrated in her purse. She knew without looking at it that it was Trevor. She reached inside, felt for the button to switch the phone off, and pressed it.

Thirty-seven

※

Annaliese saw no one as she sped along the A-deck corridor, Simone's convincing insults still ringing in her ears. The grand staircase was empty of other people, and only a few lingered on the exterior of the promenade deck as she made her way outside. The closer she got to the stern, the quieter and more isolated her surroundings became. Simone's demand that no one see her had been easy to comply with. She exited the covered promenade deck, opening one of two double doors, and was met with an immediate icy chill. She wrapped her cardigan tighter around her middle and headed for the metal staircase that led to the last visible deck before the hull hit water. The night sky was speckled with starlight and the wake behind the ship sounded like a waterfall. Annaliese hurried to the railing and peeled off her cardigan, a gift from Mama many years ago. Without it, she was immediately freezing. She tied the knitted arms loosely to the railing with numb fingers, looking over her shoulder to make sure no one had emerged onto the deck.

She rose to her feet and for a moment considered what it might be like to actually do what Simone was planning to tell everyone: climb over the railing and jump. She looked out over the railing to the inky water below. The frigid Atlantic was a lacy black swath, glistening here and there as moonlight and starshine touched it.

The velvet blackness seemed welcoming, in a detached kind of way, almost aloof. The water seemed to beckon her with unspoken promises of empty relief and an end to all sensation—good and bad.

It would be so easy to just fall and forget.

Forget what the war had taken, what Rolf had taken, what an icy road had taken when the car Katrine had been driving tumbled end over end into the ditch.

She leaned out farther to gaze at the water's serene beauty, and she sensed a tugging on her torso not to give in to the cold pull of oblivion. Annaliese closed her eyes as a strange strength within urged her to come away from the edge.

She stepped back, numb with cold. Her cardigan on the railing fluttered and waved, bidding her good-bye, it seemed. She turned to look toward the crew door she'd been instructed to go through.

Go, now! the force all around her seemed to say.

Annaliese took one last look at the water and then headed for the door. It opened noisily but there was no one about.

Take the hall to your right and then the first set of stairs you see, Simone had told her, after she'd spoken to Marc and secured his assistance. *Keep going down until you can go no farther. There will be a passageway that leads to storage berths for the kitchen and laundry. Go along the corridor until you see a door marked* Holiday Decorations. *Make sure no one sees you. There will be a torch lying just inside on the floor. Don't turn it on until you've closed the door and then only have it on long enough to find the farthest corner to hide in. Marc will have blankets and a pillow waiting for you there. Don't make a sound, Annaliese. Especially when the ship docks in the morning. It will be quiet belowdecks when the propellers aren't turning and the engines are still. Marc will come to you when he can. Do not leave the room, or you will incriminate us all.*

"When will I get off the ship?" Annaliese had asked.

"You're not getting off the ship. You are going back to England."

Annaliese had stared back at Simone in disbelief.

"Everyone will think you are dead. No one will be expecting to see you in Southampton. Or Paris."

"P-Paris?" Annaliese stammered.

"I know someone in Paris who can help you. Someone who can help you with false identity papers. Her name is Celeste Didion and she helped me when I needed to escape. She will help you. You need to get across the channel and into Paris. If you can do that, you don't ever need to worry about Rolf again. Marc will keep you hidden on the return voyage to England, bring you food, empty your piss pot."

"Empty my . . ." Annaliese had gasped, unable to finish. "I couldn't possibly!"

"Oh, yes, you can. I peed and pooped in a pot for four months when I was stuck in a wine cellar," Simone had replied. "You can manage it for five days. When you get into Southampton, Marc will bring you a maid's uniform and help you get off the ship and onto another one."

"Another one?"

"You need to get to Cherbourg, and you need to get there without a passport. He says he can do it. He has a friend who works on one of Cunard's other ships. When you get off at Cherbourg, you will make your way to Madame Didion in Paris. I am going to send her a telegram when we get to New York, so she will be expecting you." Simone had handed her a slip of paper with an address on it.

"Are you sure she will be willing to help me?" Annaliese had asked as she glanced at the paper and then placed it in her skirt pocket.

"She will if I ask her to."

The two women had been quiet for a moment.

"What if we get caught, Simone?" Annaliese had asked, her gaze on the vast blue sea.

"What if we do?" Simone had shrugged. "What is the worst they can do to us? We shouldn't be seen talking. I'm going to leave now. Don't follow me."

Simone turned to go then, and Annaliese put her hand out and touched Simone's arm.

"I can't thank you enough for what you are risking for me, Simone. I know I don't deserve it."

Simone had smiled faintly. "We don't deserve a lot of the things that happen to us, Annaliese."

Now, as Annaliese made her way down the several flights of stairs, down into the heart of the ship, she wondered if she would ever see Simone Robinson again. It didn't seem likely. The thought filled her with sadness even as she crept down the stairs as quickly and quietly as she could.

She found the closet that had been prepared for her, and the flashlight. She followed the instructions she'd been given, clicking on the light only long enough to find the far corner where a pillow, several wool blankets, and an empty soup pot were waiting for her. The little room was cold but not as freezing as the open deck had been. She wrapped herself in the wool blankets and huddled against a wood crate marked *Garlands and Ornaments*.

She did not think she would be able to sleep for the cold and the fear of being discovered, but the gentle rocking of the ship's belly wooed her to slumber.

ANNALIESE AWOKE WITH A START.

For a moment she couldn't recall why she was immersed in darkness, nor why in the nightmare that had roused her from sleep, Katrine's husband, awash in rage and grief, had been shouting at her. As she rubbed the terrible dream from her eyes she remembered why she was hiding in a closet far below decks, as well as why her mind had conjured the tortured image of John Sawyer: In the frenzy of activity the night before, Annaliese had neglected to tell Simone there was a letter of explanation for John, hidden in the lining of her suitcase.

As this profound disappointment fell across her, Annaliese heard voices in the corridor. The crew was now up and about and talking among themselves as they walked past her door. The voices trailed away save for one.

"You in there. It's me. Marc." The whispered voice floated past the tiny seam of light at the door frame. "Don't come out. Don't make a sound. I'll be back later."

Her arms and legs were stiff and sore but she crawled toward the doorway.

"Am I safe?" she whispered.

"I don't know yet." He started to move away.

"Wait!" she said, as loud as she dared. "Please tell Simone there's a letter in my suitcase for John. She'll know who that is. Please! Tell her she can say that she found it among my things. Please tell her."

"I'll try."

And then the voice was gone. A moment later the great propellers fell silent. The ship had docked and an eerie silence filled the little room.

Annaliese rewrapped herself in the blankets and waited, mentally picturing every dance step for *Swan Lake* to keep her mind occupied in the odd silence.

Then she moved on to *Sleeping Beauty*.

And then *Giselle*.

And then *Romeo and Juliet*.

Sometime later she climbed out of the blankets, stretched her arms and legs, and clicked on the flashlight to use the dreaded soup pot for a toilet. As she settled back into her corner, she noticed a basket behind the crate that she had missed the night before. Inside was a bottle of water, three apples, and a half loaf of bread.

Annaliese clicked off the light, ate an apple, repeated the ballets in her head, and waited.

The account of her suicide must have been believed. If she'd been spotted coming down to the bowels of the ship last night, the harbor police would have already been ushered aboard and the ship searched. But several hours had passed since the propellers went quiet and the ship stopped moving.

Annaliese dozed for a bit.

When she awoke, stiff and numb again, she stood as quietly as she could and exercised her limbs. She ceased when she heard voices in the corridor again. This time, they were close. The storage berths across from her were being loaded with items for the return trip to England. She heard laughter, shouting, the shuffling of feet and boxes and handcart wheels. She caught the faint whiff of cigarette smoke. But no one came near the storage berth for the ship's holiday decorations. After a while the corridor was quiet again. She ate some bread and an apple and used her makeshift toilet.

An hour or so later she heard movement at her door. The knob turned and the door cracked open.

"It's only me," said a whispered voice. The door closed and Marc switched on a flashlight. He had a wool pullover in his arms, some cheese and nuts, and warm coffee in a flask.

"Sorry I can't bring you hot food. The aroma would draw too much attention." He bent down and handed her the food and pullover.

"I can't thank you enough," Annaliese whispered back to him as she took the garment and pulled it over her head.

Marc stood and reached for the soup pot. "I'll take care of this and be right back."

"I am so sorry you have to do that," Annaliese said, feeling her cheeks grow warm despite the cold.

"S'all right."

The young man disappeared and then returned a few minutes later, setting the pot back down. "Need anything else?"

"Maybe a watch or a clock?"

"I'll try to bring you one tomorrow. We are leaving for the return trip in the afternoon. When the engines are running, it won't matter so much if you make a noise. But until then you need to sit tight. Understand?"

She nodded. "Did it work? Does everyone think I am dead?"

He stood. "It worked."

"Thank you, Marc."

"Simone told me you are wanted by the Nazis."

Her heart skipped a beat. She wondered what else Simone had told him. "Yes."

"She told me you swam across a river into Belgium to flee Germany during the war."

"I did."

In the semidarkness she saw him crook an eyebrow. "They're not in power anymore."

Annaliese swallowed a knob of fear. "The one who wants me is."

This seemed to satisfy the young man.

"It takes five days to go back across. It's not safe for you to come out, even at night, to stretch your legs."

"I know. I will be all right."

Marc nodded and then headed for the door. "See you tomorrow."

"Good night, Marc. And thank you."

He opened the door carefully, peeked through the seam of light to make sure the corridor was empty, and then he was gone.

For the next five days and nights the ritual was repeated. Annaliese would spend her awake hours either mentally or physically performing the dance steps she knew. Marc would come each night around midnight—he had found a watch in the lost and found for her to use—and bring her cold leftovers from the evening meal, plus fruit and bread for the next day's breakfast and lunch. She missed the sun and the sensation of light on her face, but with each day that passed she knew she was that much closer to getting to Paris and Simone's Résistance contact.

On the last night before they were to dock at Southampton, Marc brought her a maid's uniform, a woman's coat, and a pair of sunglasses.

"I will come for you when it's safe for you to get off the ship with the rest of the crew. Your eyes won't be used to the sun, so the glasses will help you get off without looking like you've spent the last six days in the dark. My friend's ship leaves for Cherbourg a couple of hours after we dock, so we don't have a lot of time to sneak you aboard his ship. And for God's sake don't say a word to anyone. I'll tell anyone who might see us that you're Danish and you don't know English."

"You could lose your job," Annaliese said as she fingered the maid's uniform. "So could your friend."

"Clive and I spent the war hiding out in bomb shelters with our mothers. We wanted to do more, but no one would let us. This feels like our chance to do something."

The risk the young man was taking was too great for her not to tell him the truth. "I don't know what else Simone told you about me, but I am not a double agent."

Marc shrugged his shoulders. "Are you wanted by a Nazi?"

"You."

"Then don't spoil it for me."

And with that, he turned on his heel and left her again in darkness.

As when they had docked in New York, the moment came when

the engines fell silent and the massive propellers stopped turning. Annaliese rubbed talcum powder over her skin and scalp to rid herself of any body odor from not having bathed in a week. Then she put on the maid's uniform, plaited her dirty hair, and pinned the short braids in a coil around the back of her head.

Soon she heard movement at the door and then Marc's familiar voice.

"Put the sunglasses on. We need to go right now."

Annaliese shoved the glasses onto her face and emerged into the brightly lit corridor. Marc took her arm and hurried her down the hallway and to stairs that led upward.

"Remember. Don't say anything. You sound too much like a German," Marc said.

That is what I am, Annaliese wanted to say.

She kept her head down and the coat tight around her body as she let Marc guide her down unfamiliar passageways and finally to an exit and gangway that was for crew only. They emerged from the ship to gray skies and a sun hidden in a bank of clouds, almost as if it knew Annaliese was not ready for its brilliance. As they walked down the platform among other disembarking crew members, Annaliese turned to take one last look at the *Queen Mary.* The stately ship filled her field of vision, and Annaliese was overcome with a desire to bid farewell to the serene vessel that had saved her.

Her footsteps faltered and Marc tugged on her to keep moving.

"Danke," Annaliese whispered over her shoulder to the ship. She brought her fingers to her lips, kissed them, and blew.

"We have to hurry," Marc said.

Tears of gratitude mixed with sadness rimmed her eyes as Annaliese turned around to face another Cunard ship moored nearby: the one that would take her to France, to Madame Didion.

To freedom.

Thirty-eight

Brette immersed herself in work after returning from New Mexico, and in going to the gym before heading to the hospital each morning, and in making complex meals for dinner each night to distract herself from her warring thoughts. Keith said nothing more about returning with her to the *Queen Mary*, and Trevor's calls and texts finally stopped. Her mother had called the day after she got back, and when Brette told her everything that Simone had said, Nadine had asked Brette what she was going to do next.

"I'm not going to do anything," Brette had answered.

"But you said you thought this situation with the ghost on the ship was tied to your decision about whether to start a family," Nadine had replied.

"I was wrong. It's not tied to anything. I am clearly in over my head. I won't make that mistake again."

She thought her mother would be happy to hear her say that, but Nadine's tone was one of maternal concern when she asked next if Brette wanted to meet for coffee to talk more about it. Brette had told her the last thing she wanted to do was talk more about it. The weariness that had come over her in New Mexico had stayed with her, even as she attempted to distract herself. She told her mother the same thing she had told Keith on the way home from the airport.

She was tired.

While she wanted Keith to just let her slide back into the way things had been before he started talking about having a baby again, she could see that he was tired, too. He was weary of her way of handling what she didn't want to handle. The Sight was pulling on them even when she wasn't using it, and when she mentioned this to Keith the second week after returning from New Mexico—as a way of proving to him it was not something to wish on a daughter—he'd muttered as he left to go on a run that it wasn't the Sight that was yanking them apart.

She watched him jog away from the house that Saturday afternoon, and she lowered herself onto the couch, her heart heavy. He was blaming *her* for the tension between them, not her bizarre ability. She could almost hear his voice in the room telling her that you don't deal with something by pretending it doesn't exist. Her phone rang then and she slowly rose from the couch to retrieve it.

Nadine was calling. She hesitated and then tapped the icon to answer. "Hi, Mom."

"Are you doing anything right now?"

"What? Why?"

"There's someone here at the inn who wants to talk to you."

Brette raked her fingers through her hair. "I don't want to talk to Trevor. I can't help him. I can't—"

"It's not Trevor who's here. It's Maura."

"Maura."

"Lucille's daughter."

For a second Brette was at a loss for words. "She's there? At Willow House?" she finally said.

"Yes. And she'd really like to see you."

"How in the world . . . ?"

"She's living in Mexico now. In Baja. I flew her up so you could talk to her. I really think you should come over."

For years Brette had wanted to have a family member to talk with about the Sight. The opportunity was suddenly right in front of her and she felt more alarm than excitement. What if she was to learn there was no way of coming out on top, of being in charge of the Sight instead of being mastered by it? What if Maura told her the best she could hope for was that it didn't drive her mad?

"I don't know . . ." Brette began, but the sentence fell away half-spoken.

"Please come talk to her."

She agreed, left a note for Keith, and grabbed her purse and keys. Twenty minutes later, she arrived at Willow House as the sun was inching toward the horizon and the Pacific. Her father had told her once that if she caught the sun setting over the ocean, at just the right moment, there was a green flash that lit the horizon for a fraction of a second. She'd watched the sun set over the sea a thousand times growing up, looking for the green flash, and had never seen it. But her gaze was drawn westward even as she walked up the path to the front door, as if she still believed it could happen at any moment.

Brette stepped inside, past the main room and lobby, and headed toward the kitchen, where she heard voices. As she rounded the corner she saw her mother standing near the stove and pouring from a teakettle into a cup. A few feet away stood a woman who seemed about Nadine's age, perhaps a little younger. Her graying hair, still mostly brown, was long and frizzy and held back from her face by a tattered scarf wound across her head like a gypsy might wear it. Her skin was wrinkled and brown and sun-kissed, and she wore a denim skirt, a man's button-down dress shirt tied at her slim waist, and a fringed vest that looked like it had come straight off a 1970s movie set.

"Brette! You're here." Her mother set the kettle down and turned to the stranger in the kitchen. "This is Maura."

"Hello." Maura stepped forward with her hand outstretched. Silver and turquoise bracelets jangled on her wrist.

"Hi." Brette shook her hand.

"I was just getting Maura caught up on the family," Nadine said cheerfully, as if Maura had just been out of touch for a few months instead of three decades. She handed Maura the mug. "Cream or sugar?"

"This is fine. Thanks." Maura took the cup but directed her attention back to Brette, looking deep into her eyes.

Brette found herself wanting to look away.

"Maura and her husband, José, own a vineyard in Baja," Nadine said cheerfully, as though the three of them were neighbors on a cul-de-sac meeting each other for the first time.

"Where can Brette and I talk?" Maura said to Nadine, apparently uninterested in small talk.

"Oh. Well, there's the back porch there," Nadine answered, her brow crooked a tad. Clearly Maura wanted to talk to Brette alone.

"Is it private?"

"Guests don't have access to it."

Maura turned to Nadine. "And what about moms and dads?"

Nadine smiled weakly. "I can go find something to do."

Maura smiled back. She motioned to the back door. "After you, Brette."

They made their way to the porch and Maura closed the door behind them so that it latched. They took seats on two cushioned chairs with a wooden table between them. Just past the wooden railing ahead of them was a bit of rocky ledge, then a drop, then sand, and then the lacy surf.

Maura looked about the railings and slats as if she had lost something. "Who comes here?"

"Beg your pardon?" Brette said.

Maura turned her head to face her. "It's a woman, isn't it? She's been here a long time. But she knows you don't like her."

Brette's mouth dropped open.

"She's still here but she hides when you come."

"I never said I didn't like her!" Brette managed to say.

"Just because you didn't say it doesn't mean it's not true. She knows you don't."

"Aunt Ellen told me not—"

"Yes, yes, I can quite imagine what Auntie Ellen told you. And how'd that work out for you? Life's been a breeze, has it? Is that why your mother searched the globe for me, bought me a plane ticket to come here when I've heard nothing from anyone in the family for God knows how long?"

"I . . ." But Brette had no response at the ready.

"What is it about the Sight you want to know?" Maura's gaze on her was compassionate and yet perturbed, as if she was both happy and annoyed to have been asked to come to Brette's rescue.

"What has my mom told you about me?" Brette asked.

Maura took a sip of her tea and then set the cup down on the little table. "Everything."

"Everything?"

"She told me you saw your first ghost here at this house when Ellen was visiting, that Ellen told you they would ruin your life if you paid any attention to them, that there was nothing you could do for them anyway and the best you could do was pretend you didn't see them. She told me that you've pretty much lived your life as though you didn't have the Sight, but now your husband wants to start a family and you're afraid you'll pass it on to a girl. And on top of that, you tried to do a favor for a friend by scouting out a ghost on the *Queen Mary* but ended up meeting an entirely differ-ent ghost who latched on to you but you've no idea what it wants or even who it is. You've had no one to talk to about the Sight and you feel like you're doomed to an existence of toil and trouble with no one to show you how to take control of your life. Do I have that about right?"

Brette frowned. "More or less."

"And what do you know about me?" The woman relaxed back in her chair as if calmly ready for whatever Brette would say.

"Only what my mother told me a couple of days ago when I found out about you. You are like your mother. Aunt Ellen told my mom you indulged in the Sight."

Maura tossed her head back and laughed. "Indulged!? That's good. I haven't heard that one. Tell me, what do you think it means to indulge in the Sight?"

Brette shrugged her shoulders. "I don't know. You actively use it. You spend a lot of time with the Drifters."

"Drifters? Is that what you call them?"

"That's what Aunt Ellen called them. She said your mother had to be institutionalized because of how much time she spent actively using the Sight." Brette sheepishly added, "She thought you were headed for the same fate."

"And that you would be, too, if you *indulged* in the Sight?"

"Yes."

"First off, my mother was an alcoholic and a drug addict, and on top of that she had a mental illness," Maura said. "Having the Sight didn't make her crazy and it didn't kill her. My mother's lifestyle choices destroyed her body, and the mental illness is what put her in that institution. Second, it is not an indulgence to use the abilities you've been given. You can misuse or abuse an ability by being stupid with it, but it's not a mistake to make use of a skill when you clearly have it."

"But it doesn't feel like an ability. It feels like a curse. I don't understand it."

Maura laughed lightly. "Whose fault is that? You don't understand it because you ignore it. Treat a gift like a curse and of course it's going to make you miserable. Why do you think you've been given eyes to see the space in between this life and the next?"

Brette had never known the answer to that question. "I don't know."

"Why do you think heaven allows some souls to hang back when their mortal lives end? Why do you think there's a place in the in-between where they can do that? Haven't you ever wondered these things?"

"I didn't know where to go for the answers!"

Maura sat forward in her chair. "Okay. Look. Some answers in life you can certainly find by asking. Some you find only by searching. Those answers come when you look for them, not when you ask for them. You haven't even looked."

"That's not true. In college, I tried to be more active. I tried—"

Maura threw up a hand to silence her. "Your mother told me what happened to you in college. That was not you looking for answers, that was you being stupid. You were looking for affirmation among your peers by messing about with Ouija boards and ghost hunting. You of all people should've known the spiritual realm isn't populated solely by earthbound souls. That was a foolish thing to do. Do you really think that's what I am talking about?"

Anger and frustration boiled up inside Brette. But so did a spurt of hope. "I don't know how to control it, Maura. I want to, I really do. I'm tired of pretending this isn't who I am, but I don't know what to do. I can't give this to a child! How can I?"

Maura was quiet for a moment. "Control, then. Is that what you want?"

Brette nodded as she flicked away tears that had sprung to her eyes.

"Well, no wonder you're so unhappy and unsure. Control is an illusion. No one has it. I don't even have it. You can't wish for control; you can only learn to play your part in a world where nothing is truly certain. And you do have a part to play. Do you really think that if you didn't have the Sight you could guarantee yourself a perfect child with no flaw or defect, or that you will be the perfect parent? No one has the control you say you want with regard to having a child. People who decide to bring children into this imperfect world take the same chance as you do every day. They always have. And who's to say our world isn't made the richer by having people within it who are less or more than normal—whatever normal is. You've been given an ability few people have, and you've done nothing but ignore it and complain about it. There are a great many people in this world who would give anything to know this life isn't all there is. You and I know without a shadow of a doubt that there's more, that we aren't just a twinkling light in the universe one moment and then nothing the next."

Brette turned her head to face the water and the pearl horizon. The flaming sun was sinking low into the line of separation between water and firmament. In another moment it would disappear. If she blinked, she'd miss the snatch of time that the green flash might electrify the sky, for just that breath of a second. She closed her eyes to hold on to the hope that it wasn't just a legend. When she opened them, the orange orb was gone and only a subtly glowing shadow marked the spot where it had been. She turned to Maura.

"I don't know where to begin to do what you are suggesting," she said.

"Begin by letting go, Brette. Ellen was afraid her whole life. She was the one whose life was ruined by spending too much time thinking about the Sight. She never married, never had children. She lived a life of fear. She was so afraid of what the Sight might do to her that she never stopped to consider what she might do with it."

"But I don't want to live my life half in this world and half in the next."

Maura reached across the little table and squeezed one of Brette's hands. "That is not what I am telling you to do! I am not telling you to rush after every Drifter you see to ask them what they want. I am suggesting that you keep your eyes and hands and heart open to what God might bring your way. A baby, a fuller life, a lost soul now and then who needs a word of encouragement. You and I can offer it in a way few others can."

Brette had never thought of herself as having anything remarkable to offer the world. "There's a woman in New Mexico who thinks I'm a fraud."

"So do you spend much time worrying about what other people think?"

Brette smiled. It felt good. "You make all of this sound easy."

"It is much harder to pretend than it is to simply be who you already are."

The two women were quiet for a moment.

"There's a Drifter on the *Queen Mary* who I was sure was the ghost of a woman who died falling overboard a long time ago. But it's not. I don't know who it is or what she wants. She won't show herself. But she wants something of me."

Maura said nothing for a moment; she seemed deep in thought. "How do you know it's a woman, then?"

There was no doubt in Brette's mind that the Drifter was a woman. "I just do."

"Well, I've never known a Drifter to stay hidden when it wants something. That's very interesting, actually. I'm pretty sure you can guess what I would do."

"You'd go back to the ship and ask."

"Here's the thing, Brette. Most of us don't ask the right questions. And I don't mean just people with an ability like ours, I mean in general. You're probably thinking you need to ask that Drifter what she wants, but the question really is not what she wants but why has she stayed behind?"

Brette thought for a moment. "I'm not sure that she knows why."

"And that is precisely why you might be the one to perform a great act of kindness by figuring that out."

"Is that what you do? Do you help them figure out why they've stayed behind?"

"I've always believed if it was in my power to help someone out, it was wrong of me to stand by and do nothing."

"But how? How do you help them? They never want to listen."

Maura picked up her teacup. "It's you who needs to listen." She took a sip. "Your Drifters, as you call them, don't want advice. They don't want someone to tell them they don't belong here. They truly already know that. When you are afraid to do something, the last thing you want is someone telling you to stop being afraid and just do it already. Certainly you can relate to that."

"Yes," Brette murmured. So many questions she'd had for the last twenty-five years seemed to be finding their answers.

"My mother exploited them, Ellen ignored them, and your grandmother tried to tell them what to do. All I've done is listen to them. I know what fear is like, especially when you feel like you're all alone with it. What the lost souls lack most is validation, not courage. You'd be surprised how brave you can become when someone simply affirms that what you are feeling is real."

Images of the Drifters she'd come into contact with in recent days came to her mind. The mother at the baby shower. The man with the beard on the walk with Keith. The young woman in white on the ship's bridge. Brette had not considered for a moment offering empathy. A ribbon of regret twirled about her mind. "When you listen, do they cross over, then?"

"Sometimes. They don't haunt my every step if I show them compassion, if that's what you're afraid of. They usually move on in one way or another."

The gathering twilight was turning the sky a sleepy shade of violet. "I need to go back to that ship," Brette said. "If I go tomorrow, will you come with me?"

Maura set her teacup down on the table between them. "Absolutely not."

"Why?"

"This is how you begin to learn how to be you. And just because she appeared to you doesn't mean she would appear to me. You need to go alone."

"But Keith said he'd come with me. He wants to come with me."

"That's very nice of him. But not a good idea. Have him wait in the parking lot if he insists on driving up with you. I doubt this Drifter will seek you out the way she did the first time if you aren't alone. Be a shame to drive all the way up there for nothing."

"I suppose." Brette thought for a moment. "I'm not sure what to do when I get there. This Drifter doesn't actually speak. I'm not sure how to listen to her."

Maura again seemed to find this detail perplexing. "Is it true the ship is full of lost souls?"

"I saw several. One spoke to me. I don't know how many there are, probably not as many as ghost hunters would have us believe. But yes, the ship seems to be a thin place where Drifters filter in and then stay."

"And the one that you saw that did speak to you. What did she say?"

"I asked her why she and so many others were on the ship. This was when I was still looking for my friend's wife. She told me, 'She lets us stay.'"

"'*She* lets us stay'?" Maura echoed. "Who is this 'she'?"

"I've no idea."

"You might want to think about who that 'she' is. I would imagine she is the one who sought you out. Think about it, Brette. Why
would this ghost care about the supposed drowning of someone
else?"

"I don't know," Brette said quickly.

"No, no," Maura said. "Your problem is you want the answer as
soon as you pose the question. Think about it. Why does this ghost
care about that other woman? There has to be a reason."

Brette had no idea how to tackle that question. "What if I can't
figure it out?"

"I don't think that question matters until you've tried."

"They don't usually care about anyone but themselves . . ." Brette
said, partly to herself and partly to Maura.

Maura stood and started to head back inside.

"Wait! I'm only just starting to get this!" Brette said.

Maura half-turned. "We've a lifetime left to us to get to know
one another better, Brette. Anyway, this bit with you and the ghost
on the ship, it's not my nut to crack. It's yours. And your mother
promised me your grandmother's stroganoff for dinner."

Brette rose to follow her.

Nadine asked Brette to stay for dinner, but she wanted time to
think. She knew she'd be going back up to the *Queen* the next day.
She needed to do some pondering.

"You're not returning to Mexico right away, are you?" Brette
asked as she fished her car keys out of her purse.

"Your mom has given me the nicest room in the inn and a return
flight for Friday if I'm agreeable to a little vacation. I think I am.
José and the vines can manage for a few days without me." Maura
turned to Nadine. "And it's nice to be with family again. I'd forgotten just how nice."

"I'm sorry about all the lost years," Nadine said.

Maura waved a hand to dispel the regret. "Years are never lost. You and I know exactly where they are. I'll walk you to the door, Brette."

The two women made their way to the front entry. "I know you think you're not up to this tomorrow, but it's always better to feel a little underequipped than to go into a situation thinking you know it all," Maura said.

"I'm so glad you came," Brette replied. "I can't begin to tell you how much."

"Your mother was insistent that I come. I honestly thought I was done with everything having to do with this family. I haven't been back to the States in five years. But your mother wouldn't take no for an answer. That's mother-love for you. Even my mom, with all her problems, loved me. She would've walked through fire for me."

"Did you ever . . . did you think about having children?"

"I thought about it all the time. I wanted them, Brette. I would have had ten were it up to me. But I only ever had miscarriages."

Brette heard the sorrow in Maura's words. And a silent admonition not to let fear rob her of a full life. "I'd like to stop by the inn tomorrow on my way home from the *Queen Mary*. You'll be here, won't you?"

Maura assured her she would.

Thirty-nine

A cloudless, Tiffany-blue sky canopied the Long Beach harbor as Brette and Keith drove into the *Queen Mary*'s parking lot. As Keith switched off the ignition, Brette turned to look at the ocean liner's black, white, and red length ahead of them as the vessel sat at the dock, her prow pointed toward the open sea.

"You still want to go on deck alone?" Keith asked.

"Just until this Drifter and I have a chance to connect. I will know better after we've had a little time together if I can text you to buy a ticket and come on up."

Keith exhaled a breath of mild disappointment. "You are quite sure this . . . ghost can't hurt you?"

Brette curled her fingers on the door handle, eager to step on the gangway now. "She's not like that."

"But you don't even know who it is."

Brette could not explain how she knew the Drifter she was hoping to reunite with would never hurt her. "I'll be fine. Keep your phone close. I will text you the minute I think it's okay for you to come." She leaned toward him to kiss him on the cheek.

"This is a good idea, right?" he said.

"Of course."

Keith cupped her chin in his hand. "You just look tired, Brette. I mean, you're beautiful as always, but you look tired."

She knew she did. "I know. I think this might be the beginning of me finally figuring it all out. Not just for me, but for us, too. I'll be all right."

She stepped out of the car into the midmorning sunshine and began to walk to the dock. Brette had told Keith everything Maura had said when she got back to the condo the evening before, including the shift she was feeling inside about having a baby. Today was the start of letting go of fear and grasping instead the strings of hope. But it had been an arduous journey to this point. And she hadn't slept well.

She'd spent hours on the Internet, scouring online articles and blog posts about the inexplicable way the past clung to the *Queen Mary*. She'd made notes of what she had learned about the ship and the people who had been a part of its history, and everything she'd read or been told about the 1946 war brides. She refamiliarized herself with the ship's storied lifespan as a luxury liner, a warship, a transport for immigrant brides and their children, and a floating hotel, so that she could imagine every kind of passenger or crew member or guest who would have walked its decks. She went over every minute of her first trip to the ship—every pressing touch, every swirling presence, every ardent nudge.

As she lay in bed in the deepest hours of the night, an idea came to her, unthinkable at first, but the more she pondered it, the less impossible it seemed. When she awoke that morning, with the outlandish notion still spinning about her and gathering strength, she thought for a moment of calling the B and B and asking Maura what she thought.

But no. This was her grand moment of making peace with the skill that had been woven into her being. Maura would tell her as much. This was to be her discovery and no one else's.

She didn't even tell Keith what she was going to do when she got on deck. First she would need to reconnect with the Drifter who had met her the first time and tell it she knew Annaliese was alive. Then she needed to find the Drifter on the bridge who had spoken to her and ask her another question.

She knew what she would do next, assuming she was right. She could only hope it was the right course of action. It seemed like it was. Maura had said earthbound souls hunger to be understood.

Brette paid for her pass onto the ship and then made her way to the entrance and the elevator that would take her to the main gangway. Her heart was pounding in her chest. She stepped off the elevator and let the other ticket holder who'd ridden with her walk ahead so that she could step onto the burnished deck of the promenade alone.

She closed the distance from current-day concrete to weathered wood and stepped over the seam, taking a few steps to the right so that she wasn't blocking anyone's way but so that she could stand still and wait if she had to. Brette had no sooner made this adjustment when the hairs on the back of her neck and on her arms were suddenly charged with electricity. A gust of energized air swirled about her, and Brette felt the unmistakable pulse of welcome. A guest walking by put a hand to his fedora to keep it from being tugged off.

"I've come back," Brette whispered.

The warm presence pulled her away from the windows and toward the length of the promenade as if it wanted to take her down to the stern.

"I have news for you," Brette murmured as she responded to the gentle tugging and moved forward. She was being led to the back of the ship. "I know Annaliese is alive."

But the drifting presence pulled Brette along and out to the outside and the white metal steps that would lead to the isolation wards and the placard that bore Annaliese Kurtz's name.

"She's not dead!" Brette muttered, mindful of other guests and not wanting to attract attention.

Still the ghost led her down to the old sick bay and the corner room where the list of the dead hung in quiet testament to the frailty of the human body.

Annaliese Kurtz, suicide, February 1946

"She's alive," Brette said. "Surely you must know that!"

The ghost seemed to hover suspended between the poster and Brette, between the words on the placard and Brette's words.

"I don't know what it is you want. Annaliese isn't dead. You have to know she walked off the ship. And I don't know what was in that little cabinet in the stateroom. Whatever it was is long gone. I'm sorry I can't tell you more, but I can assure you Annaliese is still alive. She's fine."

Still the ghost hovered, as though Brette were the one who lacked understanding.

She had to talk to the Drifter on the bridge, and she could only hope that she wouldn't meet with resistance.

"I need to ask someone a question," Brette whispered. "It's important."

She turned to go and felt nothing barring her way. She sped out of the isolation ward, ascended the steps, and made her way back to the promenade deck. Minutes later, after covering the length of the ship and climbing more stairs, she was inside the captain's bridge. Guests taking the self-guided tour were listening to headsets and taking pictures. No one seemed to care that Brette was looking about the room as if she'd lost something.

The Drifter from before was nowhere in sight.

"Please, please, please," Brette mumbled to the air around her.

She stepped out onto the other side and scanned the length of the ship as far as she could see. Only other mortals were milling about. She hadn't wanted to spend an hour or two combing the decks looking for the ghost of the young woman, but it seemed like that was to be her only option. Brette turned to head back into the bridge and nearly ran into the Drifter with the flowing gown. She was perched on the stanchion that kept guests from messing with the ancient navigational instruments.

"Please just stay a moment," Brette whispered in the Drifter's direction as a couple of tourists snapped a few pictures and then turned to go. When the bridge was empty, Brette turned to the Drifter to quickly ask her question. She was fairly sure she now knew who the young woman had meant when she'd said the time before, *She lets us come*. What Brette wanted to know was why.

"Please," Brette murmured to the apparition of the young woman, who was staring at her. Time was of no consequence to the Drifters. She knew she could continue their conversation as if none had passed. "You said to me last time I saw you, 'She lets us come.' Why does she let you come here? I need to know."

The Drifter cocked her head, as if to indicate the answer was obvious. She started to float away.

"Please tell me!" Brette pleaded. "Why does she let you come?"

She loves us, the ghost said, and she glided away as if on a breeze.

Clarity fell across Brette in a rushing wave.

It all made sense. All of it.

She knew why the ghost that had first found her didn't speak or take bodily form. She knew why she'd been certain this ghost would never harm her. She knew why Trevor's daughter thought Laura was on the *Queen Mary*.

She knew why Annaliese's name had to come off that placard.

This ghost was a parent who'd lovingly tended those in her embrace and found great purpose in her life as a provider. The lives of those for whom she was responsible had mattered a great deal. She'd been stripped of that role when her life was taken from her in 1967.

The ghost was a caregiver.

The ghost was a mother.

This ghost was the ship.

"I know who you are," Brette murmured to the air around her, and she felt a soft breeze swirl about her body. "You didn't lose Annaliese Kurtz. You saw her safely home, didn't you? She's safely home. You made that happen. I understand now. And I understand what you did for my little friend Emily."

The breeze ruffled her collar as if to ask a question.

"I'll find a way to get Annaliese's name off that list," Brette said. "But I need to do something else first. And then I will come back. Not today. I need to get proof and it may take a while. But I will be back someday. I promise."

She pulled out her cell phone and texted Keith.

I'm coming back out. We need to go.

Everything okay?

Yes.

Then she texted Trevor.

Are you still in Los Angeles? Can I come over? There's something I need to tell Emily.

His answer was swift. Can you help her?

I think I can, she wrote.

BRETTE SAT ON A PAISLEY-UPHOLSTERED COUCH NEAR A PICTURE window that looked out on a manicured backyard lawn and rows of hummingbird feeders hanging from a patio cover. Emily Prescott sat next to her. Trevor sat on an armchair on the other side of the sofa, and Keith and Trevor's mother were standing just off to the side. Trevor's mother looked pensive, unsure, and ready to jump between Brette and her granddaughter at a second's notice.

"I'm sorry I didn't come sooner. I know this has been hard for you," Brette said to the little girl. "But I didn't really understand what had happened to you until today."

"I know what I felt and heard," Emily said, clearly ready to defend her belief that the ghost of her dead mother had embraced her on the *Queen Mary*.

"I believe you. I know what it's like to know something is real when no one else believes it is."

Trevor shifted in his chair. Brette looked up at him, admonishing him with her eyes to say nothing.

"Can you really see ghosts?" Emily said, curiosity deflating some of her defensive tone.

"I can. But they're not as scary as most people think."

"I know that."

Brette pondered for a moment what to say next. "Not everyone who dies stays here as a ghost afterward. Most don't, actually. The ones that stay behind are usually afraid to move on. They need a little time to get used to the idea that they don't belong in this world anymore. They drift around while they figure things out. That's why I call them Drifters."

Emily blinked and said nothing.

"You see, Emily, there are places where the space between our world and the one we go to after we die is thin. Drifters hang out in those places. And it's these thin places that I can see. I can't see heaven or the angels or other people who have died. Only Drifters in a thin place. Do you understand?"

Emily furrowed her brow and nodded.

Brette leaned forward and took Emily's hands in her own. "The *Queen Mary* is a very special ship. Ships aren't just made of steel and wood. Captains and sailors know this; they've always known this. For a long time, the *Queen Mary* carried people across the wide ocean, sometimes in stormy weather, sometimes during wartime. She was like a mother, carrying everyone to safety, you see? But she doesn't sail anymore. That purpose was taken from her. That was her life, and this is why she still has the heart of a parent. She still longs to be a mother. That's why you felt her hugging you when you were there."

"It was my mommy," Emily said, a silvery line of tears appearing in her eyes.

"I know you miss your mom, Emily. You were given a touch of mother-love on that ship because you needed it so very much. We all do at times."

"But it was her!"

"I'm not a mom yet, but I very much hope someday that I will be. I don't know everything about moms and their little girls, but I do know that love is always what you get to keep when someone you care about dies. You will always have that love, Emily. And sometimes something will happen that will remind you of it. Maybe the next time it won't happen on a ship. Maybe it will be when you smell your mom's perfume on someone, or when you eat something she used to make for you, or when you hear her voice in your dreams. And for a moment it will be like she's there, because in a way, she is. The love is still there. It always will be."

Two tears slid down Emily's face. "She's not on the ship?"

Brette shook her head.

"I was afraid for her there," Emily whispered, a sob warbling her words. "It's not home. I didn't want her to be stuck there."

"She's not."

Brette instinctively held out her arms and Emily fell into her embrace. She held the little girl, stroked her hair, and whispered that everything would be all right in time.

BRETTE AND KEITH HEADED HOME AFTER HAVING DINNER WITH Trevor and his family. On the way back down the coast, Keith asked what Brette was supposed to do with the knowledge that the placard in the isolation ward was wrong.

"I don't know how I'm going to do it, but I've got to find a way to get that name off there," she answered. "I think it bothers the ship that that placard bears the name of someone who supposedly died on her watch who's actually still alive. Annaliese Kurtz isn't one of those lost at sea. The *Queen* saw her safely home."

Keith shook his head. "You'll pardon me if I don't jump on the wagon of people who think inanimate objects can think and hear and see. No offense, Brette, but that's just bizarre."

"I know it is. But just think, Keith. You men of science discover new things all the time. I think it's amazing that a ship can feel like a person who cares about you. Phoebe said as much about the *Queen Mary* when I talked to her on the phone. And I've read that ships often come across to people as having hearts and souls. It explains perfectly why this ship lets the Drifters come. She sees them as anxious travelers who want safe passage to the next place but are afraid to let go. Letting them come aboard and stay as long as they want is exactly what a loving mother would do."

He smiled then, reached across the seat, and took her hand. "You seem to know a lot about mothers these days."

She smiled back. "I'm learning."

They rode for a few minutes in easy silence. Brette tipped her head back to the headrest to contemplate how she was going to persuade the City of Long Beach to correct the placard in the old isolation ward on the *Queen Mary*. Proving that Annaliese Kurtz hadn't jumped was going to be difficult without Simone Robinson's help. And yet she had no doubt the spirit of the ship, moored to the glory of its past and yet hollowed of its original purpose, wanted the world to know this one had not been lost. Not this one. As Brette pondered how she might convince the *Queen Mary*'s owners that there was a mistake on the list of the dead, her eyelids grew heavy. Perhaps Simone could be persuaded some other way to tell her the truth. Perhaps there was a way to convince the old woman that the vessel that had carried her to America so long ago was no ordinary ship. Perhaps . . .

The tiredness she'd been battling the last couple weeks—a subtle sign of a pregnant woman's first trimester—caught up with her gently, ushering her into a dreamless slumber.

RMS *QUEEN MARY*

LONG BEACH, CALIFORNIA

MAY 1969

I don't know what is happening.

I am afraid.

I am being emptied of myself.

The boiler rooms are gone, and the forward engine room, both the generator rooms, the stabilizers. All but one of the propellers. The empty fuel tanks have been filled with mud to keep our center of gravity. Only the aft engine room at the stern remains.

The heart of me has been torn out. I am sinking but not sinking. The sea surrounds me as always but it is as if I have ceased to exist.

I am dying.

I am dying and I am afraid.

What will become of me? What will become of me!

I hear the others, calling out to me from the mist of my agony.

You are one of us now, *they say.* Stay.

But I only know how to carry my passengers to safe shores. This is all I know. I am nothing now. I am nothing.

You are as you have ever been, *the others tell me.*

And at the moment of my deepest despair I realize they are right. I am still a vessel. Still.

I can still bear travelers of another kind to safe shores. I can still do that.

I am empty.

An empty vessel.

Come to me.

Forty

※

The elderly woman folded the letter from America and put it back in its envelope, fingering the lacy script of the return address. She let the letter drop onto the table in front of her. It landed in a band of sunlight cast by a low-lying afternoon sun slanting inward from an open window.

"Will this paper do, Maman?"

The woman turned toward the voice. Her daughter, Giselle, was coming toward her with a notepad and pen.

"I thought I had some stationery in the bottom of the drawer of the desk. But I don't," Giselle continued. "And we haven't unpacked your boxes yet."

"That will be fine. Thank you, dear." The woman took the paper and pen.

"So. A letter from America! How mysterious." Giselle took her mother's teacup to freshen it. "Wouldn't Papa have been jealous!"

The old woman laughed lightly. Sébastien had never been one to get jealous. *Jealousy is weakness,* he'd been fond of saying in his younger years. *When you want something you don't have, you work to get it, it's that simple. And if it's yours already, you work to keep it.* They had worked hard, she and he, for the life they had carved out for themselves, their children, and grandchildren. It had been a good life, a better life than she had ever dreamed could be hers. And now she was old and in need of care and the little chateau that had been their home was up for sale and she had moved in with Giselle and Pierre.

"I doubt he would have been jealous about a letter from a woman in America," the old woman said.

"So who's it from?"

The old woman cast a glance at the envelope, golden and warm in the sunlight. "From a very old friend."

"Who?"

The old woman looked up at her daughter. "I'll tell you in a bit. But first I need to write the letter."

Giselle smiled wide. "You are more mysterious by the minute, Maman. What's this all about?"

She nodded and raised one finger upward. "In a moment. I want to write the letter first."

Giselle looked at the envelope on the table. "You're writing back to this Simone Robinson from America?"

"No. Not yet. I need to write to someone else first. I need you to stay and help me with the English, though. And then I will tell you."

"Tell me what?" Giselle laughed.

"Everything."

October 11, 2016

Dear Mrs. Caslake,

My name is Anna Maillard but you know me as Annaliese Kurtz. I am writing to you because my dear friend Simone told me your very amazing story and I am much intrigued. She does not believe your story, but I want you to know that I do.

She thinks you are hoping to get money from me by threatening to take my story public, but I have realized I don't care if the world knows what happened the night everyone thinks I died. In fact, as I feel my mortal life slipping away, perhaps it would be a good thing to lay it all out in the open. In any case, you can lay to rest any notion that you are crazy. You are right, obviously. I did not jump. What Simone told you is true. She helped me escape, but not inside America. She told me you spoke to Phoebe, too. But we couldn't tell Phoebe what we were doing because she wouldn't have been able to keep the secret, God love her.

I went back to England on the Queen Mary. *I hid for six days in a decorations closet. A steward on the ship who was sympathetic to my plight brought me food and water and helped to smuggle me onto another ship, this one bound for Cherbourg.*

From there, I traveled to Paris, where I met up with the woman who had helped Simone escape after her father and brother were executed by the Gestapo. I ended up at the same vineyard in the south of France where Simone had hidden during the last months of the war, and where she met the American pilot whom she later married. I was given new identity papers and worked hard to scrub my voice of its German accent. I worked for the vintner and I took care of his and his wife's children. A year later, I fell in love and married one of the men who had also been in the Résistance during the war. Sébastien was a friend of Simone's, in a manner of speaking, and while we didn't write to each other very often, Simone found it entertaining that I married him. He was a mechanic, and I taught dance to the little girls in the village. God gave us three beautiful daughters. My beloved Sébastien passed away some years ago and I now live with one of our daughters and her husband. The others and our grandchildren and great-grandchildren are here and there. The closest is down the lane, the farthest is in Prague.

I rarely think of the girl I was before the war, and even less of the girl I was during it. The woman whose name is on that list on the Queen Mary *no longer exists, except in the thinnest of memories. I was her once, but so long ago; she is more phantom to me than anything else.*

So there you have it. You are right.

I trust this letter brings you satisfaction. I truly do not care to whom you show it. If you step aboard the Queen Mary *again anytime soon, throw her a kiss. She was a good ship to me.*

Regards,
Anna Maillard

P.S. I know you are telling the truth about having been told by some kind of apparition that I did not jump. The old passenger manifests have me listed in a cabin on B deck. But your ghost took you to the room I really stayed in, A-152. I had switched rooms the day we boarded the ship in Southampton. Now about that little cabinet. I left the ship thinking the husband of my dear friend Katrine would never know why I had left her the way I did, dead in that car. A letter I had written for him had been in the lining of my suitcase, which was in that cupboard. It was most distressing to me that he would never get it. But Madame Didion in Paris wrote to Simone at my request and asked her to contact John and tell him that before I died, I'd told her I had been heartbroken when Katrine was taken from me and was very sorry for his loss. She told him there had been a note for him from me, but after my suicide it had been lost. Simone told me some time later by letter that he not only got the message but eventually fell in love and married again. So you see? Tell your little ghost all is well. This is how it is for all of us. Life will send us across a bridge we did not want to cross, but when we finally open our eyes on the other side, we see that there had been nothing to fear after all.

Acknowledgments

It is always the insights and contributions of other people that enable me to carve out a novel from the rock of an idea. I am beyond grateful to the following individuals:

June Allen, a British war bride who crossed the Atlantic on the RMS *Queen Mary* in February 1946, thank you for the hourlong phone calls, the messages, the letters, the sharing of your life and heart with me, the lovely lunch on the *Queen Mary*. There would be no book without you. I am so glad researching this story led to the genesis of our friendship.

To my editors, Claire Zion and Jackie Cantor, thank you for loving this story and trusting me with the telling of it. I am also so very grateful to Berkley's Ivan Held, Craig Burke, and Danielle Dill for much support and enthusiasm, and the amazing art department for such a hauntingly beautiful cover.

Elisabeth Weed, literary agent extraordinaire, there aren't enough words to express my gratitude for who you are and what you mean to me. Thanks for being my champion.

To all my colleagues and friends who answered my question, "Do you believe in ghosts?" I am indebted to you for your candid answers. Thank you for sharing your personal experiences regarding the unexplainable. You made my fictional ponderings all the richer.

To Kendra Harpster, your insights on that first early draft were invaluable to me. You are a gem.

Thanks to Elizabeth Musser and Karen Mesch Cassidy for the

foreign-language assistance; and to my mother, Judy Horning, for the expert proofreading; and to Michele Thomas for her excellent website, uswarbrides.com.

Rene Gutteridge, fellow author and friend, that lovely chat we had while walking in a forest of redwoods changed the course of this story. You began a sentence with "What if," and what you said next made me itch to run home and write this book. I owe you one.

Lastly, I am grateful to God, who has assured me beyond all doubt that this life on earth is not all there is.

A BRIDGE ACROSS the OCEAN

Susan Meissner

1. *A Bridge Across the Ocean* opens with a spectral encounter aboard the RMS *Queen Mary* on the first day of her maiden voyage, followed by Brette's unwanted meeting with a ghost in the present day at a baby shower. What was your initial reaction to these two scenes? Have you ever experienced something that had no earthly explanation? If you had Brette's strange ability, what do you think you would do with it?

2. Which of the three war brides—Annaliese, Simone, or Phoebe—did you most connect with emotionally? Why?

3. Talk for a moment about the friendship between Annaliese and Katrine. What do you think drew them together? Have you ever had or do you have a friend like these two had in each other? What do you think Katrine would have thought of Annaliese's decision to board the *Queen Mary* the way that she did?

4. Would you have made all the same life-changing choices that Simone and Annaliese made?

5. When Katrine falls in love with John, Annaliese remarks that they've only known each other a short while. Katrine says that it seems like longer, "as if to suggest Annaliese surely knew that love didn't take

note of calendar pages." Do agree or can you relate? Why do you think Simone and Everett also fell in love over a stretch of just weeks?

6. Early in the book, Aunt Ellen tells Brette that the Drifters are "afraid of what they can't see, just like us. It's as if there's a bridge they need to cross. And it's like crossing over the ocean, Brette. They can't see the other side. So they are afraid to cross it." Have you ever faced a figurative bridge you had to cross where you couldn't see the other side? What did you do?

7. As Simone prepares to leave her old life behind to board the *Queen Mary*, she reflects on the people who stood in as parental figures when she desperately needed them: Madame Didion, Henri and Collette, the older British couple who helped her prepare for the sailing. How do you think these people made their mark on Simone? Why do you think Simone thought it best not to stay in contact with Phoebe after they immigrated to America? Was it the right choice?

8. Were Brette's fears about passing on her special ability completely understandable? Would you have had the same fears? Would you have had children anyway, if you were Brette?

9. When Annaliese is about to be detained on the ship and Simone decides to intervene and help her, she says to Annaliese: "If I do nothing when I know I can help you, I can never again be the girl that I was, I will only ever be that other girl, the one the war tried to make of me." What do you think she means here? What is at stake for her?

10. Discuss the idea that the ship is an entity with a soul. What was your reaction to this revelation? Do you have a special fondness for a place that feels like it is more than just a mere location?

A COMPELLING TALE OF A YOUNG FAMILY
WHO INHERITS A PHILADELPHIA FUNERAL HOME
ON THE EVE OF 1918'S DEADLY SPANISH FLU . . .

Under the Canopy of Heaven

BY SUSAN MEISSNER

Pauline

AUGUST 12, 1918

The sun is just starting to peek out from an apricot horizon as I stand at the place where my baby boy lies. I would've come to the cemetery last night but there was still packing to do. When this same sun sets tonight, I will be miles away in an unfamiliar house and there will be no reminders anywhere that Henry had ever been mine. Not visible ones, anyway.

I look at the little marble slab that bears my son's name and the etching of a sweet lamb curled up among lilies, and I'm reminded again that he was my angel child, even before he flew away to heaven.

I knew from the moment I held Henry, glistening and new, that he wasn't like the other babies I'd borne. He wasn't like my girls. They'd slipped out annoyed by the noise and chill and sharp edges of this world. Not Henry. He didn't cry. He didn't ball his tiny hands into fists. He didn't shout his displeasure at being pulled out of the only safe place he knew.

When the doctor handed him to me, Henry merely looked at me with eyes so blue they could've been sapphires. He held my gaze like he knew who I was. Knew everything about me. Like he still had the breath of eternity in his lungs.

He didn't care that I parted the folds of his blanket to look at his male-ness, or when I marveled at the pearly sheen of his skin against mine. I could scarcely believe I'd given birth to a boy after three girls and so many years since the last one. I just kept staring at his body and he just let me.

When Thomas was let in, he was just as astonished that we had a son. The girls were, too. They followed in right after their father, even though it was the middle of the night, and we all just stared and smiled at the little man-child, the quiet lad who did not cry.

My father-in-law came over the next morning, as did Thomas's brothers and their wives, all of them smelling of dried tobacco leaves and spice. My parents came, too, and my sister Jane, who was six months along with her own child. They all marveled at how beautiful Henry was, how calm, how enchanting his gaze and how sweet his temperament. My mother and Thomas's sisters-in-law stared at him like I'd done the night before, amazed as I had been at how serene this baby was. They had known, too, without knowing, that something wasn't right.

The few months we had with him were wonder-filled and happy. Henry did all the things a baby does that make you smile and laugh and want to kiss his downy head. When he needed something, like my breast or a clean diaper or affection, he didn't wail, he just sighed a sweet little sound that if it was made of words would have started with, "If it's not too much trouble . . ." We didn't know he didn't have the physical strength to exert himself. His perfectly-formed outsides hid the too-small, too-weak heart that my body had made for him.

And yet had God asked me ahead of time if I wanted this sweet child for just shy of half a year, I still would have said yes. Even now, five weeks after Henry's passing, and even when I hold Jane's sweet little newborn, Curtis, I would still say yes.

I don't know if Thomas feels this way, and I know the girls don't. Evelyn is still sad, Maggie is still angry, and Willa is still bewildered that Henry was taken from us. I can't say why I am none of those things anymore. What I feel inside, I'm not sure there are words to describe. I should still be sad, angry, and bewildered, but instead I feel a numbness regarding Death that I've told no one about. Not even Thomas.

I no longer fear Death, though I know that I should. I'm strangely at peace with what I used to think of as my enemy. Living seems more the taskmaster of the two, doesn't it? Life is wonderful and beautiful, but oh, how hard it can be. Dying, by contrast, is easy and simple, almost gentle. But who can I tell such a thing to? No one. I am troubled by how remarkable this feeling is.

This is why I changed my mind about moving to Philadelphia. I'd said no the first time Uncle Fred made his offer, even though I could tell Thomas was interested. Back then I couldn't imagine leaving this sleepy little town where I've lived all my life. I didn't want to move to the city where the war in Europe would somehow seem closer, didn't want to uproot the girls from the only home they'd ever known. Didn't want to tear myself away from all that was familiar. Uncle Fred wrote again a couple months after Henry was born, and Thomas had told me we needed to think carefully before turning down a second invitation.

"Uncle Fred might take his offer to one of my brothers," Thomas had said.

I truly would have given the matter more serious thought if Henry hadn't begun his slow ascent away from us right about the same time. When my son's fragile heart finally began to number his days, nothing else mattered but holding on to him as long as we could. Thomas hadn't brought up the matter again when the third letter from Uncle Fred arrived just last week. He didn't think I could leave this little mound of grass.

But the truth is, I have come out from under the shroud of sorrow a different person. I no longer want to stay in this place where Henry spent such a short time. I don't want Thomas shading a view of the wide horizon with hands calloused from binder leaves. I don't want the girls to end up mirroring this life of mine, in a place where nothing really changes but the contours of your heart.

More than that, I want to know why Death seems to walk beside me like a companion now rather than prowling behind like a shadowy specter. Surely the answers await me in Uncle Fred's funeral parlor, where he readies the deceased for their journey home. Thomas would have gone to his grave rolling cigars for other men to smoke, but now he will one day inherit Uncle Fred's mortuary business and then he won't be under the thumb of anyone.

I don't know what it will be like to be the wife of an undertaker. I only know that I need to remember how it was to keep Death at a distance.

I kneel, kiss my fingertips, and brush them against the *H* etched into the cool stone.

And I rise from the wet ground without saying good-bye.

A STORY OF FRIENDSHIP AND HEARTBREAK
SET AGAINST THE GLAMOROUS BACKDROP
OF HOLLYWOOD'S GOLDEN AGE

Stars Over Sunset Boulevard

BY SUSAN MEISSNER

AVAILABLE IN PAPERBACK AND eBOOK
FROM NEW AMERICAN LIBRARY

Hollywood

MARCH 9, 2012

Christine unfolds the tissue paper inside the pink-striped hatbox and the odor of lost years floats upward. She is well acquainted with the fragrance of antiquity. Her vintage-clothing boutique off West Sunset overflows with stylish remnants from golden years long since passed.

"I thought you were going to hold off estimating that lot until this afternoon," her business partner, Stella, says as she joins Christine in the shop's back room. The two friends are surrounded on all sides by the wearable miscellany of spent lives.

"Mr. Garceau, the man who brought this stuff in last night, just called. There's apparently a hat in one of these boxes that wasn't supposed to be included. He told me what it looks like. I guess the family is anxious to have it back."

Christine withdraws a paper-wrapped lump from inside the box, revealing at first just a flash of moss green and shimmers of gold. Then she pulls away the rest of the layers. The Robin Hood–style hat in folds of soft velvet, amber-hued fringe, and iridescent feathers feels ghostly in her hands, as though if she put it to her ear, it might whisper a litany of old secrets.

She has seen this hat somewhere before, a long time ago.

"Is that it?" Stella asks.

"I think so. He said it was green with gold fringe and feathers."

Stella moves closer, brow furrowed. "That hat looks familiar to me."

"It does to me, too." Christine turns the hat over to inspect its underside for signs of its designer—a label, a signature, a date. She sees only a single name in faded ink on a yellowed tag:

Scarlett #13

One

One

A brilliant California sun bathed Violet Mayfield in indulgent light as she neared the soaring palm tree and the woman seated on a bench underneath it. Legs crossed at the ankles, the woman rested her back lazily against the skinny trunk. She held a cigarette in her right hand, and it was as if the thin white tube were a part of her and the stylish smoke that swirled from it an extension of her body. The woman's fingernails, satin red and glistening, were perfectly shaped. Toenails visible to Violet through peep-toes winked the same shade of crimson. The woman wore a formfitting sheath of celery green with a scoop neckline. A magazine lay open on her lap, but her tortoiseshell sunglasses hid her eyes, so Violet couldn't tell whether the woman was reading the article on the left page or gazing at handsome Cary Grant, whose photograph graced the right. A wad of wax paper lay crumpled on the bench beside her handbag and a bit of bread crust poked out of it. She sat in front of the Mansion at Selznick International Studios, the stunning white edifice that moviemaker Thomas Ince had built back in the twenties to look like George Washington's Mount Vernon.

The woman under the tree didn't look at all like a fellow studio secretary, but rather a highly paid actress catching a few quiet moments of solitude between takes on the back lot. Violet glanced around to see whether there was someone else sitting outside the

Mansion on her noon break. But the woman in front of her was the only one eating her lunch under a palm tree, and that was where Violet had been told she'd find Audrey Duvall. She suddenly looked familiar to Violet, which made no sense at all. Violet was two thousand miles away from anything remotely connected to home.

"Miss Duvall?" Violet said.

The woman looked up drowsily, as though Violet had awakened her from sleep. She cocked her head and pulled her sunglasses down slightly to peer at Violet over the rims. Het luminous eyes, beautiful and doelike, were fringed with long lashes she couldn't have been born with. The casual glance was the wordless reply that she was indeed Audrey Duvall.

"My name's Violet Mayfield. I'm new to the secretary pool. Millie in accounts payable told me you are looking for a roommate. I was wondering if you'd found one yet."

Audrey smiled and her painted lips parted to reveal moon-white teeth. "Good Lord," she exclaimed, her voice rich and resonant, almost as deep as a man's. "Where are you from?"

"Pardon me?"

"You're not from around here."

"Um. No. I'm from Alabama. Originally."

Audrey's smile deepened. "Alabama. Never been to Alabama."

Violet didn't know what to say. Had the woman not heard what she asked?

Audrey patted the empty space next to her. "Have a seat. What did you say your name was?"

"Violet Mayfield." She sat down, and the cement beneath her was warm from the sun despite it being early December.

Audrey lifted the cigarette gently to her mouth and its end glowed red as she inhaled. When she tipped her head back and released the smoke it wafted over her head like a feathery length of gauze.

"Want one?" She nodded toward the pack of cigarettes peeking out of her handbag.

"No, thanks."

"Don't smoke?" Audrey puffed again on the cigarette and smiled as the smoke drifted past her lips.

Violet shook her head.

"My last roommate didn't, either. She was always leaving the windows open to let the smoke out."

"Did you not like it when she left the windows open? Is that why you need a new roommate?"

Audrey laughed. "You're kidding, right?"

Violet said nothing.

"She got married."

"Oh."

Audrey pushed the sunglasses up onto her head, fully revealing shining tea-brown eyes that complemented her shimmering brunette hair. She seemed to study for a moment Violet's navy blue dress with its plain white collar. Violet's mousy brown hair—far less wavy than Audrey's—was pulled back into a beaded barrette she had bought in a five-and-dime on the day she started heading west.

"So you just moved, then? From Alabama?"

"I came by way of Shreveport, actually. I've been working for my uncle the past year. He's an accountant."

"And how long have you been here?" Audrey asked.

"Two weeks."

"And you found a job that quickly?" Her tone held a faint edge of sly admiration. "Good for you!"

"I've worked in an office before," Violet said quickly. "And I went to secretary school."

"I've heard there's a school for what we do," Audrey said, amused. "What are you? Nineteen? Twenty?"

"Twenty-two."

"That will come in handy here, looking younger than you really are," Audrey murmured. "I'm thirty and can still pass for a twenty-year-old if I need to."

"Why would you need to do that?"

Audrey tossed back her head and laughed. Even her laugh was low and rich. "You seem to have a knack for humor, Violet from Alabama." She arched one penciled eyebrow. "So. Did you come to Hollywood to be a movie star?"

Violet startled at the question. "No!"

"That's why most girls your age come here."

The thought of performing in front of people didn't interest Violet in the least. Hollywood had beckoned her for a different reason. "That's not why I moved here."

"No?"

Her motivation for coming to California apparently mattered to Audrey Duvall. "I met one of Mr. Selznick's talent scouts at an audition in Shreveport. He said he'd put in a good word for me if I wanted a secretarial job at the studio."

"You went to that audition?" Audrey's eyes widened in measurable interest.

"Only because my cousin Lucinda insisted I come with her. She found out people from Hollywood were coming to Shreveport to search for a young woman to play Scarlett O'Hara. I let her talk me into being interviewed along with everyone else. I think by the time Mr. Arnow got to me he was just relieved to talk to someone who had actually read Margaret Mitchell's book and wasn't fawning all over him."

"You don't say!"

"I told him I was a much better secretary than I was an actress and that I knew stenography, and that I'd lived in the South all my life. He told me if I wanted a job at Selznick International in

Hollywood, he'd put in a good word for me. He said it would be handy to have a Southerner in the secretary pool during the filming. So I came."

"Just like that?" Audrey seemed both intrigued and dubious.

Violet nodded.

"You have a family back there missing you right now?"

"Just my parents. And my two brothers, Jackson and Truman. They're both married now and raising families. I doubt they think about me much."

"But your parents?"

Violet's thoughts somersaulted back to the strained phone call she had placed from Shreveport, telling her parents she'd been offered a job in Los Angeles and was taking it. They had begged her to reconsider.

"Come back home to Montgomery!" her mother had pleaded.

"Come back home to what?" Violet had responded. "There's nothing for me there."

Daddy had asked what California had that Alabama didn't. She hadn't known how to express that Hollywood didn't have expectations of her.

Or sad memories of what might have been.

"I suppose they miss me," Violet answered.

Audrey cocked her head. "So, what made you come all this way, if you don't want to be a star?"

But Violet's reason was too personal to share with a virtual stranger. She was not going to tell someone she'd only just met that fully realizing she could never have the life she'd been raised to live and wanted to live had sent her scrabbling for a new foothold on a meaningful existence.

"I was ready for a different life with new opportunities," Violet said, with a slight shrug of her left shoulder.

For a stretched moment Audrey stared at her. "Then you came

to the right place," she finally said. "Are you allergic to cats?" She took a long pull on her cigarette.

Violet shook her head.

"You don't have any furniture, do you?"

"Just a suitcase. I've been staying at a hotel."

"The rent is sixty dollars a month. Plus half of the utilities." Audrey dropped the stub of the cigarette to the pavement and ground it out with her shoe. "My place is a bit out of the way. Eight miles by way of bus and the red car. It's a very pretty neighborhood, though. Close to the hills and the Hollywoodland sign. It was my aunt's house. But now it's mine."

"The red car?"

"The trolley. The streetcar. It's a good thirty minutes getting there in the morning and just as long or more at night. Still interested?"

"Yes. Yes, I am."

Audrey smiled. "I'm on loan to one of the assistant art directors the next few days, so how about you meet me out front at quitting time? We can take the red car together so you can see the place and decide." She rose from the bench, clutching the magazine and the handbag. "C'mon. You don't want to be late getting back."

Audrey strolled confidently to toss the wax paper into a trash can some yards away and Violet had to quicken her step to catch up. Audrey's attention was fixed on the people they passed, some wearing elaborate costumes, some street clothes, some moving leisurely, some rushing as though desperate to catch a departing train. A few of these people Audrey greeted by name; some she did not. But everyone was given a look.

Amber Dawn Photography, 2008

SUSAN MEISSNER is a former managing editor of a weekly newspaper and an award-winning columnist. She is the award-winning author of *Secrets of a Charmed Life*, *A Fall of Marigolds*, and *Stars Over Sunset Boulevard*, among other novels.